To

THE PHANTOM'S SONG

my Hero my military

Big Brother

DOUGLAS M. FAIN

I met him and told him about you!

Love Kim

Enjoy the Book

iUniverse, Inc.
Bloomington

The Phantom's Song

iUniverse books may be ordered through booksellers or by contacting:

iUniverse
1663 Liberty Drive
Bloomington, IN 47403
www.iuniverse.com
1-800-Authors (1-800-288-4677)

Because of the dynamic nature of the Internet, any Web addresses or links contained in this book may have changed since publication and may no longer be valid. The views expressed in this work are solely those of the author and do not necessarily reflect the views of the publisher, and the publisher hereby disclaims any responsibility for them.

ISBN: 978-1-4502-7331-2 (sc)
ISBN: 978-1-4502-7333-6 (dj)
ISBN: 978-1-4502-7332-9 (ebk)

Printed in the United States of America

iUniverse rev. date: 11/11/2010

This book is dedicated to the men and women who served in an unpopular war and came home to an ungrateful nation. The honor they earned is their own. Those who did not return are not lost; they live in the hearts of those who fought beside them.

"In life there will always be men who stand up while others sit down. Salute the men who are standing."

James Allen Fain, Sr. 1968

Doug brings back the thrill of flying a mach 2 aircraft, the adrenalin rush of combat, the warmth of new love, and the emptiness of loss. His novel takes the reader through the jungles of Vietnam, the bitterness of the Siberian winter, and the politics of indecision in Washington. This is a story of human courage and fear, of hope and despair, of tragedy and perseverance. Doug brings his characters to life and weaves their personal stories into a rich fabric of human struggle and triumph. It is obvious he knows them well. Doug was there and has told the story of so many of us who served our country in that forgotten war. I salute him for bringing that period of our lives back into focus, and reminding us of the pride of all those warriors who flew the "Phabulous Phantoms" into harm's way.

B/Gen. Steve Ritchie, USAF, Ret., America's last fighter pilot Ace Brigadier General Steve Ritchie is the only Air Force pilot Ace since the Korean War; he downed five Mig-21s in Southeast Asia, a record that has yet to be equaled.

PART ONE

PASSION AND REALITY

CHAPTER ONE

<u>Thailand, September, 1968</u>

The two groups passed quietly in the staggering heat. Those climbing from the metal bowels of the giant C-130 aircraft squinted into the early afternoon glare as they struggled under their heavy loads toward the gate with the large, faded sign—"Welcome to Nubat Royal Thai Air Force Base, home of the 8th Tactical Fighter Wing and the world's greatest fighter pilots!" Of the men leaving the transport, only one paused to watch the group that was boarding for the return flight.

Robb Barker watched the procession silently, and only the pounding of his heart interrupted the whispered murmurs of his mind. These were the men he came to replace, the men who had started the job he was to continue, men like him who had left their families and homes to come halfway around the world to fight on unknown soil. The young captain frowned, and small lines etched themselves across his reddened face, stopping just short of his tousled blond hair. Small beads of perspiration glistened on his forehead and occasionally merged to trickle along the furrowed wrinkles. In his heart there was an emotion that shook him visibly. There was compassion and pity that clouded his vision slightly, but it was the ugly demon called fear that crawled from within the darkest dungeons of his soul to scream obscenities into the hollow recesses of his mind.

The perspiration ran more freely in the humid jungle heat. The drops became trickles, and the trickles became a great staining wetness, filled with the salt of man. He would have liked to ask these men how it had been, how they had fared with themselves. But the emotions that rose and filled his throat spread throughout his entire body and clouded his mind. He stood there, silently, and watched them being stacked roughly onto the loading platform. Only the tags taped to the ends of the long boxes linked them with life and those waiting for the sad burden back home. Less than a year before each of them had climbed from a similar plane and perhaps watched a similar spectacle. Now they were going home – for them the war was over.

*   *   *

His eyes were locked on those of the small man facing him in the dripping jungle. He could feel the weight of the child in his arms; he could smell the pungent odor of blood flowing from the boy's head as it soaked into his shirt, mixing with the sweat and mud; he sensed the quick movement to his left as someone entered the small jungle clearing; but mostly he focused on the weapon in the man's hand. Captain Robb Barker had been in Thailand less than a week, but time becomes irrelevant in a war. The ticking of his watch slowed as the beating of his heart intensified. The two men's eyes were locked in a silent, timeless moment that had captured them both. It was a moment that would change their lives forever.

The small man moved slowly backward, but his dark eyes remained locked on the taller American. The rain intensified, soaking both men and the small child in the taller man's arms. Robb opened his mouth to speak, but there were no words. What does one say to a man who has lost everything, when his language, like his suffering, is incomprehensible?

He watched the man's eyes, expecting hatred, but he found only confusion and pain. Only an hour earlier their lives had been so different. He had been in the airport control tower as mid afternoon thunderstorms grew in intensity around the air base. The F-4 fighters shattered the early afternoon peace as they screamed across the horizon like large sleek raptors, returning home, gliding toward their resting places for a brief respite from the war to the east. The giant storm continued to grow above the jungle in lofty gray columns spread randomly across the foreboding dark sky. In the tower the base controllers watched the cloud formations and the planes that flew around and occasionally through them. Master Sergeant John Henderson watched a flight of four F-4s as they approached the base. They were flying at fifteen hundred feet, directly over the runway. At midfield the first aircraft banked hard and "peeled off" from the flight. Four seconds later, number two did the same as they turned downwind and prepared to land. When number three pitched, Henderson came off of his seat. "Cobra Three, this is Nubat tower. Be advised you just lost something off your aircraft in pitchout. Check status on downwind and advise."

"Roger tower."

"Oh shit!" The sergeant did not realize that he still had a "hot" mike. "Look at that!" A large explosion sent fire and smoke into the afternoon sky. It appeared to be northeast of the base, just beyond the perimeter fence. "Cobra Four this is Nubat tower. Request you break out of formation and checkout that explosion. Three, did you have a hung bomb?"

"Don't think so; damn sure wouldn't be in this landing pattern if I did."

"Cobra Four, heads up for a chopper that will be in your vicinity in five minutes. Stay above two thousand feet."

"Roger, two thousand."

"Status Four?" There was a long pause. "Four do you have the impact in sight?"

"Roger."

"Status!" The sergeant's voice was tinged with impatience.

"Cobra Four is circling a hooch on fire." There was a long silence on the radio.

"A hooch?" The thought of a 500-pound bomb hitting one of the small Thai dwellings near the base was an image none wanted to consider. This was a friendly village; Thailand was an ally in the war.

"Roger, a hooch."

In the tower the crew looked at each other in disbelief and shock. "Damn!" Henderson ran to the window and began shouting orders as fast as he could talk. "Call the Chopper; tell them to expedite. Call the Wing Commander and Base Ops. Call the Air Police, and tell them to get a crew out there ASAP. And, oh yes, alert the hospital." The tower crew looked helplessly at the rising smoke on the horizon. "Damn, a hooch. I sure hope nobody was home this afternoon."

* * *

The early afternoon rain pounded the blue Air Force Powerwagon as it bumped to a stop in the thick brown mud. The heavy vegetation surrounding the small road drooped toward the muddy earth, heavy with dampness. Six men inside the faded truck stepped out into the rain soaked road; they were silent; they were shocked; none of them had seen the terrible effects of a 500-pound bomb at such close range. It had been a near direct hit; the lost bomb had landed beside a small house on the outskirts of the Thai village. What had once been a home was now a pile of broken and twisted wood. Around it lay the bodies of those who had lived there. The young officer walked slowly forward as his team stood motionless and stared at the destruction. Like the falling rain, the silence only served to focus the visual image of the horror that had occurred only minutes earlier. In the distance a clap of thunder flashed across the small clearing, shocking the men into action. Following the captain they, too, began to move forward.

The Americans approached slowly, walking through the thick foliage until one young sergeant gasped aloud. He stood frozen, looking at his feet. The arm of a child lay in his path like the appendage of a lost and broken doll. He turned abruptly and vomited into the dense foliage.

Then a small cry brought them back to reality. The men looked quickly at each other; the tall captain began to run toward the wrecked home, his heart beating rapidly. Abruptly he stopped as he entered the clearing before the small hut, his eyes locked on a scene that would haunt him the rest of his life. There in the small yard beside the wrecked hooch stood a small man with brown pants and no shirt. His black hair was stained with blood and rain. A tiny boy was in his arms. Beside him, lying in disarray, was what remained of his life—the bodies of his wife and three of his children. He turned slowly to look at the stunned Americans.

As Robb stepped forward, the small child cried out again. Blood covered his head and ran down his father's arms, mixing the blood of father and son. "It was all a mistake. We didn't mean to hurt your family. It was a mistake. Oh God, help us."

The small man raised his head and opened his mouth to speak, but there was no sound. With effort he focused on the men standing around him, then on the child in his arms. The young captain reached for the boy, but the man pulled the child away and held him close to his own bleeding body.

"We've got to get you both to the hospital. Please. Let me help

you." There was sadness and frustration in his voice. "Please…
Please." Forcefully the captain took the boy and handed him to one
of the sergeants. "Careful."

The small man sank to his knees in the rain, his head hanging
as if exhausted beyond measure. Finally he looked up and with great
difficulty crawled to his dead wife. Carefully he lifted her body and
held her in his lap and began speaking to the dead woman. He spoke
softly, brushing her matted hair from her bloody face. He talked to
her as if she were seated at his table, feeding his children. He looked
at her lovingly and stroked her pale cheek as he spoke to the woman
he loved. Then he bent and kissed her gently. When he sat up, his
body was shaking as the sobs overcame him.

The young Americans stood helplessly in the rain and watched,
their own eyes moist as they witnessed the unbearable pain of another
human being. Two of the airmen turned away as tears streamed
down their own faces. As the small man buried his face in his bloody
hands, Robb walked to him, placed his hand on the man's shoulder,
and began to pat him. As the man wept, Robb sat beside him and
put both arms around the man's shoulders. It was all he knew to do.
Together they sat in the clearing as the airmen began to move the
bodies under a large tree for shelter from the rain.

Finally Robb rose and took the small child as two sergeants
gently lifted the injured man and started toward the trucks. As
they moved forward, the farmer jerked away and ran back toward
the hooch. Robb turned to coax him back but stopped when he
saw the bleeding man standing amid the remains of his family,
holding the sergeant's pistol to his own head. Balancing the child
with one arm, Robb raised his hand high into the air. All of the
men froze. He spoke slowly, deliberately as he stared into the dark,
blank eyes. "No, don't." He watched the small farmer carefully, then
suddenly shifted his eyes to a movement on the left. It was a young
boy of fourteen or fifteen walking from the jungle, returning to

his home, his family. Instead, he found a scene his mind could not comprehend. He stopped abruptly, looked at this father, his mouth open in silent protest.

A strange inertia settled over the tall captain as he turned back to the man with the gun. It slowed his movement; it slowed the world around him as he stared again into the dark eyes of the sad face before him. "Don't. Please, don't."

The sorrow in the man's eyes reflected the pain in his heart. It was simply too great. Everything he loved was strewn about him in pieces. The dark eyes looked upon a reality that the man could not bear. Somehow Robb understood that. It was a father's eyes that looked at the small boy in Robb's arms. He nodded toward the child. "Somboon." He said it quietly.

The captain nodded and pointed at himself with his right hand. "I will take care of him. I promise." The man seemed to understand; he nodded, then pulled the trigger. His pain was over; he was once again with his family.

As the shot rang out in the jungle, the scream from the boy on the edge of the clearing startled the shaken men. It was one of unbearable pain and unspeakable rage. Robb turned quickly, speaking in a broken voice that he did not recognize as his own. "I'm so sorry, so sorry." But before he could finish, the boy turned and ran back into the jungle. He was sobbing as he disappeared into the wet green growth.

Robb handed the small boy to the sergeant standing beside him and walked haltingly to the body of the small man. "Sarge, stay here until the detail arrives from the base. Watch for the boy in case he returns." He paused for a moment and looked at the devastation around him. "If he does, call me on the radio." The tall captain stood there briefly then removed his fatigue shirt, knelt, and placed it over the dead man's head. He picked up the weapon and handed it back to the sergeant as they walked toward the truck.

"I'm sorry, sir, I didn't see him get it."

"It's okay Sarge. This wasn't your fault."

"Captain Barker, why didn't he shoot at us?"

The officer walked toward the truck in silence; finally he looked up and answered. "Because he was a good man." They both looked back as the men continued to collect the bodies beneath a large plastic sheet as the rain intensified. "He was just a simple farmer who loved his family. We took them from him. Dear God, how could this happen?"

*   *   *

The hospital doors flew open with a crash as three men ran up the narrow ramp with the bleeding boy. The captain's eyes were desperately searching the halls when a young woman in hospital greens ran to meet him. She reached for the child, but the captain turned away, holding the child to his breast. "Quick, get a doctor!"

"Let me see him." She reached again and began checking the boy's wound.

"Dammit, nurse! I said to get a doctor!" His voice had risen to an angry shout, one filled with both anger and fear.

Two brown eyes looked into two blue eyes and sent icicles in response. The young woman grabbed the child as she spoke. "I am a doctor, sergeant; now give me this child and get the hell out of my hospital." With a turn, she ran down the hall cradling the small boy in her arms.

The red faced young man shouted after the retreating figure. "How was I supposed to know? And I'm a captain!"

"And I'm a major! Now get out!" For the first time that day he smiled.

*   *   *

Major Kerrie Marie Jernigan, surgeon, walked into the cramped waiting room to face the captain she had ordered from her hospital. She was braced and ready, but he was asleep. She studied him carefully. He was seated on the one couch in the tiny room that was crowded with furniture. His flight boots rested on a worn table. He sat upright, his head forward, short blond hair tousled in various directions. His muddy fatigues and T-shirt were spotted with blood and outlined a young, strong body with wide shoulders and narrow hips. She interrupted his peaceful nap. "He's going to be okay."

The sleeping man jerked into wakefulness. "What?"

"I said he's going to be okay."

"Great." He was rubbing his eyes with his hands. "Great. There was so much blood. I was worried."

"What happened to him?"

The waking eyes narrowed instantly as his mind remembered the scene at the small home on the edge of the village. "Hung bomb. Shit!" The last word was almost a shout.

"I'm sorry."

"Yeah."

Kerrie studied the young man briefly. "Was it yours?"

He looked up in surprise. "No, I was in the tower. But it was one of our planes; they lost the bomb during pitchout." He looked up at her, studying her reaction. "It was an accident, a damned accident."

"Where is his family?"

"All killed but one other boy—about fourteen or fifteen I'd guess. We tried to stop him, but he ran away into the jungle." There was frustration in his voice.

She studied his face carefully as she spoke. "Do you know this child's name?"

He thought for a moment. "Somboon; his name is Somboon." He was talking mostly to himself.

"He'll be okay in a few days—physically—but he'll have a scar on his forehead. I did the best I could under the circumstances." She paused then added. "What becomes of him?"

"I really don't know." He looked up at the woman standing before him. She was dressed in surgical "greens," and there were several small bloody spots on her bosom. From under the green cap, strands of dark brown hair escaped and curled around her face. He noted for the first time that she was beautiful. Her eyes were large and dark and matched her hair. As he looked at her, he noticed her cheeks redden. Was his stare so obvious? "I'm Robb Barker." Awkwardly he rose and extended his hand. "Sorry about the mix-up before."

"That's okay. It happens often. I'm Kerrie Jernigen." She shook his hand briefly.

"We just don't see too many female Flight Surgeons over here."

"I understand."

He rose and started for the door. "Take good care of him."

"Will you be back for him later?" Robb stopped at the door and looked back at her again. The question had surprised him; he had not thought past the hospital. "I guess. Yes, yes, I'll be back." He thought a moment, his face suddenly serious. "I made a promise."

"I just wondered who will take care of him when we're through here."

"I'll find out. There are a lot of details to consider, I'm sure. In the meantime I'll take care of him. Somboon." He spoke the name carefully as he turned and walked toward the door.

Kerrie watched from the window as Robb jogged across the small grass lawn before the hospital and jumped the short fence beside the gravel road. He was strong, the planes of his body well muscled. She smiled, the blush still on her cheeks.

* * *

The sweet earthy smell hung heavily in the air as the somber group stood before the rain-drenched graves; beside each was a small wooden coffin. Like toy soldiers they were lined up, the longest on the left, five feet long, the shortest on the right, barely three feet long. The rain fell and splashed softly on the rough boxes, but the rain was not salty. Unlike sweat or tears, it had not taken on the imperfections or the greatness of humanity. It represented neither toil nor grief, but rather, like the silent soil, it merely gathered in the torn pits and waited to join the repair of the opened earth. Salt was there, however. Tears stained the cheeks and bit the tongue and fell with the rain into puddles. And the puddles were stained with the pain of suffering; the suffering soaked into the soil; and the earth swelled with its burden.

Somboon said his last farewell, but his childish mind could not comprehend the tragedy that lay stretched before him in the afternoon drizzle. It was only later that the shocking reality shook his small frame with sobbing cries. Robb stared into the darkness, bewildered. His was a life among men; he had little experience with children. He did the only thing he knew to do; he held the small shaking body next to his own and prayed in silence. Finally, the river in Robb's heart overran its banks, too, his tears overflowing and falling with those of the boy to soak the worn floor in the small room at the pilots' hooch. Together they sat and cried, the tall blond captain and the small blackheaded boy. One wept through innocence and loss, one through pity and understanding. Their tears filled a void far deeper than the small graves in the village, and they were drawn together in a way that surprised them both.

And that is how she found them, still clinging to each other, asleep. The tired doctor saw the peaceful beauty on the tear stained cheeks. In their slumber they had left the current pain for the refuge of happier dreams, and the loss vanished with reality and moved into the darkest recesses of the mind where it was not allowed to return until the body roused the troubled brain and released the captive reality to wound and scar again. She was turning quietly to leave when she met the blue eyes. They were sad, confused eyes she thought, and perhaps embarrassed too, but like the sunburned hands that held the child, they were strong and kind. She spoke quickly as her eyes turned to the floor. "I'm sorry…" His eyes lowered too, and she left.

Skovorodino, The Soviet Union

In a desolate forest on the Siberian steppes, Colonel Dmitriy Mihail Ruchinsky sat in a cold, sparse room and stared dumbly at the uncomfortable young man who stood stiffly before him. When the nervous soldier finished his report, the colonel rose slowly and ushered him to the door, thanking him for transmitting the news he had yet to process, yet to fully comprehend. When once again alone, the older officer slowly turned the lock on the door and returned to his desk. He sank heavily into the bare wooden chair, held his head in both hands, and wept.

Dmitriy's life was crumbling around him. His career had already been irreparably damaged, the result of an unfortunate decision by a superior in a highly political environment. A career that had once seemed destined for advancement and position had fallen into disfavor. Moscow and the Kremlin had been exchanged for a remote outpost in the far reaches of the Soviet system. It would be impossible to be farther from the excitement of a career in Moscow than in Skovorodino. The blow had been devastating, but Dmitriy still had his wife, Dariya, or Dasha, as he affectionately called her, and his son, Nikolai, a bright young pilot in the Soviet Air Force. His career had resulted in undeserved failure, but his personal life had been a success. Dasha doted on him still, and Nikolai regarded his dad as a hero of the people. Nikolai, who graduated very near the top in his class at the university, had also graduated top in his class from flight school. Like his father he was a military man. He had not selected transports, but fighters. He had not selected Moscow, but Vietnam. With a select group, Nikolai had secretly left for the war to test the American will, their skill, and their equipment. Now he was dead.

In his own grief Dmitriy thought about Dasha, the woman he had loved from childhood. How would he tell her that her only child was dead? How could he stand her pain? If only he could bear it for her, but he knew he could not. He could hardly bear his own pain. The shock was setting in; he could feel the numbness enveloping him. He could feel his mind slipping back into the past, unwilling to admit the present or face the future without his son. Desperately he tried to force his mind to concentrate on the present. Could it have been a mistake? Perhaps Nikolai will call to correct this unthinkable report. Perhaps he had parachuted into the jungle and would be rescued later. No! No. His discipline took over, and control was momentarily regained. The young soldier had been specific. There was no parachute. There was no beeper. The plane exploded—shot down by an American pilot. Those damned Americans! How could Dmitriy live knowing some smug American pilot was celebrating the death of his dear Nikolai? Dmitriy slammed his fist on his desk; it was an old, large, brown desk, and like Dmitriy it was not without scars. He rose but then sat back down before he could move away. The discipline faded and crashed—like his career, like his son, like his life. Somewhere from the faded pages of his memory he heard the excited voice of a young boy calling him. It was a voice he had loved, and like the small boy in his memories, it invited him to a happier time in his life. Dmitriy's mind responded and escaped the raw pain of reality; he smiled and whispered his dead son's name.

* * *

The Soviet colonel walked out of the two-story wooden house into the bitter evening cold. He stood alone in the night on the weathered porch and breathed the cold, dry air. The crisp smell of evergreen branches mixed with the pollution of coal smoke that permeated the environment and bit at his nose. He leaned on the wooden railing and hung his head in despair. Dasha had always been the foundation of his life. When he was angry, she was calm. When he was confused, she guided him back to reality; when he was afraid, she was strong. He depended on her to preserve order amid the chaos of his world. But he had just walked into her peaceful, ordered life with a message she could not accept. He had explained all he knew without withholding any details; she had simply looked at him, silently, unblinking. Finally she had risen, walked to her room, and closed the door. She cried for hours behind the locked door as Dmitriy stood helpless outside. Then she emerged, composed, and began asking the practical questions required to bury her child.

"When will we receive his body?"

"They haven't found him, Dasha; they probably won't."

"Why not? Didn't he crash in North Vietnam?"

"Yes, but…"

"Then why can't they send him home?" Her voice was expressionless.

"Dasha, his plane exploded! They may never find him." Dmitriy's voice was barely a whisper. He was watching her face, measuring her pain. She was calm, but Dmitriy knew her well. He could feel her struggle hidden below the surface of her blank face. He could feel the pain; it added to his own and weighed his soul with a giant anchor that dragged him down to the very brink of hell. She rose calmly and walked into the kitchen, returning with two cups of tea. Dmitriy raised his head and looked again into her eyes. He opened his mouth, but the words would not come. He was aware that tears were streaming down his own face, his shoulders shaking as his body gave way to sobs. Dasha's blue eyes blinked repeatedly as she watched her husband falling apart before her. He had always been her stability in life, the vibrancy that made life as a military wife worth living. Her world was colorless without him. He was the artist that gave her the morning sun. It was he who colored her life with flowers. She loved him desperately; she always had. One tear rose in her right eye, reflecting her pain, her soul. Slowly it grew, finally brimming over her eyelid, rolling slowly over her cheek. It was the impetus that bridged her will and broke the dam of her emotions. Tears streamed across her face as she rose and walked slowly to her husband. Dasha pulled Dmitriy's face to her breast like a child and held him as his body shook with emotion. Together they wept, holding each other in the dim light of the small room.

CHAPTER TWO

<u>Nubat Royal Air Force Base, Thailand</u>

The men stepped from the air-conditioned operations building into the bright sunlight and the oppressing heat. They walked briskly across the small road, crossed the concrete parking ramp, and turned right toward the long rows of camouflaged F-4 fighter-bombers. In the distance profuse white clouds sprinkled the clear blue sky. They walked like men with purpose. The weight of war clung to their bodies: g-suits, survival vests, .38 Smith and Wesson revolvers, knives, radios, camouflaged flight helmets, and, as always, smiles. These were not men bored with lives of quiet desperation. These were men driven by excitement. They lived with adrenaline racing through their sweating bodies. Their lives were an adventure; they flew mach 2 fighters into combat. These were men who envied no one.

The new man in the group walked beside his laughing comrades, watching their easy strides, listening to the casual jokes. Robb Barker tried to smile; he wanted to fit in, but unlike these veterans, he was still a "new guy." This would be his fifth combat mission, and he still had butterflies in his stomach. The first four missions had been relatively easy "milk runs" with little opposition from the enemy. Today would be different. They were going "uptown," and Hanoi was always heavily defended. He looked down at his hands swinging easily by his side. They appeared relaxed, ready, but the tension inside his body was rising. He could feel it. The other men were laughing and relaxed. Was that simply experience, or were they just better at masking their own doubts?

The crews walked on through the heat, their flight suits wet beneath the vests and equipment. Robb slapped his friend and roommate, Joe Wilburn, on the back as he turned into the first large concrete and steel revetment where his plane was parked. "You sober, Joe?" Robb teased his friend, knowing that no pilot violated the drinking before flying regulations, not even Joe Wilburn.

"Hell no! I'm going uptown today. You don't think I'd do that sober do you?"

"You wouldn't do anything sober if you had a choice." Robb grinned and searched Joe's face. He could find no fear, only excitement. And why not? Joe Wilburn was the best pilot he knew, better even than he. Robb turned left several revetments later and inspected the large fighter-bomber waiting for him and his navigator. It was a large bird, and like the raptor it was, it even looked fierce. Large eyes and vicious teeth had been painted on the nose, an obvious copy of the Flying Tigers of World War II fame. They had been feared, but their weapons were minor compared to the craft before him. He would be carrying more bombs today than any bomber that existed in World War II. Robb studied the large black numbers painted on the tail of the plane—three-three-six. He grinned to himself; the three numbers didn't add to thirteen. He wasn't especially superstitious, but he also didn't like to take chances. Only last week Two-seven-four had gone down over Laos. He increased his pace; he had an airplane to preflight.

Checking the bombs hanging beneath the wings and fuselage of his aircraft, Robb watched Wayne Compton, his navigator, busily writing a message to "Uncle Ho" on one of the 500-pound bombs with fuse extenders. It occurred to the pilot that his own father had once been on the receiving end of a bombing mission somewhere in France. Surely he had felt fear, but he had done his job, and his unit had held against a massive attack. Robb calculated quickly. His father had been only eighteen then, a boy ten years younger than he. In a moment of discovery he realized that he had never thought of his own father as a courageous man. It had simply not been an issue in his life. He knew his father as a kind and gentle man, one he respected and loved, yet surely he had known fear and probably even had his courage tested. He had fought and undoubtedly killed other men. It was an amazing revelation, like opening a door one has passed frequently without thought for years. He pondered why his father had never broached the subject of courage or fear, even as he was leaving for war himself. Perhaps he would pursue this subject with his dad someday. Perhaps. It might depend, he concluded, on his own performance today. It would be difficult to face his father with shame. Then it crashed upon the screen of his mind. Could that be why his father had never touched this subject with his own son? Had he felt shame, or had the horrors of war been so great that he dared not unlock that compartment in his mind? It was a troublesome question, one with implications for his father, and after today, perhaps for him as well.

The preflight was completed quickly, and one by one the ground crews connected the auxiliary power units and started up the powerful jet engines. Robb sat in his cockpit and watched the flight leader taxi out of the parking area; three minutes later he pushed his throttles forward and felt his own plane accelerate slowly. The crew chief stepped back and saluted smartly, and Robb returned the gesture as he turned toward the runway. As the plane rolled forward he forced everything from his mind and focused on the aircraft he was flying. Thoughts of his father and even his own doubts were put aside. Flying required his full attention; for that he was thankful.

An hour later the three F-4s were engaged in their business; Copperhead One, Two, and Three were dive-bombing a bridge that crossed a small meandering stream just south of Hanoi. The stream snaked through the thick, green jungle foliage and shimmered in the sunlight, winking at the aircraft circling above. The small bridge was an unlikely structure, obviously made from locally available materials. Yet despite its meager size, the deep ruts on either side indicated that it was, indeed, a busy crossing. Unlike strategic bombers, the fighter-bombers did not fly level over their targets and drop their bombs from a high altitude; instead they would dive down at forty-five degree angles and drop their bombs closer to the targets. It allowed greater accuracy, but it also made them more vulnerable to the anti-aircraft gun sites on the ground. Major Bill Adamson made the first pass and released a string of three five hundred-pound bombs. All three hit short of the bridge. The last of the three hit the stream about one hundred feet from the bridge, showering it with water from the blast.

"Damn, One's off south, I'm short."

"Two's in from the west." As Copperhead Two plunged toward the target, a bright string of 37 MM anti-aircraft rounds streaked upward from a gun site just north of the bridge. Like the F-4's, his aim was also bad. His rounds passed far below the racing aircraft. "Two's off to the east. Damn, short again!"

"One's got the gun site! He's below the ridge just north of the bridge, roughly 50 yards!" The voice was fast and professional. Before he could call his position, the airwaves crackled on the Guard channel of their radio, a channel specifically designated for emergency transmissions.

"Copperhead flight! Copperhead flight! This is Hillsboro One on Central track; you've got bandits closing fast from the north! I repeat, you've got bandits closing fast from the north. Heads up!" Somewhere in the distance a controller sat in the rear of an

RC121 aircraft and tracked the enemy planes with a very powerful airborne radar.

"Hillsboro, Copperhead One, distance?"

"Ten miles, closing very fast!"

"Shit! Copperhead Two, jettison everything, climb west, ASAP!"

"Roger." Robb leveled his aircraft and punched off both external tanks and all of his bombs. As he felt the weight drop from his plane, he thrust both throttles forward with his left hand, igniting both afterburners. The aircraft sprang forward and began a rapid climb to the west.

The next radio transmission was that of Lt. Colonel Andrew Bennett, the squadron Operations Officer and leader of this flight. His voice rose with excitement as he asked for directions to the approaching enemy fighters. "Hillsboro, Pigeons?"

"Less than a mile, northeast, closing fast!"

"Two, where are you?"

"Climbing through eight thousand, turning north." Both Robb and his navigator were straining their eyes to the northeast. He spotted a Mig approaching from his four o'clock position. "Wayne! Four o'clock, high!"

"Got him!"

Robb pulled hard on the control stick and began a six-g turn to his right, straight into the Mig. It appeared that the two enemy aircraft had started their pass from over twenty thousand feet and were diving, making a fast pass at the three American fighters.

"Three's got a bandit at two O'clock." Joe Wilburn's voice was fast and tense.

"Two's got one at four." Robb's voice had the strange sound of a man pulling six and a half-g's. He was also straining hard to keep the Mig in sight. He watched the enemy plane over his right shoulder, carefully judging its rate of closure and its relative position. He could see that it was closing far too fast. "He's streaking."

From the backseat, "Right. One pass—haul ass!"

"Wayne, snap left, Ready?"

"Ready!"

Robb pulled the "stick" into his stomach and felt the immediate onset of the additional g's as they pressed him toward the floor of the aircraft. They quickly built in intensity--pushing him, thrusting him, into the seat. As his legs flattened against the survival pack, the g-suit fought vainly to counter the forces on his body. The cheeks on his face sagged toward his chest. Still, his eyes watched the approaching Mig over his right shoulder, the muscles in his neck straining with the effort. His mind timed the approach, measuring the distance--as he had done so many times in training. It's the same maneuver, he thought, but this time it is for real, and that guy is no Walt Burkette; this guy is a novice; I can take him easily. He fought the g's, listening to his navigator's strained breath in the intercom. He knew that Wayne was twisting in his seat, too, watching the enemy aircraft streaking through the blue sky toward his own. Every muscle in Robb's body tensed against the "g" forces as his vision began to narrow on the Mig. *Now!* he thought, and with the precision of a professional, he smoothly pulled the control stick into his lap as hard as he could. He snatched the aircraft from six to nine g's almost instantaneously. In doing so, he slowed the aircraft from 350 knots to barely over 250 in a fraction of a second. That sudden change of speed was enough. The Mig, already overshooting, had no time to react. It passed below and behind his aircraft at a very high rate of speed, its guns firing into the empty sky. *Now,* Robb thought, *Now!* With a slight smile on his straining face, he initiated the next move in his plan. Releasing some of the pressure on the control stick, and being careful not to engage either aileron, Robb pressed smoothly, but hard, on the top rudder pedal. Then, almost violently, he thrust the stick to the right, opposite the rudder. Instantly the F-4 rolled up and to the left, rolling inverted directly behind the fleeing Mig. "Oh, Yes!"

"Shit hot!"

Robb released the g forces on his aircraft as he watched the Mig accelerate away from him. He shoved both afterburners to full power and felt the thrust drive him into his seat as the large fighter lurched ahead, suddenly closing the distance with the Mig. Pulling the throttle out of afterburner to 100 percent power, he stabilized the rate of closure and finally established his aircraft about 200 yards behind the fleeing enemy. Now the hunter was the hunted. "Wayne, get him!"

"Roger that." The navigator leaned forward and peered into the radarscope before him, attempting to lock his radar onto the escaping aircraft. Suddenly the Mig turned hard right in a six-g turn; no problem, the F-4 had the cutoff position. Robb yanked his stick right and turned inside the Mig, then to the left as the Mig maneuvered around the sky. It made little difference; this event was already decided. There was no escape. "Got him!" grunted Wayne, obviously straining with the "g" forces and short of breath. "Radar's locked on!"

"Aim 7's up. One's away." The missile dropped from the right center of the aircraft's belly and streaked off at mach 3.5. Robb watched the contrails as the missile overtook the enemy aircraft. In fractions of a second it intercepted the Mig. Before he could arm a backup, the Mig was a disintegrating mass of fire before him. The explosion surprised the pilot; the fireball was larger than he had imagined, and he was headed directly into it. Large pieces of metal flew through the sky before the F-4. Robb had daydreamed this moment a thousand times, but always the daydreams had ended with the missile flying into the exhaust plume of the enemy aircraft. He had never envisioned the explosion. "Shit!" He yanked hard on the stick, thrusting it to his right while pressing the right rudder pedal as hard as he could. Simultaneously, he pulled both throttles aft to slow the aircraft's speed. The F-4 rolled to its right and started into a steep dive. "Splash one!"

"Yes! Yes! Yes!" Three feet behind him, his navigator celebrated their success.

On intercom, "Wayne, where are they?"

A groaning voice from the backseat answered. "Don't know; I'll check the radar."

"Three, your position?"

"Bandit's six o'clock! Hang on!"

"Need help?"

"No!" There was a grunting in his voice, indicating heavy g forces. A few moments passed as both Robb and Mark strained to see the other two aircraft. Robb finally spotted a small dark dot on the horizon to his west. It was the distinctive marking of an F-4 afterburner ignition.

"I've got your position Three. I'm on the way."

"Son of a bitch!"

"Three, this is One; what's up?" The colonel's voice was calm and professional.

"The pilot just bailed out! He abandoned ship!"

"Smart little bastard. He wants to fly again."

"Stand back while I put a missile up that Mig's ass. I'm getting credit for this." There was a short pause. "One's away." An even shorter pause. "Splash one!"

Somewhere in the distance the RC121 Sector Controller flew circles in the sky over Laos, monitoring the battle miles away. An excited voice interrupted. "There were two bandits; do I understand that both are down?"

"Roger that." It was Colonel Bennett's voice. He was pulling up to Robb's right wing. In his cockpit he was looking over at the young captain with his thumb up.

"Great work, Copperhead flight. Go home and find the paint can." The excitement remained.

"Two red stars for the good guys." Colonel Bennett's voice had lost some of its professionalism. "One has the lead."

"Roger One." Robb eased back into formation on Colonel Bennett's left wing.

"Three, do you have us in sight?"

"Roger, Three's rejoining on your right from 7 o'clock low." Almost immediately Joe was on the colonel's right wing.

"Good work, men. We party tonight!" The two pilots maneuvered their aircraft to within two feet of the lead plane's wings and saluted their leader. The colonel held his right thumb in the direction of his mouth with his fingers closed and made the sign of drinking. He was inquiring about the other aircrafts' fuel situation. Robb gave him a thumb's up, as did Joe, and the lead pilot nodded. Slowly they turned toward the southwest and headed home. "Thanks for the heads-up Hillsboro, we owe you one."

"Congratulations guys."

"It's Miller time."

"Have one for me."

"How about several?"

"Sounds fair to me."

So fast and it was over. Robb had trained for this moment for so long. In a brief few minutes the battle had ended. He was flying home the victor, and another man was dead. He had been attacked and had destroyed the attacker. Briefly he wondered about the other pilot. Had he also loved flying? Had he also dreamed of flying home a victor? Was he young? Who would mourn his death? He pushed the thoughts from his consciousness. He had to concentrate on his flying. He pushed them into a small file in the darkest recesses of his mind and locked that file carefully. The key to that file, like the missile, was then fired off into the vastness of the summer sky. Like the Mig, it exploded and was lost forever, or such was his hope. Then another thought crept quickly from his subconscious and pulled the corners of his mouth into a deliberate smile. Fear had been absent during the skirmish with the Migs. The training had prevailed. He had done his job like a professional.

"Shit hot, Robb! We got one! That roll worked like clockwork."

"Yes it did." Robb glanced over the nose of the lead aircraft. The deep blue of the afternoon sky contrasted sharply with the bright white and dull gray clouds that hovered on the horizon, stacked randomly upon each other like large moss covered rocks strewn below a crumbling mountain. Far in the distance the sun's rays danced among the towering thunderstorms to the south, sending a kaleidoscope of colors across the afternoon sky. Below, the landscape was already changing hues as the afternoon shadows darkened the vegetation of the jungle, giving it a foreboding shade of green that was almost black. He was glad to be skipping among the clouds, bathed in the waning sunlight. It was right to be above the darkness below, above the war on the ground. This had been a day of challenge and success. It had been one of discovery; soon it would be one of celebration. And yes, he thought, I will have that man-to-man chat with dad someday, when we both are ready.

*   *   *

Robb was a veteran now; he had ten flights on the books. He paused as he walked toward his aircraft and looked up as three F-4s flew into the airbase flight zone and headed down the long runway at 1500 feet. The formation was tight—one, three, and four. Number two had not returned.

Across the base, all ears were attuned to the returning planes. In the tower, in the control room, even in the squadron ready room, men listened, waiting. A truck of crew chiefs and mechanics raced to their positions on the parking ramp and in the revetments.

"Tiger flight, you're cleared to land."

"Roger, one's pitching."

"Three!"

"Four!"

The three planes jerked ninety degrees and turned rapidly to downwind, paralleling the runway. All three pulled six to eight g's in the pitchout, showing their professionalism. They were the best pilots in the world, and they were returning one shy. This was no time to be sloppy. One by one they turned final and landed in the stifling jungle heat.

"Tiger, this is Nubat tower, move expeditiously off of the runway. Crow Three is limping in behind you."

"Roger, tower."

"Tower, this is Crow Three; I'm two miles out."

"Roger Crow Three, we're ready for you." Already the large fire trucks were lumbering into place with the crews who would remove the crippled aircraft from the runway.

"Crow One, how's Three's gear?" It was Colonel Bennett's voice.

"Looks good from here. I checked him over; he's still burning in the right engine, wingroot area."

"How are his flaps?"

"This is Crow Three, I can't get more than a few degrees of flap extension."

"Put them all the way up, then. We don't want them to change on approach."

"Roger, flaps up."

"Watch your airspeed. You'll be coming in fast. Recalculate now."

"Roger." In the aircraft the pilot calculated his approach speed carefully. "160 knots!"

"Make that 165. You'll be hot as hell; try your hook on the first barrier. We'll have all three up for you."

"Roger." The voice was surprisingly cool.

"How are your hydraulics?"

"Fluctuating like hell. PC-2 shows 800 psi; PC-1 is bouncing between 2500 and 3000."

"Okay Joe; bring it on in. I'll meet you in the bar. Beer's on me."

"Bring your wallet, Colonel."

"You bet."

Men and women stood in the glaring sun as the heat rose like waves from the concrete ramps and taxiways. All across the base, they were watching the aircraft approaching from the east, trailing smoke. The colonel turned to the young lieutenant beside him. Unlike the colonel, the junior officer wore khakis—not a flight suit. He was the base Admin. Officer and was not pilot qualified. "Jeff, call the club and tell them to put six in the freezer."

"Is he going to make it?" The young officer studied the colonel carefully.

"Hell yes, he'll make it. He's a fighter pilot isn't he?" The colonel smiled to the younger man. "Jeff, if that plane can be brought back in one piece, there's five or six men alive who could do that. Joe Wilburn is one of them."

"He's the best?"

"No, dammit. I'm the best." Bennett smiled broadly, "but Joe Wilburn is damn close."

"That's reassuring." The lieutenant observed the tightly squinted eyes and the growing stain of sweat on the colonel's back. Was it the heat, or was it tension? The colonel might curse the former, but he'd never admit to the latter. That was his job, to be cool, to lead his men; he managed to do that quite well. He maintained the act, and the pilots would follow him into hell.

"Make that call—six on ice."

Joe coaxed and cajoled the damaged plane onto final approach. Those below saw the burning plane lurching through the sky. One engine was groaning loudly; the other was shut down, trailing smoke and flames.

"Crow Three, you're cleared. Good luck!"

"Roger that." There was tension in his voice for the first time. He was fighting the controls skillfully. The airwaves became suddenly silent as the plane descended toward the long asphalt strip in the jungle clearing. Beside the apron of the runway the fire trucks stood patiently, red lights flashing, waiting. Maintenance crews edged closer in their pickup trucks. The crews in the escort aircraft, flying in loose formation beside the damaged plane, watched for visible failures on the crippled bird.

With utmost precision the F-4 descended and tentatively touched the right main landing gear onto the pavement and then the left. Immediately the large drag chute popped from the tail structure to slow the plane. The tail hook fell simultaneously but bounced over the first Bak 9 arresting barrier. The burning aircraft continued down the runway at high speed. Joe clamped down on the brakes with both feet, but little hydraulic pressure was left. It slowed only slightly before the hook engaged the barrier at the center of the runway. The aircraft jerked abruptly to a halt, crumpling the right main gear. Like a large, broken toy, the plane fell to its side and slid slightly backward as the barrier tension overcame the plane's inertia.

The air was filled with sound as the fire crews merged on the stricken plane. Maintenance crews followed closely behind. On board the aircraft, both pilot and navigator scrambled from the wreckage, running from the burning plane. Before they could reach the grass beside the runway, the fire crews were covering the plane with foam.

The two men turned to look at what remained of their aircraft. "Damn, Joe, you broke it."

"They're cheap. We'll get another." Joe smiled at the older man who was watching the fire crews at work. "Fly with me tomorrow, Pete?"

"Damn right. That was great flying out there. Nice job, Joe."

"Thanks. By the way, what was that song you kept humming while we were on final approach?"

"*Guantanamera*. Sorry, I hum when I'm nervous."

"It must be on your mind. You were whistling the same tune while we were preflighting the aircraft."

"Yeah, I hum when I'm nervous; I whistle when I'm happy."

"Sounds good to me. I drink beer when I'm sad; I drink beer when I'm happy—same thing." Both men turned as Colonel Bennett's familiar pickup approached. The colonel jumped from the truck and walked quickly to the two men. He said nothing but extended his hand to Joe. Finally he spoke. "That was shit-hot flying, Joe."

"Thank you sir."

"Get in the truck; I owe you both a beer."

"Sounds great to me. I could use one right now."

"Me too."

As the truck pulled away, several large pieces of mobile equipment approached to drag the crashed plane off the runway. Already other flights were holding overhead, waiting to land.

"Ops One, Colonel Bennett."

He keyed the radio and waited for the reply.

"Roger, Colonel, what can we do for you?"

"After that plane is removed, I want twenty-five men to walk that entire runway to remove any FOD that might be left."

"Already underway, Colonel."

"Thanks, Glenn. Drop by later for a cold one."

"Roger that."

*　*　*

Dear Mom and Dad,

I've been thinking of you a lot recently. I miss you guys. In the midst of all that is happening here—I fly a sortie most every day—I met someone really interesting. She is one of the surgeons on the base. Her name is Kerrie Jernigen. (She's a major — she outranks me!)

The flying is great, but the weather is unbearably hot. Sure would like a ski trip to Winter Park! I bought an old bike to help me get around the base. Most of the guys got new ones and have to lock them to keep them from being stolen. Mine is so old no one else would want it, so I don't have to bother.

Joe sends his love. He says he'd give a month's pay for one of your pies, Mom.

Got to run for a flight briefing. I'll write more later.

Love, Robb

P.S. I'm getting a Distinguished Flying Cross for a mission I flew last month. Just thought you'd like to know.

Skovorodino, The Soviet Union

Dmitriy observed the dramatic changes in Dasha as the weeks passed. His own heart was heavy, but Nikolai's death had brought even another blow to his now frail grasp on reality. Dasha was living each day in his world, but she was dead. It was as if the very life had drained from her. She never smiled; her singing had ceased; and she spoke only when necessary. As he watched her, his own soul shrank as well. Slowly, but surely, the colors of life dulled into an interminable gray—the numbing of a soul.

The morning was cold and steel gray, tinged with the ever-present dull orange tint of the pollution that permeated everything. Dmitriy stood on the porch and breathed deeply the brisk morning air. He had slept little the night before, lying in his bed beside the still figure of his wife. He wondered whether she were asleep or not but dared not ask her. If she were asleep, he did not want to awaken her. If she were awake, the silence between them, like her pain, would have been unbearable. So he lay there wondering, wondering and planning. He would go to Vietnam and return with his son's body—even if it were a box of sandbags. Perhaps then Dasha would find the closure she needed so desperately. Perhaps together they could start the long difficult process of healing. He knew his life and Dasha's would never return to what they had known and shared, but perhaps, perhaps, it could be a life they could at least survive.

He looked beyond the snow-covered yard to the white mountains in the distance. He had learned to love this land—cold and bleak. It had always invigorated him and brought him such joy. Today, however, he found no pleasure in the fresh snow or the small birds that flitted through the large evergreens that populated his yard. Like everything in his life, the landscape was monochrome. All color, all joy was gone, as was all of his hope for the future. He turned slowly and walked back inside. The smell of strong coffee and frying bacon wafted through the house. He was not hungry, but the coffee would help him through the day. There was still much planning to do. "I'm going to Vietnam next Monday." Immediately Dasha raised her face. It was expressionless. She said nothing but waited for Dmitriy to continue. "They've found Nikolai; I'm going to bring him home. He will be buried here with full honors." She nodded and rose quickly to attend the bacon. He watched her carefully and noted that she wiped her right eye with her apron. It was a small move, but it brought him hope. Perhaps he could break down the wall she had built around her heart, around her very soul. Perhaps he could hold her, and they could weep together. Perhaps each could ease the pain for the other.

The eggs, heavy bread, bacon, and coffee were consumed without comment. Dmitriy was a large man and had always enjoyed Dasha's cooking. Today it was tasteless, but he ate anyway. He did so for Dasha and also for the strength he knew he would need. It would be a difficult day; he had a large region to administer, and he had arrangements to make. He had lied to Dasha; he knew there was no body, but he would bring back a casket to bury in the cold Siberian earth, and he would find answers to questions that had plagued him about the circumstances of that fateful day. Where had it happened, and how? Was his aircraft functioning as it should? It seemed impossible that a pilot like Nikolai would have lost an engagement with an American pilot. Perhaps the mechanics had not done their job. Perhaps Nikolai had been ill. Perhaps. Perhaps.

As he walked around the small table he placed both hands on his wife's shoulders as he had done so many times before. Dasha looked up at her husband. He kissed her forehead and turned for the door. He walked slowly, praying that she would call his name and run crying into his arms. But she did not. Dmitriy took his great coat from the closet in the hallway and glanced briefly at the rank on the shoulder boards. He had once dreamed of the general's boards; now it seemed so insignificant. He struggled into the heavy coat, reached for his hat and leather gloves, and walked slowly toward the door. He stopped briefly and pulled on the heavy gloves. He waited still a moment longer. Perhaps she would call his name. Perhaps she needed him as he needed her. In silence he waited, but she sat silently staring at her plate. Finally he opened the door and stepped out into the cold winter morning.

Dasha watched the broad, strong back of her husband as he walked toward the door. She noted that his normal gait was slower today. He seemed somehow smaller. She watched him, longing for him to turn and come to her. She needed his strength, but she knew how vulnerable he was. She was barely clinging to reality in her own pain. Surely he was equally burdened, and men had such difficulty handling grief. In time, he would prevail and once again give her the strength to live, but today he, too, was hanging by a thread. She could not disturb that. Her own existence depended upon him, and she would give him time--if only she could wait that long. How she needed him now, but she had noted how slowly he had walked to the door, how silently he had left the house. When he closed the door she rose, went to the window, and wiped the frost from the single pane of glass, watching her husband climb into the rear seat of the official car. The soldier closed the door behind his colonel and scrambled into the driver's seat, glad to be back in the relative warmth of the sedan. As the car accelerated down the street, Dasha waved weakly. She had loved Dmitriy since her early teens when she had watched him excel at sports and then struggle with math. He had been an awkward boy but totally devoted to her. Together they had grown into young adulthood, experimenting with sex, experimenting with love. Both had blossomed, and by the time he was commissioned a lieutenant, they were married with a child expected before his first operational assignment. It was a small, delicate little girl. Lidiya they had named her. She had lived only three months. Her frail little body had been no match for the cold, bitter Russian winter. Together they had buried her under a large fir tree. They had wept together and held each other close for comfort in the long dark nights that followed their loss. They persevered and vowed to have another baby as soon as the summer ended. But eight summers passed before Nikolai was born. He had been an ugly baby, but he had pulled the two together and made them a family. Efforts for a brother or sister had failed repeatedly. One miscarriage in the years after Nikolai's birth was all they could produce. But Nikolai was their joy. He was a bright boy, giving them love and respect and filling them with great pride. When he graduated from the university and was accepted into flight school, Dmitriy had strutted like a rooster. It had given Dasha such pleasure to see the two, father and son, talking strategy, politics, or simply snow shoeing in the vast forests, hunting rifles over their shoulders. She had always packed their lunches. She knew how much Dmitriy loved the black olives she saved just for him. Nikolai would always comment on the special cheeses she would select. It pleased her to watch the two men she loved interact with each other as father and son and as two very competent officers.

The cheese, he always loved the cheese. Dasha sat heavily into the stiff living room chair and surveyed the room around her. It was filled with things. There were plates from Moscow, a clock from Berlin, wooden carvings from Poland, lace doilies under everything. The doilies she had made herself. How important they had once been—how unimportant now. She rose and walked to the window again, looking to see Dmitriy's car, but it was gone. Gone, like her son, Nikolai. Gone, like Dmitriy's closest friend, like all that was important. She wiped the window with her hand again to clear the frost and peered down into the empty road. She probed her mind and measured her resolve. She was sinking into an emotional abyss as surely as the coming winter storms. She could find nothing to grasp onto, nothing to stop her slide. Dmitriy? She pondered that idea briefly and dismissed it. He was struggling himself. She could not bear to drag him into the abyss with her, as surely she would if she reached out to him. Dmitriy was barely navigating his own pain. She had lain beside him and felt the anger and the despair as he struggled with demons that only military men must know. If only Nikolai had chosen medicine or engineering. He had made such high marks in math and science. But no, he wanted the military, like his beloved father. Such fun they had together, drinking and eating cheese. How Nikolai had loved cheese.

Thailand

The blue Air Force truck lurched to a stop before a rambling building surrounded by an expansive bare lawn. A small metal fence ran the length of the yard and intercepted a tall hedge on either side. Lengthening shadows dispelled the sunlight, lending a sense of stillness to the late afternoon. Two occupants emerged from the truck. Before them was a rusted gate, hanging loosely from one hinge. The other had long since given way to the laughter and swinging of small children. The path to the wide porch on the building was worn. Large eyed children peered silently from the open window frames in the unpainted wall. There were no windows, only wooden shutters held back to let in light and air.

They stood beside each other, hand in hand, and looked at the opened door before them. They were a living contrast—the man, tall and blond, the boy, tiny and dark, his hair as black as coal. They found the reassurance they needed in each other's grasp, a bond of trust from a man to a boy, one that transcends race or creed and served to strengthen the relationship that was growing between them. Robb walked slowly toward the steps with Somboon clinging to him like a small monkey. Suddenly there was laughter inside, but it died quickly as the children watched the American approach with the small boy clinging to his neck.

Robb had researched the orphanage carefully and had expected to see nuns there. What he had not anticipated was their size. Barely taller than most of the children, two small Thai nuns approached. They said nothing but, after bowing, reached for the child. Somboon screeched in protest and clung even more tightly to Robb's neck. The small nuns looked at each other, spoke rapidly, but incomprehensibly to Robb, and indicated that he was to follow. As they started up the stairs to the orphanage, the children in the yard watched the pair silently. Robb noted several of the older ones were washing babies in a large metal tub in the shade of the porch; as they squatted in the dust, they too stopped their splashing to stare at the incongruous pair that passed.

The office surprised him. It was large and uncluttered, two chairs for guests, a desk, and a wall of books. A fan hummed above and provided some respite for the late afternoon heat. An old nun was writing and singing to herself, completely unaware of his presence. One of the small nuns spoke very loudly and both bowed deeply, their hands together as in prayer.

Startled, the older woman looked up. Her eyes met Robb and a smile spread across her wrinkled face. Carefully she screwed the cap on the old fountain pen, placed it and her letters aside, and with an effort she stood and extended her hand. She was tall, almost as tall as he. Tufts of blond gray hair protruded from her habit. Her face was ruddy; her eyes a very light blue. As she spoke the accent was unmistakable; she was English. "Would you care for coffee or tea, Captain?"

"Robb, please, and yes. Yes, thank you, sister. Tea would be nice."

Her eyes moved to Somboon. His eyes were very large. She smiled. "I'll bet he would like a biscuit."

"A biscuit? Oh yes, a biscuit." Robb smiled. She spoke rapid Thai to the two younger women and they left, bowing. Robb studied her carefully. She appeared to be in her late fifties, but he knew his judgment about a woman's age was only reliable to approximately thirty-five. He was also aware that she was reading his lips; her hearing was obviously limited. He made a mental note to speak louder and also to speak to the staff at the base hospital. A pair of hearing aids should be an easy task for them.

"Do you have the paperwork for the child?"

"Yes, but it is in English. Is that all right?"

She smiled, "Yes, I can handle English." There was a twinkle in her eye.

She has spirit, he concluded. Then he chuckled to himself at the pun. He wondered what she had been like as a young woman. Probably very pretty, he concluded. "Your Thai is remarkable; it's a difficult language."

"I suppose. Do you speak any Thai, Captain?"

"Robb, please."

"Robb." She tested his name; it was comfortable.

"A little," he paused, "very little."

"Perhaps," she referred briefly to the papers before her, "Perhaps Somboon can help you."

"Yes, and I can help him learn English." He glanced at the boy in his lap.

"Why?" She was looking at her papers and only glanced quickly to see the expression on his face. He felt the unrelenting gaze but had no answer to her question, his own mind confused.

The young nuns returned with steaming tea and rice cakes. Sister Estelle fished through the single drawer in the old desk and produced a large yellow candy wrapper. She held it to the child who grasped it with one hand while continuing to cling to the man with the other. The tea was hot and sweet. In typical British fashion, milk and sugar were offered to be mixed into the bitter black liquid.

"How long have you been here sister?"

"Fifteen years. And you?"

"Three months."

"The accident. Were you the pilot?"

"No, I'm the Civic Actions Officer for our squadron; I know the village and was the one who found him after the accident." He paused briefly. "It was a tragic accident. Everyone regrets it-- especially the pilot who was involved." He tried to explain; he felt a great need to explain that it was an accident--that such things were never done willfully. Instead, he simply said again. "It was a tragic accident."

"Of course." Sensing his discomfort and seeing no practical benefit in the current direction of the conversation, she shifted the focus to the child. "He seems rather attached to you."

"Yes, I think he is. We've become very close." Robb looked at the child while she studied his face--their faces. What she saw planted a small seed that sprang forth and grew rapidly in her mind. She smiled, muttering to herself. "God's ways are strange and mighty indeed."

"Pardon?"

"Nothing. Isn't this proper tea?"

"Yes, it is good." And he meant it. After three months of beer and coffee, the tea was a welcomed break.

The afternoon sun was dipping lower in the sky. Shadows in the room stretched slowly across the wooden floors as they talked. In time, the boy slept and was taken to his new cot by one of the smaller nuns. How strange a pair, the nun thought, one tall, the other so small. One brown, the other blond and sunburned. Yet, she thought, there's a bond there. God showed me that. And I know what to do with it. With His help I cannot fail. She smiled at Robb as he turned from the sleeping boy. Before he could speak, she assured him. "Don't worry, we'll take good care of him. But you'll need to visit very often for the next few weeks so he won't feel abandoned. That is very important."

"Fine, I intend to visit regularly anyway." He reached into his pocket and handed the woman an envelope. "Something from the Squadron; I'm sure it can be helpful." He looked out across the yard, "And I expect there will be much more from the government. I understand that the paperwork is in process."

"Thank you, you're right, we can always use the help." She took the envelope and placed it on her desk, unopened. "Let me walk you to the door."

As the blue pickup pulled away, the old woman walked back into the building, painfully climbing the steps. The arthritis was getting worse; she could vouch for that, but there was so much to do. She couldn't think about the pain, or the increasing difficulty to simply rise each morning. So much to do, and a new plan to devise. She smiled and walked into the small, deserted chapel. She sat before the beautifully carved crucifix and bowed her head. She had not knelt in over two years; she missed that, but she could forgo that personal joy to avoid the inevitable pain later. She knew that God understood; she needed her knees for other ways to praise Him. As she prayed, she smiled.

* * *

Dear Son,

This morning Frank Hutchinson stopped me at the store to inquire about you. He still remembers you from scouting. He mentioned how proud he was when he saw the article in the paper about your Distinguished Flying Cross. Son, I know you all hear about the demonstrations against the war. Well be assured that there are a lot of people here who respect all of you for the job you are doing. I'm proud of you, and you can be proud of yourself.

There is fresh rhubarb in the grocery store right now, but I'm not making any more pies until you get back to eat them.

I love and miss you so much.

Mom

PS. You need to write a note to Jason; he's worried about you over there. You know how seriously he takes his "big brother" role.

Robb, I just wanted to add something to this letter before Mary mailed it. I'm proud of your DFC; Barkers have always been men of courage and honor. You're carrying on that tradition in fine form. Someday when you're older, you'll look back with pride on the fact that when your country called, you answered, because you felt it was important. Just don't take too many chances over there. Do your job, as I know you will, but come home soon. Until then, just be safe.

I love you too,

Dad

* * *

The three aircraft flew off into the hot afternoon sky. It was a beautiful late afternoon. Small clouds hung over the green jungle below as the flight climbed toward the distant hills. Colonel Bennett led the flight, Robb was in number Two, and Joe was in number Three. Four had aborted prior to takeoff due to munitions difficulties.

Robb watched the sun sparkling off the lead's wings as he eased his F-4 into formation beside the colonel. "Two's in."

"Three's in."

Robb looked over across the lead aircraft at his best friend. Joe was probably smiling, though it was difficult to tell under the mask and sun visor. But Robb knew he was smiling. Joe always smiled when he flew. It was when he was most alive. Robb had never really seen Joe smile as he flew, but somehow he just knew that he did. He could not imagine it any other way. Robb knew many fine pilots, but Joe was the best, had always been the best. Somehow when he climbed into the plane, he became a part of it—no, rather, it became a part of him. When once asked how he performed a maneuver, Joe responded that he did not know how he did it; he simply thought about it, and it happened. Everyone had laughed, except Robb. Robb had known that it was true. Joe had merely to think of a maneuver—then it just happened. The plane was simply a part of his body, the same as his hands.

A sense of elation rose in Robb's mind and heart. He felt so free and so alive. What was it about the day that caused the blood to flow through his body so fast? What had piqued his mind, even his emotional state? He checked his oxygen; perhaps he had been on 100 percent. He watched the planes slicing through the skies as the late afternoon sun danced on the clouds below, the blue contrasting with the growing thunderheads off to the north, the great white clouds climbing silently in the sky.

The aircraft flew on in silence toward their target, a weapons storage area south of Hanoi. There was an electricity to the day that all the men felt. Ammo dumps were fun targets. The area would be heavily defended, but that was something they would face on most any mission near Hanoi.

"Cheetah flight, this is Moonbeam. How do you read me?" The evening sector controller was flying a circular track over northern Laos in a RC121 aircraft. His powerful radar had the fighters' exact location and the controller crew knew their exact mission details.

"Cheetah reads you five by."

"Roger Cheetah, you are cigarette on boxcar. Proceed to tango and execute Ford. Contact candy on Pepsi."

"Roger, Moonbeam, Cheetah is cigarette on boxcar. Will proceed to tango and execute Ford. Contact is candy on Pepsi." It was Colonel Bennett's navigator on the radio.

Col. Bennett keyed the intercom and spoke casually to his navigator. "What's that about, Hank? Sounds like a divert."

"Stand by, Colonel." Quickly he deciphered the coded message, then keyed his mike. "Moonbeam, this is Cheetah, leaving your frequency. Cheetah, go Pepsi."

Each of the three planes immediately switched frequency to that designated by code name "Pepsi".

"Cheetah Lead."

"Two."

"Three."

"Kangaroo, this is Cheetah."

"Kangaroo has you sixty-five miles southwest of my position. Continue on a heading of 045 degrees."

"045 degrees, Roger. Cheetah awaiting instructions."

"Roger Cheetah, stay this frequency and standby." The planes flew on in loose formation. They had entered enemy airspace earlier; all crews were alert and monitoring the sky before them. "Cheetah, this is Kangaroo. We need your help ASAP. We have 57 friendlies on Delta 17 manning the Tacan station there. They are under attack from an enemy battalion. We've got a chopper on the way, but it won't be there for another hour. How fast can you get there?"

"Standby Kangaroo." In his intercom, "Bill, dial in the coordinates for Delta 17. What's our ETA?"

"Seventeen minutes."

"Kangaroo, Cheetah can be there in ten."

"Expedite as fast as you can, Cheetah. Those boys need help—Now!"

"Roger Kangaroo, do you have ground frequency?"

"Compass on 181.6"

"Cheetah is leaving your frequency; we'll call you later when we clean up this mess."

"Good hunting, Cheetah."

"Cheetah, go 181.6."

"Lead's up."

"Two."

"Three."

Robb pressed forward on his throttle as the Colonel increased his speed. All three planes were accelerating through the darkening sky, rushing to save men outnumbered and outgunned.

Hank's voice broke the silence of the lead aircraft. "Coordinates are checked, we're twenty-five out, begin descent."

"Let's see if we can raise the troops on the ground." Bennett keyed his mike button. "Compass, this is Cheetah flight, can you read me?"

The voice on the reply was excited and frightened. "Boy are we glad to hear you guys. Where are you?" Lt. William Hartford watched the advancing army and wondered why he was standing on that mountain. His was a world of music. He was an accomplished violinist with a career of great promise ahead. Yet, for some strange reason he had felt the need to volunteer to serve his country. Perhaps it was his one chance to prove to his father that he was truly a man, even if he did choose music over engineering. Perhaps it was Billy Barton's death, killed during the first week of his tour of combat. Really, it did not matter. He was here, and he was frightened. But somehow he had to keep that fear from his men. They depended on him, and he could not fail them.

"Ten out, descending through twelve thousand."

"Hurry!" Over the background of the radio rifle fire could be heard with an occasional burst of machine gun fire. It was getting darker; the enemy had chosen a particularly difficult time to attack a mountaintop.

The F-4s began a large arc above the target area. All eyes were straining to see the mountain tops below. Like a huge reservoir filling with water, the darkness was slowly moving across the valleys and up the sides of the mountains. Soon it would be impossible to see anything below. "Compass, do you have a log?"

"Yes, red ones."

"Good, light one at your location."

"Now?"

"Now." In a few minutes, the red glow of a brightly burning flare shone through the evening shadows. "I've got your log." On the intercom, "Hank, how's it look down there? Have you checked the mountain tops?"

"Hold on, I'm plotting the site on my map right now."

"Alright, guys, arm for three 500 pounders per pass."

Hank's voice. "There's mountains to the northeast and south. All passes will be from east to West. Pull off southwest. Questions?"

"Let's do it!"

"Hurry damn it!" More rifle fire, more fear in the voice. "Do something fast! They're coming up the hill!"

"What is their location from the log?"

"Northeast, about two hundred yards! Shit! There's thousands of them. Oh shit! Hurry up!"

"One's in from the East."

Robb watched the lead F-4 bank abruptly and begin its dive toward the mountaintops below. "Two's in."

Eight seconds later. "Three's in."

The first string of bombs hit approximately 150 yards northeast of the burning flare. Three explosions rocked the side of the mountain. Ten seconds later three more struck nearby; another ten seconds and another three bombs. The airwaves were suddenly alive with chatter. "Shit hot! Wow! Look at that! They've stopped. Hot damn!"

"One's in from the east."

"Two's in."

"Three's in."

Pass after pass the planes dived at the ground, leaving behind their loads of bombs. With each pass the cheering on the ground increased as the 17 Americans and 40 Laotians watched the overwhelming enemy being crushed by the planes above. "They're retreating! They're retreating! Look at them go!"

"Compass, now what is the enemy's distance from the log?"

"They're retreating!"

"What is their distance from the log?" Colonel Bennett was shouting; he was also smiling.

"Oh, 250 to 300 yards and moving fast—northeast."

"One's in—250 yards northeast."

"Two's in—300 yards."

"Three's in—splitting the difference." The bombs followed the retreating troops, raining death on the soldiers caught on the open mountainside.

"Three's Winchester." There was a long silence as Joe announced all ordnance expended.

"Cheetah, they're turning around! They're coming back! Oh shit!"

"Hang on Compass. Cheetah, say status."

"Two's Winchester on bombs."

"Three—samo."

"They're coming back, they're coming back! The voice was

almost screaming now. Are you guys out of bombs?" Small arms fire sounded in the background over the radio.

"All we've got are four CBUs each."

"Drop them. Fast!"

Joe spoke what was on all of the aircrews' minds. "If we drop the CBU's we'll throw bomblets across that entire mountain. We'll get you guys too."

Colonel Bennett's voice was cool and heavy with authority. "Stand by Three. Compass, do you have any bunkers?"

"Yes!"

"Now listen up, Compass. If we drop the CBUs it's going to be a mess down there. We can't confine them to the enemy. You'll be hit too."

"If you don't get us they will. Drop them!"

The colonel paused for a moment; when he resumed, his voice was cold and commanding. "Listen up Compass. I know this will be hard for you to do in the face of enemy fire, but you'll have to trust us. Get all of your men in those bunkers. Cover the doors with anything you have. These munitions are not particular who they kill. Do you understand? No one is to stay outside. Now, where are the enemy right now, and what is their approach direction and speed?"

"They're heading back uphill, that is southwest, at about walking speed. They're 200 to 250 yards out now."

"Get in that bunker—now—everyone! Do you understand?"

"Yes sir."

"Do it! Now! Cheetah, listen up; push your delivery 1000 feet. These CBUs are on timers and they'll open at 2500 feet instead of 3500. We'll choke the dispersion—just like an old 12 gage. Hank, mountain problems with that strategy?"

"Keep pulling to the west and southwest. If you pull north or south you'll be an ornament on some karst formation."

"One's in from the east. And for the asshole who's monitoring this frequency down there, this one's for you."

"Two's in. So's this."

"Three's in. This too."

The advancing troops were caught in the open with hundreds of small bomblets raining down on them. On the mountainside it was chaos and death. For four passes each, the F-4's dove at the small flare on the ground and dropped their loads. When the last CBU was dropped, there was little left of the enemy force below. Bodies were scattered everywhere, men crying in pain and screaming in anger. Six men above them had demolished an entire battalion of Hanoi's finest troops.

Twenty minutes later two Chinook C-54 helicopters arrived and picked up seventeen grateful Americans and forty Laotians and carried them safely to Thailand.

* * *

Dear Mom and Dad,

Last night we got diverted and arrived in the nick of time to save a platoon of GIs and about 40 friendlies surrounded on a mountain top. What a great feeling. All the good guys were rescued by helicopters.

Mom, sure do miss your cooking; can't wait to get home for one of those rhubarb pies—don't forget the recipe! I've lost about 10 pounds. (Dad, want to come over?) Ha! Tonight we're having a steak cookout at the club. Jack Treadeau says he can grill the best steak in the world. Well, Dad, he hasn't tasted one of yours yet!

Love you both,

Robb

* * *

Sister Jean Patrice Estelle stood before a small, dark mirror. She glanced in it, wondering if the mirror really was as bad as it appeared, or were her eyes simply tired, or was eyesight dimmed by pain, love, sacrifice--or age. She dressed quickly, wishing she could go bareheaded. But the veil, like the black habit, had truly become a part of her life. She smiled and prayed quietly as she looked into the small dark mirror. Today would be a day with the Americans. She reflected on the two—so young and so talented. It was still dark outside, but already the heat had enveloped her tiny room. Oh, for an air conditioner, she thought. But how could she spend so much money on comfort when there are so many needs, so many mouths to feed. That thought alone brought her great comfort, for she had more blessings than she felt she deserved. And she knew each one by name, every smile, every cry. They were her gifts, granted by a loving God in return for her devotion and her life of struggle and commitment. Who could be more blessed than she? But today she was worried. She had spent most of the prior evening observing her newest blessing, watching him and struggling with the vague shape of a plan, a plan that could insure his future--one small success in a world of many failures.

A small, young woman entered with a hard roll and a cup of steaming black coffee. It was Sister Estelle's one luxury. She had never adjusted to the tradition of tea in that part of the world. Coffee had been her choice of drink for over forty years. She was too old to change now; besides, a generous benefactor kept her well supplied with the finest coffees found in the local markets. In return she was raising two of his illegitimate children. Two more blessings. "Thank you, Letok." The hot coffee was black--no sugar, another luxury she could do without. Scalding hot and bitter, it sharpened her mind and braced her for the day ahead. Check the children first, oversee breakfast, review the weekly inventory of food, visit the market, decide what to do with the American money that was suddenly coming from the Air Base. And Somboon, he must be baptized. There was no one to speak for him, so she would decide that herself. He *would* be baptized – immediately. Her gift to the God she served. She smiled to herself. Such a fine gift from such a poor woman; no queen could offer more.

"Letok, Is the American doctor coming today? The woman doctor?"

"Yes sister."

"Good, please get me my pen and paper. I have a note I wish delivered to Captain Barker at the American Air Base. Ask our most trusted messenger to meet me in my office in an hour."

"Yes sister."

"Bless you Letok; you are a wonderful helper."

The young woman smiled and lowered her head. "Thank you sister."

"Now hurry, I have much work to do today. God has placed an idea in my mind, and I must act quickly."

The young woman smiled and rushed from the room. She was deliriously happy. She had a gift, too, and it would arrive the following spring. How wonderful God is, she thought, and how handsome the shopkeeper's oldest son.

Chapter Three

Hanoi, North Vietnam

The Vietnamese colonel spoke softly but with the authority of a man who had seen much war. Colonel Tien Van Tran was barely five feet six inches tall, but his mind and his will were great. He watched the Russian colonel across the table. The Russian was a large man, but Tran knew he had been made small by pain. His eyes bespoke a sadness the Vietnamese colonel understood, and the pallor of his skin indicated far too much alcohol. Like the impressive uniform, Dmitriy Ruchinsky was suddenly old and a bit worn. Tran liked him immediately. He also recognized that Dmitriy might be used to assist him in his constant struggle for ammunition and supplies. The Russian was wounded, and he was also angry. That was a combination he might use. Tran glanced at the young bar maid whom he had briefed earlier, and she rushed forward with more of the vodka that both men were drinking—or so it seemed. In reality, Dmitriy was drinking vodka; Tran was drinking water. The young waitress would be well rewarded later.

The alcohol was finally working, and the Russian was beginning to talk more freely. He had been silent when Tran had given him the bag containing his son's things. Tran had watched the Soviet commander of the entire Southeastern Siberia Region, commander of thousands of men, a man like himself, silently withdraw each item and examine it carefully. In the very bottom of the cloth sack was the item he least expected, his son's ring, given to him by Dmitriy himself when Nikolai had graduated from the university. Dmitriy looked at it briefly, withdrew his handkerchief and wrapped it carefully and put it in his breast pocket. It took him several moments to regain his composure. He simply sat there staring into the distance, a huge struggle raging inside his heart and mind.

"We found those things in his room. I knew you would want to have them."

At last the Russian spoke. "Yes, thank you."

Dmitriy drank the vodka quickly. It was not the quality he was accustomed to, but at the moment, that mattered little. Finally he looked at his comrade in arms and broached the question that he had come to discover. "How was my son killed? Do you have any information that I might know?"

Tran looked sadly at the man before him, his mind racing back over two years when he, too, had asked the same question of another man. He had planned such an elaborate lie for this Russian, but now he knew he could not use it. Tran was shocked at his own reaction to this situation. He had devoted most of his adult life to the struggle for his country; there was no price he was not willing to pay, but now he felt some strange kinship with this fat Russian before him. Perhaps it was the common bond of military men the world over; perhaps it was a bond far stronger. Hadn't he, too, lost sons in war? Hadn't he, too, been given just such a sack? He understood Dmitriy's pain. He had two sacks hanging in his own small house. His own heart had scars similar to the fresh one the man before him was trying to handle. Tran wondered if Dmitriy's wife cried at night as his own did. He guessed most women were the same regarding their children. He looked at the face of the man across the small bar table and determined that he could not tell him the lie he had planned. He couldn't tell him that the equipment had failed, allowing the Americans to kill him mercilessly. That might earn more supplies and better planes from the Soviets, but he could not do it. Dmitriy was a man of honor, a military colonel who had lost his son. Tran could not lie to such a man; neither could he tell him the truth—that his son had actually died of an infection that neither of them could understand or even pronounce.

Tran looked straight into the face of the man slumping in his chair before him and placed his hand on Dmitriy's arm. "He died a hero, my friend. He was flying with two North Vietnamese pilots. They were defending Hanoi against what we estimate to be a force of over twenty-five American jets. Your son downed two American planes and damaged two more before he was lost. He is to receive North Vietnam's highest award for valor. Your son was a man of great courage—like his father, I suspect." Dmitriy's face was expressionless, but behind the green eyes a great battle was raging. When he had won it he shifted his body in the small chair; Tran noticed that he sat taller now.

"Thank you, Colonel Tran."

"We should thank you, Colonel Ruchinsky."

"One more question. Was his body recovered?"

"I'm sorry, no."

"I have a favor to ask—for his mother." Dmitriy explained his plan.

"I understand. I, too, buried a box of sand in my village."

"I'm sorry. I should have guessed."

"In war, the civilities of life are often put aside while we fight and grieve, and then fight again. It was three years ago. I live each day to fight in his memory." Dmitriy drank the remaining liquor in his glass. It was refilled immediately by the smiling barmaid. Tran watched the Russian carefully. He had done what he had to do, but there was still a chance to push his agenda. Perhaps his chances were even enhanced by the new friendship. There were many avenues to approach the issue of material support from the Soviets. Dmitriy was downing the vodka like water, but it appeared to have little effect on the big man. The water, however, was having its predictable effect on him. He rose suddenly. "I must make room for more vodka. Will you excuse me?"

"I think I'll join you." Dmitriy rose, a bit unsteadily, causing the young barmaid to grin largely behind his back.

"Come friend, I'll show you the way." As the two men walked from the room, Tran winked furtively at the young woman and began to try out the new approach he had been formulating with his new agenda in mind. "I drink to all the brave men who fight for the freedom of Vietnam, and I piss on the American dogs who bomb our cities and kill our children."

"As do we." The two men walked down the small hall and out into the warm Vietnamese night.

Nubat Air Base, Thailand

Kerrie watched the two playing in the water, man and boy. What differences are there between men and boys she wondered. Probably just age and size. It made her smile. Well, there are a few differences, she thought as the tall young man lifted the small boy over his head. The muscles in the man's arms were impressive, she noted. Medically speaking, she thought, he's a very handsome and sexy man--medically speaking of course. The thought caught her completely by surprise. If only he weren't so obnoxious. She smiled. I wonder if he's married. She knew that none of the pilots wore jewelry. It was a safety factor for fighter pilots; they also needed and wanted none in combat. But there was another way; she knew an old trick. All she had to do was feel the underside of his third finger, left hand. If he had worn a ring there, the indentation would remain. Kerrie paused; why was she in the least concerned about this brash young man? She looked again at the muscular young body and the shape of his butt stretching the thin fabric of his faded swimsuit and flushed slightly as her mind imagined the remainder of his body. It was young and strong and tanned, so different from the scarred and damaged limbs she worked over each day in the operating room. Immediately she chastised herself. What was a doctor, a surgeon, doing with such wild visions dancing in the shadows of her mind? Then she smiled. Of course, she must be ovulating. It was that time of the month. Wasn't she still a woman? And yes, she decided, he was beautiful. What a strange adjective for this brash young man, but how apropos—he was beautiful.

The tiny boy splashed water on the man and laughed as the pilot chased him into the water, both laughing loudly. They stopped and waved at her briefly. She waved back, smiling, and turned to the older woman seated beside her. "Sister Estelle, this was a great idea. It is so good to get away from the hospital and the base." They were seated on a grassy knoll overlooking a large, shallow river that moved lazily through the soggy jungle.

"I'm glad you could come. Frankly, I love the opportunity to speak English more often." She unwrapped a small basket by her chair. "Would you care for a sandwich?"

"That sounds great. Shall I call the kids?" She motioned to the two in the water.

"Don't worry, as soon as they see we've got food, they'll come in a hurry." More shrieks came from the water. "They have become very close." She said it carefully and thoughtfully. Kerrie grasped the significance immediately.

"Yes, they have."

"He's a sensitive young man. Somboon needs that." Again, deliberately spoken.

"Yes, I think you're right." Both women fell suddenly silent, each weighing the intentions of the other.

* * *

The sandwiches were wrapped in brown paper and tied with heavy string. Robb finished the last one and threw the ragged crust toward the brackish river that slowly floated on its silent journey toward the sea. He adjusted his position against the scrubby tree and relaxed luxuriously on the grass while Kerrie busied herself with gathering the remains of the picnic into a large bag. Sister Estelle had made her apologies when she left earlier.

"Aren't you worried about the kids being so close to the water?"

"Those kids? They were swimming before they could walk. Did you ever see Thailand from the air? It's about ninety percent water. Looks like a great big mirror divided into small rectangular plots." He pushed the sunglasses back from the tip of his nose. "Sometimes at night you can watch the reflection of the moon as it slides across the paddies; really eerie with dark clumps of trees that move like clouds on a wet sky."

"That's almost poetic. You must be happy."

"I just feel good today. I'm not on the schedule tonight; I'm full of great food and Portuguese wine; and I have a beautiful woman for company. What more could a man want?" Before she could answer, the children down by the river began to shout excitedly. One of the older boys motioned toward Robb. "Cap! Cap!" He climbed reluctantly to his feet and patted his full belly as he walked down the small hill. He was back in a few minutes followed by the throng of kids. "They found a turtle. You'd think it was the treasures of King Solomon himself."

Kerrie had taken his place against the tree, so Robb squirmed in beside her. "Sort of reminds me of when I was a boy. Somehow when you watch them it seems to bring all that enthusiasm and excitement for life back, but only for an instant, just long enough to remind you that there is something exciting about a turtle or a leaf, the beauty of spring, or the first snow of winter. It's all there, wrapped up in the laughter or wonder of discovering a tadpole in the process of growing legs." Robb checked his watch and began waving at the children. "We've got to get this outfit in gear. I've got to go out to Ban Pla Duc after dropping them off at the orphanage. Want to come along?"

"Sure, I'm scheduled to spend an afternoon there next week to evaluate the locals; this would give me the chance to get to know them."

*　*　*

The dark blue pickup glided smoothly along the newly finished highway that led through the green jungle. On either side of the black streak was the muddy sore of the torn earth. Already the sticky jungle growth had begun to creep back across the deep scars and threaten the new construction. Robb was deep in thought, the creases on his forehead lined against the brown tan. Kerrie watched him intently, speaking quietly. "This is a nice road. Did we build it for the local people?"

"Pardon?" Robb's mind was focused on the trip he was undertaking. He wondered how the villagers would regard him now. He had not been to Ban Pla Duc since the bombing. Would they understand the accident; would they understand that the same intellect than can successfully build and pilot these large machines is also capable of mistakes, of panic, of indecision? Would it really matter if they did? The sound of the young woman's voice snapped his mind back to the present.

"Did we build this road for the Thais? It's the best one I've seen around here."

"It just leads to the bomb dump. Stops about a mile and a half from here. After that it gets pretty rough."

"Oh."

The road stood proudly above the creeping jungle and represented the incursion of civilization as it marked a path across the green wilderness. The truck slowed perceptibly as it rounded a corner; Robb swerved sharply to avoid two water buffalo that plodded along the center of the road. The two small boys riding the beasts waved happily to the two Americans and then looked suspiciously as the truck began to slow down. It stopped and then backed slowly towards the foursome. Robb said nothing but reached into a blue handbag at his feet and produced two candy bars. He extended them and watched the eyes widen with the broad smiles. They all nodded formally and the blue Dodge pulled away. No words were spoken, but a message had been conveyed.

"I wondered what you had in that bag."

Robb shrugged as he drove. "Well, kids are kids the world over. Candy and smiles are a hell of a lot cheaper than bullets." The two officers passed the bomb dump and turned off onto a narrow dirt road. After several minutes of bouncing along the deep ruts, they turned into a clearing before the river. Her eyes followed the sandy road; then she saw the bridge.

Doctor Kerrie Jernigen peered at the narrow, rickety bridge that lay before the truck and turned pale. "Are you sure that thing will hold the weight of this truck? It doesn't look sturdy enough for a bicycle. It's made of sticks."

He looked at her as earnestly as he could while smiling inside. "I don't know; it looks like it might handle this truck."

"Might?"

"Well, maybe."

"Maybe?" Her voice was rising as they approached the bridge. "That's not good enough for me."

"Well, if one of us got out and walked across, the truck would weigh less." He looked to the left so she could not see his face. "I'll get out if you want."

"Stop the truck and let me out. You drive across; I'll walk."

"Alright, if you wish." She climbed from the truck and started to walk across in front of the truck. He watched her walk toward the bridge, a slight bounce in her stride. He evaluated the woman before him and considered that she must have a lot of spirit to be here in the jungles of Thailand. She had a lot of spunk. He smiled as she looked back at him, watching to see what he would do. Slowly he proceeded behind her, watching her trim figure in the tight fatigues.

On the other side, she watched as he pulled off of the bridge to pick her up. As she got into the truck, she looked at his smiling face. "How many times have you crossed that bridge before?"

"Oh, probably a dozen or more." He watched to see her reaction.

"Smart-ass!" She reached over and shoved his shoulder playfully.

Robb was smiling broadly. "Actually, the first time I crossed that bridge I also did so on my own two feet while my Thai assistant drove across after me. In fact, it was only after I'd seen several trucks cross it that I would ride over in one. But you did look great from behind."

*   *   *

Silently the pair looked at the large hole filled with water. After a few moments they turned and proceeded towards the small village. Behind them the open sore festered in the rotting earth; the decay around them slowly filling it and erasing the visible evidence of a tragic event, leaving nothing more than painful memories in the frail minds of those left behind.

The village was not at all what Kerrie had expected. It sprang suddenly from the jungle and surprised her. One moment she was walking along a white sand path; the next moment she was surrounded by small frail houses set on poles and elevated from the hot ground. Swarms of naked children jumped from the thick undergrowth and surrounded the pair of Americans. Then the old people appeared, and lastly, the middle aged adults. Robb produced the bag, and in a gesture that is understood around the world, he distributed the goodies to the children. For the most part, they were shy and quiet around the strangers, but the small eager hands quickly accepted the gifts. They didn't eat the treasures immediately; for long moments they merely studied the wrappers and sniffed at the delicious morsels. The adults watched them longingly, swallowing frequently from the sudden profusion of saliva.

One large chocolate roll was held back. "Sorry kids, this is for Mai Dee. I made a promise." The children didn't understand the language of the visitor, but when he put the candy into his pocket, their hands were immediately withdrawn. Robb glanced at his watch and, signaling Kerrie, turned quickly from the throng of giggling children. He turned down one of the smaller paths leading into the jungle; after five minutes walk they came to a small clearing with a rotting structure in the center. Beside it was a small creek covered with the slimy growth of green, foul smelling algae. Several skinny chickens scurried around the brown crumbling structure, careful not to leave the small clearing and the protection it afforded. Robb stopped at the edge of the clearing and waited for Kerrie to join him.

The young girl who stepped from the leaning bamboo building was beautiful. She reached barely to Kerrie's shoulder. She was small and graceful, and her face had the serenity of a person much older. The large dark eyes were soft, and the long dark hair flowed to her tiny waist. She wore a patched blouse that permitted an occasional glimpse of her smooth stomach and a sarong that reached to her ankles. She was barefoot; only the large hardened feet broke the perfection. Silently she led the two visitors to a cool shaded area beneath the hooch. There on a makeshift cot lay Mai Dee. She was a withered old woman, and the skin clinging to her face was as brown and worn as an old saddle. She was blind, and the smile she offered was toothless. "Mai Dee expects her Tootsie Rolls whenever I visit. She'd consider it a big insult if I forgot." Robb smiled as he placed the candy into the weathered hand. "And I've heard she has influence with the spirits around these parts." The old woman smiled broadly and began to shake her head up and down at the familiar voice. Her wrinkled hand found Robb's arm and squeezed it firmly as she mumbled something that neither of the two Americans could understand.

"Do you know what she said?"

"It's either thank you or a blessing. I guess I could use either." With a nod they turned and left.

As he started back up the path, Kerrie watched his back and wondered about this man before her. Here was a man who flies combat and bombs enemy he can't see, yet here in the jungle he cares for even the weakest in the village. What makes a man like that tick, she wondered. In her own world it was simple—heal all who needed it. That was her goal; that was her oath. What were this man's goals? Can compassion and anger coexist in the same mind and heart? Can a man be both gentle and violent? If so, what is the dividing line between them? She increased her pace to keep up with his longer strides. "Robb, how does she live? I mean, what does she eat? They don't have baby food here; what does she do without teeth?"

Robb pushed a large, intrusive limb from his face and held it carefully as Kerrie ducked under it. "They do what they have to do. The young girl, the pretty one? Well, she eats for the old woman. She chews the food, places it back into a spoon, and then gives it to the old woman to swallow." The young doctor grimaced at the thought. "It's not too bad; it's a damn sight better than starving." He slowed his pace to facilitate the shorter woman. "You'll get used to it after a while. I'll come back with you when you visit the village if you want. They need to trust you; you have so much to offer them. Basic medical care is non-existent out here."

The woman looked at the man walking beside her. "Yes, it would be a good idea if you came along. I have a lot to learn about these people."

"I'd love to." He was smiling broadly.

*　*　*

For over a month the two had spent much of their free time working together at the village or the orphanage. Initially they had found themselves together per the secret magic of Sister Estelle's superb planning. After several weeks, however, they began coordinating their visits on their own, much to the older nun's delight. They worked together with the local population. Whenever the doctor checked the young or the ill, the pilot was generally nearby organizing the villagers for some project. Whenever Robb and his friends were busy repairing a roof or building a shed, Kerrie was nearby coordinating her work. Their work drew them together, and the closeness blossomed into a deep friendship. All the while the nun watched, prayed, and smiled secretly to herself.

The warm Thai evening surrounded the five people sitting on the large porch. Letok brought tea, which no one drank. Robb brought a bottle of wine that he, Kerrie, and Sister Estelle were enjoying, along with the music from an old record player that had been at the orphanage longer than anyone could remember.

The conversation had lulled when the small nun placed another record on the old turntable. It was a waltz. As the music began,

Robb jumped to his feet and grabbed Kerrie, sweeping her along with the music.

"I don't know if I can waltz." she exclaimed.

"Nonsense, anybody can waltz."

The small boy clapped his hands and the two nuns watched as the young couple danced across the porch. The music rose and swept the two along. Though she was reluctant at first, Robb guided Kerrie expertly across the uneven boards and around the various chairs and the swing at the end of the porch. When the music finally faded, he swung her back into place beside the smiling boy and the grinning nuns. She was breathless, her eyes shining, her cheeks flushed.

"There. How was that?"

"Exquisite!" she exclaimed, looking at him strangely. "You dance well."

"Of course, I'm a fighter pilot," he laughed.

"And you waltz like a pro."

"Care for another?"

She looked at him briefly. "Yes, Yes I would."

"Sister, strike up the band."

They held each other more closely as they glided across the porch to the music. Sister Estelle smiled at the two. She watched them; they were oblivious to the world. Their eyes were locked, and their arms clung to each other tightly. When had she last danced, herself? It was so long ago. As the music died into the evening air, she reached and started the record again. The young pilot and the young surgeon never even noticed. They simply danced through the soft breeze that wafted across the yard and onto the five people swaying to the music's spell. When finally it stopped Robb reached down and kissed Kerrie gently. She stood on her tiptoes to reach his lips and kissed him back. On her face was the look of utter surprise. Neither was even remotely aware of the blushing women or the grinning child who watched them. He held her long after the music had stopped, after even the kiss. Like her, there was a strange look upon his face; like her, he was a little breathless.

The older woman watched them intently. Outwardly she was smiling; inwardly she was praying, a prayer of thanks. Her request had been granted. The plan was working, and it was beautiful, far more beautiful than she had imagined. The looks on their faces were so clear to her; her plan was progressing far faster than she had even imagined. And it was beautiful--like the two young people before her. The blood rushing to the nun's face was evident, even to her. Sister Estelle reached her hands to her own face. The heat, the color-- she knew they were there, like the spreading smile. "Thank you," she whispered silently into the evening sky as the young pilot smiled into the face of his dance partner. As she turned away, she noted that his dance partner was still on tiptoes, and her smile broadened.

Skovorodino, The Soviet Union

The young officer stood stiffly at attention, afraid to look at the red faced colonel who stood beside him shouting. He could feel the hot breath of the older man on his neck as perspiration ran down his face and dripped from his chin, despite the cold temperature in the room. There was pain on his face and fear in his heart. "What do you mean you lost a shipment of ballistic missiles? How does one lose a shipment of missiles 20 meters long?" The colonel walked around the young officer in circles as he shouted at him. "Is there no competence in this army anymore? Lose missiles? That's outrageous! Are you some imbecile?" Dmitriy was shaking with anger and frustration. "Get out of my office and find those missiles at once! Don't sleep; don't eat; don't take a piss until those missiles are found and accounted for. You may be a captain today, but if those weapons are not under my control by tomorrow morning, you will be a sergeant in charge of latrines. Is that understood?"

"Yes, colonel."

"Now get out! Out! Now!" Barely breathing, the captain did an abrupt about face and marched out of the door. He left the drab, gray building and cut across the snow-covered parade ground. His lieutenant joined him and hurried alongside as he sprinted across the bare, windswept field. Above them the cold winter sky brooded, the dark gray clouds heavy with moisture, waiting to dump their white burden on the frozen landscape below.

"What happened, Captain Odnoralov?"

"I got my ass chewed; that's what happened." His face was still red, and he was sweating in the cold morning air. "The old fart has not been the same since his son died. But that gives him no excuse to treat me like an enlisted man." He snapped his head toward the younger officer. "And what the hell are you doing here anyway? Why aren't you out checking all of the rail yards for those damned missiles? Round up all of the men in the company; get them out of bed and on this assignment right away. I want those missiles found before dinner or there will be no dinner. Do you understand?"

"Yes sir."

"The man who finds those missiles gets a week's leave. Pass the word."

"Does that include officers?"

"That includes every swinging dick in the company. Now get your ass over to the command post and get started." The lieutenant sprinted off in one direction while the captain walked briskly in the other. From the window in the second floor corner office, Dmitriy Ruchinsky watched in dismay. His face was still red; he was still angry. How could men of such little capability serve as officers? The bigger question in his mind was one that had taunted him for several weeks. How could such inept young men laugh and drink with their friends while his own son lay rotting in some Vietnamese jungle? Dmitriy was not a man of faith. He had rejected religious faith, not because of the state position but because of his own intellectual assessment of the world. He believed in no God except man's own sheer intellect. Nikolai's death was even more proof of his position. How could any logical spirit allow the survival of such idiots as those he watched from his window each day while his own son, a man of such promise and capability, was dead. It made no sense at all. Surely there could be no logic in such a god. If such a power did exist, Dmitriy wanted no part of it.

The colonel walked to his desk and pulled the bottle of vodka from his lower left-hand drawer. He poured a small amount in a glass and drank it quickly. He had never been a man who drank during the working day, but recently he needed something to calm him. He knew the small amounts he was drinking would not affect his logic; neither would it become obvious to those in the offices around him. After all, he was still the region commander—even if it were one of the more remote posts in the army. Dmitriy sank heavily into his chair and stared at the blank faces on the pictures that adorned his sparse office. What ugly men they were. True, they may have been great leaders, but why were all leaders such ugly men? He pondered that momentarily to calm himself. Perhaps they became great in order to compensate for their dire lack of physical attractiveness. Yes, he concluded, that was it. If they had been attractive men they would have probably lived common lives of desperation—like his own. Dmitriy pondered his last thought. Desperation? Had his life been one of desperation? Had he not accomplished the rank of colonel? His only son had died, but he had died a hero. Desperation? No, not desperation. Sadness, perhaps. Yes, sadness for what might have been. All that he had lost—then it hit him. He had lost his grandchildren in that fiery explosion. He would never be a grandfather, and Dasha would never hold her grandchildren like the other women did. Dmitriy walked to his door, closed it, and turned the lock. He went back to his chair, poured another vodka, a larger one, and sat quietly in his office with only the ugly men to watch his pain while he waited for the vodka to dim the hurt.

*   *   *

The sun had been down over an hour when the Soviet captain walked stiffly into the office and saluted Dmitriy. "Sir, we have found eight missiles. The idiots at the rail yard sent them to the wrong siding. They were fifty-five kilometers from the rail yard where they were expected. I have two detachments guarding them around the clock. They will not be out of our control until safely secured at the base." He stood stiffly, but Dmitriy noted that he stood with pride.

"I thought there were twelve missiles missing."

"Yes sir, but I believe the invoice is inaccurate. I'm checking."

"Thank you, captain. I want you to personally stay with the guards until the missiles are offloaded at Warehouse Five. If you need any additional assistance, you have my authority to commandeer any help you need. Do you understand?"

"Yes sir."

"Dismissed."

"Sir?"

"Yes?"

"The paperwork for the missiles." He handed over a large leather folder with stacks of paperwork inside.

"Thank you, captain. You did well to find them so fast. I hope you realize the importance of such cargo. With the Chinese buildup going on in Qiqihar, we must maintain our military readiness. That's only 700 kilometers from where we stand. Do you know how long it would take those Chinese hordes to knock on our doors?"

"Yes sir, I do."

"Let me know as soon as you reconcile the number disparity."

"Yes sir, I will." The young man relaxed somewhat and turned sharply and left.

Dmitriy was tired, very tired. He considered his fatigue. Was it the pain of suffering that caused the weariness that hung over him like a heavy blanket; was it the vodka, or was he simply getting older? Did it matter? Suddenly he felt hungry and wanted to go home. The thought of home was the first pleasant thought he had experienced all day. Home was warm, and Dasha would have dinner on the stove, waiting. She was slowly recovering from Nikolai's death, as was he. Once in the night he had awakened to her crying. He had reached for her, and she had clung to him in her pain. Somehow that had given him strength. He loved her so, and he had to be strong to help her through the difficult days ahead. It gave him purpose in his life. Together they would get through the terrible fate they had been dealt. He stopped and felt a sudden pain in his soul. Had she realized the loss of their grandchildren? Had that awful thought penetrated her damaged spirit? He hoped not. She had suffered enough. Surely she would one day realize that additional loss, but not now. She had load enough to carry through her painful days. He picked up the reports and walked slowly to the old safe in the corner of his office. It took three tries to open it, frustrating him and encouraging several curses. As the safe's door finally swung open, he perused the first few pages of the reports. Twelve SR-04 Short Range Ballistic Missiles (SRBMs) were being shipped to his sector. They were armed with small nuclear warheads and had a range of over 1500 kilometers. The target information would be sent by classified means later. Dmitriy shrugged— 1500 kilometers—had to be Beijing. What other targets would they hit from this sector other than Qiqihar? The simple fact that he could hit Beijing was enough to ensure the buildup across the border would be held in check. He tossed the file into the safe and slammed it shut. His mind was tired and he wanted to go home.

* * *

The relentless ringing of the phone roused Dasha from her sleep. She, in turn, shook her husband; after all, it was highly unlikely that one of her friends would call in the middle of the night. Dmitriy groaned loudly and rolled from his warm bed. The cold floor caused him to search for his slippers. Once found, he stumbled awkwardly in the dark for the stairs that led down to the phone in his small study. He fully expected it to stop its relentless ringing before he could reach it, but it did not. That simple fact shot adrenaline into his waking body. Only some emergency would require such diligence. "Col. Ruchinsky."

"Good evening Colonel. I apologize for calling at this late hour. As you can probably imagine, the hours of the day mean much less in a war zone."

"Colonel Tran, how good to hear from you. I want to thank you for your diligence in having my son's award here in time for his funeral. It meant much to both me and my wife."

"It is I and my country who should thank you and your wife for your great sacrifice for Vietnam. You may note that our great leader signed the commendation himself. That is a great honor here in our country. You may be very proud of your son and his service to us."

"Yes, thank you."

"I called to pass along some information that you asked about while you were here in Hanoi. We have determined that the horde of planes that shot down your son and many of our own brave pilots on that day were from Nubat Airbase in central Thailand. We lost four aircraft that day; they lost seven."

"Nubat? It was not a Navy pilot?"

"No, it was an American Air Force group."

"I see." Dmitriy rubbed his eyes and tried to concentrate. Tran's Russian was heavily accented, and it required his full attention to discern the message he was hearing.

"It will take time, but the Americans will pay for their cowardice."

"You will attack Nubat?" There was surprise in Dmitriy's voice.

"Oh no. That would be impossible. Nubat is over 400 kilometers away and heavily guarded. No, we will make them pay, but unfortunately, not at Nubat."

"Did you say 400 kilometers?"

"Yes, from Vihn. It is far too distant for us to attack now. But someday we will find a way."

"Only 400 kilometers?" he reiterated. In the back of his mind Dmitriy's subconscious began to calculate. He had no idea that it was a shorter distance from Vihn to Central Thailand than from his own sector to Beijing.

"Yes."

"Perhaps there is a way."

"I'm sorry; I do not understand."

"Maybe there is a way. Let me think about this for a few days. I will get back to you then."

"If you wish. Thank you again, Colonel. And give my regards to your wife."

"Yes, I will do so. And thank you, too, Col. Tran." Dmitriy lay the phone back into its cradle and stood quietly in the darkened room. He reached for the light switch and began searching through his desk for his booklet of maps. Dmitriy was an Army officer. He understood maps, but he knew very little about Vietnam. He quickly found the map he wanted and began to study it carefully. As he did, he opened the drawer on the old desk he had used throughout his career and shuffled through its contents until he found his ruler and a pencil. Quickly and expertly he began measuring and marking the map. Absently he began speaking to himself. "Of course. Yes, it would work." The cold realization of what he was thinking soaked over him, and he stopped abruptly and looked up from his work.

Did he dare even think the thoughts that were rushing through his mind? As a career officer of the Soviet Union, could such ideas even be allowed into his conscious thoughts? He began to rub both temples with his fingers as if the very effort would drive the thoughts from his mind. As he did his eyes focused on the only photograph in his office. There on the desk was a picture of him and Nikolai, arms around each other, standing over a dead buck. Such happy faces; such happy times. Slowly Dmitriy placed the instruments back in the cluttered drawer and closed it. The cold, dark room closed around him and sent a chill up his spine. He reached for the picture and turned it face down on his desk and turned to leave the room.

"Who was it?"

"One of my junior officers."

"Why was he calling at this time of night? Was it so serious that it could not wait until morning?"

"He is an idiot. It was a small matter that I must decide in the morning. Go back to sleep my dear." Dmitriy fumbled in the darkness to find his bed and considered his last statement. Yes, tomorrow he would decide. For tonight he would crawl back into his bed and hold his wife to warm his body and his soul -- suddenly both were very cold.

*   *   *

When Dmitriy walked into his office the two young officers jumped to attention and stood silently awaiting his wrath. "Yes captain, what it is you have to report?"

The young man spoke quickly. He was trying to sound professional but his voice was strangely high in pitch. "Colonel, I personally talked to Missile Command last night. They said they shipped twelve missiles. The military escort was with the eight we found at the rail siding, so I suspect there was an error in the Missile

Command's number. In any case, I have my entire company out searching for four more missiles. In addition I have calls into the shipping depot to get their shipping instructions in case the shipment was divided and sent on two different trains."

"Do I understand that we may have lost four of the missiles?"

"Yes sir, but I do not think so. We've checked every possible location within three hundred kilometers. I have also interrogated the escort troops; they feel there were only eight."

"We will succumb to the Chinese or the Americans—whoever decides to attack us first. We will not even be able to find our own ammunition in time to fight. Are we all mad? We can't even confirm how many missiles were shipped?" Dmitriy's tone was no longer one of rage or anger. He was suddenly tired. He sat in his chair and turned to look out onto the frozen parade ground. The men watched him suspiciously, anticipating his next move. When he turned to face them, his face was one of resignation—not anger. He looked at each of them carefully and said nothing for several minutes. Finally he spoke, very clearly, very deliberately. "Captain Odnoralov, go to your command post and prepare a dispatch alerting my office, Missile Command, and the shipping depot of all that has transpired. Explain the missing missiles and ask their help in finding them. Furthermore, list all of your actions to date to find the cargo. Finally, advise them that you will notify them as soon as the missiles are found." He thought a moment then added. "You might also ask them to verify if they did, indeed, ship the intended twelve. Perhaps only eight were shipped." He waved the two men away with his hand. "You are dismissed. And keep me informed." After they left he stood a long time looking out onto the cold morning. Dmitriy and Dasha had buried Nikolai on just such a cold February morning. Now Dmitriy had reached a decision. The death of his son would be avenged. He had thought it through carefully. It was not a sudden decision; it was not some rash moment of unrestrained anger. No, it was, in his mind, a rational choice after considering all the facts at hand. His son had fought in a war that he, himself, had been denied. The enemy had killed his son and now sat with impunity far from the battlegrounds of death. They could fight and then return to their havens of safety, and there they could not be reached, until now, because Dmitriy might possibly have the weapons to reach them. The only question that remained was whether he had the will. His son had the will to fight. Could he do less? He considered the ramifications. His career? What career? How could that measure against his honor, his duty to his son? The colonel rose and walked slowly around his desk. Everything finally came down to one question. Did he have the will that his own son had demonstrated? What had Colonel Tran said? He suspected Nikolai had come from men of courage. Certainly he had descended from men of will. Dmitriy stopped his pacing and walked back to his desk. His decision was made. "Clerk, get me Captain Sergei Iskhakov. Now! Tell him to report to my office as quickly as possible." When he returned to his desk his face had a strange look of both despair and determination. He had made his decision, but it was one he feared more than any decision he had ever made.

Nubat Royal Thai Airbase

Kerrie was seated in a wooden chair under a large sprawling Cinnamomum-Camphora tree beside the orphanage. Like the building, it was old and worn from the many small hands and feet that had crawled over it. Overhead the bright fuchsia of the bougainvillea stood brilliantly shimmering against the blue afternoon sky. The colorful leaves were thick, surrounding the tiny yellow flowers that peeked from their brilliant surroundings. It was cooler here, and the early afternoon light aided her inspection of the children lined up before her. Like children everywhere, they laughed and peeked excitedly at the American woman doctor. She sensed their wariness and had come prepared, a box of Tootsie Rolls at her side. She paused as a flight of F-4's roared overhead. She watched and listened carefully. The F-4 Phantom had its own sounds, sometimes wailing, sometimes shrieking, sometimes simply roaring into the endless sky. To many it was an obnoxious sound, perhaps even frightening, but to the men who flew these large, powerful planes, it was beautiful, indeed; it was the Phantom's song. It was a melody they knew and loved. Quickly she glanced up in time to see the belly of one of the aircraft in a four-g turn to final. The landing gear were just extending; the flaps were also coming down, the engines wailing. She watched in fascination and wondered if one of the pilots were Robb. What was it about these machines and the men who flew them? They were both a strange lot, she considered. The men, strong and boisterous, like the planes; they were different, a swaggering lot--all of them--including Robb, she decided. They were boys who had never grown up, lost in some strange time warp that left them forever young, forever delighted in the sensual pleasures of life. The thrill of flying and the love of speed were different from her own commitment to science. Yet they had found a joy that few could understand; how fortunate for them, she thought.

As the children paraded one by one to her, Kerrie wondered about the men she had met at the base. She, herself, was a surgeon in search of science. But they--they were in search of that exhilaration of flight that gave them a thrill she didn't even understand. What must that be like, she wondered, as another aircraft descended in the warm afternoon air. So much power to control. She had heard the pilots talk of the thrill; once she overheard one say it was only surpassed by sex with a beautiful woman. Another had emphasized that he might be right if the woman were extremely beautiful.

They did it for personal gratification, she concluded. Not a selfless act at all-- a purely selfish act of personal joy. Could that be wrong? Maybe that is why they are supposed to be such great lovers, she thought. After all, sex is really an act of satisfying ourselves, she concluded. In the act of finding and enjoying beauty, perhaps that is where joy and beauty are best shared. Her own mother had once joked that no woman should marry a man who couldn't dance. These guys dance, she thought. They know the exhilaration of life and joy. She was thinking about Robb when she glanced up into the eyes of the tall approaching nun. She felt her cheeks redden and wondered if Sister Estelle could, indeed, read her thoughts. No, she concluded, not these thoughts; she's a nun. She was wrong.

Sister Jean Patrice Estelle looked up at the jets overhead when she saw the young doctor watching the planes. It was strange, she thought, that she had never noticed them before. They were simply a loud raucous noise that woke the children and frightened the animals. Like Kerrie, she wondered if Robb were flying one of the aircraft screaming overhead. To fly and see the world as a bird; that would be wonderful she thought. Floating, that was what she envisioned flight to be--not power, not speed, but floating slowly through the clouds, looking down on a tiny world below. God had given man the ability to do such amazing things. She frowned; leave it to men to figure a way to use that gift to destroy each other. She thought of Somboon, the lonely little boy who cried for his mother in the night. Sister Estelle would hold him and rock him until the fear left and sleep closed his large eyes. As the months passed he would soon call her "Mother" as the other children did. It gave her great pride to be the surrogate mother of so many small souls. It also caused her to wonder about the many dead women who had carried these children in their bellies and delivered them in both pain and joy into a strange and difficult world. Did their souls cry out when their own children called another woman "Mother?" Perhaps they blessed her for loving their children and taking care of them when they, themselves, could not. She prayed for these women every night.

It was her hope that they did the same for her. Their work was over; hers remained until at last she would join them.

∗   ∗   ∗

The look on her face was one of surprise. Then she smiled, and the blood rushed to his face. He had been staring at her, openly, unconsciously. He had been memorizing that moment, filing it forever in his mind. The soft evening breezes replaced the sweltering heat of day, and the world felt at peace as the blue skies faded into purple, then black--so far away from the bombs and the guns. Kerrie was rocking gently, singing some lullaby he had never heard. Somboon was asleep in her lap.

He had memorized that moment in all the finest details; the texture of the wooden floor of the porch; the sounds of tropical insects in the distance; the curve of her nose, the size of her eyes, the rise and fall of her breasts in the sleeveless T-shirt--all of it. It was not a sudden shock; there were no bells or lightening, he just became aware of it--softly, like the evening. He was in love with this woman. It was peaceful, and soft, like the woman, like the Thai evening, like the breath of breeze across his cheeks.

She looked at him, her dark eyes penetrating his soul. She read his every thought; she knew his every emotion--he could feel it. He was emotionally naked before her; he didn't resist. It was peaceful, knowing that she knew. He smiled at her and she replied in kind. Their eyes met, and they both recognized the same truth, together; they were in love. Suddenly they were both grinning like two kids in a park. Grinning, then laughing. No words were spoken, but an understanding as clear as the evening sky passed between them.

Kerrie rose from the chair, still cradling the small child, and walked to the stoop where he sat. She sat beside him and kissed him. She wondered if he had noticed how she had watched him, studying the small things he did by habit, the way he wrinkled his eyebrows as he walked the lost pathways of his unspoken thoughts. She smiled to herself. He's so unlike any of the other men I've known, but then, I've never been in love before. Her eyes widened slightly. She savored the last thought carefully, weighing it within her mind and heart. It was the first time she had admitted that she loved him, even to herself, and strangely, it made her want to cry.

He had never known such emotions as were dancing through his heart. He reached out to touch her face and felt the tears that were flowing down her cheeks. She reached both hands for his face and nearly dropped the child. They collapsed into each other's arms, the child between them--laughing hysterically. How simple it was, and how complex, and how lovely and soft and beautiful--like the soft touch of the Thai evening.

From the far end of the porch, Sister Estelle peered from the open window. The laughter had interrupted her prayers. She watched the two young people kiss, and she smiled, too. Love is beautiful, she thought. "Thank you Lord," she said aloud, barely murmuring. "What a strange and beautiful and powerful gift you gave us to share," she prayed. Love--was it from the heart as mythology proclaimed, or from the brain, or from both? Perhaps it was from a lesser gland, she thought. "No matter, it is a gift above all others."

The three were embracing and laughing--even Somboon. The older woman watched them, smiling. Thoughts from many years ago flooded into her mind, reminding her of another night and another love. He had been a young and handsome man--full of youth's vigor, and he had loved her desperately. How wise was the decision she had made? Had it been the right one? For her, yes, perhaps. She wondered about him, the young man who had held the one threat to her vows. Where would he be now? What would he look like today in his late fifties? Would he still remember her? Would he be disappointed to see an older woman, one whose beauty had long since faded? Would he love her still? Had he loved her all these years? Outside the two young Americans kissed again, long and passionately. The nun moved away from the window, still smiling and a little perplexed at her own feelings. Somehow the joy of young love made her strangely sad; a single tear slid over her cheek and fell to the front of her habit.

Sister Estelle forced her mind to concentrate, a skill she had developed over many years of life in a world she barely understood. God's ways are strange, indeed, she thought.

*   *   *

When she stepped back from him, he gasped slightly. In his life, he would never know what that had meant to her. Kerrie smiled; no, she beamed. She had never felt beautiful in her life. Competent, yes. Cute, yes. But totally beautiful, no. She stood before him totally naked and unashamed. She stood before him beautiful in her own mind, and the look on his face affirmed every emotion she felt. She was relaxed and smiling, her shoulders back, her breasts forward. It was not a suggestive stance, but one of pride. It was a feminine pride she had never known before.

Robb looked at her carefully, his eyes moved up her body, down, and back to her eyes. She felt glorious. The emotions welled in her; she could feel the small hairs on her arms and neck, the blood rushing through her legs, her arms, her breasts, the steady rhythm of her pulse in her temples. Every nerve, every inch of her being was alive with joy and focused on that one moment in her life. The euphoria that swept them both was overwhelming.

There were no mirrors in the small room. It was a room where men lived. It had the rough appearance of life that was lived very quickly with little regard for the trivia of space. She never looked at herself that evening; yet she knew she was beautiful; she saw it in his eyes.

That was all the mirror she needed, and in it, she saw herself far more clearly than at any other moment in her life. And the vision pleased her greatly; it was far more beautiful than she had ever imagined.

He reached to touch her breasts and a shudder of pleasure coursed through her body. When he reached, she felt his touch; she also sensed his reaction to her body. The pleasure was almost more than she could stand; it surrounded her with passion, emotion, and physical joy. So this is love, she thought. Oh God, how wonderful, how beautiful!

Then came the tears. They were tears of joy that rushed from her eyes, ran down her cheeks, and fell splashing to her breasts. She was laughing when he reached for her, pulling her to him, cradling her in his arms. Gently he led her to the small bunk. She lay down and pulled him to her, her hands tracing every detail in his face and body. He looked at her in amazement; somehow he understood and felt her joy. Gently, carefully, he cupped her face with both his hands as he lay beside her. It was a night that neither would ever forget, and he wanted to remember every detail. As he kissed her, the salt of their tears, like the sweat of their bodies, mingled, changing the taste of their lives forever.

*   *   *

Dear Barb,

I need a favor, and please, no questions. I don't want to ask this of my mother, as you will understand, so I knew I could count on you. I need you to buy me five pairs of panties and three bras—the sexiest you can find. (Who else could make such a selection other than my sexiest friend? Certainly not my mother!) My panty size is a 5, and my bra is a 34-C. And Barb, please get pretty ones. I know you'll have better taste in this than I would. (I'm including a check that should cover everything.) Thanks.

Life is crazy, indeed. Here I am in the middle of a jungle and a war, and I've never been so happy in my life.

Miss you.

Kerrie

*   *   *

Dear Son,

Thanks for your letter and the picture. They mean so much to us. We can't wait to meet Kerrie; she sounds like a very smart young woman. A surgeon! She really is accomplished, and she is a beautiful young woman.

Yesterday I saw Frank Jones and Dave Middleton. They are opening a law office here this week. Can you believe they are doing that? It seems like last week you kids were playing in the back yard. They both asked about you. Dad told them about your DFC. By the way, you never told us what you did to earn that. Is that something you're allowed to talk about?

I saw Polly at Safeway yesterday. She asked about you.

We miss you son; Be safe.

Mom

Me, too.

Dad

Skovorodino, The Soviet Union

Captain Sergei Vladislav Iskhakov stood outside the dark gray buildings, shivering in the cold morning light. Behind him the dark green firs bent toward the earth with the heavy burden of snow from the evening storm. He was irritated; the men delivering his cargo were late, and the morning light was approaching soon. All had been planned so well--and executed so poorly. Even half of the guards were asleep. Was there no discipline at all anymore? The mission itself was bad enough, but the damned cold was awful. At least it was better than the unbearable heat in Afghanistan. How he hated that place and all the people there. Idiots all, he thought. They live and die worshiping a god that wills their own deaths. How strange. But at least they had discipline. His own troops were a shiftless group of dullards who merely did what they were told with the least effort possible. It is a bit like our entire economy, he reflected, everyone doing the least he can get away with. It is no wonder that we live like dogs. Sergei smiled to himself and wondered how different he, himself, was from the others. Probably not much, he considered. He began walking down the long rows of rail tracks that led into the dark buildings. The wind increased, blowing under his great coat, and chilled him further. The rail stock before him stood desolate in the twilight, guarded by a small band of young soldiers. "Wake up you sleeping dogs or I'll have the entire detail placed on report. If you think this is cold, how would you like five years guard assignment in a gulag?" The young men jumped to attention and eyed him carefully. "Now listen to me you shiftless bastards. No one is to mention a word of what we have been assigned to do. Understand? This is a top-secret mission assigned to us by top officials in the Army. You will follow orders, keep your mouths shut, and do as I tell you. Anyone who disobeys will be shot. If you think the Army doesn't have the guts to do that; well, I do." He watched the young soldiers carefully looking for any sign of question or disrespect. He saw only fear. "Good! It took us only three hours to find something the entire Soviet Army could not locate in three days, so we get a special assignment for our reward. I am also advised by top command that if we pull this off without incident we will all receive a special pass to someplace warm. I don't know about you, but I'm tired of this godforsaken place—so don't screw up!" The men stood quietly and shivered in the cold morning air. "Get this cargo covered; keep it covered. I don't want anyone to know what we are moving — including you! If you want to get dumped into the brig for a thousand years, just tell one of your whores in town about this task. I'll personally break both of your legs first—then I'll ship you off to Vietnam to rot in the jungles in that hellhole. Any questions?" He spat upon the ground and narrowed his eyes as he looked menacingly at the group. "Now get to work! Get this rail car into warehouse number 16 in the old tractor factory and keep it out of sight. A train engine should be here within the hour with Sergeant Kochkin. He'll be in charge until I return." Sergei turned to leave but returned after two steps. "One other thing. You will remain with Sergeant Kochkin until this mission is complete. No one leaves; no trips to see your whores; no vodka. Understand?"

"Yes Captain."

"Now, for the first time in your miserable lives, do as you're told. I'd hate to have to shoot one of you. That would require me to clean my pistol." Without smiling he left.

Nubat Royal Thai Air Force Base

Robb walked wearily back to the hooch. He was smiling in the dark and whistling softly. It had been a magnificent night to fly. The moon was full and the night sky had been filled with tiny white rays of light from the countless stars that populated the night sky. The mission had been routine; all aircraft returned without incident. One more flight into the endless sky, one more thrilling day of excitement, one more memory of joy on file in his neatly organized mind. He was tired, but he was happy.

"Kerrie?" She was seated on the top step of the hooch, staring off into the evening sky. She looked beautiful in her fatigue pants and the T-shirt that she stretched so alluringly. He looked at his watch. "It's two fifteen!"

"Couldn't sleep."

He slid onto the step beside her and put his right arm around her shoulder, drawing her to him. "And why not, my beautiful lady?"

"It was lonesome in the trailer." She faked a pout.

"That could be a lonesome place." Both were smiling.

"Yes it can."

"Any lonesome goblins there?"

"Probably."

"Did you know that I'm a licensed goblin exterminator?"

She laughed softly. "Really? Well I could sure use your help. What's your price?"

"That depends. When do you have to be at the hospital in the morning? What is it you doctors do—rounds?"

"What does that have to do with your price?" She rose and pulled him to his feet.

"Everything."

"In that case, tomorrow evening—late."

He answered, surprised. "Really?"

"No, but sleep is of little consequence when I have you to myself. It's only precious when I'm alone." He pulled her close and kissed her softly for a long time.

"You are so beautiful." She smiled and kissed him again.

"I'm so happy." She spoke quietly.

"Me too; what a night." He looked up at the clear sky and the large moon floating over the hooches where the forward air controllers slept.

"It is just beginning."

"Yes, it is." Together they walked off toward Kerrie's trailer as the soft warm breeze of the evening caressed them both. Behind them four F-4s roared off into the night. The two red afterburners of each plane gradually merged into one small red dot in the black sky as the planes climbed Northeast toward the waiting war.

*   *   *

As they lay in each other's arms, exhausted from the lovemaking, a strange peace settled over the small, candle-lit room. Only the sound of the air conditioner interrupted the silence and the sound of her heart beating next to his.

He looked at her, memorizing again--another file in his mind, a moment of beauty in a world of chaos. She smiled and snuggled closer to him, her head resting on his left shoulder. Softly he touched her cheek, tracing it with his forefinger. Her eyes looked into his and said a thousand sentences far more clearly than vocal speech. "I love you," he said quietly.

"I know, and I love you too." She stretched and kissed his lips. Robb brushed the long brown hair from Kerrie's cheeks and kissed her again. "I worry about you," she said softly, but with feeling.

"Me? Why?"

"The flying and all."

"Oh, I'll be okay. They've never even come close. Besides, I have a lot to come back to."

"Yes you do." She grinned at him. "And he needs you to read to him every night."

"Yeah, Somboon's a great kid. He's become a very important part of my life." He looked at her carefully. "But you know what I meant." He rolled to his back and looked off into the darkness. "I love you, and I have come to love him too."

"The Three Musketeers." She smiled at him and tickled his ribs.

"Careful there lady, you're playing with fire."

"I hope so." She leaned over him, her breasts hanging over his face. Robb pulled her down and kissed her breasts, her neck, her lips. "You asked for this."

"Yes I did. It's just what the doctor ordered." She pulled him over her and wrapped both of her legs around his hips, feeling his passion rising between them. She laughed softly and kissed him very hard, hoping that the silk tie she had bought him was still wrapped around the doorknob inside the trailer.

If I were to die today, she thought, *I would have known more joy than most people would know in a lifetime. Why have I been so fortunate to be so blessed?* She wondered about this exciting young man who had taken her heart--just as surely as she now owned his. She knew so little about him, and yet she was so comfortable in love. Were there important things about him that she did not know? She looked deeply into his clear blue eyes and saw her own reflection smiling back as he entered her. She gasped slightly; the joy was almost unbearable. She wanted to watch his face as his passion grew; she wanted to experience his pleasure, but she could not. She was lost in her own ecstasy, falling into a physical pleasure she had never understood before. The sounds and sights of her world faded into the depths of her mind. She did not see the look on his face, or hear the moan in his throat. Even the sound of her own voice crying out was lost in that moment.

While Dr. Kerrie Jernigen's body was lost in the physical passion of sex, her body, mind, emotions, and spirit merged, sealing her heart with the discovery of love -- a totally unexpected and exciting adventure in a life that had only known disciplined order and intellectual certainty. The song of her life had taken on a melody far more beautiful than she had ever imagined, and she was lost in a symphony of joy.

*   *   *

Dear Kerrie,

I found just what you'll need. I hope you like the colors I chose. (The black is my favorite—bought a bra just like it for myself—

except in a slightly smaller size! Ha!) Somehow I just can't imagine how these will work with regulation uniforms or your standard hospital "greens," but who will know? By the way, what is his name? How serious is this?

Love you,
Barb

P.S. Is it true that they issue you underwear that is that awful army color?

P.P.S. Kerrie! I am not a Pharmacist—you may be a doctor, but if you intend to communicate, you need to work on your penmanship. It's awful. Wow, how stereotypical. Who was your third grade teacher? Your folks should have sent you to a Catholic school where they teach penmanship! Sure do miss you, kid -- Barb

*   *   *

Phillip Brady had never been in love before. It was something that had simply never occurred to him. He understood women--but only in a scientific, biological way. He was a doctor, and a damned fine one, but that did nothing to help his lack of understanding about the beautiful woman before him, even though she, too, was a doctor.

All of his life Phillip had wanted a career in medicine. He had wanted to help sick people get well, and he needed to see their faces when the pain was gone. Medical science was okay; he could handle, even excel, in that arena, but his real joy was that of seeing people get well. He had once saved a small girl while interning in a large hospital in Cleveland. He would never forget the parents--their relief, their joy--and a little, he conceded, their admiration for his skill, for his special gift to them, the life of their child. He had come to serve, and he had worked diligently and hard for many long years. Now he had his reward, "Doctor" before his name and the opportunity to do what he loved most, make people well.

Then one hot, sweltering Thai afternoon his life had taken an abrupt turn, one he hardly understood, but one that filled him with wonder. He had fallen madly in love. He had never expected it to happen like this; he certainly never thought it would feel as it did. How does one describe such joy, especially when you are a doctor? It made no sense to Phillip at all--at least not medically, and that was the only reference he had.

"Doctor?"

"Yes." He looked up and wondered if she could see the color in his face changing to crimson. It was a simple surgery, a strong nineteen year old with an appendix close to rupturing. It was routine, no risk, but his mind had wandered. It's her, he thought, dammit. I can't concentrate around her. He wondered if it were as obvious as he feared. Did she notice the times he stopped in the hospital to stare at her, unconsciously? He suspected that she knew, and he fought his own emotions. Still, when he looked over the operating table into her large brown eyes, he felt his own spirit soar and his resolve melt into utter joy."

"Nice job, Phillip."

"Thanks." He finished closing the surgery. You should see me when I'm not distracted, he thought.

She reached and touched his arm. "You have good hands, Doctor." He tried to speak, but the words were not there. He smiled at her and nodded. His eyes met hers briefly, but she was moving quickly, preparing for the next operation. Phillip stopped to watch her walk briskly from the room. She always seemed in a hurry. She always knew where she was going and what she was doing. Her control was absolute. And now he, too, was under her control. Did she suspect?

The second operation was difficult; the risk of death was high; and the team was tired. Phillip's mind and his hands labored over the twenty year old lying on the table before him. Kerrie worked with him, struggling to maintain the ebbing life. It had been a simple accident, but a dangerous one--a motorcycle and a truck. The truck always wins.

Both professionals worked together, talking rapidly, giving terse orders to the staff assisting them, struggling against overwhelming odds. Phillip glanced at the vital signs on the heart monitor machine repeatedly, trying to imagine them stabilizing into normal, healthy rhythms. He tried to will the machine into submission, but the numbers continued to fall. He wanted to see this young man's face in a recovery room. He wanted to know he had helped save this life. He wanted to write the letter home saying he had saved their son and that all was well. He wanted to win again.

It was a difficult operation and both doctors were totally engrossed in their work. Phillip looked up at Kerrie to ask assistance with a particularly difficult procedure. He froze; his hands paused from their labor, then began to shake visibly.

Kerrie's eyes were locked on his hands; when they stopped abruptly, she looked up, into his face. He was staring into her eyes, and even with his surgical mask in place, she could see the surprise. What was it that had shocked this professional so greatly? He was looking into her eyes. What message did they send?

Phillip struggled with the vision he saw. What did it mean? Kerrie had never worn makeup before--only a little lipstick. But today that had changed. Yesterday she had the clean scrubbed face of a professional, a doctor. Today she literally glowed, and there was eye shadow and blush on her cheeks. Yesterday's doctor was today's woman. She had changed. Yesterday he had dared to dream; today those dreams came crashing to the floor. Phillip was not a sophisticated man when it came to women, but neither was he a fool. Kerrie had changed; she looked like a woman in love, and he knew it wasn't with him. For a moment his heart sank; he knew it; and she saw it. He could hide his expression beneath the mask, but the eyes were windows to his soul.

"Doctor?" She spoke softly, her eyes looking into his own, questions unspoken.

"Yes. Yes." With the force of his will, Phillip focused his mind, his energy, and his eyes on the battered limbs below his scalpel.

It was a strange pact; it made little sense, but at that moment Phillip Brady vowed with all his mental and spiritual might that this young man would live. He needed that more than he had ever needed anything in his medical career. He needed to see that young face alive. Saving this young man had become a journey for his own salvation. There had to be one absolute, one truth that he could cling to, and saving this young man was now it. His medicine was all he had left. It was all he had brought to this base; it was all he would take away. He knew unequivocally that he had lost his chance with Kerrie. He sensed it. The game was ended, and he had never even begun. He motioned for a nurse to wipe his face and refocused all of his energy to the task at hand. The young man on the table before him was suddenly the most important patient in his career. If he could save this life, he could, perhaps, salvage his own.

✳   ✳   ✳

Kerrie stepped forward and hugged the exhausted doctor. "That was fantastic, Phillip. I've never seen anything quite like it. I'm so impressed. That young man in there owes his life to you. You were great."

Once more he tried to speak but found his voice mute. He simply stared at her and nodded. He searched within the recesses of his mind; could there be justification, reason, in all of this? He was a doctor first. That was the absolute in his life; it was the thing that mattered. Could he smile back at the beautiful woman facing him? No, not today. Maybe tomorrow, after he had looked at the face of the young airman in the recovery room. Maybe then.

*   *   *

Dear Barb,

How did I ever get to be 30 without learning to dance? What did I do with my life—except learn to become a surgeon?

Oh Barb, I never knew I could be so happy! His name is Robb. He's a captain—a pilot here—and he's still single. He's tall, handsome, and he's really a good man. I had no idea I could feel this way about someone. It all happened so suddenly, and it is so amazing. I can't wait for you to meet him.

P.S. Could you send me a lipstick? I like shimmering pink, unless you have a better idea. Just not too dark. I like lighter shades—you know what I wear.

> Thanks loads,
> Kerrie

Kerrie,

You've got it bad kid. Is this the same woman who said men were such a pain in the ass? Really, I'm so happy for you—and it's about time!! Can't wait to meet him.

> Love ya.
> Barb

P.S. I know this sounds crazy to tell a doctor (especially a great one!) but you guys are being careful aren't you? Love can do weird things to your head. Be safe, dearie! (Do I sound like your mom?)

CHAPTER FOUR

Nubat Royal Thai Air Force Base

Robb felt the smooth thrust of the giant J79-GE-15E engines beneath him. In his hands he held the strings that made the powerful puppet dance to the tune he chose. The exhilaration was almost overwhelming. Below, the green sea of towering trees stretched as far as he could see, bathed in the early afternoon sun. Above, the sky was etched with faint white streaks of cirrus clouds. Only the black patches of ragged karst interrupted the peaceful scene. Like dark, broken teeth they lined the rugged jaws of the broken mountains, stretching in the early afternoon sunlight, casting long blue shadows across the green valleys below. The flight commander was a gruff and unfriendly man, but he was also a good pilot, and that alone was enough for Robb. Personality quirks were annoying, but they wouldn't get you killed if the man were a good pilot, and there was no doubt about Major Pace's skill in that area. There was also little doubt among his men about his being an ass.

Robb was flying as number Four in a four ship formation targeted against an enemy command post and storage area located far north on the Vietnamese-Laotian border. Joe Wilburn was in number Three, and Clem Roberts was in number Two. Clem had placed both of his hands high on the glare shield to indicate that his backseater was actually flying the plane. Robb's thoughts were interrupted by Major Pace's voice over the radio. "Green 'em up. Take spacing, Rattlesnake." The lead started a wide right turn around the target area. Robb glanced at his Loral inertial navigator (INS) and noted that the target was less than a mile off his starboard wing. Pace increased his power setting to facilitate the spacing as the planes arced through the clear sky around the target area. The target below was a large cave in the face of a lone karst formation that occupied the center of a large green valley. Numerous roads crossed the valley from all directions, several of which ended at the mouth of the cave. "Does everyone have the target?"

"Roger that."

"Lead's in from the south." Suddenly the entire valley floor erupted in a fusillade of fire. Streaks of red tracers raced through the sky like strings of neon lights.

"They're shooting!"

"No shit!" The lead aircraft flew straight through the white cloud of smoke from the exploding shells. Orange puffs seemed to encircle the aircraft. Down it plunged toward the target, then, abruptly, it changed its course and strained for altitude. Puffs of smoke followed the jinking aircraft as it danced through the sky.

"Two's in from the east." Clem's voice was cool and professional as his aircraft rolled into the afternoon air and plunged toward the ground. Lead's bombs had impacted short of the target, partially obscuring it with a growing cloud of dirt and debris. Guns seemed to be firing from all locations around the target as Rattlesnake Two flew into the hell below.

"Get those damned guns! Get those guns!"

"Four has three gun sites north of the road running east and west just south of the karst formation. Four's in from the east." Robb rolled inverted and saw the entire valley below him as he looked from the top of his canopy. He rolled upright and was diving directly at the gun sites he had spotted. Three red "beer cans" passed directly over the canopy, and small white puffs blossomed in the air around the aircraft. Robb was breathing hard and cursing as his navigator called altitudes to him.

"Seven thousand, six thousand!"

More puffs filled the air before him as the target gun sites moved across his heads-up display and into the pipper sight for his weapons.

"Five thousand!" A brief pause. "Pickle, Pickle!" Robb pressed the bomb release button on his stick and pulled violently to climb from the valley. As he did, he violently jinked left and then right to disrupt the gunners' tracking. The g forces were pulling on every nerve in his body as the plane darted upward, away from the guns below. Behind him his navigator, Wayne Compton was thrust against the sides of the cockpit as the plane jerked through the afternoon sky. When they finally reached altitude, all he could say was "Shit!"

"Nice bombing four."

Rattlesnake Three, who had rolled in just behind Four, climbed to altitude as his bombs walked up the main road leading to the cave entrance. "Short, Dammit!" Even Joe's ordinarily cool voice was high with excitement.

"Lead's in on the cave; keep an eye out for the location of those guns." Major Pace rolled to his left and dived again toward the target in the valley. As he pressed his F-4 toward the enemy below, the sky glittered again with the savage response.

"Four has guns between the karst and the trees beside the road. Four's in from the south." Robb rolled the aircraft and pointed the nose toward the ground below. He glanced at his attitude indicator as it rolled upright and indicated a 45-degree dive. Two large red flashes passed off his right wing. Suddenly the entire aircraft lurched as hard steel ripped through the belly of the plane and gutted its delicate entrails with the sharp jolt of an explosion.

"Four's hit!"

Another impact slammed into the aircraft and ripped huge pieces of molten metal from the gaping holes. Smoke and flames lapped at the left wing and spewed from the burning guts of the machine.

"Four, you're on fire!"

Robb scanned his instruments quickly and pulled the left throttle to idle. Breathing hard, he ignited the afterburner on the right engine. His words over the intercom were quick and irregular but determined. In a barely audible whisper he commanded. "Altitude?" Then mumbling, "Those sons of bitches!"

"Four, pull out; pull out!"

In the backseat, Wayne listened to the mumbling of his pilot. "Those bastards!" Instantly he knew what Robb was going to do. Three feet behind his pilot, he knew he was also committed to that same plan.

"Nine thousand, eight thousand!" The ground jumped up at the burning plane. Wayne looked around and saw that many of his circuit breakers were out. Vainly he tried to reset them. "Seven thousand! Six thousand!" The aircraft fell through the sky. "Five-five! Pickle, Pickle! Pull dammit! Pull!" He felt the entire load of ordnance remaining on the aircraft leave with a thump—nine five hundred pound bombs and four CBUs released at once. The aircraft climbed slowly upward. Robb could feel Wayne pulling on the control stick with him. The plane began to roll abruptly to the left. "Oh shit! Right rudder! Right rudder!" Slowly the aircraft rolled upright and began to climb from the valley.

"You're on fire, Four; bail out!"

"Bullshit! Not here." Robb was straining in his seat to look over his left shoulder to determine the damage to the aircraft. Smoke billowed behind him and occasionally he could see the bright orange and red flames that raged from within the left engine.

The radio crackled. "You got the guns! You got 'em!"

On the intercom, Robb was speaking quickly with Wayne. "I don't think this buggy is going to get us home, Wayne. Be ready to punch out at any time. I'll try to get up to the karst mountains to the east. If we go down, head for the mountains and climb as high as you can."

"Get as far from here as you can, Robb."

Already Major Pace had started Search and Rescue (SAR) procedures and had joined the crippled bird on its left. Joe Wilburn was on its right. "We've got a chopper on the way to Holding Point Three. He's out of Delta Seventeen so it shouldn't take long. Eighty-seven miles, heading two-three-zero."

Robb had just looked over at Joe to inquire about his assessment of the plane when the loud growl in the right engine began to increase. He saw Joe jerk suddenly away from his aircraft and knew that the plane was dying under him. His voice was rapid and tense as he reached for the ejection handle between his legs. "Wayne, heads up; we're punching out!"

Robb's mind was racing with fear as the parachute descended slowly toward the green jungle below. As it rolled lazily in the hot humid air, he tried to will it to fall faster. This was one time he didn't want to delay his descent. To his right, South if his bearings were correct, Wayne drifted down toward a green clearing. Robb jerked his body violently to the right, trying to change his direction of descent. It was useless, the wind, gravity, and the large umbrella shaped parachute were in control. Every muscle, every sinew in his body was tensed, but it was his mind that raced faster. He was heading into large trees below. If caught in them, suspended helplessly above the ground, he would be a great target for rifle practice. He sensed the buck knife in its sheath on his right calf. How wise his dad had been, though he had laughed when his dad gave it to him. Both had hoped that it would remain sheathed until some warm summer fishing trip high in the Rockies. Now its job was far more real, far more necessary.

Quickly he grabbed the knife and cut two of the nylon risers off his left side. Immediately, the angle of descent changed, air slipping through the collapsed area on his chute caused him to fall to his right--and at a faster rate. But that, too, was okay. Hanging in the air made him far too vulnerable. If he could only make it to the small clearing, it would enable him to reach the ground, escape the parachute, and look for Wayne. Then they would race up the Karst mountain to the east and try to avoid enemy troops. Troops! He searched the jungle below. He knew they were there, but he couldn't see any. Wayne, south of him, was descending toward the large clearing. He made a mental note of its direction and prepared for his own landing. He smashed into the ground far harder than he had anticipated. Staring at the parachute latches, he sat for several seconds, unable to release them and rid himself of the harness and chute. Slowly his mind began to function, driven by panic and trained determination. It began to react and reconstruct the moments preceding his present predicament. An aircraft roared overhead and slapped his brain, reeling it back to the present. He released his equipment and, climbing to his feet, began to survey the terrain around him. Off to his left he could see the tops of the karst mountains—his goal.

Robb looked back at the parachute as he ran in the direction of Wayne's last sighting. Did he need it? In survival school it had provided shelter and rope for many uses. No! It would only slow him down. That was theory--this was real! Get away as fast as possible, that was his only thought. Would it mark his location? He raced back and rolled it quickly into a large ball and stuffed it under some thick underbrush. Hopefully it would not be found soon. Run! But be careful! He unbuckled his .38 and checked it. It was fully loaded. Any injuries? Ankles okay? Yes. Run!

A surprising thought raced through Robb's mind. What if he could not find Wayne? What if Wayne had already started to flee up the mountain? Why had they not discussed this in more detail before? Damn!

They had discussed the karst mountains. Surely he would head in that direction. Even the enemy would know that. How long would he search before he headed east himself?

Robb tore at the thick underbrush as he struggled through the jungle growth that pulled at his body and slashed at his face and hands. "Damned flight suits--not worth a shit in this environment." After fifteen minutes he stopped, exhausted. The burning in his chest died slowly as his gasping breaths grew smaller and less frequent. Then came the thirst. Automatically he reached for his water bottles that were zipped securely in his g suit pockets. Of the two original plastic flasks, only one and a half remained. He downed one of them with large gulps and then placed the containers back in his pockets. Nervously he looked at the huge swath he had made through the underbrush on his trek thus far. He pushed a large leaf from his face and stood before a small clearing. Robb stopped. "Mustn't enter the clearing," he thought. Too easy to spot. "It will take longer to go around through the brush," something in his mind argued, "and it will be more difficult."

"Can't risk that" something else answered back. He looked carefully across the clearing. No indication of Wayne. He crouched, cursed the thick jungle growth that gave him cover and started off to his left. He had covered about 100 yards when the sound of gunfire stopped him in his tracks. Instinctively, he fell to the ground. Control the panic he thought. Must not panic now. Need all my wits. What he had heard was six or eight shots -- small arms -- off to his right. But they weren't close--maybe 300 yards away. Suddenly more shots. Had they found Wayne? The familiar sound of an F-4 roared overhead. He had never thought much about the sound of his beloved F-4. It was not a smooth sleek machine, and its voice was neither smooth nor sleek. It roared and screamed as it dashed through the sky, an angry spirit that spit dark smoke behind as it accelerated in the warm moist air. A series of three shattering explosions ripped the jungle floor near the area of the gunshots. More rifle shots and shouting that he could not comprehend. He scrambled to his feet and began to run bent over around the clearing. Each twig that snapped sounded like a falling tree and each leaf that crunched under his boots were like the clatter of a freight train. Several more shots were fired, and the adrenaline responded, enabling him to scramble even faster. This time he was scanning the trees. Wayne had to be somewhere in this area. He spotted the chute first. Hanging in a tree thirty yards from the clearing, Wayne was suspended thirty feet off the ground. At least it's not 100 feet, Robb thought. He shouted up to Wayne in a strange whispered voice. "Wayne, you okay?"

"Yes, but I'm caught. I can't get loose."

Robb scanned the area to his west carefully. "You've got to get down fast! They'll be here soon!"

"How?"

Suddenly there were more rifle shots as the enemy fired at the fighters overhead. The nearness of the shots alarmed them both. "Jump!"

"I can't, it's too far."

"You've got to. It is your only chance. Cut yourself loose, I'll break your fall."

More shots, closer now.

Wayne fell with all his gear on. If calmer, one or both would have realized that twenty-three pounds of ammo, radios, etc., can be a dangerous load when exiting a tree. When the last small arms were fired, he simply cut the shroud lines and dropped like a rock, atop his pilot. When he landed, he let out a muffled cry. When he tried to stand, his grimace told the sad truth. His left ankle was injured--badly. "Come on, lean on me." Robb grabbed him around his shoulders and started forward. Wayne winced but hobbled as fast as he could. Fear quickly overcame the pain.

The two men struggled through the dense jungle, heading East toward the mountains. The plants, Robb thought, are on their side. They hold us back, and they show where we've been. The thought frightened him so badly that he stopped suddenly and turned back to look at his path. Wayne moaned with the effort. Behind them was a clear trail of broken and twisted plants, a clear trail to mark their path. It was only a matter of time before the enemy crossed this path and followed it to them. They were hobbling; the soldiers were not. "Shit!" Robb said it aloud. The pause gave him a moment to think. "Think dammit!" he told his mind. No panic! Wasn't that what he had been taught in pilot training—don't panic. Think your way through the problem; be logical. Robb took the small survival radio from his vest pocket. "Rattlesnake!" the radio squelched, and he cupped it in both hands while adjusting the volume. "Rattlesnake flight!" He spoke quietly, but forcefully. Both men were crouching in the dense growth.

"Roger Rattlesnake. Callsign?"

"Four."

"You guys okay? Where are you?"

"Don't know yet, but we're following plan A." He planned to climb the mountains to the east.

"Can you give us any idea where you are? We're dropping live ordnance down there."

"Do you have the chute in the trees?"

"Roger that. We followed one of you in."

"We're about 200 yards from the chute. Chute's in Colorado; we're in Kansas."

"Roger, I've got a fairly good fix."

"We're moving; they're close. We're going silent for a while."

"Keep your heads down. We'll keep them busy." Just then an F-4 swooped close to the ground and dropped three 500-pound bombs. The explosions were deafening and close. More rifle fire followed the bombs, and more screaming. The enemy were approximately 250 yards to the west.

Both men began moving again. The small arms fire had given Wayne more energy. He leaned heavily on Robb as they broke through the jungle and came to a small path that led up the first range of mountains. They looked quickly at each other and started up the trail. "What the hell," Robb muttered, "They'll find us soon enough anyway. If we can just make it until the choppers get here." The trail made progress easier, but it was uphill and difficult work for Wayne.

The sound of voices brought them both to a stop. They were soldiers, and they were close. Somehow Robb expected them to be loud and excited-- excited and scared, like him. But they were not. They were laughing and shouting what seemed to be the good-natured insults that men share with each other the world over. One thing was sure, they were getting closer.

Then it changed. The shouting became louder--and excited. The soldiers had found their trail. Robb concentrated. Could he count the voices? Would that even be useful? His mind was racing again, smoothly. In pilot training his T-38 Talon had once lost hydraulics on final approach. It wasn't a drill or a test; it had been real, and he had been alone--solo. He had focused then--his entire being. "No panic. Just focus." It had worked then; he depended upon it now. Robb noticed that Wayne was shaking. He felt it as the other man leaned against him. He didn't know if it were fear or pain--probably both. He was shaking too, and he felt no pain.

One hundred yards down the path, the soldiers were running and shouting now. Robb knew they could not escape. He focused— can't run. Then fight! They have AK-47s most likely. A .38 is no match for that. What to do? What about surrender? Then he saw the large hole ten yards away, up the path. "Surprise! It's our only chance." He said the words aloud. Wayne nodded. "In that hole." Dragging Wayne with him, he crawled into the hole, pulling green leaves and a large limb behind them. "Get your gun; we'll ambush them when they round that curve in the path. Don't shoot until they're right on us. I'll take the ones on the right; you take the ones to the left. Maybe we can surprise them if there aren't too many. It works in the movies." Quietly he prayed that there weren't more than five or six of them. If there were, surrender was the only alternative, and not a very good one.

Robb lay poised, ready, frightened. He looked at Wayne who had two pistols, one in each hand. His .38 issue and a smaller .32 caliber that he had brought with him from the States. Somehow that and the calm look on Wayne's face gave him a strange sense of confidence. Wayne was a recent graduate from the University of Texas law school; he intended to go into politics when the war ended. Robb surmised that the look of confidence was a practiced look. It was also probably false. But three guns are better than two, and confidence was what they both needed now. Wayne glanced at him as the voices came nearer. Quietly he muttered; "good luck buddy. It's been great."

The first soldier rounded the curve in the path and did something totally unexpected. He stopped to wait for the others. Robb was hardly breathing. Wayne had both eyes squinting as the soldier fished a cigarette from his wet shirt pocket. It was wrapped in a piece of plastic, as was a match. He tried to light the cigarette but the match was damp and wouldn't strike. The soldier cursed; neither of the Americans knew what he said, but they could guess.

The raw smell of dirt, mold, rotting decay, and broken plants surrounded the silent men. It doesn't smell like home, he thought, is dirt different here?

Four more soldiers rushed up and stopped to smoke as well. One of them found a workable match, and soon all were puffing and talking at the same time. Five soldiers, three AK-47s and two rifles versus three small pistols. What the hell! Robb listened to his heart pounding; couldn't they hear it too? He could smell his own sweat soaking through his wet flight suit. Couldn't they smell that too?

The conversation grew louder. The soldiers were little more than twenty yards from the hiding airmen. The senior man was pointing down the hill while looking at one of the younger men in the group. Sullenly, the boy got up and started off down the path. He was walking slowly until the older man shouted after him. Grudgingly he walked back to the older man. The leader handed the younger a cigarette that he had been smoking and produced another for himself. The young man smiled and puffed on the stub of a cigarette, coughing uncontrollably. The other men laughed, and the younger was obviously embarrassed. The older said something and pointed again, and the young soldier trotted down the mountain trail. Several of the others shouted obscenities at him. He spat on the path and disappeared around the corner. The other four soldiers laughed again and relaxed against the trees along the path. They propped their weapons against the trees and began to smoke in earnest.

Like a cold wind that brings shivers down one's spine, the realization of the event that had just taken place unfolded in Robb's mind. The kid was going for more soldiers. He and Wayne couldn't wait any longer. Decision time was now. This was as good as it would get -- two frightened men against four smokers with weapons stacked against trees.

Robb looked at Wayne. Their eyes met, wide with anticipation. Somehow he sensed that Wayne was reading his thoughts. Robb touched the barrel of his pistol. It was cold. Even in the jungle heat it was cold. Soon it would be hot, he thought. It would smell of powder and death. Four men smoking in the jungle, two hiding in an overgrown hole-- probably from a stray bomb, he surmised. Six men, some or all would soon be dead--rotting in the soft jungle soil. He counted out with his fingers. One, two, three!

The gunshots rang out in the sweltering jungle. The four smoking men were caught completely unawares. In the first round of shots, Robb and Wayne fired quickly, rapidly. Two of the four were down; another was hit but moving. The leader had miraculously dived behind the large tree he had been standing beside and was reaching around for his weapon. Robb fired and splinters flew from the tree. He aimed again, pulled the trigger, and was answered by a loud click from his .38. It was empty. Wayne's .38 also sounded the unmistakable sound of an empty cylinder. The older soldier knew this was his chance. He jumped from behind the tree, grabbed an AK-47 and charged the twenty-five yards up the hill.

Robb was cursing and praying at the same time as his shaking hands jammed bullets into his gun. It was not fast enough. The soldier ran the first twenty yards, then stopped and walked slowly toward his prey. He was grinning broadly. He stood at the ledge of the small fortification and kicked the large leaves away. Slowly and deliberately he raised his weapon and aimed it at Robb.

A million things are supposed to go through your head as death stares you in the face. Your entire life is supposed to flash before your eyes. For Robb, it was a long, slow motion image of a grinning enemy, one who was uneducated and illiterate. For some reason that infuriated him--to be killed by such an unworthy opponent. He braced himself as he continued to force bullets into his pistol.

The three shots caused him to wince; then he realized he felt no pain. Was that the way it happened? Was that how death happened? No Pain? He looked up and the soldier stumbled backwards, a large bloodstain on his chest. The small caliber pistol had not killed the soldier, but it had stopped him momentarily. He stumbled to his knees but lifted his weapon and fired one burst into Wayne who was standing in the pit. Wayne's eyes were wide, blood flowed from several holes in his torso; a small trickle of blood flowed from the corner of his mouth. He fell forward, firing his last round into the soft soil of the pit.

Robb was out of the hole and attacking the soldier in an instant. He was clawing toward him even before he fired the burst into Wayne. As the soldier fired the last round, Robb had hit him across the face as hard as he could. The injured man went down, still holding the weapon. He looked up at Robb and grinned again, raising his weapon. Wayne's last shot diverted him just long enough. Robb's kick caught him in his left side and lifted him from the ground. He grimaced in pain. Before he could recover, Robb's second kick sent the AK-47 several yards down the trail. In doing so, he slipped and fell himself. Both men were struggling, one injured, the other exhausted, adrenaline flowing wildly in both. The two men scrambled for the weapon. The soldier reached the AK-47 first and rolled to his back, ready to fire. But standing over him was the American, a rifle and bayonet raised over him. Robb thrust it into the soldier's chest with all of his might. The rusty bayonet sliced through the man's body, the thrust so powerful that it forced the muzzle through as well. It was a loud crunching sound, then the whoosh of air as the dying man's lungs collapsed. His eyes were opened wide, but he was already dead. The grin was gone. Robb collapsed beside the dead soldier and gasped for breath. Tears streamed down his face, mixed with the sweat, and left small streaks in the jungle mud that covered his face. When the shaking stopped, he crawled to Wayne who was laying face down in the pit. "Wayne?" He rolled him over; his eyes were opened, staring blankly at an unseen world. Robb grabbed him and cradled him in his arms like a small child. Slowly Wayne's eyes searched him out. His lips moved slowly, but no sound came from the dying man.

"Hang on Wayne! Hang on!" But Robb knew it was useless. He

wiped the tears from his eyes; in that amount of time Wayne was gone. He exhaled softly, his eyes still locked on Robb's face, and died in his arms. Robb looked at him briefly, then he began to shake his friend. "Wayne? No! No!" It was more a moan than a cry.

Shouts down the mountain brought him back to reality. "Quick, focus." his mind shouted. "No! It's too late."

Another voice responded. "He saved your life. Live to tell his story. You owe him that. Focus! Focus!" The voices were in his head, but they was as clear as any conversation he had ever had. In Robb's mind Wayne spoke clearly and with control. "Run, Robb; get the Hell out of here!"

"Okay, focus."

Robb crawled to the body of the soldier with the rifle sticking through his body. He had seen hand grenades hanging on his belt. They were still there, three of them hanging limply at his side. He grabbed them, putting one in his pocket. The other two he placed carefully under the soldier and Wayne. He pulled the pins on both, but left the spring in place, held there by the dead bodies--traps for the troops coming up the hill. They would get an unpleasant surprise when they moved those two bodies--and no one would parade Wayne's body through Hanoi for pictures to feed the American Press. It would also allow him a few more precious minutes to escape.

Grabbing the AK-47 and two clips of ammo from the dead troops, Robb turned to leave. As he extracted the ammunition, he noticed one eye blink to look at him. The third soldier wasn't dead. He looked down at a trembling, bleeding boy. That's all he really was, a boy. He pointed the weapon, and the boy murmured something, then he began to cry. Like a small child, he sobbed.

The shouts were getting closer. They were excited; they had heard the shots. Robb grabbed the pistol with one hand and the boy's hair with the other. With a swift chop he bashed the pistol into the boy's head. Instantly the boy went limp. How hard do you strike a person before it's too hard? How many injuries can the human body take? The mind? The soul? The boy was breathing, but he would be out for a long time. Carefully he rolled the boy to his back. There was a large bloodstain just below his right shoulder. It was bleeding profusely. Reaching into his flight suit, Robb pulled a soiled handkerchief and gently pushed it into the bleeding wound. It immediately soaked with blood. "Good luck kid. I hope you make it."

Robb turned to run up the hill but stopped and looked back at Wayne. It had been a long time since Robb Barker had prayed or felt a connection with his God, but there in the jungle he stopped, walked back to his friend and traced a cross on his forehead. "Thanks, Buddy. You've got my vote." Then he turned and ran up the hill without looking back again.

*   *   *

Phuong Huynh was a North Vietnamese officer, and he was proud of his status. He didn't have a fancy uniform or a staff office, but his men respected him. Like him, they were peasant farmers, uneducated and ignorant of the technology of war. But Phuong had proven himself as a brave and resourceful fighter. He had spent months carrying supplies down the Ho Chi Minh trail, outsmarting the American bombers that pursued them daily. It was no bullet or bomb that had stopped his long hard trips. It was age and arthritis. He was getting older. Somehow 48 didn't seem so old, but his body was betraying him. The constant pain he could endure. The slow pace and awkward movements he couldn't. The local colonel had promoted him when the captain of his unit was killed in a bombing attack. They had given him a captured .38 revolver to show he was an officer now. No more rifles. That was a blessing. The .38, heavy as it was, fit snugly into his belt. How he wished he had a holster, how much easier the walking would be.

He watched his troops firing their weapons at the aircraft overhead. What a waste of ammunition, he thought. Small arms are useless against the fast jets of the enemy. Yet he knew that it gave the young men a sense of pride to shoot back. They yelled curses and screamed threats, boldly proclaiming their invincibility. "Invincible, indeed!" He stood quietly in the shade of a small tree watching the spectacle before him. He had troops scattered throughout the valley, looking for the two downed pilots. They've probably pissed in their expensive pants by now. The thought made him smile. How brave are these Americans when they face you man to man, without their technology to defend them? He wondered about that, about the men in the sky above. Do they have hooches and kids and rice fields? What do they eat? What do they think? Who is their God?

Phuong glanced east to the Mountains. "That's probably where they will head if they get through our net." But he had already thought of that and had a team of troops looking there as well. That was why he was the leader. That was why he carried the pistol. He pulled it from his belt and stroked it lovingly. What a beautiful gun, he thought. He looked skyward again. The Americans do make excellent weapons, he concluded. If their will to fight were as great, we'd be finished by now. How strange. Why do they even care about this small country? The gunfire in the mountains broke his thoughts. Slowly he rose and signaled his troops. Damn, the pilots must have landed nearer the mountains than I thought. Thanh had said they landed near the center of the valley. Phuong frowned. Why do I listen to him? Thanh is a fool, always has been.

The men surrounded their leader and slowly began their trek through the jungle toward the mountains. Phuong slapped Thanh lightly on the side of his head. "You fool, you said they landed in the valley. Did those shots come from the valley?"

"Sorry Captain. Perhaps they ran fast, like small boys running from their mother."

"Thanh, let's see you run fast. Take three other men and check out those shots. Don't wait for an old man like me."

"Yes, captain." And with that the four men ran ahead.

It was suddenly quiet on the mountain. The four soldiers peered cautiously at each other and slowed their pace. One called out. No answer returned. "Quiet you fool, do you want to alert the enemy?" Their pace had slowed to a very deliberate walk. A noise in the jungle! All four dropped to their bellies. An animal scampered across the path. Laughing quietly, they rose and proceeded carefully up the trail.

It had been ten minutes from the last shots when the trio rounded the small curve and found the remnants of their unit. Again, the men dropped to the ground and crawled for cover behind trees. Finally, after several moments one rose and stepped forward carefully. The other three watched, then they, too, followed.

Tien Dung, the leader of the first group lay on his back, a rifle protruding from his chest. Two others lay nearby. "Thanh," one of the troops called. "Look, they killed one of the Americans!"

Thanh walked over and looked in the pit. The first thing he saw were the boots, then the holster. "My lucky day. Boots for me, a holster for Phuong. Maybe even another pistol. He won't call me a fool after this." He turned and addressed the three other soldiers who were standing over Tien Dung, wide eyed. "Bring him and the others over here. We'll bury them in this hole. I'll take care of the American."

Phuong stopped briefly in his trek toward the mountain when he heard the two grenades explode. How strange, he thought. Grenades? No gunfire? Have those idiots come to war with no bullets? I'll kick all their butts, even with these bum legs. Then there was silence on the mountain. When they reached the trail, the group moved more rapidly. Two men were sent ahead, young and faster, to scout the way. Five minutes later they returned, breathless and frightened.

"Dead! They're all dead!"

"Who's dead?"

"All of them!"

"Any signs of the Americans?"

"Looks like one of them is dead too."

"Only one?"

"That is all we saw. It is hard to tell—grenades."

Phuong pushed his aching knees, nearly running now. "You two--secure the path 50 yards beyond the dead men--and be careful or we'll be burying you too. You two--same north and south. He reached the bodies five minutes later. Six of his men lay strewn around the path. In the pit, twenty yards up the path was what appeared to be the remains of two men--one American, the other Vietnamese. Both were unrecognizable, a mass of blood and torn flesh. Grenades, he reflected, make a terrible mess up close. One of the younger men was bent over, vomiting in the bush. Phuong patted his back but said nothing.

"Comrade Captain, Minh is alive!" Phuong walked painfully over to look at the youth. The young soldier was moaning softly, barely conscious. Phuong looked at this wound; it was still bleeding, but controlled. He reached his hand and touched the bloody handkerchief stuffed into the wound. It had been placed there and held in place by the empty ammunition belt. Someone cinched it tightly in the back-- a deliberate move. Thanh? No, someone with the initials RB. The boy opened his eyes slightly and began to mumble. "Quiet, my boy. You're going to be fine."

"Thanh must have thrown himself into the pit with a grenade to kill the American." one of the soldiers exclaimed as he studied the bloody pit. Parts of Thanh's scarf were scattered throughout the hole.

Phuong rose slowly and considered the carnage before him. No, Thanh was a fool, he thought, but he was dead now, and his family would live better with a dead hero for a father. What a waste, he thought.

"Call in the troops," he ordered. "Bury these dead in the pit with the others. Get Minh down the mountain to the medical team."

"Bury our men with the American?"

"It doesn't make much difference now, does it?"

"What about the other American?"

"He's probably still in the valley. We got one; perhaps we'll find the other. If I'm lucky, he may not kill off the rest of my miserable unit." He looked again in the pit, murmuring to himself. "Well, RB, whoever you are, you're very clever. That's an old trick, but it still works. You saved your friend's body from being desecrated in the streets of some village; you gave yourself a good 30-minute head start, and you saved an innocent boy. That's not all bad. I know a little more about you now. You are a lot like me." He turned to his men and spoke with authority. "Now quick, collect all of the weapons and get Minh down the mountain. He's from my village; I know his family. Quick, and be gentle. And don't move that rag until I get down. It is holding the blood flow; leave it in place. The rest of you, put the bodies in the hole and bury them together. Then everyone report back to me. Understood?"

"Yes, Captain."

"Now move!" He started down the hill, the pain in his joints throbbing, but unnoticed compared to the pain in his heart. Thanh was a fool; he was also his son-in-law. He had many messages to convey to the village tonight. That one was personal. He looked once over his shoulder up the mountain and nodded his head, then turned and walked away in pain.

* * *

Robb watched the sun rise slowly over the mountain and illuminate the valley below. He had slept little and was exhausted. It had been a night of terror and sadness. Thoughts of his parents, Kerrie, and his life at the base raced through his mind as he lay curled under a thicket of bushes, listening to his own heart beat. The fresh horror of Wayne's death moved silently in and out of his conscious thought, causing him to shiver in disgust and sadness. The vision of his friend's eyes, staring at him in death danced across the screen of his mind, punctuated by the eerie smile of the soldier holding the weapon pointed at him. A sound in the jungle caused him to tense suddenly, every sense heightened, his breathing held in check to better discern the source of the sound. Then silence. Were there enemy soldiers creeping through the night searching for him, or were the creatures of the jungle simply going about their normal lives, oblivious of the frightened American huddled in the forest.

Robb thought about Joe and his friends at the base. They would be taking off about now, their morning preparations complete, sitting in their planes at the end of the runway, watching the same sun rising, anxious to climb into the sky and begin their flight. He wondered if they were coming for him. He thought about Kerrie. Surely she knew he was down by now; did she know that he was still alive? Had anyone told Somboon? He hoped not.

The first flights of the day would be around daybreak; it was time to try the radio. He read the instructions twice though he had read them countless times before. A nervous finger pressed the transmit button and released it with a jerk when the radio squawked loudly in response. He trembled slightly as he very carefully read the instructions one more time. He could never remember hearing a survival radio make such a loud noise before, and he had tested this one just prior to the flight. But then, he had never heard his heart beat quite so loudly either. He finally pressed the operate button once again. Through the squawk he heard a voice shouting to him. "Rattlesnake Four, this is Playboy One, How do you read?"

"Loud and clear." He whispered.

"Sorry we couldn't hang around last night, fuel got low. Chopper's on the way. You got flares?"

"Roger." His voice was distant, far away, professional.

"Both okay?"

"No, Nav's dead."

"Shit!" There was a long pause. "Hang in there buddy, we'll get you out. What is your position?"

"I'm up on the mountain. I'm south of the A-1's position now."

"How far up the mountain are you?"

"I don't know."

There was a long silence then a new voice came over the tiny radio. "Rattlesnake, this is Sandy Lead, I'm going to drop a smoke on the side of your mountain. I'll be coming in from the west. Try to see where it hits. We'll use that for reference." There was a silence for about thirty seconds. "Sandy's in."

Robb peered from under the bushes and saw the aircraft bearing down towards the ground. A flash trailed from under its left wing and the aircraft pulled hard from its dive. He watched the smoke rocket plummet into the ocean of trees. "Your smoke is about two hundred meters northwest of my position. It seems to have alerted the bad guys. I hear more small arms."

"Where's Charlie?"

"Sounds like they're three hundred to four hundred meters west of my position."

"Playboy, do you have my smoke? Charlie is approximately two hundred fifty meters southwest of my smoke. Standby while I make a pass." The A-1 banked hard left and dove again at the ground. " I'm in." It was like watching a midnight movie version of a World War II drama. The old aircraft beat at the sky with a powerful propeller. When it lunged at the ground, it didn't shriek like the newer jets or groan loudly through the air; rather it hummed almost happily, thankful to be flying freely through the air instead of crated and rusting in some forgotten warehouse in Arizona. The A-1's were slow, but they were deadly accurate.

"Rattlesnake, this is Playboy, do you have flares?"

"Yes."

"Get it ready, Jolly Green's coming in for you after Sandy's next pass." There was a moment's hesitation. "By the way, what was your first car?"

"It was a truck. It was a '56 Ford."

"That's affirm. Keep your head up; Jolly's coming in. If you hear any big stuff down there, let us know. We've got a flight of Fox Fours up here just itching for a fight."

As he watched the bright blue skies through the dark jungle growth, the familiar whop, whop, whop of the Jolly Green helicopter reverberated across the valley. As the powerful rotors hammered the hot jungle air, he guided the chopper in. "I've got the Jolly Green in sight. To your left. Ten o'clock."

"Tallyho!"

The mind summoned weary muscles to action again; he crawled from his hiding place and began waving frantically. It was surely, he thought, the most beautiful sight in the world. At that moment, the large green monster with the rope dangling down toward him was the most beautiful aircraft in the world. As strong hands pulled him into the safety of the belly of the chopper, he reflected that no fighter or trainer in the world could match the beauty of this fat, ugly helicopter.

He sat silently in the chopper and stared at the large black sergeant who had pulled him aboard the craft and the winch that had lifted him from the jungle floor. The sergeant's face was one of shock. "You okay, Captain?" He was staring at Robb's chest. Robb looked down and saw the huge bloodstain on his flightsuit. Instinctively he placed his own hand inside and examined his chest. "Oh, my nav."

"Sorry we lost him."

Robb said nothing, he only nodded wearily. He was staring absently at his bleeding hands. Slumped against the cold steel bones that held the giant reptilian monster together, he could feel the tension draining from his body. Inside the helicopter was cool and dark except for the small beams of light that streamed through the dirty windows. Fatigue hung heavily upon his entire body; even the cold hard floor felt comfortable. He felt as if he were in a bad dream. Was this something that had never happened, something that had merely been imagined? Only his torn hands and the raw burning in his lungs separated the reality from the nightmare.

*   *   *

Kerrie Jernigen stood on the small wooden porch of the trailer where she lived. Unlike the pilots she lived in a small cluster of trailers reserved for the Wing "brass." It was comfortable and considered appropriate for a female flight surgeon stationed on a base with three squadrons of fighter pilots and their support crews.

It was still dark as she watched the large helicopter lift off from the ramp adjacent to Operations. She knew their destination; it had been the prevalent topic in the club the night before. She had gone for dinner but had left soon after arriving at the club. The talk of the downed crew had shaken her visibly, and she had wanted to be alone. They were going to try to rescue Robb and Wayne. The fact that they were going at all was good news. Perhaps they had contact; perhaps they were simply moving into position in case of a radio call that might never come.

Kerrie wiped her cheeks. They were wet. She was a doctor, but she was surprised that a human could cry so many tears. Surely there must be a limit to the production of bodily fluids for tears. She walked back into the trailer and sat down on the uncomfortable overstuffed couch, the same one on which she and Robb had made love. Without thinking, her hand reached and touched the rough surface of the fabric. For a moment she smiled, thinking of that night together and the fabric burns on her hips and back. More tears followed. She looked at the small clock on the table in the room. It was almost five AM. She wondered where he was, if he were alive, wounded, in pain? Was he afraid? Certainly she was. For a moment she thought of all the wives waiting back in the States. How did they do it she wondered? The "not knowing" must be terrible. At least the information here was "real time." Five AM and she had slept less than two hours. It was a nightmare she would never forget. Kerrie walked to the door and looked out again. The helicopter was gone. "Godspeed," she muttered and walked back inside. "He'll be back," she said aloud to comfort herself. But something in her subconscious mind threw a large cloud of doubt over her momentary optimism. "He has to. I love him; I need him." She sank back onto the couch, rubbing it violently with both hands.

In the distance four F-4's were preparing for takeoff into the dark morning sky, interrupting the silence of the night. It was a sound she had heard so many times; this morning she heard it as never before. Each of the planes ran the throttle to 100% for 45 seconds, the pilots checking their instruments carefully. Then there was the brief interlude between the takeoffs. Each plane's engines roared off at 100% thrust, then the afterburners were ignited. The roar shook the entire base as the planes raced down the runway at five-second intervals. In less than twenty seconds they were airborne, heading northeast.

Kerrie looked at her fingers, her hand; they were red and irritated from the rough fabric on the couch. They were also shaking. She held her right hand before her face and studied it carefully. It was, indeed, shaking slightly. The lack of sleep and the emotional strain had taken their toll. She rose and walked slowly to the small counter by the sink, still looking at her right hand. She lifted a blue piece of paper and squinted at it in the dark room. It was the hospital schedule for the day. She scanned it quickly:

0730, Operating Room A, Sgt. John Harris—hernia.

Kerrie dropped the piece of paper and placed both hands to her forehead. Forcing herself to concentrate she measured her alternatives. They were few. She looked back at the clock. It was 0530. She walked back to the tiny bedroom and fell across the unmade bed. Just two nights before they had made love in that bed. She rubbed the sheets with her left hand and raised the right again into the dim light. Finally she rose and walked to the door and into the early morning light. The sun was just rising and could be seen on the trees adjacent to the base. The rays were clearly visible on the tops of the trailers; from the sounds around, she knew the base was coming to life for yet another day of war.

In less than two minutes she stood before the metal door of another trailer. She inhaled deeply and paused for a moment to regain some measure of composure. After wiping both eyes and cheeks, she knocked on the door. She had to knock several times more before a sleepy face greeted her at the door. It was Phillip, and she noted that he actually wore pajamas. They were gray with small green figures of men playing golf.

"Kerrie?" He awoke abruptly.

"Hi. Look, I need a favor."

"Sure."

She continued hastily. It was apparent that she had rehearsed the dialog. "I don't feel well—that time of the month—you know. Anyway, I've got surgery at 0730. It's Harris, the hernia. It could be dicey, and I really don't feel up to it." She was looking down the entire time she spoke, her words rushed. Phillip reached out and gently lifted her chin to face him. Tears glistened on her cheeks; dark circles were under her eyes.

"Sure Kerrie. I'll take Harris. You get some rest."

"Thanks Phillip." Instinctively she reached and hugged him. As she did, he felt the wetness on her cheeks and the tension in her body. Embarrassed, she stepped back quickly. He didn't want to release her.

"Don't worry, Kerrie, everything's going to be okay."

She looked at him for a moment without speaking. A small voice finally answered. "You're sure?"

"I'm sure."

"How do you know?" It was the voice of a child.

"I'm a doctor; I know everything." He forced a smile. She hugged him again and left quickly.

Phillip watched her disappear into the morning shadows and then walked slowly back into this trailer. He stared at his visage in the small mirror; he looked frightful. He hadn't even combed his hair. He stood momentarily looking at the reflection. Suddenly he grasped the small sink with both hands and leaned forward, staring into the widening eyes that stared back at him. "Robb Barker." He said aloud. "Of course, it must be him." Phillip didn't know Robb well but had seen him around the base. He seemed a pleasant fellow, tall and good looking, athletic. Phillip looked again into the mirror and moaned aloud. He didn't even know the man, and he hated him.

Phillip picked up his watch and checked the time—ten minutes until six. Operation at 0730. He had work to do. As he shaved he wondered about Robb Barker. Phillip knew he had parachuted behind enemy lines. He also knew Robb's chances of recovery were not too good. Did he really want Robb to come back? He stopped and looked into the mirror closely. How could he have even thought such things? Besides, would it really matter? He studied the face in the small mirror and suddenly threw his razor across the room.

Chapter Five

Skovorodino, The Soviet Union

The worn military truck bounced along the rutted street in the darkness. Captain Sergei Iskhakov sat anxiously staring into the night. "Stop!"

"Here?"

"I said stop, idiot."

"Yes, sir."

"Listen carefully. You are not to mention to anyone that I rode in this truck tonight or even where you went. Is that understood?"

"Yes, Captain." There was fear in the young man's voice.

"Good. Now turn around and drive back to the base as I instructed. If anyone asks where you were, tell them you were delivering colonels to a whorehouse." Sergei smiled at his own humor and stepped from the truck. "That should be enough to avoid further questions." In a moment he was left alone in the dark. He reached into the pocket of his great coat and produced a crumpled cigarette pack but on reflection he put it back unopened. He didn't want to risk being seen in the dark. It was cold, and the wind was blowing along the open road. He cursed the cold, and he cursed the wind as he pulled the collar up around his neck. Snow was just beginning to fall lightly on the deserted road. At least he had thought to bring his large fur hat. He pulled the earmuffs tight against his head and tightened the string under his neck. Perhaps he should have volunteered to serve in Vietnam. At least it was hot there, but the thought of two years in the stinking jungles with the Vietnamese was more than he could stand. He smiled at the thought. He would probably end up shooting several of them and help the American war effort.

At exactly 2200 a darkened truck could be heard approaching. Sergei turned and walked back into the trees beside the road. It was a dark night combined with snowfall, and he could not distinguish the markings on the truck. The driver pulled forward slowly and stopped twenty meters ahead beside a small road sign. He killed the ignition and sat in the dark as instructed. Sergei walked slowly to the back of the truck, recognized his contact, and spoke to the driver. "Good work, Illarion, you are right on time."

The young man jumped at the sound and turned to see his captain standing beside him on the road. "Yes, Captain Iskhakov. Thank you, sir."

Sergei walked around the truck and got into the front seat by the younger man. "Let's go. And drive slowly; I would not want to run into a snow bank and have to walk to the warehouse. It is as cold as a metal toilet seat out there." There was mirth in his voice; the young man smiled carefully. He was not accustomed to humor in his captain. "Did the train engine arrive per schedule with Sergeant Kochkin?"

"Yes Captain."

"Are the missiles secure in the warehouse?"

"Yes, sir."

"Did you see anyone around the warehouse or the deserted factory?"

"No sir, it was deserted as you said."

"Good, the colonel will be pleased." Sergei relaxed into the seat and peered through the window. He started to ask about the security plan and posting of guards, but he knew that was not necessary. Vadim Kochkin was a professional, as was he. His sergeant would have already thought of such things, and they would be implemented carefully. How lucky he was to have such a man working for him. He had been very careful to insure that Vadim did not get promoted to higher positions; Sergei could not afford to lose the one man he trusted. After all, had he not taken care of Vadim? Did he not live like a colonel? Sergei smiled to himself. He also had more money than most colonels. There were many ways to accomplish the same end, and he had all the connections. He had even considered ways to funnel some of the rewards to his beloved colonel, but Sergei had decided against that. Ruchinsky was a man of principle and might not understand the rules by which Sergei played. While he had grown up and survived in the Eastern Region, the colonel had only come here recently. He had yet to learn the ways of this cold, desolate countryside where survival is the rule of law. But perhaps after their mission they could talk about such things as money and how it was made in this cold dark country.

The young man stopped the truck and looked carefully behind to see if they were being followed. He made a major issue of straining out of the truck to peer into the darkness. Sergei recognized that the act was strictly for him. He wondered how many times the soldier had checked on his way to get him. Finally, after circling back once to check the roads, the pair pulled up to the deserted warehouse. Sergei stepped out and looked at the area. As a boy he had played here when the factory was a major operation in the area. It was here that he had stolen his first beer and had almost been caught as a result of drinking it on site. It was a lesson he had learned not to repeat. When the factory had finally closed down due to the constant lack of materials and parts from Moscow's planners, it had robbed him of his finest loot. It is hard to pilfer a deserted shop.

The old factory was quiet, dark, and cold. Sergei could not see the faded letters high on the side of the crumbled building, but he knew them well. He rapped twice on the door that was built into the sliding rail doors. The door opened quickly, and Sergei found himself face to face with a rifle barrel. "It's me you fool; don't shoot that thing or you might kill the only good soldier left in Russia."

"Yes, Captain, come in." The two entered quickly with the sentry looking outside quickly to see if anyone else were around the building.

"Where is Kochkin?"

"Follow me, sir." The captain followed the young enlisted man through the cold, dark warehouse. On the right was a set of rail tracks that entered from the large sliding doors which held the smaller door through which Sergei had just entered. On the left was a concrete loading dock approximately waist high. Further down the track, in the middle of the building, were the missile container and the engine. Between the two was a standard boxcar with men entering and leaving with supplies. Standing at the rear of the missile container was the sergeant. Sergei immediately recognized the short, balding man standing with his right hand on his chin, gazing at the container. He was obviously lost in thought.

"Vadim, I'm glad to see you here, old friend. And how was Vladivistok?"

"Always the same. Drunk."

"Well, it appears you will get another chance to visit that wonderful resort." Both laughed at that. "We're headed back."

"To Vladivistok? With this cargo?"

"That is correct."

The old sergeant smiled at his captain. "Did you sell these? If so, what is my share?"

"This is official, old friend, but it is Top Secret. We have been chosen by the colonel to help him get these to the port without being seen or detected. No one is to know what we're doing."

"Are you sure you haven't sold these?" Kochkin's grin broadened.

Sergei laughed and slapped his friend on the back. "Are you afraid I'm trying to cheat you?"

"Of course not. I have always trusted my captain and my friend."

"As well you should." Suddenly Sergei became very serious and stepped closer to his old friend. "Vadim, if we pull this off successfully you too will be a captain within a year, and I will be a major. This is our big chance. Who knows, in time we could even run this sector for Moscow. Any idea how much that could be worth?"

The sergeant smiled. "I'll not start calling you major just yet."

Sergei laughed. "That's probably a good idea. We've got a difficult job to do first. That's why I called you."

"What are we going to do with these when we get them to the port?"

"Put them on a ship; what else?"

"A ship? What would the navy do with these?"

"It's not going to be a navy ship."

"It isn't?" There was surprise and disbelief in his voice.

"No, I'll brief you on all the necessary details as we proceed. For the time being, just figure how to get these missiles from here to the port without being detected. That's going to be tough. By the way, who's driving the train engine?"

"I am, plus I'm teaching young Illarion. He's a bright enough kid."

"Good. I worry a great deal about our own troops. They must keep quiet about this. No leave, no trips to town."

"I understand."

"That means us too."

"Us?"

"Yes, I need you here to keep things under control when I have to leave to arrange the ship and to meet with the colonel to plan our mission."

"Is the colonel going with us?" There was a sudden seriousness in his voice.

"Yes. This operation is very important to him and he wants to lead it himself. Or at least we will let him think he's leading it." Sergei smiled. "Now enough of this. What are your thoughts on getting to Vladivistok?"

"It is going to be very difficult. First we have to get rid of this container. It is sure to alert the entire world of our cargo. Second, we must travel at night so that detection is minimized. That means we must know the details of the regular train schedules on a real time basis."

"Good idea."

"I've already taken the action to put one of our men in the rail scheduling dispatch office. Unless Moscow changes something at the last minute, we should be okay there. And by the way, he knows nothing of our mission and is totally trustworthy."

"Are you sure?"

"He's my son-in-law. He married the one beautiful daughter I produced."

"Good for him."

"When we leave, we must take our troops with us, so I commandeered a boxcar to carry them along. They cannot be seen escorting the missiles without causing questions."

"You have thought of everything my friend."

"No, I have just started to plan. How much time do we have?"

"Unfortunately, too much. I must arrange the ship, and that could take quite some time. I can get support from the colonel if needed, but I'd rather that we do most of the planning ourselves." The sergeant grimaced. He was thinking of his plump wife and his warm home. He didn't like the idea of long assignments in a cold warehouse. Sergei knew his old friend well and understood his reluctance. "Don't worry, you and I can take time off now and then. With two of us here, one could get a day in town now and then when the planning is complete." Kochkin's face brightened. "One last thing. We don't know when the ship will be secured, so we have to be ready as soon as possible. Then we wait."

"I'm going to need some things. After looking at the container car, I've decided that the missiles should not be moved to a standard rail car. Instead, we'll just take the top off of the container car. It will take some work, but it must be done. It is the only safe way. I was hoping there would be an overhead crane in one of the warehouses, but what was left has been long since cannibalized or parts pilfered for other uses. Besides this equipment is so old I wouldn't trust it. Removing the top of the container car is the only alternative."

"Then how will we cover the missiles?"

"With tarpaulins. That way no one would guess we have important cargo underneath. We certainly can't pull this container car in the open without advertising that we have missiles."

"Yes, you are right. What do you need?"

"I can find the equipment most easily. It should take me a day or two." Kochkin was again thinking of his plump wife, and Sergei was aware of that fact.

"Very well, but hurry, and remember that this is Top Secret. Not even our wives are to know."

"Of course."

Nubat Royal Thai Air Force Base

The HH-3 helicopter circled the parking ramp twice. Below the crowd cheered and waved. The pilot, obviously enjoying this portion of his work, smiled broadly at the accumulation of people below.

There were pilots, mechanics, and airmen, all of the groups that enabled the base to function. In the back of the crowd stood one woman, dressed in the faded green garb of a hospital. She was smiling; no one noticed as she wiped her eyes repeatedly, brushing away tears that simply would not stop.

Softly, the large green chopper settled onto the ramp. The crowd converged; someone opened the door; and from the dark bowels of the helicopter, Robb stepped into the bright sunlight. His flight suit was torn and muddy. He had two days' beard and a forced smile on his face. What the crowd saw instantly was the blood that stained a major portion of his chest. At once the crowd grew silent as he scanned the accumulation of faces, squinting into the morning sun. Joe barged through the crowd, followed by Colonel Bennett. He placed a cold can of beer in Robb's hand and held it high as the crowd roared again. Still the blue eyes scanned the crowd; then their eyes met and locked. In the midst of the laughing people they were suddenly alone; blotting out the sounds and sights of the morning. All they saw was each other.

She had read the forced smile, the tired face, and then she saw the blood. Her face went white and she felt her knees buckling under her. She leaned heavily on a young airman beside her, watching carefully as Robb jumped to the ground. The men raised him to their shoulders and began to march toward a waiting pickup, his carriage to the club. There would be a party tonight. As the men cheered and shouted, Robb felt a hand touch his. It was soft, but strong. He recognized it instantly and grabbed it and pulled her to him. Joe and the others stopped, unable to carry both Robb and Kerrie. He dropped to the ground and took her in his arms, kissing her. The men cheered even louder. While they were kissing Robb felt her hand exploring his chest through the flight suit, searching for the wound. When she could finally speak she said simply, "The blood?" He looked to where her hand searched his body, and his face became suddenly sad. The joy drained away; reality struck with full force.

He simply answered, "Wayne."

She squeezed his arms and whispered, "Oh, Robb, I'm so sorry." With that short, private exchange, the crowd put them both into the truck and started for the club. The truck lurched to a stop at the entrance of the worn building where another group was waiting, more pilots and airmen. Standing aside, the small Thai waitresses stood holding hands, watching the strange Americans celebrate.

"First a hamburger; then beer. This man's been without food for two days." Several of the waitresses ran off to the kitchen at the colonel's bidding.

She touched his wrist. "I've got to get to the hospital." She leaned closer and whispered. "See you at 2100?" His smile was answer enough, and she hurried out the door toward the hospital.

And now the celebration would begin in earnest. One of their own had been plucked from the enemy's back yard. There would be time to grieve the loss of another friend, but that would be later. Tonight was time to celebrate. Tonight the cares of war would be put aside. Tonight they would laugh and sing and perhaps even dance. Who knows what might happen when a group of fighter pilots celebrate a successful recovery. Tomorrow they would think about Wayne, but only for a brief few moments. It is too hard to dwell on such things when one flies every day into that same hell that took him. But tomorrow they would fly with vengeful purpose.

*   *   *

The pilots lived in small "hooches" or buildings that were constructed with four rooms, each room opening to the outside and accommodating a pair of pilots or navigators. They were placed in a circle with a long, narrow bath building in the center. This "latrine" had toilets on one end, a line of sinks with mirrors in the center on both walls, and a shower room on the opposite end. Between the sinks and the shower room was an area with hooks on the wall and several short benches for removing the heavy flight boots that all aircrew members wore. Robb was seated on one of these benches, tugging at his boots. He was exhausted and a little high. He had consumed three beers--rather quickly--with and after the hamburger at the club. The adrenaline had finally washed from his body, and the alcohol was taking over. It felt as if he had finished two six packs. Finally, the second boot released and fell to the floor. He looked at it for several moments as his mind wandered. With great effort he stood and began to remove his flight suit. As he did, the dark red stains of dried blood and sweat appeared across his chest, in violent contrast to the dull white of his undershirt. He quickly stepped out of the flight suit and stepped in front of the last mirror on the wall to his left. His eyes widened as he stared at the stains. Instinctively, he reached his hands to his own torso and felt for wounds that were not there. His fogged brain struggled, remembering. "Wayne!" A groan escaped his mouth and his mind simultaneously. His shoulders slumped. Then he saw the other red stain on his right shoulder and for the first time felt the slight twitch of pain there. He grabbed his sleeve and pulled it over his shoulder. There was a small wound, about an inch in length, barely penetrating his skin. "One of the bullets on the hill," he surmised. "Dodged one more." He touched it carefully. The sting increased. It had done no real damage, but it would leave a scar.

As waves wash upon the beach, an idea far back in his subconscious burst upon his conscious mind and shook him into sobriety. It was the vision of Wayne, gasping his last breath in his arms. The picture of blood rushing from four or five red holes in Wayne's chest and the sound of his last exhalation--these washed inexorably across his mind and his soul. Robb staggered to the last sink in the long row, grasping it with both hands to steady his shaking body. Through the tears that welled in his eyes he looked once more at the tiny scar on his shoulder. After a few moments, he tore the undershirt from his body and threw it to the floor. He stumbled into the hot shower with one realization--for the rest of his life he would see that scar on his shoulder, and every time he did, he would see and hear Wayne dying on some hillside in North Vietnam. With both fists, he pounded the wall as the hot water washed the soil, the sweat, and the blood from his body.

$$*\quad*\quad*$$

The weary man walked across the yard between the hooches and the latrine. The party had been long and loud. He was exhausted, still a little high, and much in need of sleep.

When he opened the door, she was there, sitting on his bunk. She ran to him and held him tightly. "I was so afraid!" He hugged her in silence. "The waiting was so terrible." They held each other, standing in the center of the small dark room. "Thank God for Phillip; I don't know how I would have made it without him." She looked up into his eyes. "Are you okay, Robb?"

"Yeah, I'm fine."

"When I saw all of that blood, I nearly screamed."

"It was Wayne's." Robb was suddenly looking into the distance, far away.

"I know now. Joe told me what happened." She buried her face in his chest. "How awful."

He cupped her face in his two hands and lifted it to his own. For minutes he studied her face, the horrors of war receding from his mind. "You are so beautiful." He bent and kissed her softly, passionately. "I'm so glad you're here. I need to hold you, to feel your breath on my cheek, to know something beautiful still exists in this crappy, rotten world." There was anger in his voice.

"There is nothing in this world that could have kept me from you tonight." He was running his fingers through her hair, staring, memorizing every part of her face. Kerrie pulled away from his grasp and walked back to the small bed. When she turned she had a bottle of wine and two tumblers. "They aren't crystal, but they'll have to do." He smiled. "I thought you might want something to unwind, but you'll have to open it. I can handle a scalpel, but a corkscrew is your business."

"Thanks, but I've had more than enough to drink tonight. All I really need now is to hold you. Can you stay here tonight?"

She read the message in his eyes, the message left unsaid--he did not want to be alone with the shadows in his mind. "Sure."

As they lay together on the small bunk, she listened to his breathing as it slowed. Sleep finally came for him, but not as easily for her. She clung to him desperately, and to the newly found joy that had changed her life. She knew how closely she had come to losing that joy, and in the cool dark room she was wrestling with that specter. The two had become inseparable in her life she thought--Robb and love, Robb and life. How could one exist without the other? Dark demons clouded her mind and brought a fear she had never known before. But she fought them. She was a woman of science, a woman of intense control. And besides, she had made a deal with God, her first. If He would protect this man she loved, she would relinquish enough control to open her heart to his greatest gift--love. Wasn't that what He wanted for her? Wasn't that what she wanted? Love. But that meant giving up the most precious possession of her early life--the control she strove to build and protect. If God gave her His greatest gift, could she do less? In the dark room she smiled, Robb stirred, and a sudden warmth flowed over her. Surely God had understood. It was so right. Could He not agree? The thoughts in her mind slowed their pace; fatigue and the warmth of his body brought her closer to the sleep that had evaded her. She caressed him in his sleep and joined him in restless slumber. In their sleep, they held fast to each other, both fighting demons from different worlds—for one, witnessed, for the other, imagined.

At 0430 his hand reached out into the darkness and felt cautiously around the alarm clock on the small table beside the bed. Consciousness invaded his brain gradually. He sensed the woman lying beside him, her arm across his chest. The smell of her hair was pleasant, with it came mental images of the soft brown curls bouncing at her neck as she walked. Robb smiled and shifted to his side carefully in order to see her more clearly. He noted that the sheets were damp where his back had laid. The air conditioner had maintained the cold temperature in the room; still the bed was damp with sweat. Perhaps it was the closeness of two bodies in the night, or perhaps it was the nightmares in the darkness--a grinning man with a weapon, a wounded boy crying in the dirt, Wayne struggling to talk as he died, blood on his hands, his clothes. He forced his mind to the present. 0430! Briefing at 0515; takeoff before 0600. Today he would get back on the proverbial horse that had thrown him. He let his mind toy with that idea a while. Would he be okay? Decisively he knew that yes, he would be fine. He would fly again; he would fight again, but he would be different; he would always be different. "God help me," he prayed quietly, "I <u>will</u> fly today, and I'll be okay."

Sliding gently from the bed, Robb stretched, turned on the small table lamp, and looked back at Kerrie. She was wearing one of his T-shirts and her panties, lying on her side, facing the wall. Her hips were silhouetted against the dark wall. The light was soft, like her. He smiled to himself as he grappled through the metal locker for a clean flight suit. He had learned two things that night. He knew now what he could endure; he also knew how that had been possible. His life had taken on a new purpose. It had found a new reason for existence. There were others who depended on him in a new and different way. And while the responsibility was overwhelming; it also brought a sense of contentment and purpose that he had never felt before. She rolled over and looked at him sleepily in the dim light. "Go back to sleep. It's only 0430. You can sleep another hour and a half." She smiled, rolled back to face the wall and in a few moments was breathing deeply. He wanted to touch her but decided to let her sleep. When he walked out into the early morning light, he was whistling softly.

*   *   *

Colonel Bennett watched the young captain as the team of men studied maps and target photos. They talked quickly in the ready room, then listened to the weather briefing and the target description. Each man made notes for the mission. Printed forms were also filled to reflect the various codes of the day, target coordinates, refueling locations, strike frequencies, etc. Throughout the process the young captain appeared normal. He even joked with the weatherman, but the test was coming fast--crew assignments. Bennett had anticipated this situation and had arranged for a senior navigator to be paired with Robb. Tall, thin, and affable, Major Jack Trudeau was a pro. He had chatted briefly with the Ops Officer and knew his job well. He would fly the mission with Robb. For all practical purposes, it was a normal mission, but there was one other duty to be performed. Trudeau would also assess the young pilot to verify his status. Everyone understood this, including Robb himself. No one doubted his capability to perform, least of all Robb, but it still had to be verified.

Three hours later the sweaty crews returned. The fighters flew in formation over the airfield and pitched out in succession to downwind. Colonel Bennett stood on the hot ramp and watched with pride as they roared overhead. One by one, they landed and taxied off the runway toward the waiting revetments and the maintenance crews.

He had monitored their progress. It had been a routine flight; one bridge destroyed, minor antiaircraft fire from the area, no damage reported. Four more birds ready to "turn." It might be a war, but he still had quotas to make, sorties to be counted, and tons of bombs to drop. He wondered if the Pentagon really understood his problems. It was damned hard to meet their sortie rates when the jungle and the enemy kept damaging his aircraft. That was why he had the best maintenance crews in the Air Force. The pilots get all the glory, but it was the maintenance crews who kept his planes in the air.

The first of the fighters pulled into the revetments and parked at the direction of the waiting crewchiefs. Two, Three, and Four were immediately behind. Colonel Bennett rode by the aircraft in a blue Dodge Powerwagon and waved at his crews. From the back seat of the second aircraft a wave and a thumbs up were all he needed. One more potential problem solved; now he could concentrate on the long list of others that loomed before him.

Robb walked out onto the small porch of the hooch in his shorts. It was late and already the bugs that swarmed around the lone light cast a dark, dancing shadow across the dim stoop. He watched them flutter back and forth, constantly battering the light bulb. They would fall away, only to ram it again. They never seemed to realize the uselessness of their endless pursuit of the bright warmth. Nor did they see the stealthy lizards that edged slowly and unobtrusively closer and closer. Patiently the reptiles stalked their prey while the insects dazzled themselves with the bright security of the warm light. Slowly and surely the attrition was whittling away their ranks until the lizards were satisfied and gorged. Yet the insects kept coming, and they would forever fly to the bulb until the light was finally extinguished or faded by the early morning sun. Only then would the sacrifice stop. The sleepless man pondered the attraction that drew the insects to the brilliance of the light and to their early demise. He lay a pad upon his knees and after a moment's hesitation began to write.

Dear Jason,

This week I lost my plane and one of my best friends. You may remember Wayne Compton from RTU training. We went down behind enemy lines, and Wayne was killed saving my life in a gunfight. I've frankly had a rough time getting through this, but I keep remembering our conversation on the back porch just before I left.

It was all such a freak chance. We were hit by groundfire in Route Pack 5. I kept thinking of what you said about keeping my cool when the chips were down. Well, they were, and I did. I wrote Wayne's folks a long letter. That was one of the hardest things I've ever had to do. We were really close friends; we had flown together through RTU and then here. I'm going to miss him.

They say you only have one time to crash. Well, I've had mine, so I should be good for the duration now. By the way, please don't mention this to Mom or Dad, I don't want them to get upset and worry.

Take care,
Robb

* * *

Dear Barb,

I'm sorry I haven't written recently. It has been a difficult week. Robb got shot down over North Vietnam last week. He made it back (God bless all rescue teams!) but he lost his navigator. They were close, and it's been hard for him. I don't know why, but I feel such guilt about Wayne (Robb's friend). Robb said Wayne saved his life, yet his death has brought us into an even deeper relationship. Does any of this make sense?

Thanks for being my personal shopper. Please let me know if I need to send extra money. By the way, I like the black ones best, too. (So does Robb—hey, I'm blushing!)

I guess you think all I do is play. The work is going fine, and there's a lot of it. I'm working with a great surgeon named Phillip Brady. He's a very intense man, but his skills as a surgeon are amazing. At first I thought he was a klutz, then suddenly he seemed to work miracles in the operating room. I feel like I'm back in training again though he's only four or five years older than I am. I'm learning a lot from him.

Got to go; there's a formal dining-in tonight. I really should go in uniform, but Robb made me promise that I'd wear something else. (Doctors aren't real officers, I guess.)

Love,

Kerrie

P.S. Thanks for the warning—but yes, I am a doctor. Seems like I did study human reproduction back in high school. I think I remember the key points. (I just didn't know it was this much fun.) Oh yes, good news! I've lost 12 lbs. since I got here. You wouldn't recognize me. By the time I leave here I'll look like a model.

*   *   *

The knock on the door was both harsh and urgent. Robb jerked his head toward the sound and moved gently from the sleeping woman cuddled beside him. He hurried to the door, but not before the pounding resumed. Behind him Kerrie moaned and raised her head to peer toward the intrusion. "Robb, are you there? It's Joe!"

Robb swung the door wide to see his friend standing in the rain, drenched. He reached and grabbed his shirt, dragging him into the small room. As he did he held one finger to his lips to calm the noise and protect the sleeping woman. It was too late. "What the hell is going on Joe?"

Kerrie climbed from the bed, the sheet held to cover her. "Joe?"

"Guard at the front gate just dropped this at the hooch." He handed Robb an envelope with his name neatly written on it. "Guard said it was delivered about twenty-two hundred. I figured it must be important." Robb reached for his watch as Kerrie handed Joe a towel. He looked at her and smiled. She certainly was beautiful; Robb was fortunate, indeed.

"Damn!"

"What's wrong?" Kerrie was watching his face as the lines of concern darkened his expression.

"Somboon's gone." He sat suddenly on the chair beside the small table and perused the short note again in case he had missed something.

"Gone?" The flush had left Kerrie's cheeks.

"He's missing; they think he went into the jungle. Sister Estelle thinks he may be looking for me."

Kerrie looked rapidly between the two men. "Does he know that you went down?"

"I don't know how he could have known."

Kerrie walked over to Robb and placed a hand on his shoulder. "Maybe he thinks you left him." She watched Robb's face then added. "He lost his family—maybe he felt he lost you too."

"When did you say this arrived?"

"Twenty-two hundred."

"How long has this monsoon storm been here?"

"It's pretty nasty out there."

Robb looked at the puddle under Joe. "Yeah." He opened the door to the trailer and looked outside. "Damn!" Robb turned and grabbed his fatigues and boots. Kerrie watched as he struggled into his clothes. Kerrie began collecting her clothes as well.

"Turn around, Joe."

"Huh?"

"I said turn around."

"Oh, sure."

"You go back to bed Kerrie; I'll find him."

"I'm going too. I care about him just like you do. Besides, I'm a doctor."

Joe grinned at the wall. "And a damned pretty one I might add." She threw a pillow at him.

"Keep facing that wall."

"Yes, ma'am!"

*   *   *

Robb ran across the dark orphanage yard and splashed through several puddles on his way to the truck. He opened the driver's door and jumped in quickly, dripping water over the seat and Kerrie. He sat shivering momentarily then slapped the steering wheel in frustration.

Joe looked over. "Well, any news?"

"No, he left sometime after dinner. They have eight or ten people out looking for him in the area. They think he went into the jungle, but I don't agree." He started the truck and pulled away from the orphanage fence. "I think I know where he is." Robb headed northeast, driving slowly as sheets of rain pelted the truck. All three young officers strained their eyes peering into the darkness as the truck bounced through puddles and streams crossing the narrow muddy road. Ten minutes later they pulled out of the small village and turned off the main road onto a smaller road that was little more than a trail through a dark jungle cavern. At one point Robb stopped abruptly and studied the road before him. It was completely flooded as water rushed across the worn tracks in a small muddy river about 50 yards wide. "What do you think, Joe?"

"Looks like crap."

"I know; what do you think?"

"This old Dodge can make it, but use four wheel drive."

"Right." He paused and looked at Kerrie. "By the way, Kerrie, do you swim?"

"Of course."

"Good." With that he down shifted the truck and plowed across the stream.

The rain was still pouring when the truck pulled to a stop about fifty yards from the battered remains of the tiny hooch where Somboon had lived with his parents and siblings. Robb tested two flashlights and handed one to Joe.

"Joe, you check the shed out back. I'll check the hooch and the yard. And be careful, there's a large hole on the left side of the hooch; my guess is that it's still there and filled with water." He kissed Kerrie on the cheek. "Stay in the truck. If you see anything, blow the horn. Let's use that as our signal to return to the truck." In less than a second both young men jumped from the truck and disappeared into the darkness and the downpour.

The rain was surprisingly cold for Thailand. Robb guessed that it must have been falling from the top of the storm clouds in excess of fifty thousand feet. It was a hard, cold rain, and it made the darkness even more difficult to navigate. The forest glistened in the evening storm. The broad green leaves winked at the small rays of light that emanated from the flashlight and reflected from the fine mist that fell from the leaves as the two men pushed their way through the underbrush. The pungent odor of the decaying jungle surrounded them as the rain soaked their fatigues and the mud caked their legs and boots. Ahead a small curl of white smoke wound through the broken hut and floated slowly skyward. By the time it reached the tops of the trees it was invisible in the heavy rain. Robb heard the child before he saw him. Somboon's familiar childlike voice was shouting, shrill with anger and frustration. As Robb raced toward the sound, a giant bolt of lightening crashed through the sky and lit the small clearing beside the mangled remains of the small dwelling. For an instant the jungle was bathed in a flash of bright light. Then it was black again. He approached the broken structure slowly as his eyes adjusted to the darkness. He could see the tiny clothes hanging near the fire and the figures of two boys huddled close together beside it. He recognized Somboon immediately; he was naked, as was his only surviving family member, a boy of 14 or 15, Chusak. Chusak was the oldest of the Ranguak children; the last time Robb had seen Chusak he had been a boy; the eyes of the youth before him now were those of a young man, a young man who had known much pain. Robb carefully surveyed the smooth features of his face; they were expressionless, but the eyes were cold and angry.

The lightening had faded, and only the firelight and the small light of the flashlight penetrated the monsoon storm that raged around them. Robb stopped and stood quietly behind the two boys. Both turned instantly, surprised by the dim glow of the light in his hand. Somboon shouted, this time in fear. The young pilot sensed the boys' confusion and turned the light to illuminate his own face as he spoke their names. A shout of recognition rose from the smaller boy, and he started to run toward the man. Suddenly he stopped and looked back at his older brother. Chusak stood facing the tiny boy as pelting water fell through the remains of the collapsed roof. They were obviously arguing again, but Robb could not understand them. For long minutes the tiny naked boy stood between the man-child and the man. Robb held out one hand and said simply, "Come, Somboon." Still the child stood and watched the older boy who studied the pilot closely with deep, dark eyes. A sound behind him startled Robb; he turned to see Kerrie approaching carefully in the rain. She was soaked, her hair flattened against her cheeks. He held his hand up as a signal to her but said nothing. Somboon wiped the rain from his face and eyes then shivered slightly; Kerrie started to move toward him, but Robb grabbed her arm and stopped her. He whispered quickly. "No Kerrie, let them decide." Then he looked long and hard into the eyes of the older boy. "Sawatdee, Chusak. Chusak come; Somboon come." Finally the older boy appeared to make a decision. He walked forward, grabbed his brother, turned him toward Robb, and shouted rapidly as he pointed toward the pilot. Another clap of thunder lit the wrecked hooch in blinding light. Both boys shrieked in fear. The two adults also winced at the noise and the bright flash of light. For a moment Robb's eyes were blinded; he could feel Kerrie's grasp tighten around his arm. Slowly his focus returned in the darkness. In the dim light he saw only the child walking slowly toward him. Robb moved the flashlight beam and called after Chusak, but he was gone. Kerrie looked at the spot where Chusak disappeared.

"What about the other boy?"

"I'm afraid we lost him a long time ago, Kerrie. Did you bring the candy from the truck?"

"Do you think he'll come back?"

"He'll be back. See the spoon and that cloth? There's probably meat or jerky in there; he'll be back." While Kerrie gathered the damp clothes for Somboon, Robb fished in his pocket and withdrew a large, brown handled pocketknife. He placed it and a handful of Thai money beside the candy. Lifting the small child he turned toward the truck and shelter from the storm. He shouted for Joe but to no avail in the howling wind and rain. The truck's horn would be signal enough.

Kerrie cradled the tiny boy in her arms and brushed the water from his hair as the truck drove slowly through the pouring rain. "Are you sure it was Chusak?"

"Yes."

"But he wouldn't come with us." It was a simple statement.

"No." Robb paused for a moment and considered his words as the truck navigated a large hole filled with mud. "It was strange. I could see absolute hatred in his eyes, yet he sent Somboon to me."

It was Joe who answered "Well, I can certainly understand why he might hate us."

"Yeah. I just wish I could talk to him. Damn. If only I could speak Thai."

"Do you really think that would help?" Somboon's large brown eyes were locked on Kerrie's as she spoke.

"Probably not. I just want to try."

*   *   *

Dick O'Brian had chosen the small mountains to his east before ejecting. What he had not known was that the prevailing winds closer to the ground would blow the parachutes back to the West. "Owl One is going down! We're losing altitude fast!" Dick had given up the idea of sounding professional; his voice was fast and at a considerably higher octave than normal. "Bill, get ready! We're punching out!" He reached for the ejection handle between his legs and tugged sharply. The rear canopy flew into the air, and less than a second later the navigator flew his rocket seat into the Vietnamese sky. Less than three seconds later, Dick felt the jolt of nine and a half g's as his own seat ejected him from the burning plane. It all happened so fast. In mere seconds both men had ejected and were separated from their seats by the automatic mechanisms installed for that purpose. Now they both hung suspended in their parachutes, drifting lazily toward the jungle below.

The early morning sky was surprisingly beautiful. Streaks of orange tinged the Karst mountains to the east, in bright contrast to the dark green of the vegetation. Soft puffy white clouds were already forming in the northeast as the moist air rose from the jungles below. But neither of the men saw or noticed the beauty of the morning sky. They were focused on the ground and the dangers below them. Dick struggled with his risers, pulling various combinations to attempt some small measure of control over his descent. He looked quickly around and finally spotted Bill drifting slowly toward the jungle on his left. He cursed the winds; they were blowing them both back toward the valley between the mountains. That's where the danger lay. That's where the enemy were. Dick forced his mind not to panic. Quickly he inventoried his equipment. He had his .38 Smith and Wesson which was not loaded. He would decide between bullets and flares when needed, but his personal .32 was fully loaded in the shoulder holster strapped inside his flight suit. In an emergency, it was ready. He hoped he would need neither.

Dick was drifting toward a small clearing near the base of the hills. That would be dangerous. Landing on a slope is dicey business for well-trained paratroopers. Surprisingly, Air Force pilots receive little training in the skill of parachuting. They are expected to fly planes, not jump from them. Off to his left, Bill was descending into the dense jungle.

Rifle fire on his right and the whiz of a bullet over his head spun Dick's body around. Two soldiers about 150 yards away were running in his direction. One had a rifle, the other a pistol. Dick looked down; he was approaching the ground very quickly now. He considered releasing his harness and falling the remaining distance, but he was still too high. The soldier with the rifle stopped to aim again. Dick waved both arms at him in surrender, but the soldier fired once more. The right harness strap snapped above Dick's head as the bullet slammed through it. Dick struggled with his .38 and began firing at the two soldiers. It worked; they stopped firing and ducked behind several small trees. A minute later Dick rolled to the ground, released his chute, and started to run along a ravine in the opposite direction from the soldiers. As he ran, the rifleman took aim and fired. The bullet struck Dick in the left shoulder, spinning him around. He fell backwards into the ravine and tumbled down its side, finally landing face down beside a small creek. The pain was terrible, but the shock was worse. He was hit badly, bleeding profusely, and unable to move. For a moment consciousness hung like a cloud over his head. He heard the shouts above him and was vaguely aware of the gravel that fell down the ravine as one of the soldiers raced down the steep slope. The second soldier stood above with his rifle ready should the American move.

Sieu was a squat man, shorter even than his fellow Vietnamese. But he was powerfully strong and unpredictable, and everyone in the village feared him. He had long since learned that reckless courage and violence would intimidate most men. Willingness to accept pain in physical combat earned the respect of the others. His smile was mostly toothless, a loss he was more than willing to sacrifice for the respect of bigger men. He was small; he was also fast. He ran and slid down the ravine, his pistol ready, though he could see the blood on the lifeless figure below. The American was dead or dying. To Sieu, it did not matter which. Still, he approached the pilot carefully, a little surprised at his size. This American must have been almost a half meter taller than Sieu, still, like most big men in his life, it was Sieu who stood with the gun while the larger man lay dying in the dirt. He walked over to the pilot, cocked his pistol, and placed it on the back of the American's skull.

Dick O'Brian felt the cold steel on the back of his head. He wanted to scream, but he couldn't. It took all of his power to keep his mind functioning at all. So this is how it ends, he thought, killed by two ignorant peasants! We have the greatest military in the world and the best equipment, and I'm going to be killed by some rusty pistol. From within a rage emerged and poured adrenaline into his body while he waited for the bullet to end his life. Jane! he thought, Oh God, Jane.

The soldier pulled the trigger, smiling and stepping away. He didn't want to be splattered with blood--even if it would gain him more respect in the village. The gun clicked--a misfire. He backed away two steps, examined the gun, aimed and pulled the trigger again. Another misfire. He cursed the gun and the ammunition he had been given. Perhaps it was old; perhaps the ammunition was made for a different gun. He reached for the pilot's gun in the holster at his side. He placed it at the base of the pilot's skull and again squeezed the trigger. Again it clicked; the gun was empty. Sieu shrugged, looked at the lifeless figure, stuck both guns in his belt, and began unlacing the pilot's boots. From above on the ridge of the ravine, the other soldier shouted obscenities at Sieu. Laying his rifle on the rocks above, he too scrambled down the ravine for his share of the loot.

Dick O'Brian prayed for the first time in many years as the gun clicked above his head. Tears of anger were running down his face as the enemy soldier began twisting his legs and tearing at his boots. Suddenly the soldier dropped his leg, the boot still intact. Had he seen Dick breathe? Had he moved or moaned? The answer became obvious as the two soldiers behind him began to argue loudly. Both wanted the prized boots. The argument grew louder, and predictably, Sieu moved into the physical confrontation mood. He shoved the younger soldier who stumbled and fell backward.

Dick listened to the two men arguing. His body ached all over, and his mind was drifting in and out of consciousness. He forced his mind to concentrate, to think. He knew this might well be his last chance. Would they leave him alive after stripping his body? Could he endure the pain without groaning? Probably not. It had to be now. His left arm was crumpled under his chest. He tested it carefully; the arm was practically useless, but his left hand responded. He grasped the zipper on his flight suit and moved it downward carefully. It was then that he felt the sticky dampness on his fingers. It took a moment to realize it was his own blood. He tugged again, the zipper moved further.

Dick was not certain what caused his sudden resolve. It most certainly was partly related to his fear. He had never known such terror in his life; his cold logic also led to only one conclusion--he had to use this last opportunity; but it was his rage that flooded his body with adrenaline and heightened every sense in his pain wracked body. He fought the rage to control it, otherwise his entire body would shake with malice for the two men who had shot him and especially the one who had coldly tried to finish that job. The .32 was fully loaded; he was sure of that. It was a small caliber pistol, but six shots at close range should do the job. If only he could reach it, roll to his back, and surprise the two men who were fighting over his boots. One chance; might as well be now, he thought. With all of his remaining energy, Dick marshaled his last remaining strength and initiated his plan.

The two soldiers were glaring at each other when the movement behind them caught their attention. They both turned simultaneously to see the American lying on his back, a pistol in his hand. Dick began firing and did not stop until his pistol was empty. With great difficulty he reloaded without moving from where he lay. Both of the enemy were down. Painfully he rolled over and crawled toward the two downed men, his gun ready for any movement. The younger soldier was dead. The shorter of the two lay moaning in a pool of blood. As Dick crawled toward him, he saw the two pistols in his belt. The soldier was lying on his back, breathing with great difficulty. Dick looked into his eyes, placed the .32 to his forehead, and whispered. "Same chance you gave me, Asshole." The soldier's eyes were wide with fear when Dick pulled the trigger; it did not misfire.

The wounded pilot put the .32 in its holster, retrieved his .38, loaded it, and began the difficult chore of climbing out of the ravine.

The effort to crawl to the top of the ravine was far more difficult than Dick had expected. Bleeding badly, one arm useless, and drained of energy, he started climbing in the soft, moist soil. One third of the way up, his right foot slipped on a root and he rolled backward down the hill. His descent was stopped by the bloody body of one of the two soldiers he had killed.

He lay beside the dead man breathing hard. Exhaustion shrouded his body. Stop. Think. Must get away from here. Those gunshots will bring more soldiers, he thought. He rolled to his back and looked up into the cloudy sky. Two F-4's roared overhead and brought his mind back to reality. He looked again at the dead soldier. Two bullets had obviously hit his chest; another had crashed through his throat. Dick wondered for a moment which had killed the man. Did it really matter? More F-4s, this time dive bombing some target south of his location, screamed through the sky. He watched the planes swoop down, release their bombs, then strain back into the heavens to climb again to safety. From somewhere off to his left a .37mm anti-aircraft site opened fire. The rounds rattled off in clips as the jets jinked through the summer sky to avoid the enemy rounds. Dick wondered if that were the same site that downed his own aircraft. More gunfire shattered the afternoon. This time it was small arms, about 200 yards west of his position. Realizing the nearness of the enemy troops, Dick rolled abruptly to his stomach and began the long climb back up the ravine. Moaning, panting, and cursing, he climbed steadily--dragging his left arm. His concentration focused on every twig, every root, every rock as he climbed. The chore became both deliberate and painful.

More shots were fired to his west, approximately at the same location as before. That was good, they were not moving in his direction. The top of the ravine loomed before him. He grunted and swore at the soft soil that crumbled under his right hand and his boots. With the last of his waning energy, he topped the ravine and fell gasping into the thick, wet grass. He lay there gulping air. The pain in his left shoulder was intensifying, he knew he could control that, but the clouds invading his mind were unmistakable, consciousness was absolutely necessary for his survival, and he felt it slipping away.

Dick crawled slowly into the thicker underbrush. As he did, he felt his hand on something hard, metallic. Through bleary eyes he slowly focused on the rifle left behind by the second soldier he had killed. "I've got to take it; might need it; it would direct them to this area." Dragging the rifle as he crawled, he disappeared into the thicker underbrush and fell unconscious into a small hole in the thicket.

Consciousness came slowly, like waking on a summer Sunday morning. Through the fog in his brain, he became aware of his body and the throbbing in his left shoulder, and then the damp grassy smell of his uncomfortable bed invaded his nose and added to his structure of conscious thought. Finally, the cool, hard barrel of the rifle pressed into the flesh of his neck and reminded him of the reality he wanted to forget. He lay there a long time, feeling, listening--not even moving the rifle that his muscles strained against. Think. Must think. Are there any soldiers around? He held his breath to quite his own breathing and listened. Nothing. No airplanes, no ground fire, no soldiers laughing or calling to each other. Nothing. But they were there; he sensed it. How long had he been unconscious? He looked up at the sky. It appeared the same--clustered clouds building in the afternoon heat. He probed his left shoulder carefully. It was still bleeding, but not as profusely. He would have to do something about that. With his right hand he unzipped his flight suit to his waist and began tearing at his undershirt. It was far more difficult than he had thought, so he reached for his survival knife for help. He stuffed the rags into the wound on the front of his shoulder. He could not reach the entry point on his back. He mumbled to himself quietly. "That will have to do for now. What is my situation?" He felt both of his pistols then reached for his radio. Carefully he pressed the switch. But nothing happened. He tried it again. Nothing. He studied it carefully; it was caked with mud and dirt. He brushed it against his flight suit and tried again. Still nothing. Dick shook the instrument violently and tried again. "Shit! I'm wounded, no radio, and have limited time without help. And oh yes, surrounded by enemy." Dick closed his eyes momentarily and groaned. "How do I get help? Bill! I must find Bill. He has a radio." He sat up and reached into his g-suit pocket for his water bottle. It had survived intact. He drank most of it with large gulps, then with renewed energy and a plan, the wounded pilot slowly rose to his feet, looking quickly in all directions for danger, and headed toward the thick jungle before him. That was where he had last seen Bill descending into the trees.

Trudging through the jungle required far more effort than Dick had imagined. The thickness of the undergrowth would challenge a strong man. It was almost impenetrable for a wounded one. The trees overhead blotted the sun from the dark, damp jungle floor. But Dick sensed that the darkness was changing. He pulled his limp left arm painfully to check his watch. It was covered with blood. He rubbed his hand across the face and checked the time. It was nearing 1600. Fifteen minutes later he found what he had been searching for. To his left he spotted a parachute hanging in the treetops above his head. Frantically he fought the jungle vegetation that blocked his path and his vision. As he broke free of the tangled vines and walked under the tree he saw Bill, hanging in his harness thirty feet above the ground. He was slumped forward, his face down. He looked as if he might be asleep. Dick rushed forward calling his name. "Bill!

Bill!" Then he stopped abruptly, looking up. Three bright red circles were clearly visible on his chest. The blood ran down his body and dripped from his right boot. A small puddle formed on the ground below him. He was dead.

The wounded pilot slumped to the ground, cursing, tears in his eyes. Bill had not had a chance. Dick looked up at the lifeless body. Bill's pistol was still in its holster. They had shot him like a hanging target. He had no chance at all, suspended high in the trees. He had probably tried to surrender, but they had killed him like the trapped animal he was. Dick slammed the rifle butt into the soft wet soil repeatedly. "Dammit, they could have spared him; they could have taken him prisoner. He was fucking helpless up there. Those bastards!" He sat in the mud below his friend and watched the drops of blood fall into the puddle and seep into the rotting leaves on the jungle floor. He wanted to vomit, but his rage would not permit it.

The sounds of war again drove his mind to focus. "The radio! Must get the radio!" Dick looked up again at his friend. There, in its proper place on his vest, was Bill's radio. How to retrieve it was his problem.

Dick studied the tree trunk and then his useless left arm--the thirty feet might as well be five hundred. He was still very weak, though the bleeding was almost controlled. "Thirty feet." What were his options? Not many. Could he find a long enough limb to reach Bill? Then what? He could never dislodge the radio from that vest. It had been made to withstand ejection forces; it could certainly withstand a one armed man's attempts to dislodge it. Could he make a torch and burn the nylon risers of the parachute? That might work, but it would almost certainly alert the enemy, and how would he reach the risers? He walked slowly around the bottom of the tree, searching for ideas and examining every bit of physics he had learned. Finally, he slid to a sitting position beside another tree twenty yards away. He looked at his dead navigator. "Well, Bill, it looks like we go together--like always. You're thirty feet from my only chance to freedom, and I'm too weak to cut you down." Tears again filled his eyes. He saluted his friend and reached for his gun. The .38 would be better. He didn't want to botch this, and he didn't want to slowly bleed to death either. It would be even worse to be captured later when his strength was almost gone. Dick pulled the pistol from his pocket and flipped open the cylinder. It was loaded. He suddenly remembered an old book he had read from James Clavell. There was a strange Japanese custom of the Samurai warriors in which they composed their life's poem before their impending death. Dick was an engineer by training, a man of science and numbers. Words were not his long suit; still, he had time to reflect on his life, his goals, his failures and successes. How would he assess it all? He pondered this while staring at his friend, dangling above the jungle floor. "Poor Bill, you never had time to think about your own death. It came too fast. But, perhaps that is better."

As he sat there, the wounded officer was suddenly startled by the sound of footsteps. He quietly lay to his side and rolled behind the tree he had been propped against. An enemy soldier approached, looking up at Bill. As he approached, he shouted at the body. He walked closer and Dick saw he was smiling. The soldier stopped beneath the body and looked up at the dead officer, studying the situation, unaware that a rifle was pointed at his back.

Dick squeezed the trigger carefully, slowly, for he had no left hand to steady the weapon. He almost reached the firing point when the sound of more voices stopped the steady pressure from his finger. Two more troops arrived. The three men stood beneath the body, pointing and talking. The first pointed his hands and fingers like a rifle and made the sound of a gun firing. The other two men watched excitedly. Then all three stopped and looked again at the body, talking quickly. Finally, the first soldier started for the tree, motioning for the others to follow. The younger of the remaining two soldiers boosted him into the tree. From there he climbed quickly, panting and cursing as he climbed. He had barely reached the first limb when the oldest of the group aimed and fired at Bill. The bullet struck him in the head and jerked his entire body sideways. The impact exploded the skull and thrust his head backward, leaving the body swinging gently in the air.

Dick cursed silently and aimed for the older soldier's head, then cursing again, he lowered the rifle. The older soldier would live a little longer--at least until they cut Bill from the tree. That was his only chance of escape. Then, God willing, all three would die.

The first soldier cursed loudly, screaming at the two below. The rifle fire from them had surprised him and had ricocheted off the tree trunk thirty feet above his head. They laughed and began walking deeper into the jungle, shouting back at their comrade. Five minutes later they were gone, while the first soldier climbed steadily up the large tree. Dick watched and waited.

Finally the soldier reached a limb that extended into the shroud lines of the parachute. As he climbed carefully out its length, Dick lay in the moist jungle growth, silently urging the man on. At one point the soldier slipped and almost fell. Cursing, he threw his leg over the limb and swung his body back over it. Dick was scarcely breathing as the soldier resumed his trek toward the parachute's lines. For approximately fifteen minutes Dick watched the soldier climb and finally reach the lines that suspended his friend. One by one the shroud lines were cut. As they dropped away, the body in the harness dangled, jumping like a man alive trying to escape the web of nylon lines. Finally, enough of the lines were cut, and the body plummeted to the ground. It hit with a thump, crumbling into a heap in the small pool of blood below. From above the soldier shouted in relief and excitement. His task was finished. Now to gather the spoils of war, the price for his work, the evidence of his skill as a warrior. His captain and the others in the village would respect him now. Boots, a pistol, probably even money, maybe even jewelry. But first--the climb down. It would be faster, but also more dangerous, he knew. Carefully he climbed from the top of the tree. That part was easy; there were many limbs near the top of the towering tree. As he neared the ground, however, the limbs were farther apart and harder to reach. He also had no help from his friends. But that was okay. It also meant that he didn't have to share the booty. The last limb was still twenty-five feet or more from the ground. He sat on the large limb and pondered his options. He could jump, or he could try to slide down the trunk that appeared too large for his arms. He did neither; he tumbled backward from the impact of the rifle bullet and fell crashing to the ground below. Another pool of blood formed under the tree and seeped into the rotting leaves on the jungle floor.

Bill's body was cleared of all jewelry, his gun, and his radio. Dick squeezed his friend's hands between his own, while tears dimmed his vision. "I'll miss you, Buddy." Slowly he turned and staggered toward the clearing he had left two hours earlier. He never looked back. The pain had returned to his shoulder, and like the pain in his heart, it slowed him, but it also drove him onward.

* * *

Captain John Singletary had wanted to fly since boyhood. He had lived that fantasy when other boys were dreaming of homeruns and touchdowns. What a surprise it had been when he entered flight school and discovered that he was prone to airsickness. John had struggled and vowed he would not quit even though his weight had dropped fifteen pounds and his face had taken the pallor of the clouds through which he flew. But he prevailed and graduated near the bottom of his class. He earned his wings, but he would not get the prestigious fighter slot he dreamed about. That went to those at the very top of their class--a select few. He, instead, found himself assigned to rescue helicopters. At first it nearly caused him to turn in his wings, but after chopper training, he found it to be a mixed blessing. Flying a helicopter is far more difficult than flying a fighter--or at least that was his opinion, and somehow in the calisthenics of controlling so many variables at one time, John forgot to get sick. Within a week his airsickness was gone. After confirming that fact, he had begun the serious process of volunteering for a tour of duty in Vietnam. With a year's tour in "Jolly Greens," his chances for a fighter might yet be revived. First he had to survive for a year in a large, slow helicopter floating over enemy territory – the perfect target for enemy gunners.

"Captain! Scramble! We got a call from one of the crewmembers on that F-4 that went down this afternoon."

John Singletary threw down the latest copy of Playboy and ran from the ready room. "How far out?"

"If we're lucky, we may get a shot at pulling him before dark."

"May?" The two men were grabbing gear from their lockers. A truck waited outside for the drive to the waiting chopper. "May, hell! We'll get him out. Trust me."

"It's going to be close. I sent Len to get a medic. Pilot's hit; sounds bad. We may need him. "

*   *   *

Dick stumbled and fell face down into the jungle brush. Exhausted, he lay there in the soft grass as fatigue drugged his mind. He tried to stand but fell back to his knees, then he sat, then he lay back on the wet brush. The throbbing in his shoulder seemed far away as he looked through the canopy of leaves to the tiny blue patches of sky. Funny, he thought, that evening was coming so early. Darkness closed slowly over his vision as the comfortable earth beckoned him to sleep.

The voice that rang out in his mind was clear, and it was unmistakable. "Get up son. You've got to keep going. Don't forget that you're an O'Brian, and O'Brians never quit. We just don't quit."

"Okay, Dad." Dick opened his eyes suddenly to a bright ray of sunlight that permeated the heavy forest canopy. The visage he expected was not there. The thick jowled man with the heavy eyebrows was not there at all—but his words still echoed in Dick's ears.

"Get up son! Get up!" The wounded pilot rose to his hands and knees. For a moment he tried to crawl, but his one arm was not enough. He fell back to the ground in pain. "Get up son; get up."

"Okay, Dad." He struggled, cursing, to his feet and stumbled forward, through the jungle. Ahead, he could see the light of the clearing. Like a beacon, it urged him onward. The rifle was left behind, but the radio was clutched in his right hand. It was his one link with rescue, his only hope.

"Keep walking son."

"Right, Dad."

"You're doing fine, son."

"Right, Dad." On he walked toward the light, while somewhere in his mind a well known voice urged him onward.

At the edge of the clearing Dick stopped and looked carefully around. Wearily he slumped to his knees, then he sat, staring at his own feet. The fatigue was overwhelming. He weighed his chances— not good if he passed out. He had to maintain consciousness. He looked at his shoulder—still bleeding. What about that left arm? Would he ever use it again? He grasped his left hand with his right, testing the nerves. The feeling was still there. I suppose that's good, he thought. The heat of the sun now covered him in the clearing. Slowly his eyes began to close. The sound that woke him was one he least expected—a man whistling. At first his mind rejected the thought, but the sound persisted, coming closer.

Dick's mind worked diligently to sort the information it was receiving. It was slowed, but it was also trained. Once released, the adrenaline rushed immediately through his body and Dick rolled quickly behind a thicket of bushes and peered carefully around the brush toward the sound that approached his position. He touched both of his pistols. Both were in place and loaded. Could he still aim and shoot? Perhaps. The whistling grew louder, interrupted occasionally by short phrases of some song he could not understand. It was a Vietnamese soldier. Dick selected the .32. It was somewhat quieter. He checked the weapon and waited. Unaware, the whistling soldier continued to approach through the waist high foliage. When he was fifteen feet away, Dick rose slowly and fired one shot. The look of surprise was replaced instantly by one of pain as the soldier grasped his chest and fell backward into the bushes.

Slowly Dick crawled to the wounded man, his gun ready. The soldier was lying on his back, gasping for breath. Dick crawled to him, stood shakily, and aimed the gun at the man's head. The soldier looked at him in pain, still clutching his chest. For a moment their eyes met. There was no hatred there, only pain. The man watched Dick with indifference. His pain was too great. His body jerked intermittently as he awaited the bullet.

Dick's eyes focused on the small front sight of the pistol, then the focus shifted to the target, the enemy lying on the ground before him. Their eyes met again, each searching the other. Slowly the view over the pistol sight moved downward until it pointed at the ground at Dick's feet. Dick looked at the wounded man, his mind filled with revulsion at the scene before him. The man gasped quickly as air escaped from his left lung. The wounded pilot turned and threw the pistol to the ground, slumping there himself in pain and confusion.

The two wounded men stared briefly at each other. Both understood the other's physical pain. Both witnessed the other's mental pain as well. In confusion, the two men struggled with the fine line between life and death, and somewhere in both a brief flame of understanding flickered amid the physical torment of pain.

Dick crawled once again to the wounded soldier. Silently he reached his hand and patted the man's boot; then he turned and crawled slowly away.

$$* \quad * \quad *$$

The hospital was quiet and both surgeons were finishing the last reports of the day. Nurses hurried down the narrow hallways with medicines and assorted equipment. Kerrie spoke first. "Through. All of the reports complete for another day. Let's celebrate. Want a beer?"

"Sure."

"I have a couple of cold ones in the fridge at the trailer." Phillip watched her for a reaction.

"How about the club? Don't you like the club?" As an afterthought she added. "You hardly ever go there do you?"

"No, not really."

"They have the only decent hamburger in 5000 miles."

He rose and began to pace the floor very deliberately without looking at her. "I just don't seem to fit in very well there. Maybe it's a doctor/pilot thing."

Kerrie was just beginning to disagree when shouting in the hallway interrupted them. A large sergeant ran toward them screaming. He did not stop until he found the surgeons. "Doc; we need a doc or a damned good medic--now!" Both surgeons were on their feet and walking quickly down the hallway toward the shouting man.

"What's happened?"

"Pilot--down behind enemy lines. We're going in for him, but he's been hit—bad. He may need help on the way back." He was breathing hard and stood impatiently between the two doctors. "We've got to go now."

"How bad is he?"

"Bad, bring your tools."

Kerrie ran to the small wooden locker beside her desk and unlocked it. She grabbed the leather bag inside and started for the door. "When do we leave?"

"Chopper's on the way, ma'am. Five minutes at most." The sergeant turned and ran back down the hall. "See you on the pad. Hurry!"

Phillip stepped between Kerrie and the door, snatching the bag from her hands. "I'll go."

"What?"

Phillip looked at her with firm resolve. "I said I'll go."

"Why you?" She looked at his face and misread his eyes. "I can do this Phillip."

"I know you can, but I'm going."

"Why you and not me, because I'm a woman?"

"No." The look on his face was somewhere between pain and determination. "Kerrie, please understand. This isn't about your being a woman." His eyes turned to the floor as if searching for the right words. He struggled with his own voice. It seemed far away when he spoke. "Kerrie, this is about my being a man--not your being a woman. Don't you understand?"

She studied the thin doctor for several moments and nodded, then she leaned up and kissed him on his cheek. "Good luck, Phillip." As he rushed out behind the sergeant she added, "Be safe." The two men ran from the hospital to the waiting helicopter. The large rotors on the chopper turned slowly, then increased their rhythm as the men checked their instruments, testing the readiness of their aircraft. "Captain?"

"Yeah."

"Redbird just called. Controller says to hurry; that pilot's in bad shape."

"Where's the medic?"

"Doc's on the way. Here he comes now." Both men turned to watch the thin young doctor climbing awkwardly aboard the helicopter.

"Checklist complete, we're off." John closed his half-finished list, pulled the collective up, rotated the cyclic clockwise, and applied backpressure to the stick. Slowly the big green helicopter lifted from the ground and turned east toward enemy territory and Captain Dick O'Brian who was fighting desperately to maintain consciousness.

"Redbird to Jolly Two, do you read me, over?"

"Roger, Redbird, Jolly Two reads you loud and clear."

"Jolly Two what is your present position?"

"Jolly Two is eight miles east of Tango 1 on a heading of 045 degrees."

"Roger Jolly Two, Redbird has you. Turn right to a heading of 052 degrees. Request you expedite."

"Redbird, Jolly Two is balls-to-the-wall. We're giving it all we've got. Pigeons to the target?"

"Pigeons are 052 degrees, one hundred seventy-five miles. You've got a flight of four Fox 4s on station and another breaking ground at Udorn. They should be there soon."

The four fighters circled above the jungle. All eyes were straining into the late afternoon haze. Somewhere below was their man. He was injured badly; a delay until the following morning could be fatal. Also, there was the potential of enemy groundfire. The fighters were there to take care of any gun sites that lay in ambush for the slower moving helicopter. The key to success was to find the pilot and snatch him out before the chopper presented too great a target.

"Any contact with our boy?"

"Not in the last twenty minutes. But we told him to keep low. What is your ETA?"

"One hour fifteen minutes. We have vectors from Redbird. Jolly Two is holding seven thousand feet."

"Roger Jolly Two, Cougar flight is holding ten thousand."

"Receive any fire?"

"Negative, Jolly; they're waiting for *you*."

John laughed and broke the tension. "Tell them we're on the way."

"Roger that. Cougar is ready and we see no roads for several miles, so there may not be any big stuff there, but watch for small arms."

"They are all big to us." The sound of the helicopter could be heard over the radio as the rescue team approached. "Did you soften the area, Cougar?"

"We've found no targets of opportunity, Jolly. We're standing by in case any triple A shows." One hour and ten minutes later the chopper entered the target area.

"We've got you in sight, Cougar. Redbird, Jolly Two is signing off for now. We'll give you a call when we're headed home."

"Good luck Jolly Two. Get him out."

"Will do. Jolly Two out. Okay Cougar, let's raise our boy."

"Owl One, Owl One, this is Cougar lead, do you read me?"

"Cougar, this is Owl One - alpha. I read you loud and clear." It was almost a whisper over the radio.

"Owl One, any bandits around?"

"None in sight. But there are troops in the field on my left. I've heard rifle fire."

"Do you have the Jolly Green in sight?"

"Roger, he's about two miles southwest of my position."

"Are you in the clearing or in the bush?"

"I'm on the edge of the clearing. There are two large trees about one hundred yards south of me in the middle of the clearing, and there's a ravine about fifty yards west of my position."

"We've got your general location. Keep down until we tell you what to do. Now, everyone cease all radio chatter. Jolly Two will coordinate all activities from this point. Owl One, we will circle your location from the south. When we cross over your position, click your radio twice. Understand?"

"Roger."

"Jolly Two is descending to one thousand feet. Cougar, descend to five thousand and keep an eye open for groundfire. If you get a target of opportunity, strike at will, just keep us in sight at all times."

"Cougar, Roger."

Sweat drenched John Singletary's already stained fight suit. He watched the altimeter drop toward one thousand feet. The chopper was performing well; he decreased his speed from one hundred twenty to forty knots and looked over his right shoulder to his team. The young men in the back smiled and gave him the thumbs up. The doors were opened and all of the crew began to peer into the green jungle below. Over his intercom, John talked his men through the drill. "I think he's 360 degrees ahead of our position, in the edge of those trees just ahead. Len, get the winch ready. Are you ready to go down? He may need help."

"I'm ready, captain." A second later two clicks were heard on the radio.

"We've got you Owl One. What is your status? Can you make it up alone?"

The wounded officer watched the big helicopter pass overhead. "You're taking small arms from east of my position. Estimate two hundred yards, maybe more."

"Cougar one has that location and is in. Strings of three boys."

"Cougar three Roger. Two's in behind One." The second

aircraft banked hard and then dived toward the target, following the leader.

"Owl One, what is your status?" John was shouting above the sound of his own aircraft.

"I'm going to need help."

"Help is on the way!" The large sergeant peered out of the helicopter and began preparations to lower himself toward the jungle floor.

The bullets were not heard until several machine gun rounds penetrated the chopper. One passed through the forward fuselage doing little damage. The second struck the sergeant in his right leg, and another hit the co-pilot in his right buttocks. The door had slowed the round, but it still was sufficient to lift him in his seat. The last bullet smashed through the windscreen and exited the chopper just above the pilot's head. "Shit!"

"You okay captain?" The helicopter lurched suddenly in reaction to the pilot's sudden moves. Singletary instinctively pushed the stick forward while applying right rudder to take advantage of the engine torque. He simultaneously pulled the collective up to increase speed while rotating the cyclic clockwise. As the chopper gained speed, he pulled back on the stick and climbed rapidly toward safety.

"Jolly Two, Cougar, you okay?"

"Don't know; we've taken a few hits--small arms! Hold on while I check!" Over his intercom he shouted. "Len, how's it back there?"

"He's hit, but he'll make it."

"That you doc?"

"It's me."

"Crap!" There was a short pause then more. "Crap, crap, crap!" His voice grew louder with each word. "Owl One alpha, what's your condition?"

"Not good. Left arm's out of service, and I'm pretty weak."

Over the intercom again. "What are we going to do now? He

can't make it up by himself, and Len can't go down. Shit!" There was anger in his voice mixed with frustration.

"Are you hit up there?" Phillip's voice was strained.

"I've taken one in the butt!" The co-pilot was moaning softly.

"Hold on; I'll check it out."

"I'm okay!"

"I'll check, dammit!" In seconds Phillip had checked the leg. "You'll make it. Nothing important was hit, but keep this bandage tight to stop the blood loss."

"Jolly Two, this is Cougar. Status?" The pilots in the fighter-bombers were watching the helicopter circle slowly below them.

"Hold on, dammit!" The chopper pilot was breathing hard and shouting quickly. "What the hell are we going to do now?"

"I've got a plan." Phillip spoke slowly, deliberately. "I'll go down for him."

"You? Are you kidding?"

Phillip screamed back at the helicopter pilot in anger. "Fuck you, dammit! Don't you think I can handle that?" Phillip's voice surprised him. It also strengthened his resolve.

"What the hell do you know about rescue or that harness back there? Have you ever hung suspended over enemy snipers before?"

"Not before today." Phillip started aft.

"Where are you going?"

"Back to talk to Len. I need a quick lesson in rescue." Phillip was excited and frightened at the same time. He was moving without thought, reacting to the situation in which he found himself.

"Dammit, doc, you don't know what you're doing!"

"Look Captain," The thin doctor was suddenly calm and totally in control. "Consider our alternatives. One, we leave him there, and he dies. With a wound like that he'll never make it through the night. Two, you go down to get him and I'll fly this buggy. We know how well that would work don't we? Three--I go down and try to get him out. You see, it's not good, but it's all we've got." He looked the pilot straight in the eyes. "Can you fly off and leave him there without at least trying?"

"Doc, you've got balls."

"I just hope I still have them tomorrow."

Swinging out of the helicopter on the end of the rescue cable was the most frightening thing Phillip Brady had ever done. He had not anticipated the sound or the beating air from the blades rotating over him. He didn't hear the rifle fire, only the wild beating of his heart. Adrenaline rushed through every pore of his body; he felt every hair blowing in the whirling air; he sensed every pulse, every gasp. His chest heaved as he choked the air that rushed into his lungs. And suddenly he felt himself suspended above the world, slowly descending into the evening mist below. In that moment Phillip Brady found something he had never known before. He met himself--as a man, a man of courage. The fear subsided and was replaced with determination, resolve, and a thrill he had never before experienced. He looked below at the forbidding jungle, then above at the hovering helicopter. Beyond that were the jets, circling above. All were part of the team, as was he, a team dedicated to saving one of its own, and now all of them were watching him. All of them were pulling for him. He was their man now; he was one of them, one of the guys. But most of all, he was his own man, one he could live with and respect for the rest of his days. He smiled to himself and watched the green jungle rising to meet him.

Phillip dropped the last five feet and landed in a clump. His world was cerebral, not the rough and tumble world of sports. His coordination was solely concentrated in his hands, which were thin and gangly, like their owner.

Climbing to his feet, he began searching. He knew the pilot was nearby, but he wasn't sure which direction to begin his search. His descent had disoriented him, and he was shaking with excitement and fear. Hovering in the helicopter, the world below was clearly distinguishable. In the jungle itself, all direction was lost.

The dampness of the underbrush soaked into his clothes and mixed with the sweat that soaked him. The heat was oppressing, and the thick growth was an impenetrable barrier that impeded his work. Phillip looked at his watch for reasons he could not explain. His hands were still shaking. "Adrenaline," he thought. "Good."

The sergeant had briefed him well; he began walking in a circular pattern, each turn increasing the diameter ten yards. He walked and fought the jungle. In less than five minutes he found the pilot, barely conscious, lying beside a small tree. Quickly he raced to the wounded man, calling to him as the sergeant had explained. "Hey, I'm here to get you out. You okay?" He stopped instantly when he saw the .32 pointed at him. "I'm on your side. I'm a doctor."

"Step closer!" The thin man did as he was told, very slowly. "Okay." The pilot dropped the weapon in his lap. "Sure glad to see you."

Phillip bent over the wounded pilot and began checking his shoulder. "We've got to get you out of here." As Phillip worked on the wound, Dick cried out in pain and fell back against the tree, unconscious. Finishing his work for the moment, the thin doctor tried to lift the larger man but found him far too heavy. He grabbed the pilot again and tried to swing him onto his shoulder; again he failed. Panting heavily, he stopped and stepped back to ponder his alternatives. How could he lift this large pilot? It was a problem he had not considered earlier. As he stood there, he heard a loud moan behind him. Phillip Brady had never jumped so fast in his life. He spun around then walked carefully toward the sound. Twenty yards away he saw two legs extending from some small bushes. Cautiously, he approached; it was an enemy soldier, and he was shot. Instinctively, the doctor pulled him from the weeds and began checking his wound. He had been shot with a small caliber weapon in the chest--obviously Dick's .32. The wound was bleeding badly. Phillip stood, looking at the man, then reached quickly into his pockets. He ripped the soldier's shirt and began to work with quick, skilled hands. He didn't have time or a hospital, but he had a few minutes, a handful of tools, and a great deal of skill.

Overhead Phillip heard the chopper pounding the air; it was leaving, per plan, to return in ten minutes. In his mind he was aware of time passing; sweat poured from his brow and melted into the sleeves of his shirt as he raked it from his eyes. He ceased his work momentarily and searched his pockets for one of the remaining syringes of morphine. As he did, he looked at his patient. The soldier's eyes were open; he was alert; their eyes met in a brief moment. Nothing was said, but the man managed a weak smile. Phillip reached over and patted the man's arm. "Hang in there Buddy. With a little luck you'll make it." He injected the morphine and reached back to mop the sweat from the wounded soldier's brow, then his own. "Got to go. Good luck. I hope somebody finds you soon." With that, Phillip turned to see two soldiers standing behind him, ten feet away. The younger of the two had a rifle, held loosely at his side, pointed at him.

Phillip could feel the heartbeat racing in his chest. Fear filled him as he fought to control his shaking limbs. Slowly, deliberately, he did the only thing he knew to do; he raised his arms over his head in surrender. The older man looked at him carefully. There was obvious confusion on his face. Then he looked at the man on the ground. More confusion. He walked over to the wounded soldier and looked at his wound and the dressing that had been placed over it. He spoke briefly with the wounded soldier who was quickly losing consciousness from the morphine. Rising, he walked to the doctor and examined his bloody hands and the blood on his shirt.

As the two soldiers talked quickly to each other, gesturing wildly, Phillip watched them carefully. How he wished he could talk to them. Would that have really made any difference? How long had they been behind him? How stupid to risk his own life and Dick's. To stop and do what? To stop and do what his life was about, to heal other men. How absurd it all seemed now with a rifle pointed at him. Phillip searched his mind. What did he feel? Anger? Rage? Fear? No, it was different he concluded. Pride, satisfaction? Somewhere between the two he decided.

The older soldier walked to him and reached up to pull both of Phillip's arms down from above his head. He stepped back and spoke to the younger soldier who handed him the rifle and started to lift his injured comrade. "Wait!" Phillip walked quickly to the injured man, watching the older soldier with caution. Gently he helped lift the moaning man, placing one arm around the other's neck. "Gently. Easy. Walk slowly." He was speaking to the young soldier loudly and slowly. The young man looked at him and shook his head, then slowly started off through the thick grass. Phillip turned and faced the older man again; the soldier held the rifle loosely, pointing at the ground. From a distance, the sound of the chopper approaching grew louder. The soldier said something to Phillip that he could not understand, then the old man motioned for him to leave. Phillip looked at him with disbelief. Again the soldier motioned for him to leave. For a brief moment the two men faced each other in silence, then Phillip moved off, his eyes locked on the wrinkled face of the man with the weapon.

Dick still lay beneath the tree, unconscious. The thin doctor stood over him and studied his task carefully. Kneeling, he tried again to lift the pilot, but the struggle was futile. He stood again and cursed his own weakness. Again he reached for the larger man, tears flowing down his face in frustration. He was shaking with fatigue and despair when two more hands reached for the unconscious pilot, grasping him by the right shoulder and his waist. With surprising strength, the older soldier hoisted Dick to Phillip's shoulder and placed his arm around Phillip's neck. Once again he gestured toward the approaching chopper. Very quietly he spoke, "Easy." Phillip reached out and placed his hand on the soldier's arm. The older man looked at it briefly, then into Phillip's eyes. They said nothing as the sound of the helicopter approached. The soldier looked briefly in that direction and nodded to Phillip. Shouldering his load, the thin doctor hobbled off through the thicket of grass and jungle, the unconscious pilot dragging along on his shoulder.

Slowly the winch started to pull the two men into the sky. They were barely 100 feet in the air when Phillip spotted the old man with the rifle standing in a small clearing below him. The man stood motionless, rifle by his side, and watched the two men ascending into the air. Phillip watched him and raised his hand in a silent salute. The man nodded and turned and walked away into the jungle.

* * *

Between the wounded sergeant and Phillip, they managed to get Dick aboard the helicopter. Captain Singletary immediately began a rapid climb from the area. Above, the circling fighters climbed to escort the "Jolly Green Giant" home. The air was filled with voices calling congratulations. Another warrior was plucked from the enemy's back yard.

Inside the large helicopter, the newest rescue man in the Air Force traded his new pride for the concentration of medicine. He worked feverishly on the pilot, then the sergeant. Finally, a half-hour from base he slumped against the metal frame of the aircraft and slid to a sitting position. He was exhausted, and the adrenaline was ebbing from his body. He closed his eyes and smiled. When he opened them again, both men in the helicopter were looking at him. He looked at the faces of his patients. They would recover. Perhaps, too, the one left behind in the jungle would also recover.

Three, plus the chopper co-pilot; it had been a good day. The smile on his face grew to a grin. They would all recover, and he had done it. The sergeant nodded and spoke. Phillip could not hear him over the rotors, but he knew what he was saying, men just know those things. He smiled and closed his eyes again.

*   *   *

The crowd on the ramp stood back as the ambulance pulled up to the helicopter. The major was loaded on a gurney while the sergeant and the pilot were helped inside. The crowd cheered and congratulated the men. Someone handed beers to the mobile wounded and to Phillip. In twenty minutes it was over, and Phillip Brady stood alone outside the hospital entrance. He was staring at the large helicopter parked 100 yards away. The hand that touched his arm was familiar. He knew it instantly; he did not turn. "I heard what you did. Captain Singletary told us all about your going down to get Major O'Brian." He turned and faced her but said nothing. "I'm proud of you Phillip; that was a brave thing you did." He nodded, smiling. "You know, it's a good thing you went; I could have never done that." As they walked in the darkness, Kerrie took his arm and stopped him, facing him solemnly. "What you said earlier, did you find that man?"

He smiled broadly. "Yes, yes I did"

"And do you like him?"

"Yes."

"I knew you would." She squeezed his arm and began walking again. "How about that beer we were going to have?"

"Great idea." He looked back at her, still smiling. "At the club."

"Yes, at the club." She kissed his cheek as the two walked off into the warm Thai evening. Somehow she thought that he seemed a little taller than before.

The two doctors walked into the club amid the noise and the

revelry of a roomful of men celebrating. Suddenly, the entire room became silent. Every man turned to stare at the two who had entered the officer's club. For a long moment Kerrie and Phillip faced the room of men, then Col. Bennett stepped forward and, lifting both hands, began to clap. As he did, every man in the room stood and joined the colonel. The applause rose into a crescendo, lifting the silence and also one man's heart.

Phillip stood alone; Kerrie had stepped aside as the pilots applauded the thin, pale doctor. She watched his face as the smile broadened. Phillip had found himself in that jungle, and a fine man stood before her, blushing at the attention of men he could now call brothers.

*　*　*

Dear Kerrie,

It was good to get your letter. Things here are pretty much the same. Madison doesn't seem to change much. Just wish it would warm up a little.

I was sorry to hear about Robb's friend. I know that must be tough. Is he doing alright? It's good he has you now. Maybe this war will end soon. There was a big demonstration against it here at the university last week. It wasn't pretty, but it got a lot of news coverage. Maybe we'll end this and get you guys home soon.

Two days ago I got a call from your dad. Dr. Jernigen is fine, but he was politely digging for info on you. I don't know what you're writing home, but your folks know you quite well. They have recognized a change in you, my dear. I played dumb, of course. You decide how to handle that. They love you; it would probably please them to know about Robb—or would they consider a pilot below their daughter—the soon to be famous surgeon. (I'm smiling—don't get angry!)

Take care; keep in touch,
Barb

* * *

Robb walked into the small, sanitized room. The smell of disinfectant hung heavily in the air and assaulted his nose. Lying in a narrow hospital bed on his side, Dick O'Brian was staring pensively out the window. "Dick, you okay?"

The injured man turned to his friend. "I guess; it'll be a while before I fly again, but I guess I can deal with that."

Robb cut immediately to the topic that weighed most on both their minds. "Want to talk about it?"

Dick looked back out the window for several long minutes. "Did you read the report?"

"Yes."

"Is that why you're here?"

"No, I'm here because I'm your friend." He paused then resumed, "And because I also spent some time on the ground over there." He paused again--longer this time. "And because I also lost a friend out there in the weeds."

Dick looked up at Robb. "That's right, you did. Wayne."

"Yes."

"Could you have helped him?"

"No, and neither could you have helped Bill."

"I could if I had been a better pilot. If I hadn't flown into that triple A." There was pain on his face.

"Shit, Dick! You know better than that. They don't make better pilots than either of us. The gunners just got lucky--just dumb stupid luck. You know it had nothing to do with your flying. So just forget that crap." Robb walked around the bed and looked into Dick's eyes. "And, dammit, you know I'm right."

Dick's face was masked in pain. "They just shot him while he hung there — trapped."

"I know. Wayne killed the soldier that had us covered with an

AK47. He died in the process." Robb was looking at the tiles on the hospital floor.

"Did you see it?"

"Yes." It was almost a whisper.

"How are *you* doing?" Dick was watching the man standing before him.

"Okay, I guess. It's tough isn't it."

The wounded pilot looked up at his friend and placed his hand on Robb's arm. "Yeah, it's tough, but so are we."

The two men looked out the window in silence for a long time. Finally Robb smiled. "Hey, I came here to perk you up."

"Maybe this road's easier if you walk it with a friend."

"Yeah, I guess."

"Robb, did you ever think about trying to bring Wayne out?"

"He was dead." He sat heavily in the stark chair by the window. "You mean his body?"

"Yes."

"No, there was no way--for either of us."

"I just felt bad about leaving Bill out there."

"I know."

Outside the room, a surgeon stood quietly, listening. A single tear escaped her left eye and rolled slowly down her cheek. Kerrie quietly turned and walked down the narrow hallway. A slight red tinge crossed her cheeks and the pursed lips deliberately shifted into a smile. A second tear trickled down her cheek; she flicked it away and hastened her pace. She had a plan, and she needed to find Phillip.

* * *

Phillip Brady bustled into the room, two male nurses in tow. He was giving orders rapidly. They were both taking notes as fast as their ballpoints could glide across the paper that was bunched on the dark brown government clipboards. When the doctor finished, the two young men rushed from the room, leaving Phillip and Dick alone.

"How do you feel? That shoulder still hurt?"

"Yes, a little."

"Can you move it?"

"No, not yet."

"That's normal; don't worry about it. Can you move your fingers?"

"Yes."

"Great. That's good. The x-rays indicate that you're a lucky man." He paused and peered carefully at another clipboard before continuing. "That bullet missed everything important. Some soldier needs target practice."

"Too late; he's dead."

"Oh?" Phillip looked up from the chart and studied the wounded pilot carefully. He had been worried about Dick, and Kerrie's comments had exacerbated that concern. Now he suspected he was closing on the truth. "You kill him?"

"Yes." It was a quiet voice, very unlike Dick O'Brian. Phillip made a mental note of that. "And three others." The voice was even quieter. Dick was staring out the window at nothing. Phillip pulled a chair beside the bed and sat wearily into it. He pulled his glasses from his balding head down onto his nose and stared directly into the eyes of the other man from three feet away.

"You're mistaken. It was two others."

"No, it was three."

"Two!"

"Two?"

"Two! You're a piss poor shot Major, and I'm a damned fine surgeon."

"You're sure?" A smile slowly crossed the pilot's face.

"His wound was no worse than yours, and it was a much smaller caliber." He paused a moment then peered over the reading glasses at Dick. "And, he had the benefit of the best surgeon the US Air Force has to offer, as do you."

"Shit!" Dick was smiling broadly.

"Sorry, it was just a doctor's duty to his oath—you know, to help save mankind." Phillip was smiling too. "You won't turn me in for aiding and abetting the enemy will you?"

"Hell no. There's no crime in singing."

"Singing?"

"He was singing and whistling. I had no choice but to shoot him. He walked right up to me—with a smile on his face. I didn't know what else to do."

"Well, he's probably still singing somewhere, though his grub is not as good as yours."

"Don't bet on that." Both men laughed together. Dick's face was suddenly peaceful. He raised his right arm and saluted Phillip. Phillip smiled broadly, remembering another salute far away in the jungle—from a wise old man who had experienced and understood life, perhaps better than he.

PART TWO

LOSS AND REDEMPTION

CHAPTER SIX

Nubat Royal Thai Air Force Base

Kerrie walked outside the small hospital into the peaceful Thai night. It had been a tiring day, but a wonderful one as well. She had participated in three surgeries—all successful. She had watched Phillip perform a miracle, then he had watched her own magic. Together they had saved lives, and she had learned new techniques. She respected Phillip; he was a strange man, so talented, with so much to offer the world.

The roar of fighters on the runway to her left diverted her attention. Four F-4s were readying for takeoff. She watched them as the sheer power of their engines shook the very building behind her. One by one they began their takeoff roll—racing the wind into the skies.

Kerrie wondered about the men who designed and built such aircraft as these. They must be men driven by science—like her, men who pushed the envelope of human knowledge, human endeavor. They were serious, dedicated men she suspected—unlike those who flew the planes. Were they really different, she wondered. Yes, they were different, she concluded. One group was driven by science; the other was driven by the sheer joy of flying. One group were serious engineers, the other carefree pilots tasting the thrill of flying their crafts through the open spaces of the sky. She thought of Robb, the man with whom she had fallen so deeply in love. How different he was than she. He was a leaf floating free in the wind while she was firmly attached, clinging to the tree. His complete abandon in life, and their lovemaking, had shown her a view of life that she had never known. As his mouth explored and kissed her body, she abandoned all illusions of control, the control upon which her life had been built. It was control that got her through medical school and control that established her as a surgeon. And now it was all crumbling around her as this beautiful man carried her to passions she had never imagined. Though it would take a lifetime, she would follow that drifting leaf and somehow learn to free her own spirit that it, too, might soar.

The second fighter roared defiantly and began to roll down the runway. Kerrie wondered where they were going and what their task would be tonight. She wondered if Robb was in one of those planes. She glanced at her watch—2130. Yes. He could very well be in that flight. Another plane roared and rolled off into the darkness. Only the two large afterburners indicated its progress down the runway. She watched as it leaped from the ground and climbed into the night sky. Before the aircraft left the earth, the next in the flight was screaming down the runway in pursuit, the roar of the engines announcing the power and the skill of the men commanding the machines. She watched as the last aircraft lurched into the sky. She wondered what it must be like to sit in that forward cockpit, perched on the nose of such power, controlling that power through a night sky. The thought startled her. Control! Their control was over the plane and the sky as her control was in the operating room. She realized that Robb, too, was a man of control. She watched the tiny red dots disappearing in the black sky. A sudden warmth rose across her cheeks as she reflected that he also led her as they made love. She touched her own cheek. In the darkness she knew that she was blushing. Robb had showed her the cockpit of the F-4, and she had squeezed into the pilot's seat. It was far tighter than she had expected. The gages and instruments had been overwhelming. Truly, to fly one of those must require the same kind of training as a surgeon. A familiar voice behind her interrupted her thoughts. "Kerrie, are you ready to finish the last surgery of the day? It's a local kid—broken leg."

She didn't turn but spoke into the night. "Yes, I'll be right there."

Phillip walked to her side. "Beautiful evening, isn't it?"

"Yes it is." Kerrie turned to look at the man beside her. "Phillip, did you ever fly a plane?"

He looked at her with discomfort, reading her mind. "No, there was never time." He paused, looking into her large brown eyes. "Besides, like you, I'm a surgeon, not a pilot."

"Did you ever want to?"

"I never thought about it—until recently."

"Well, do you?"

"I think it might be fun, but I'd rather find a cure for cancer."

She smiled and patted his arm. "You know, Phillip, if anyone can, it'll probably be you. It will take a miracle to cure cancer, but I've already witnessed one of your miracles today."

They turned to enter the hospital. As they walked inside, Kerrie paused briefly to look at the aircraft that were taxiing onto the runway. Like the prior flight, they were roaring with power, or was it anticipation, or simply joy.

*   *   *

The four young officers were just attacking their spring rolls when the screaming outside the restaurant interrupted their meal. Several of the waiters ran into the late afternoon heat to investigate and returned with dismay on their faces. A young woman had been struck by a car while crossing the street. As the young man explained in his broken English, Kerrie rose without a word and raced for the front door. Robb watched her, slowly realizing her mission, then rose to follow. The scene in the street was one of pandemonium. People were crowding around the stricken woman while a kneeling old woman wailed at her side. On the opposite side of the street a very nervous man stood beside a small taxi in obvious fear while the crowd shouted obscenities at him and the uniformed policeman who endeavored to maintain calm in the street. Kerrie rushed through the crowd shouting and shoving people aside as she ran. She reached the woman and fell to her knees beside the prostrate figure. "Back! Get back!" she screamed. The crowd stopped their shouting and watched the American as she began checking the choking woman on the ground. Robb and another of the pilots arrived and began clearing the street around the injured woman. He watched in awe as Kerrie knelt over her and worked to save her life. At one point she looked up momentarily and spotted a long scarf over the shoulder of a middle-aged woman. Without a word she snatched it and went back to work. "Belt! Belt! I need a belt!" Robb pulled his own from his trousers and handed it to her. She pulled a small kit from her purse and quickly poured its contents beside the young woman. Grabbing a syringe and preparing an injection she continued to shout orders. "Call the base. Get an ambulance out here ASAP. Call Phillip. Tell him to meet me in surgery as soon as we can get there. Have all blood types on standby. And put a call out for donations of blood—we're going to need a lot." She injected the hypodermic. "Check if this woman is her mother. If she is, bring her along." The other Americans had also arrived and were rushing back into the restaurant for a phone while Robb found a waiter who could talk to the hysterical old woman who stood weeping in shock.

Robb had never seen Kerrie at work. On an intellectual level he knew she performed surgery, but this was different; this was a battle for life in the middle of a crowded street, and he could only watch. The injured young woman cried out in fear and pain; the old woman wailed in grief; the blood that covered Kerrie's hands and arms was pooling in the street. The pungent smell of the blood rose from the sun baked pavement and assaulted his senses. For a moment he was far away on a hillside in North Vietnam. The labored breath in his ears was not that of a young Thai woman but rather of his dying friend. Robb felt his head growing dizzy; the sounds of the street faded into the cloud that surrounded him. He could smell gunpowder and blood. The pounding in his mind increased in intensity and he felt suddenly faint.

The raucous sound of the siren shocked his mind back into the present. He looked at Kerrie still kneeling over the smaller woman in the street. He was glad that she was not looking at him. The crowd moved back as the ambulance pulled to a stop beside the damaged taxi. The corpsmen recognized their surgeon and raced to support her. "Plasma! Get me plasma. Fast!"

"Yes, ma'am."

"Splints! Neck brace! Careful with that right leg. It has multiple fractures. Okay guys, let's get her out of here as quickly as we can. Are they ready at the base?"

"Doc, we've got everything on standby and six airmen waiting to give blood."

"Phillip notified?"

"Roger that."

"Good work, Paul. Bill, get oxygen."

"Done."

The team worked feverishly for approximately ten minutes then moved the young woman to the back of the large truck that served as an ambulance. Robb loaded the old woman into the front seat and stood watching as the truck sped away; she leaned out the open window and looked back at him, confusion and fear on her face.

When he arrived at the hospital, the young woman had been in surgery for almost twenty minutes. Several young airmen lay on cots outside, needles in their arms to collect blood for the injured woman inside. Robb walked to the double doors of the surgery room and peered through the small windows. Inside he could see several people bending over a figure on the operating table. They worked quickly and quietly. Occasionally they would pause, and the two doctors would confer as they pointed into the broken body before them. Robb watched in fascination. How professional they were; how skilled their hands must be. He prayed silently for the small woman struggling for her life; then he prayed for the team struggling to save her. "God bless their hands," he murmured. Then on reflection he decided that He already had.

The operation proceeded into the night. The old woman sat with Robb in the waiting room, still weeping, confused, and frightened. Robb put his arm around her and held her hand. He tried to explain that her daughter had the finest care she could have. The old woman didn't understand his words, but his intent was clear, he was trying to comfort her. He walked again to the small window and watched in awe as the woman he loved continued her work. He was seeing a different person than the one he held at night. He was watching a professional. And why shouldn't they be the same he thought? He considered that for a few moments. He found this side of Kerrie so attractive. It was different from the other Kerrie, but it added ever so much to his understanding of her. He wondered how other men would react to her. Some might be uncomfortable with such a professional woman; some might even be threatened, but he was completely intrigued by the woman dressed in green hospital garb, covered with the blood of another she was trying to save. Robb smiled. He suspected that there were probably a red bra and panties under those drab hospital garments. And why not?

It was almost two AM when the two surgeons walked slowly from the operating room. They were still on an adrenaline high, but it was fading quickly. They both looked excited and tired. The old woman saw the two first and rose with difficulty and stepped forward to meet the two doctors. She had been seated for several hours without moving and her joints were stiff and painful. She walked forward with much effort, moving one leg and then the other, very deliberately, very slowly. Somewhere in the night she had found a calm that Robb had not seen earlier. In truth she had wept all of her tears; there were no more to be shed. Only the visible shaking of her hands beside her rounded body gave evidenced to the fear in her heart. Robb stood also and stepped beside the old woman, his arm again around her small shoulders. She felt small and frail to the large man looking down at her, yet her small body was rigid. Was it fear? Resolve? Or was it acceptance? Most likely, he thought, it came from a long life of many tragedies and many joys as well. In many years of life, there is time to sort such things into an understanding of balance. This was one more travail that she must endure. He noted that her face looked tired, but alert. She waited patiently as the Americans talked. She could not understand their words, but their expressions and body language told her much. Robb watched Kerrie approach—or rather, Doctor Jernigan. The idea surprised him, and he was not certain of his reaction. She was tired, but smiling at Phillip and talking quietly as they approached.

"How is she?"

"It will be a long and difficult recovery, but she will make it. She is a very strong young woman." Robb turned to the old woman who watched them with frowning excitement and gestured with a thumb up and a broad smile. It was the only Thai he could produce. The old woman looked at him briefly then turned and walked awkwardly to Kerrie and threw her arms around the young doctor. Sobbing again, the woman kissed her on the cheek and began speaking quickly, incomprehensibly. The young woman put her arms around the older and patted her back gently. The two men stood silently watching as the two women shared in the feminine mystery of life that men seldom seem to understand; every woman has it buried deep within her psyche as an integral part of her very being—that seed of creation's genius that gives and nurtures life, the very essence of life. What one woman had created, the other had saved. In their embrace was the celebration of that life, of all life, of each other as sisters in the eternal pact of creativity. They embraced while the two men stood by awkwardly and watched.

Robb approached cautiously. "Are either of you hungry? The club is closed, but we have goodies at the hooch."

"We also need to get this woman home." Kerrie stood with her arm around the older woman. "Give the AP's a call; we'll arrange for someone to take care of that. We should also get an interpreter to relay all the details of what's happening to her daughter as well."

"Done." Robb rushed off to find a phone while the two doctors sat wearily on one of the small couches in the waiting room. Kerrie waved to one of the corpsmen watching from the doorway to the operating area.

"Paul. Please take this lady to see her daughter. She's unconscious, but let this woman look at her from the prep area. She doesn't speak English, but she'll follow your lead when you take her. And Paul, don't take her into the operating room. She can look through the window. I'll be down in a minute."

"Sure, Doc." He smiled at the old woman, and taking her hand, led her down the hall. Both doctors sat holding their heads in their hands.

"Phillip, thanks—another great job. You worked magic in there."

"You were magnificent in there yourself. We really make a great team." He watched her face for a reaction, and seeing none continued. "She's lucky you were there; that probably saved her life."

Kerrie sat back and looked over at him, straight into his eyes. "When we're rested, I'd like to discuss how you handled that right femur. That was fantastic."

He was still staring into her eyes. Finally he stammered. "Sure, anytime." After a few seconds he recovered somewhat. "Yes, it did work out rather nicely didn't it?" He was looking into the distance down the hall.

"You bet. Where did you learn that?"

"Walter Reed. Had a mentor there who was the best surgeon I've ever seen. I once watched him operate for nine hours straight."

"He must have been good."

"He was great." There was excitement in his voice.

"Like you, Phillip; you learned well." She reached and placed her hand on his arm. Glancing over into her large brown eyes, he could feel her touch on his arm; he could smell the scent of her hair as it tumbled from the operating room cap she lay in her lap. She sat back and breathed deeply while he watched the rise of her breasts under the green linen garb. Phillip felt the pounding in his temples increase. His entire body was suddenly alert; every sense heightened. Her pheromones must be working overtime, he thought and smiled to himself. He was a doctor; he could analyze the operations of his body. That he understood, but the areas of the heart confused him. He felt drugged—happy and sad at the same time. He wanted to sing and to cry. Mostly he just wanted to reach over and kiss her. He felt every logical sequence of thought in his conscious mind melt as she smiled at him. Quickly he closed his eyes to regain the control he felt slipping away.

"You look exhausted. If you want to turn in, Robb and I can take care of this lady. I'll file the reports in the morning." He looked at her, his entire world crumbling around him. Quietly he rose and started for the door without a word. Kerrie watched the sudden change in the expression on his face. There was a sadness there that she noted but did not understand. "Thanks again, Phillip."

"Yeah, I'll check first thing in the morning. You sleep in." As he walked down the hall he stopped once, looked back briefly, then slowly turned and walked away.

*   *   *

The men walked in silent pairs toward the hot revetments and the waiting aircraft. It was early afternoon and the temperature was reaching its peak on the baking concrete ramp. Looking into the distance, one could see the waves of rising heat as it climbed into the clear sky. The wind was blowing to the south, and there were a few scattered clouds dotting the horizon at even intervals of several miles. Robb and Jack Trudeau walked behind Joe and his navigator, watching the busy activity around them as they peered from the shadows of their red ball caps with their squadron numbers embroidered on them. Together they walked quickly across the ramp, sweating through their clothing and the heavy equipment that they wore. All around them the weapons specialists and the maintenance men drove back and forth in their specialized vehicles. The weapons men made trip after trip on their tiny, powerful loaders, vehicles that sat squat on the ground and had the ability to spread their front extremities for added stability and maneuverability. They looked more like toys with large children bumping along for the sport. In truth, however, they were extremely precise instruments, requiring skillful operation for their dangerous job. Theirs was the task of transporting the bombs from the convoy of trailers and then hoisting them into place beneath the waiting planes. It was a tricky job, one that had to be handled carefully, but rapidly.

The maintenance men drove in their larger and more spacious vans, complete with portable command posts. The Line Chief could drive and control his domain from one seat. Above him was his radio--his link with the brain center for the base, and on his right was his status board, listing each aircraft on the line, its status, and its discrepancies. It was his job to know and understand each separate bird, each man on the line, and the strengths and weaknesses of each. He was the nerve center that connected the brain with the heart and ultimately with the muscle of the Wing. To the aircraft he was an insensitive observer, a master overseer who held the accounts. To the men he was father, friend, taskmaster, punisher -- if necessary-- drinking partner, and sometimes even mother. He was caught between responsibility to his commanders and loyalty to his men. He was the intermediary that formed the indispensable link that kept the mission going.

It was a normal day, sweltering hot, with trucks and ammo trailers moving up and down the ramp with a steady hum of hot rubber tires. The familiar sounds of men shouting, trucks racing back and forth between the planes, and airplane engines whining in the heat echoed across the ramp and throughout the revetments. That cacophony of sound was suddenly interrupted by the unexpected sound of a man screaming, then a shot, then several more shots.

The four men froze in disbelief as a projectile ricocheted off the side of a metal revetment ten feet away. By the time the machine gun began to lace its steady drum across the ramp, men were scattering in all directions. Robb turned toward the nearest revetment, the last one on the ramp. He dropped his helmet and the rest of his flight gear as he struggled with his taped .38 revolver. He had taped the pistol into its holster to prevent its loss during an ejection; now that precaution was taking precious time. He was still fighting with his holster when an explosion behind him picked him up and threw him to the concrete. Pain raced through the left side of his body as his mind fought to concentrate on the series of events that were taking place. With a loud moan, he rolled from his left side to his back. He felt the blood flowing across his forehead and reached to block its path toward his eyes. As he tried to focus he became suddenly aware of a figure standing over him. The bleary outline of a small man with a rifle pointed toward him jolted his stunned mind into panic. He blinked repeatedly and still his eyes would not focus clearly; still the figure stood over him, motionless. Time stopped in its pace across Robb's mind. A vague figure in a flight suit crouched behind a loading cart in the adjacent revetment. Robb could not see his face, but he guessed that it must be Joe. Couldn't he see what was happening? Robb tried to shout, but his voice would not come from his choking throat. He hardly recognized that he was reaching and struggling with his own pistol while he waited for the bullet that would end his life. In times of stress the mind often functions without informing the entire system of its intentions. Robb's mind was driving his body with emergency actions and was fighting for his life. The process that raced frantically in his brain had relayed all the pertinent actions to the body which raced far ahead of his consciousness. Behind it all was a realization that time was passing, and it was passing far too slowly. The wait was too long, and the raw sound of the rifle had still not destroyed his brain or its race against time. Perhaps the short bleary figure before him was frozen in the same inertia that had settled like dust over the figure behind the cart; perhaps he, himself, was the only actor moving on the stage. Then came the explosion, and the figure before him collapsed slowly over him, the rifle unfired.

Robb, too, collapsed back onto the concrete, his pistol falling from his relaxed hand. He stared at the blue sky above and then closed his eyes as the heavy fatigue of shock settled over him. He felt the weight of the enemy soldier over his lower body and the sticky dampness of blood that was soaking into his flight suit. He rubbed the rough concrete by his side with his fingertips and felt the hot, rough texture of the concrete ramp, so familiar to the reality he knew. Then that friction became slippery, confusing him. His body felt cold and heavy, but his mind felt as light as the small downy clouds that danced by overhead. Slowly his brain wound down from its frantic pace and began to assimilate the various messages that were coming in. He should have felt nothing but relief, but somewhere in his mind there was the stabbing question of the unfired weapon that he had to understand. Why had the enemy soldier frozen above him? He opened his eyes and listened to the last gunshots as they echoed down the ramp. Painfully Robb rolled onto his right elbow and pushed the soldier's body from his own. He sat stiffly and with concentration tried to focus on his gun laying beside him, the smoke still spiraling slowly out of the barrel and climbing upward in a slight gray wisp. Beside him lay the crumpled and bleeding body of the enemy he had shot, the bright red blood trickling down the attacker's chest and onto the hot pavement. Its sweet pungent smell mixed with the harshness of the gunpowder and brought memories that provoked a nausea in Robb's stomach.

Still the stark question that his mind was trying so desperately to draw into perspective remained. He tried to force his mind to concentrate, but it balked. He spoke aloud, "What?" Still the rebellious mind would not answer. The man shook his head and forced his mind, ordered, demanded that it answer, but it would not. The insurgent's left hand and arm began to twitch; he moaned loudly and began to gurgle slightly as the blood trickled from his mouth and down his smooth cheeks. Robb's eyes moved slowly beyond the blood stained concrete, over the mangled, writhing body, focusing slowly on the face.

"Oh my God! No!" The desperate cry came grating from deep within his soul, and the stunned mind climbed out of its hole and took control once again, as the glassy eyed man crawled awkwardly toward the inert body of the boy.

Joe ran to the crawling man and knelt beside him as Robb pulled the bloody body into his lap. His face was contorted with fear and shock as he held the dying boy to his breast. "Why Chusak? Why?"

The boy blinked his dark eyes and stared with the fixed glaze of death at the man holding him. He opened his mouth to speak, but no sound came from his lips. He looked once again into Robb's eyes, then his head rolled abruptly to one side; the accusing eyes still open. The anguished wail that issued forth from the captain shook the small group of men that had gathered around the two prostrate figures.

The crowd grew and the sirens began to wail in the distance as the security guards and the ambulances raced across the ramp. The men stood and shook their heads at the tall captain who sat dripping his own blood into the dark puddle that formed from the boy's body. They watched the blond officer in silent wonder as he gently laid the body upon the stained concrete and struggled slowly to his knees with the aid of the other pilot. "C'mon Robb, I'll help you over to the shade."

"No, the gun..."

"I've got your pistol."

"No, the rifle! The rifle." Dragging himself along, Robb grabbed the weapon beside the boy, propped it on his hip, and pulled the trigger. It fired into the air, and the injured man buried his face in both hands and wept unashamedly as the rifle clattered to the ramp.

The confusion that had branded the afternoon burned itself into the minds of each of the men present. Little did they understand the captain's reactions to the death of the enemy saboteur, and why did he want to fire the rifle? Only those who had seen it poised above the captain's head for several minutes--without firing -- knew, and perhaps their confusion was greatest of all.

*   *   *

She opened the door and peered inside. There was perspiration on her brow and her uniform was already stained from the heat and sweat of the tension in surgery. He sat alone, his head in his hands, staring at the floor. He did not look up as she entered. "Oh Robb, I just heard." She walked to him and sat beside him on the small bunk. When she touched him, she felt the shudder surge through him. She gently put her arms around him and said nothing as the sobs shook his body.

"He was just a boy, a kid."

"I know."

He turned to her suddenly. "I didn't know it was him; I couldn't see. I couldn't see!" He was shouting. "Dammit, my fucking eyes! I couldn't see!"

She hugged him to her. "It's alright. You didn't know." She held him close and felt the convulsions in his body. She held him tighter and waited for the tears to ebb.

Cursing, he rose and screamed at the darkness in the room. Finally, pounding his fists against the wall, he crumbled into a heap as she watched helplessly. He was sobbing uncontrollably as he lay on the floor. Her own tears joined his as she cradled him in her arms. They lay together, crying in the darkness.

The rising sun found them still laying on the hard floor, holding to each other under a worn blanket. She woke first and examined the man beside her. His flight suit was covered with the smell of blood and sweat. His hair was crumpled; there were dark circles under his tear stained eyes. She looked carefully at his face. It was distorted in pain, still plagued by demons she could not see. She sat up carefully and stretched quietly. Then she looked again at the man beside her. This was the man she would wake up beside for the rest of her life. He was hurt, but the physical injury would heal soon. The pain in his heart would take much longer, but she was a doctor, and she understood healing.

Robb moaned and rolled to his back. She was watching him when he opened his eyes. For a moment there was confusion on his face, then the pain of memory. She touched him. "It's okay."

He turned from her and rubbed his eyes, cursing. Crawling to his knees, he faced the young woman seated with her back against his door. "How long have you been here?"

"All night." She said it simply as a statement of fact.

"All night?" He sat opposite her.

"All night."

"Why?" He looked at the bed that had not been disturbed. "On the floor?"

"You're in pain, and I'm a doctor. Remember?"

"Damn."

"You okay?"

He looked at the floor a long time. "I feel so bad. If only my damned eyes had worked."

"You had a concussion."

"I did?"

"Yes."

"Are you sure?"

"I'm a doctor aren't I?"

"He was just a kid."

"I know." She watched his face. "And we both know you would have given your life rather than kill him. You didn't know. It's not your fault."

He rose and began pacing the room. Suddenly he stopped and looked at the woman before him. There was a sudden realization on his face; it was one of great pain. "How am I going to tell Somboon?" Slowly he leaned against the wall and slid to a sitting position, there was a great sadness on his face.

"Maybe we won't tell him just yet. Maybe we'll wait a while until he is older." Robb looked up at her but did not speak. "Look, first of all he loves us both, just as we both love him. We have spent so much time with him, and in that he truly has grown to accept us as family. We have that going for us."

"Will that be enough?"

"For now it will. The day will come when he will understand. Then we will have to tell him." She thought for a moment then added. "Or, maybe we won't. We'll just continue to love him. That will be the best gift we can give him—just as it has been his gift to us."

Robb finally smiled. "Yeah, he does love us doesn't he."

"Of course he does. He also knows how much we love him."

Robb stood slowly and stretched his cramped muscles; before he could speak the door moved, shoving Kerrie into the room. Col. Bennett managed to stick his head inside. "Robb, you brief in 30 minutes. Get your ass to the squadron—Now." He looked at both and nodded at Kerrie. "Morning, Doctor."

Before the surprised pair could speak, the door closed, and he was gone. Robb stood carefully, one hand braced on the cabinet. There was confusion on his face, then suddenly, resolve.

Kerrie looked at the door in anger. "Fuck you—Sir!"

Robb reached into the metal cabinet and grabbed his shaving gear. He started for the door, but she stepped in front of him. Without a word, she reached for his face, and pulling him to her, kissed him. "Be safe today. I love you. I'll be here tonight, but let's not sleep on the floor, okay?" She smiled a slight smile and walked out into the bright morning sunlight. He watched her as she walked quickly around the scattered lawn chairs between the hooch and the latrine. How could he explain the strange mixture of joy and pain that had settled in his heart? As he watched the familiar bounce in her step he knew which would prevail; he also knew it would be a difficult journey. And like the scar on his shoulder, the pain would never be completely erased. It would return as a reminder throughout his life. He looked at his watch and then walked out into the warm sunshine toward the latrine. He had a flight to prepare.

*　*　*

Dear Jason,

Thanks for your letters. It's been a hard week. Our base was attacked last Tuesday. I shot one of the sappers and later discovered he was one of the kids from the village outside the base. He was only a kid. What is this crazy world coming to? What kind of men send children to fight their wars? This has been a difficult week; Kerrie and I talked about this for hours last night. She helps a lot.

It's late and I have to go to a flight briefing. Got to run. I'll write more later.

Robb

∗   ∗   ∗

There were eight of them standing in the rain before the open grave. With closer inspection it could be noted that there were five other graves, already covered with jungle growth, beside the new one. Robb, Colonel Bennett, Joe Wilburn, Kerrie, Sister Estelle, two smaller Thai nuns, and the chaplain from the base stood silently as the small casket was lowered into the open pit.

Robb stood staring off into the distance. It required all of the control he could muster as he struggled with the conflict in his mind. His intellect told him that what had happened was simply an accident—one he had not willed, one he had not wanted. The arguments were sound, intellectually. But the emotional image of a young boy lying bleeding on the concrete ramp was overwhelming. It was another vision that would haunt him the rest of his life. The small crowd listened to the priest's words of comfort, but Robb heard only the gasping chokes of the dying boy. The assembled group saw the flowers that lay upon the small casket; in his mind, Robb saw the large brown eyes looking at him, through him, in fear and pain. Each of the people reached for a small handful of dirt to throw into the grave. Robb's fingers felt the sticky soil, and he gasped, looking at the mud in his hand. For a moment it was red, dripping through his fingers. He stood rigidly looking at his hand, his face ghostly pale. Kerrie grasped his arm firmly. "Robb?" He turned and looked at her momentarily—his eyes fixed somewhere in the distance. Slowly his eyes focused on Kerrie's face. Recognition changed his countenance, and he turned and threw the wet soil into the grave. Through the entire morning two equally competent professionals had watched him carefully from a distance. In time they both noted the other's actions and guessed the other's intentions. As the crowd dispersed in the growing rain, Col. Bennett stepped quickly to the side of Sr. Estelle.

"I think we should talk."

"I agree."

"I'll call you tomorrow. Let's have dinner and strategize."

"Good idea. Shall we eat at the orphanage?"

"No, I know a great place in town. I'll pick you up at seven. Okay?"

"Fine, Colonel. May God bless our efforts."

"Yes, we may, indeed, need His help on this one."

*   *   *

Kerrie felt the muscles in Robb's arm. He was a strong man, of that she was sure. The question in her mind was how brittle was that strength. He could handle war; how would he handle Chusak's death? It would be difficult, of that she was certain. She also knew she would somehow pull him through. The colonel would keep him busy flying during the day; she would have him at night. It was the two things Robb loved most. Kerrie blushed at her own thought; looking quickly to see that no one had noticed.

Robb turned abruptly, pulling his arm from Kerrie's grasp. He walked quickly back toward the grave where three half-naked men were already shoveling the wet dirt into the open hole. But he did not stop there, instead he walked to the first of the five graves. Kerrie watched him carefully as he stood, head down, mumbling something that none of the others could overhear. After a minute he turned and walked rapidly back toward the waiting group. Quickly they all climbed into the waiting blue AF crewcab pickups. As the rain intensified, the two trucks drove off toward the base.

"Are you alright?" she whispered.

"Yes." It was said without conviction.

Later that evening as they lay together on the small bed in her trailer, Kerrie asked about the first grave.

"It was his father."

"Oh." There was an unstated question in her voice.

"I owe him something."

"You do?"

"Yes, a promise I made to him before he died."

"I guessed that." She raised her body to her right elbow to look into his face.

"Know what it is?"

"Yes, I think so. Can I be a part of that promise?"

"You already are." She squeezed him with both arms. They lay in silence until sleep overcame them. It was the first time either had smiled in several days.

* * *

Colonel Bennett walked through the Operations building like a man with a purpose. His eyebrows were furrowed with concern. His attention was focused; he was looking for Joe Wilburn. He found him in the briefing room. The colonel stood in the back of the room by the open door and pointed in his direction several times. The pilots finally deciphered his signals and alerted Joe. Moments later the two men stood outside. "What's up Colonel?"

"I need your help. We've got a new pilot coming in today, and he's green."

"How green?"

"Fresh out of pilot training and RTU."

Joe's eyes widened. "What? You're kidding."

"I wish I were."

"Wow!"

"I'm putting him on your wing this afternoon. I want you to keep an eye on him—show him the ropes."

"Sure. Who's his Nav?"

"Barnes. One of the best."

"I know Barnes, he's one of the few pilots left in the backseat. I hear he's a good stick."

"Joe, this new kid must also be good to get this assignment." He rubbed his temples with both hands. "But combat is different." He reached out and placed his hand on the young Captain's shoulder. "Joe, you're the best pilot on this base—next to me of course."

"Of course." Joe's face beamed at the compliment.

"Just make sure he doesn't do something stupid."

"Don't worry Colonel, I'll take good care of him."

Three hours later Joe watched the new pilot walk confidently into the ready room. He walked directly to Joe. "Captain Wilburn? I'm Lieutenant Keller."

"Call me Joe."

"Yes Sir."

"And no 'Sir'—save that for the colonels."

"Okay Joe, I'm Mike."

"That's better, Mike. Now follow me; we've got a target to study."

"The colonel says you are the best "stick" on the base."

"He said that?"

"Actually he said you were the second best."

"Behind him, right."

"Right." Laughing, they walked down the dim hallway and into the intelligence briefing room. Joe liked the younger man immediately. He was young; he was fresh. His flight suit even looked new. Joe directed him through the flight planning process and stood beside him as the two men urinated on the revetment wall before climbing into their respective planes. He watched Mike climb confidently into the front seat of his F-4. How long had it been since he, too, had been so new, so fresh at this job. He reached his right mirror and adjusted it slightly to look at himself. He needed a shave; his flight suit was worn and stained. When had he changed it last? He couldn't remember. He looked closer; even his eyes were slightly bloodshot. Seeing his full face in the mirror, he broke into a loud laugh. The navigator in his back seat responded.

"You belch, Sir?"

"Right. By the way, you wouldn't happen to have a beer back there would you?"

There was mirth in his voice.

"Are you kidding—I'm the one who has to fly with you. It's me who needs the beer."

"Right you are." Joe watched Keller give a "thumbs up" to his ground crew in the next revetment. Behind him George Barnes watched with an experienced eye.

Fifty-five minutes later both pilots were involved in a bombing raid just south of Hanoi. They were on their third pass when the alert came over the radio.

"Hawk flight! Bandits, low, high speed, approaching from three o'clock low. I repeat, Bandits! Bandits! High speed, approaching three o'clock low."

Mike Keller was just pulling out of a dive bomb pass when the Migs arrived. "Break right four! Break right!" Joe was just initiating his bombing run and spotted the enemy immediately. The first Mig banked right and flew right up the path Mike had taken. With one burst of cannon fire he blew the F-4 from the sky. It exploded in a huge ball of flame and fell to the jungle below.

"Nooooo! You fucking asshole!" Joe banked left and dove into the two Migs. They were streaking across his view from right to left, but he had altitude and with both afterburners he was soon chasing them. Joe fired a Sidewinder from his left wing that caught the second Mig and ripped through the aircraft's tail, sending it cartwheeling into the jungle. The first Mig banked hard left to force an overshoot. Vainly the Mig pilot strained to get a visual sighting of the F-4 that had taken out his wingman. No F-4 could turn with a Mig; he knew his advantage and pulled hard into an 8-g turn. Behind him, Joe cursed and grunted. "You fucking bastard! I'll blow your fucking brains out!"

The Mig driver was a pro; he rolled over and began a split S maneuver, diving rapidly toward the jungle below, still looking for the F-4. As he did, he passed the F-4, gear and flaps down flying beside him, headed in the same direction.

"Got you now, asshole!" Joe was swearing into his intercom. "Lock him! Lock him!"

"Locked on!" The voice was excited and grunting from the g forces.

"There! There!" He pulled the trigger twice—nothing happened. "Shit! Shit!"

"What's wrong?"

"No fire!"

"Crap!" Both men were excited and shouting into the intercom. "What'll we do?"

"Fuck me!" Joe was angry and frustrated. In front the Mig was desperately jinking right and left searching for the F-4. The Mig pilot could not see it anywhere. Still he jinked, looking into his mirrors and straining his neck. Nothing. Perhaps the Americans had given up? He had lost his wingman, but he had also destroyed an F-4. He would be a hero when he returned. How many pilots could claim an F-4? Still no F-4 behind him. He turned hard right at 7 g's. No F-4.

Just behind and below the Mig, in close formation, was Joe Wilburn's F-4. "Joe, what'll we do?"

"I've got a plan." I still have two pods of air-to-ground rockets. It's all we've got, but I'm going to kill this bastard if I have to ram him. That's a promise."

"What's the plan?"

"Wait until he relaxes and levels out. Then we nail him. Hang on." Both planes banked left very hard. Then suddenly the Mig leveled and headed north. He never saw the F-4 fall back behind him at about fifty yards. Joe leveled his craft, selected the air-to-ground rockets, cursed quietly, and fired both pods together. The Mig burst into flames and exploded.

"Die asshole! Gotcha!" Joe watched the Mig spin out of control and crash into the jungle. "No chute! Good."

There was no excitement in his navigator's voice. He just sounded tired. "Joe, it's over; let's go home."

"Yeah, right. Whatever happened to the rest of our flight?"

"I think we left them over the target."

"Hawk Three. Hawk Three. Report your status."

"Hawk Three is somewhere north of the target area returning south."

"Status?"

"We're okay. Splash two Migs." There was no joy in his voice. "Any chutes from Four?"

"Negative chutes."

"Damn!"

"Hawk flight, this is Beacon 2. Score?"

"Hawk Four is down. Splash two Migs."

"Sorry about Four. We'll monitor radio frequencies."

"Thanks Beacon. Pigeons for Three."

"Roger, Three squawk cigarette."

"Squawking."

"Three, fly 190 degrees. You're 28 miles out."

"Roger." A few moments later—"Three has a visual."

"Hawk One is in a right hand turn. Rejoin right."

The flight back was long and very quiet. Even the bar was subdued when Joe walked in. Three beers later he was still brooding in the corner when Robb and Colonel Bennett walked into the room. Both were soaked with perspiration; both searched the bar until their eyes found Joe. They approached together, sat and began drinking their beers. Finally the colonel looked over at Joe. "I'm proud of you, son. You got the bastard that ambushed Keller." He looked at the half-drunk captain. "One question."

"Yes?"

"Did you really take him out with a pod of rockets after flying formation under him half way back to his base?"

"Those rockets were all I had left. Damn missiles wouldn't fire."

"Son of a bitch!" The colonel finished his beer and rose, patting Joe's shoulder as he did. He started to leave but stopped and turned. "You know Joe, there is an old Scottish saying that all men die, but only some truly live. It's what we do, son. Every time we strap that plane on our ass—we live. For a short while we experience what most men only dream of. That's the way Keller lived; it's the way he died. At least it wasn't a heart attack in some office." Joe and Robb watched the older man as he struggled for words. "And one other thing, I lied to Keller." Joe looked up suddenly. "You really are the best." He turned and left as a slow smile spread across Joe's face.

"Thank you, Sir."

* * *

Kerrie sat in her bed and stared out the small window. The constant sound of the air conditioner was suddenly drowned in the roar of yet another fighter aircraft roaring down the concrete runway on the other side of the base. She was alone for the first time since Robb had been downed. Loneliness had never been something she had even noticed before him. She had lived alone all of her adult life, and frankly, that had suited her just fine. Then she had met Robb. How love had changed her life. It had made her so vulnerable. She had never quite recognized the degree to which that had happened until Robb had parachuted behind enemy lines. What fear she had felt. Was it worth so much vulnerability? Yes! Yes! Yes! Had the color in life ever been so vivid, so beautiful? Never! Could she ever live without this feeling again? No. She had understood why Robb had felt it necessary to return to the Hooch with Joe after the loss of the new pilot. There was that male thing. They had been roommates in pilot training and throughout their careers. It was a bonding she could not completely comprehend, but she did acknowledge that strange relationship between men. She pondered that briefly, measuring it against her own friendships with other women. No, there was nothing even remotely similar, but she wished there were. To have a friendship like that must be momentous in one's life. How she envied them that. What was it about her that was so different? She had few female friends except Barb, and even that was often tenuous. How is it that men share such lasting relationships? Is it because they can piss on trees together? Kerrie laughed softly to herself as she envisioned Joe and Robb standing together, urinating on a large tree. Joe, of course, would be holding a beer in one hand while aiming his stream with the other. How she missed Robb. She had become so accustomed to sleeping beside him, touching him in the night, listening to the sound of his heart as she lay upon his shoulder. Did he miss her as she missed him? Did he miss her touch in the night? She could almost feel his hand upon her hip as he slept.

She smiled to herself. "Joe needs him tonight. I'll have him for a lifetime." She smiled at the thought and pulled the loose sheet over her body and closed her eyes to peaceful dreams.

As Kerrie drifted into peaceful sleep, Robb lay in his bunk two hundred yards away listening to Joe's snores. He stared into the darkness, thinking of the beautiful woman asleep in the trailer across the base. What had she done to his mind? He had always lived free of encumbrances. Flying was the only passion that had controlled his waking moments. There had been other women in his life, but he had always kept his heart closely guarded. Sex was one thing; love was entirely another. He considered the two. How surprised he had been to discover that sex was different with love, and how remarkable that difference, how much more beautiful the act. It had shocked him. Kerrie had destroyed every barrier around his heart; she had changed everything. He had never understood or felt such joy. How could he have missed that before?

He lay sweating in the hot still air. How lucky he was. He had found the truest treasure in life, he knew. Was there ever another woman like Kerrie? He envisioned every intimate detail of her body and smiled in the dark at the reaction of his own. How lucky he felt, how special. What a gift, and the remarkable thing was that she loved him too. To fly and to have found Kerrie; he was, indeed, a lucky man. Should he give thanks to God for these? It had been a long time since he had prayed. Did God hear the prayers of warriors? Did He, indeed, hear prayers at all?

Robb toyed with this in his mind as Joe started snoring louder. He wondered if he ever snored when he slept with Kerrie. He must remember to ask her. Oh yes, the prayer. His mind struggled with his own hypocrisy but was resolved. "Thank you God. You've given me skies to fly in and a beautiful woman to love, and, oh yes, a small boy who needs me. I don't deserve any of these, but thanks just the same. I'll try to take care of them like you've taken care of me.

Thanks for the gifts." Satisfied, he closed his eyes and fell asleep to beautiful dreams of summer mountains in Colorado.

Near Skovorodino, The Soviet Union

The two-ton army truck drove slowly through the blinding snowstorm. The rattling diesel and the crunching sound of its tires on the frozen ground were the only sound penetrating the howling wind in the blinding winter storm. Inside the two men peered through the worn wipers at the landscape before them as they rubbed their hands together and tried to keep warm. The road was hard enough to see in daylight; using only their parking lights for security, the shrouded landscape was difficult to perceive. Sergei cursed the storm and urged the tense driver onward. "Drive faster, Illarion, we don't have to worry about goats on this road."

"Yes, Captain Iskhakov." The truck speed increased slightly. "Shall I double back as usual tonight?"

"No, only idiots like us would be out in this storm." Sergei looked back over his shoulder into the darkness behind the truck. "We are not being followed. Drive on to the warehouse. Let's get out of this cursed truck and get some dinner."

"Yes sir." The thought of food encouraged the young soldier and the truck increased its speed appreciably.

Sergei ran from the parked truck, climbed a flight of snow covered stairs, and opened the door to the warehouse. In moments the larger door slid open, and the truck pulled inside, alongside the train cars. When the doors were closed, Sergei turned and walked briskly down the loading dock toward the small fire that had been built in an old furnace in the dilapidated office against the far wall. Most of the soldiers were there trying to keep warm. They eyed him cautiously as he entered. "Where is Sergeant Kochkin?" The soldiers all looked at each other uneasily and shrugged.

"I don't know, captain." One of them finally said.

"You don't know?"

"No sir." The young man stood sullenly and looked at his feet as he spoke. Without a word, Sergei turned and walked quickly from the room. A short time later he returned, looked into the room briefly, and walked back out onto the loading platform. He circled the missile car and checked the train engine then walked out into the snow filled night.

The wind had decreased but the snow continued to fall in the darkness. The flakes were small, but they were thick in the dark night. There was almost a full moon out, though it was barely visible through the remnants of the storm. Sergei pulled his coat tight around his neck and raised the collar to provide some protection from the freezing cold. He looped his scarf around his neck and pulled the black fur of his hat down over his ears. Without stopping, the captain turned left as he exited the door, crossed the rail tracks, and began to skirt the building. He had turned the far corner of the old structure when he found what he had been searching for—fresh tracks in the snow. Sergei stopped and looked carefully around. There were no sounds and no movement except the constant snow that was slowly filling the footprints he had discovered. He bent quickly and inspected the tracks. There were two sets, and both were made by military boots. Rising, he began to walk rapidly as he followed the tracks into the night.

The tracks were made by one obviously familiar with the local terrain. They proceeded along a straight path through the snow. There were no turns or meandering from the persons who had left the footprints. They obviously knew where they were going and were striding with confidence. Sergei studied the tracks as he walked. One of the men was tall and took long strides. The other was obviously shorter and took smaller strides; that he assumed to be Vadim. Where were they going? Didn't they understand his rules—no one was to leave the building. Could they be planning to report the mission to higher authorities? Or were they simply going into the village to get drunk? If so, would they dare disclose the cargo stored in the abandoned warehouse? The cold officer bent his head into the slight wind and tried to shield his face from the cold and the snow that hampered his progress. He squinted into the dark night, his eyelashes frozen into small white shadows. Sergei was angry; he was also frightened by the possibility of exposure of his mission. He had been given this mission by the one man he respected in the army, perhaps the one man he respected in all of Russia. Dmitriy Ruchinsky had replaced the father he had, himself, murdered. For everything his father had not been, Dmitriy Mihail had measured fully. Sergei had boasted that he had never loved anyone; he lied. The colonel was the one man for whom Sergei placed himself second; there was nothing he would not do for the colonel. The cold captain pondered these things as he plodded through the thick snowdrifts in the dark night. Was it the colonel's success he desired? Actually that was not his goal. He simply wanted the older officer's respect. He wanted the colonel to know that he would succeed with any task he was assigned. What did he really want? Was it respect, or was it love? Sergei spit into the snow as he watched ahead in the darkness. The sound of his boots crunching the snow was almost a soft screeching sound, giving evidence to the extreme cold. He hastened his pace as the snowfall slackened, allowing the moonlight to reflect off of the new snow and guide his progress. Then he saw it, the figure of a man walking ahead, probably thirty meters in front of him. Sergei pulled his pistol from his coat and began to walk even faster. As he approached he raised the pistol and shouted. "You there, halt."

Sergeant Vadim Kochkin turned slowly and faced his old friend. "My captain; what a cold night for a stroll."

Iskhakov lowered the pistol and walked forward slowly toward his friend. "What the hell are you doing out here?"

"Probably following the same tracks you are."

The officer put the pistol back inside his coat and slapped his friend on the back. "Who are we following?"

"Young Yuriy Rybikov. I think he is in love with a young girl in the village ahead."

"How long has he been gone?"

The short sergeant looked at the lone tracks ahead of his path and studied them for a moment. "I'd say he's twenty minutes ahead of us."

"The idiot. He could spoil everything for us. I'll skin him alive when I catch him." Sergei spat into the snow again. Kochkin watched him carefully.

"He's just a kid. Let me take care of this. I'll kick his ass and put him on latrine detail for a week. That will set a good example for the others."

"Or I could shoot him and hang his body in the warehouse as an example. I suspect that would leave a better lesson."

The sergeant looked at his leader with a frown on his face. He knew that Sergei was capable of doing exactly what he said. He also knew he had to prevent such violence to his own men. Leading them was difficult enough already. And hadn't he, himself, escaped into the night just last week? "My captain, don't get too upset over this. I'll take care of young Rybikov. I'll make him wish you had shot him. Besides, we need all of our men to make this mission a success. We cannot afford to lose one—even such a stupid one." He watched the angry officer for some semblance of agreement. When he got none, he continued. "After all, he is just a kid."

"He'll be a dead kid when I get my hands on him." The two trudged on in the darkness, the older sergeant struggling to keep up with the strides of the taller captain.

*   *   *

The lights of the village were like small candles glowing softly in the cold winter night. The snowfall had ceased, but the cold had only intensified. As the two men followed the tracks, they found themselves circling the village to a small building on the north side of a large river. It was frozen and the two walked across quickly, listening to the groaning ice as they climbed up the bank and crossed a small road. The lights inside the small wooden structure were warm, like the sounds of music that echoed across the cold courtyard. The smell of cooking meat, probably venison, wafted through the night air and caused both men to stop to smell and swallow repeatedly as the saliva filled their mouths. Sergei stopped his companion and looked carefully up and down the street. No one was about; it was too cold for anyone to venture out into the freezing temperature. As they approached the small wooden door, they realized that the building was a small bar. Inside men were singing and music was playing loudly. Sergei bent slightly and entered the noisy room. Inside were ten to fifteen people, six were at a small crude bar drinking vodka; the others were seated at small tables around the littered room. Most were eating and drinking and paid little attention to the two who came in from the cold night. Yuriy Rybikov sat at a table in the far corner of the room with a young girl. His back was to the door and he did not notice the two soldiers enter. He was far too engrossed with the young girl who looked at him with absolute admiration and love. The captain crossed the room with his sergeant in tow. Sergei was watching the young soldier intently; his sergeant, however, was surveying the room.

The angry officer walked to the table, tapped the young man on the shoulder, and when he turned, Sergei hit him squarely in the face, knocking him across the table into the lap of the girl. She gasped in horror, then screamed. As the officer threw a chair from his path and continued his attack, three large men at the bar rushed forward to join the fray. The first to reach the screaming girl shoved her aside, and grabbing the officer's shoulder, spun him around and smashed him in the face. Kochkin grabbed that man and swung at him, glancing a blow off of his shoulder. A second later he was on the floor with blood flowing from his nose and mouth. When he cleared his head to look up, two of the men had Sergei's arms pinned behind him and the third was beating him mercilessly. One of the men struck the officer in the stomach, and the attacker screamed loudly. He had located the pistol under Sergei's coat with his right fist. In the process he had broken his hand and was howling in pain. An older man reached into the coat as Sergei struggled against the two holding his arms. In the process the pistol fell and slid across the dirty floor. One of the younger men reached for it but was kicked by the restrained man. The young local turned and swung at Sergei but missed as the bloody officer dodged. Angrily he grabbed the captain's hair and held his head while he prepared to make hamburger out of Sergei's face. The shot stopped everyone. Three men held the captain; two sat on top of the sergeant. The gunshot got everyone's attention. Standing in the middle of the room was the young soldier, blood running from his nose, the pistol pointed at the three men holding his captain. "Let him go."

"That crazy bastard attacked you."

"Let him go."

"Kopteva, you alright with this?" The older man spoke to the young girl who stood shaking beside the wall.

"Yes father, let them go. Do what Yuriy says."

The three men pushed the bleeding officer to the floor and turned and walked to the bar. Kochkin crawled to his feet, blood covering his face, and stood shakily. He walked slowly to his companion and helped him struggle to stand. Sergei wiped the blood from his face and turned to the young soldier. "Give me that gun."

"No. Give it to me." The sergeant spoke quietly and walked to the young soldier. The young man looked at his sergeant and his captain. The look in Kochkin's eyes prevailed. Very carefully he turned the weapon over. Kochkin took the pistol and placed it in his own coat and turned to his captain. "Let's get out of here. Yuriy, you too. Move." With great resolve he shoved the two men out the door and into the cold night.

"Give me my pistol, dammit."

"No, if you walk back in there and kill those assholes you could jeopardize the entire mission—and the mission is more important that all those bastards in this stinking village." He waited a moment for that to sink in and continued. "Besides, we'll be back later. They aren't going anywhere. Next time we'll return with the entire squad and burn the whole village. But not now. We have more important work to do." Sergei said nothing but nodded affirmatively. Wiping the blood from his face he stumbled into the snow and began the long trek back to the warehouse. Beside him the young soldier trudged into the darkness and the frozen forest beside the river. Kochkin patted the pistol in his coat and watched the young man as he felt his broken nose with his handkerchief. It continued to bleed profusely. He knew that the soldier would live as long as he held the weapon. When he finally returned it, as he knew he would, Yuriy Rybikov's prospects would be much less certain. The old sergeant felt the bruises on his own face and wondered how he could protect the stupidity of youth. It would be difficult, but the fact that Yuriy had stepped forward to protect his captain might have some bearing, though how much he really didn't know. Kochkin looked up at a sky full of stars and inhaled the cold dry air. Ahead of him the two men stumbled painfully through the cold night. It was a long trek back to the warehouse and the temperature was falling. Perhaps it would just be cold enough to cool the anger burning in his captain's breast.

CHAPTER SEVEN

<u>Nubat Royal Thai Air Force Base</u>

Robb shook the raw edges of sleep from his waking mind and opened his eyes to peer into the staring face he knew and loved. He found a silence and a peace with Kerrie that he had not known since Chusak's death. The cold void of death had finally been assuaged with the warmth that glowed within their hearts as they held each other close, a refuge from the chaos and the fear they both had grown to accept as part of the outside world within which they participated for so many hours of each day. Together they waited for the lost hours together, the ones that passed so quietly, so quickly, into memories.

Robb looked into the depths of Kerrie's eyes, into the bricked security of the love they had come to share. Somehow his fingers found her hair and his lips found hers. The beauty of the silence was laced by one lone strain of beautiful music in his mind. Somewhere from the deepest shadows, it echoed ever so quietly. Then it grew in strength and became real in its beauty, and the haunting melody grew louder and stronger. Its tune rose with the wind and echoed back with a thousand voices in his head. Then it wandered away and could hardly be heard. It whispered its graceful melody and floated softly along the silence. Then it grew again, bolstered by the thundering tones of trumpets and the hammering of a hundred drums. Together they rose, and the lone strain waxed even more beautiful as the melody grew into a throbbing crescendo. Louder and stronger it grew, and the silence swelled with the one lone strain until the thundering and throbbing burst, and the song was gone, and the silence returned with its peace.

"I love you, Kerrie."

"I know; I love you too."

He stared silently at the flickering candlelight that reflected across the wooden ceiling of the small hooch. Like the tiny blaze that smoldered in his breast, it danced large and fearsome across the darkened walls of the small room. Turning to the smiling woman beside him, the tanned man stroked her side with his hand and then kissed her long and softly. "Did I ever tell you that you are more beautiful without those damned green uniforms?" She smiled and kissed him on the forehead. Abruptly he sat upright in the small bed. He stared openly at her.

"What are you doing?"

"I'm just memorizing. It sometimes gets boring up there flying." She blushed a deep, soft pink. "I never want to forget that one little freckle right there, or this mole, or the funny little fuzz that grows under your navel." He touched each of them lovingly. She blushed again, smiling in her embarrassment.

"I love you more than you'll ever know."

"Why, you silly girl?"

"Oh, for many reasons." She squinted her eyes as if thinking hard. Robb bent to kiss the fuzz on her stomach and spoke in a muffled voice. "Name one."

"Because you taught me how to love." She giggled as he nuzzled her.

* * *

Kerrie stepped from the shower and walked into the small bedroom while toweling herself vigorously. She stopped suddenly and looked left into the small mirror over the sink. She saw a smiling, deliriously happy, naked woman looking back at her. She turned and examined the woman before her, smiling at the vision. The figure was exquisite, shapely legs, almost flat stomach (Southeast Asia had helped there), slightly large breasts. The long brown hair was wavy, almost curly, and it fell across both shoulders. She crossed both arms under her breasts and cuddled herself. Her breasts rose as she watched the tiny gold cross that hung loosely between them. She grinned to herself as she remembered Robb's reaction the first time he had seen her naked. What wonder had been in his eyes that evening.

She held the damp towel before her and danced with it. She glided across the tiny floor as a young girl, lost in a dream that absorbed her. The music was only in her head, but it was more beautiful than any concert she had ever attended. It rose and swelled in her mind and in her heart as she danced across the floor, floating and twisting with her imaginary gown. She laughed aloud and turned to the mirror again, this time standing on tiptoes to see more of the beautiful woman there. She was breathing hard from the dance and the excitement of the morning. Slowly she moved the towel away and tried to imagine Robb's excitement as he had looked at her. She stood, slowly moving the towel down across her breasts, her stomach, then even more slowly across her hips to her thighs. She stood silently, staring, and then she started to sing quietly, her large brown eyes dancing. Kerrie placed her hands on each breast and then slowly slid her hands down her body. Tonight would be one neither of them would ever forget, of that she was certain.

The "greens" of the medical staff were hardly what Kerrie would have considered sexy, yet underneath she had selected peach colored panties and bra. Outwardly, she looked like a doctor; inside she felt more beautiful than she had ever felt in her life, except for her first night with Robb.

The door of the small trailer swung open, admitting the light and the warmth of the Thai morning. Kerrie literally skipped out, singing to herself. Tonight would be a special night. Robb was scheduled in the tower that afternoon with no flights until sometime the next day. She was scheduled to be off at 1630 hours, half-hour before Robb would leave the Tower. She had the evening planned perfectly. A great bottle of wine was in her small refrigerator. She had three cans of spaghetti standing beside her hot plate, and she would pick up bread at the club. A feast, to be sure. She had even borrowed a couple of great records that were already placed on the changer of her record player. An entire night together—just the two of them. She smiled even more broadly in anticipation as she walked toward the hospital. She could feel the fabric of her clothing brushing against her flesh; she could smell the early Thai morning; she could hear the sounds of the day and the song that still played in her head. How could she possibly stand waiting for the day to pass?

She glanced up as a flight of F-4s roared overhead and began their pitchouts. One, two, three, four of the aircraft banked hard left and rolled across the morning sky and onto downwind, paralleling the runway. She wondered if this were Robb's flight and checked her watch. Yes, the time was about right. He was number three in his flight. She watched the third aircraft turn sharply left, four seconds after the second plane. It looked a little "snappier" she thought—obviously the best pilot in that flight. She stopped and turned around, watching that aircraft. In the distance dark clouds were gathering to the northeast, but the sun shining on the F-4s in the pattern was bright and winked at her with a reflection from the third canopy. She smiled broadly and waved back, unconsciously. She knew he had willed that; she knew it was a signal—not an accident. Robb could do that. She knew he was the best pilot on the base. Didn't he have a Distinguished Flying Cross? And he was brave, too. She turned and started toward the hospital, a bounce in her walk. At the surgeons' room, Kerrie met a tired, but smiling Phillip. "You look happy."

"I am."

"Perform another miracle?" She touched his arm; without thinking he placed his hand upon hers and looked up into her face. For a long time he did not speak. He just looked into her eyes, entranced. Finally he released her hand and turned to remove his blood stained smock.

"Remember the kid with the cleft palate that the airmen were trying to catch in the jungle?"

"Yes."

"Well, they caught him yesterday, and I fixed it."

"Phillip, that's wonderful. Why didn't you call me? I could have assisted."

"No one ever thought we could catch him. The guys just got lucky. I had to make a quick decision."

"How's he doing?"

"Great. He's going to be okay. Now we just have to teach him to live like a human being instead of an animal in the jungle." He paused a moment and rubbed his neck. "And that may be the hardest part. He was never accepted by the villagers before. What will they do now?"

Kerrie touched his arm again. "Phillip, you're a good man and a great surgeon."

He looked at her, and suddenly he knew that all of his attempts to hide his emotions had been in vain. She knew. He could see it in her eyes, and they both had full awareness. He started to speak but stopped. She just stood there, her hand on his forearm, staring through his eyes, seeing his soul. She kissed his cheek and turned to leave. Phillip had never felt such turmoil in his life. He felt 10 feet tall and also barely two inches tall. His heart leapt with joy while tears welled into his eyes. How he wanted her to love him. His right hand thrust out uncontrollably and grasped the turning woman's right arm. Uncontrolled by his own will, the hand spun her around. In a second he reached with his left hand and placed it beneath her chin. Gently he pulled her to him and kissed her. It was over in a moment and control over his body was returned. Phillip stepped back quickly, his head down, staring at the floor. Kerrie looked at him in surprise for several moments then stepped forward and placed both hands on Phillip's cheeks. He was stammering when she lifted his face to her own. She kissed him gently. When she backed away she was smiling at him. "Phillip, you are a very special man." She turned, still smiling, and walked off down the narrow hallway. He watched her leave, the bounce of her walk emblazoned on his mind. Phillip Brady had never felt such joy in his life—or such confusion. Smiling, he walked back into the recovery room. He had one more patient to check before leaving for breakfast and some well-deserved sleep. He looked out the window at the darkening sky and hurried about his tasks.

* * *

Robb stood in the small deserted post office waiting for the rain to subside and thought about the woman he loved. The spark that flashed between them ignited a fury of passion that consumed them both with its intensity. Their love grew with the ever-present fear that the stage lights would dim and the curtains would close too soon. Each day was cherished, each precious moment was lived like a lifetime hanging in the balance of a moment; each day was filled with the sweet memories of the past and bitter fears for the future. And when at last they hid in each other's arms, time lost all dimension except for the intoxicating stupor of the present. They would hold each other and stare deeply into the eyes and souls of the other, tracing small imaginary lines across a visage that could never be forgotten in a lifetime. The wonder would awe, like heady wine floating through the heart's own soul, as they laughed at each other, at life, at love. Their love made them smile, and with their joy they forgot the planes, the lost comrades, the naked children, the anguished souls. For others, however, the war became a time of waiting, waiting for loved ones far away or lives of familiar tasks and familiar pleasures. Their lives were not moments of joy but rather months of anguish; theirs was not the exhilaration of touch and feel, but rather the constant longing for a love denied. So while Kerrie and Robb hid away with their new found love, others drank themselves into restless sleep and rose each morning to mark one more day from a worn, but familiar, calendar on their wall.

Robb walked across the small aisle to look at the hospital which was adjacent to the consolidated post office. It was raining harder now, and the falling drops smashing against the rusted screens sent a find spray across his face. The hospital was constructed of numerous small structures attached end to end into a series of wings; the entire edifice had been painted yellow to give it a pleasant look-- a monument to the work done there, an indictment to its necessity. Somewhere inside, Kerrie would be working now. With her dark hair bouncing across her shoulders, she would probably be rushing down the halls humming softly to herself. Just that morning he had awakened to her humming as she lay close beside him, softly tracing his chin, his shoulder, his ear with her finger. Kerrie tried to awaken him at the earliest possible moment, for while sleep was a precious luxury, waking was a joyous discovery of life and love once more. She jealously guarded each shared moment with Robb; she knew it was time that for her was passing entirely too quickly; it was time that was not guaranteed.

The wind ceased blowing, and the howling wail in the chapel's small steeple died with the breeze. The sheets of rain fell more slowly, and the dark clouds shifted overhead and began to track southeast. Robb looked at his watch, sighed deeply, cast one last glance at the unlikely yellow structure across the muddy road, and dashed out the door to his bike. In the middle of the road was a huge sign held slightly upright by a platform of concrete inside an old tire casing. It read simply, "Today is Sunday." He frowned as he passed it, remembering that he had forgotten to take his malaria pill for the week. Each Sunday the tiny pills were dispensed at numerous points around the base and were the reason for the signs. Without the signs, the pills would easily be forgotten, for war demands a seven-day workweek.

Robb dashed inside the tall white building and stood dripping on the irregular tile floor. This was the only modern building on the entire base and stood in stark contrast to the green jungle and the acres of camouflage around it. The white stuccoed structure served a threefold purpose: civilian airport, military tower, and combination military and civilian air traffic control agency. Robb climbed the stairs two at a time and despite his conditioning arrived panting at the locked doorway to the final set of stairs leading to the tower control room. He lifted the phone hanging beside the door and waited.

"Tower."

"Yes, this is Captain Barker; I'm the replacement for the tower officer on duty."

"Rog." A loud buzz sounded in the door and Robb pushed it open. At the top of the stairs was a familiar face.

"Hey, old man, think you're going to make it up those stairs without a heart attack?"

"Joe, where've you been for the past few days, I haven't seen you in ages."

"I've been to Hong Kong on R & R. I've got to tell you, that is the damndest place I've ever seen. They've got the prettiest girls and the cheapest booze you can imagine." He paused a moment and scratched his head in an exaggerated fashion. "Or was it the other way around?"

"Sounds like you had yourself a good time."

"Actually I had a Ming and a Sue, and a couple of others that I failed to be properly introduced to."

Four heavily loaded F4s screamed down the hot runway and climbed gracefully through the late afternoon sky. Four seconds apart, they roared down the tiny strip of concrete like small toys in some make believe world. From the cool air conditioned tower, the heat could be seen rising from the broiling concrete and asphalt below, while the tiny men sweated with their labor and scurried to prepare the next four planes to leap into the cooler heavens.

Robb picked up the senior NCO's report and examined it closely. As he did, he spoke to Joe without looking up. "Anything exciting happen today?"

"Yeah, some Navy Jock pitched out on an overhead pattern with a full bomb load about forty-five minutes ago; lost his number three bomb on the right inboard pylon. He damn near lost the entire ballgame. The Mark 82 landed in the weeds about a mile and a half over there." He pointed across the runway. "We didn't let him land with the load. I sent him up to Orange Track for gas then to the sector controller for useful work."

Robb looked up quickly. "Anybody hurt?"

"No, chopper checked it out right away and didn't see anything, we sent a truck from munitions out to make sure. He paused and watched his friend's reaction. "It missed the village by over two miles." The taller man grimaced and nodded to the unspoken words he knew to be in Joe's mind. Like many men, Joe found it difficult to show outwardly the genuine concern he felt for his friend. And so it is that men slap each other on the back and tease with no malice when they grope for some adequate method to show their true feelings. But also like all men, Robb understood the unwritten code that all boys learn on the hard trek to manhood, and the slightly embarrassed face of his friend was enough to span the distance between the two and build yet another link of friendship on an already firm foundation.

"Well, I'm off to drink all the beer in the club tonight, and then I'll terrorize the natives until they lock all their fair maidens behind guarded doors."

"After you've had four or five beers, they'd better hide those who aren't quite so fair too." Robb laughed at his friend and pointed him toward the door. "You'd better hurry before that big thunderbumper over there arrives and pisses all over this entire base. Besides, if it keeps moving in this direction, this place is going to be busier than a one legged drunk in an ass kicking contest, so you'd better leave before we put you back to work." With a smile he was off.

Robb looked off to the northeast at the giant black monster that was heading in their direction. At its present rate of speed, it would be over the field in approximately twenty to twenty-five minutes. Allowing for the wind and rain preceding and following the main buildup, the field could be below minimums for fifteen minutes or more, depending on the winds. If they started to die off, the field could be tied up even longer. For a plane returning with minimum fuel or battle damage, even five minutes could be too long.

Besides the officer, there were three other men in the tower, the normal tower crew. Sergeant Jackson ran the shift as was evidenced by the zebra stripes that covered his shirtsleeves. Helping him were two staff sergeants of exceptional ability. Like the men operating the radars below, the tower personnel were select men. Controlling the aircraft movement over the entire base required highly qualified personnel, men who could be relied on when the chips were down.

The clouds were getting nearer, looming high into the late

afternoon sky; the sun was completely blocked from the base, leaving a damp darkness hanging in the air. Already Sergeant Jackson was coping with the impending problems. "Jim, call weather and find out how long before that bumper gets here and how long before it moves over. John, you call operations and find out how many they've got out and when they estimate them back." He reached for a phone and spoke into it with authority. "Jackson here, how many tankers you got airborne? Looks like we may be covered over for fifteen or twenty minutes here." As he listened, one of the younger men handed him a note on a yellow pad. "Roger, we've got," he held the note closer, "three flights of three and one lone Wolf out right now. Two flights and the FAC are due in the next twenty minutes, so we'd better hold a little gas in a couple of tankers just in case. Will you coordinate? Rog." He cradled the phone and muttered to himself. "No sweat, baby!"

Robb smiled to himself. "No sweat, baby." That was what made the difference between the professional and the amateur. From the pilots and the crew chiefs to the cooks and the guards, they were professionals doing a difficult job, and they had reason to be proud.

"Nubat tower, Olds, flight of three, taxi."

One of the younger men picked up a microphone, keyed it, and spoke as he filled out a clearance he was receiving by telephone. "Roger Olds Flight, cleared to taxi. Active runway two three. Altimeter, two-niner-eight-two."

Robb rose and looked down at the aircraft parking ramp and the large concrete reinforced revetments where the fighters were parked. Three fighter-bombers were already moving out of their parking spaces and were making their way down the taxiway toward the armament area. He turned slowly and looked over the entire field and then the remainder of the base. It was here in the tower that the eyes of the Wing were centered. Far below, in the darkened

Command Post, lay the brain center of the base, and out on the ramp was the heart that kept the birds flying. But here in the tower were the eyes to see and direct the entire operation of the field itself. Here was the link between the brain center below and the muscle moving into position on the end of the runway. Sergeant Jackson looked over at Robb. For the first time that evening, he smiled. "Hey Captain, how're you this evening?"

"Fine, Sarge. Haven't seen you in quite some time; you been taking care?"

"Sure, I've even lost ten pounds in the past two months. And if that big black one over there keeps coming this way, I'm likely to lose ten more this evening."

The blond captain looked in the direction of the large monsoon storm. "Yes indeedy, it does look like a mean one. I'm glad I'm not flying near it."

The phone rang beside the older man and he quickly picked it up. As he listened his brow furrowed. He hung up without answering. "Cougar FAC took a hit and is about 100 out. Should be landing in about fifteen minutes. Didn't report very much damage, but you know how that goes -- never can tell just how bad those things really are." He paused and lifted the phone that was a hot line to the fire station. As he did, he mumbled to himself. "Damn those FACs take a beating."

Robb grimaced and gazed in the direction from which the damaged plane should come. More than anyone else at Nubat, the F4 Forward Air Controllers took a greater percentage of hits, and they also sustained more casualties. The Cougar FACs were a respected group; they did a tough job, and they paid high stakes. More than one of Robb's friends had taken that road, and many of them failed to finish their tour. Still the volunteer lists grew, and only the finest were selected. That was some consolation, knowing that the pilot approaching the big black thunderstorm was one of the best -- Robb looked at the flight log and recognized the pilot on this particular flight; they had been classmates at the Academy and in pilot training and were close friends. A large and burley man, Bart Loskovitch was a different man in an airplane. His gruff features hid the grace of a cat when it came to flying. If anyone could coax that wounded machine through the hell that was moving in their direction, Bart could.

Silently they waited. A small light flashed on the panel before Sergeant Jackson; he reached for the nearest phone. "He's cleared to land." He turned to the three anxious faces around him. "GCA has him 18 out. Looks like he made it through." A sudden relief swept over their faces as they watched the flash of a landing light against the foreboding black of the giant thunderstorm.

Down below the tower the radar controllers were vectoring the damaged plane toward the field. Theirs was the job of controlling all incoming aircraft as they entered the local control zone. It was a very demanding job; they became the eyes of the pilots when the weather was too bad for the pilots to see the landing strip. The approach control radar would intercept the aircraft far from the field and vector them toward the runway, being careful to align them as closely as possible with the runway itself. As the planes came closer to the field, the GCA controller would pick up the task and give the pilot precise instructions on heading and altitude in order to allow him to descend toward the runway, even though the pilot couldn't see the ground below. Using this control, the pilot would descend as instructed until breaking clear of the clouds or reaching his minimum altitude for that approach, an altitude below which it was not considered safe to descend. If the weather were initially below that altitude the approach would not be attempted, and the aircraft would be diverted to another field with better weather.

Like the men that flew the fighters, the men in the dark radar rooms worked under intense strain. Upon their shoulders rested a heavy burden, one they did not take lightly. Hour upon hour they sat before the large luminous green scopes and watched the small blips as they moved back and forth across the face of an imaginary sky. Heading, altitudes, traffic alignment, these and many other bits of information were instantly memorized and coordinated as the tiny dots moved endlessly across the scopes. "Bird dog 53, turn right to a heading of three four five, descend and maintain three thousand feet, report when level. Hoax 21, turn left, I repeat, left, to a heading of one eight zero, maintain five thousand feet. Lobo 62, turn ..." It was an endless game that moved aircraft from the skies to the ramp and then to the skies once more. Minimum fuel planes, battle damage, and monsoon storms only added to the tension in the dark cave on the second floor.

Less than five minutes after Cougar 33 landed, the black clouds slipped over the base and blackened the sky. Far below, men raced across the ramp in all directions, trying desperately to get the next flight off before the weather closed the field, but they were too late. As the torrents of rain beat down upon the sweltering land, the men sat helpless under any cover they could find and waited for the storm to pass. Up in the tower great gusts of wind beat against the huge windows and pelted them with slapping sprays of water, obscuring the vision of the tense men peering into the darkness.

Sergeant Jackson ceased his pacing and sat for the first time that evening. Nervously he lit a cigarette and watched the faces of the younger men in the room. "It's a son-of-a-bitch ain't it?"

Robb rejected one of the cigarettes he was offered with a wave of his hand. "You're right about that. I don't think I've ever seen one this bad." They sat there in silence, staring out into nothingness. Then the light flashed on the controller's panel. For a moment Jackson looked at the light in disbelief then snatched the phone from its cradle. He listened attentively and began vigorously snubbing his cigarette. "You're not serious? In this weather? I can't even see the damn runway from the tower!" He listened for a moment and then began to shout in anger. "Well, dammit, tell him to divert!" Looking directly at Robb he spoke in a desperate tone. "Slide Three-One is making an approach to the field right now."

"What?" Robb rose from his chair and raced to the forward window. "He can't land in this. Tell him he's not cleared to land. Tell GCA to divert him immediately."

"That's what everybody told him, but it didn't do any good. He said he would only try one pass and then divert. Personally, I'll bet he's too low on fuel to divert right now." He turned to the younger sergeants. "Tune in GCA frequency."

The radio crackled with interference as a large shaft of lightening flashed across the sky and momentarily blinded the crew in the tower. "Slide Three-One, you're low on the glide slope; turn right to a heading of two three five...Slide Three-One you are very low on the glide slope; turn further right to a heading of two three seven. Slide Three-One, you are dangerously low on the glide slope. Slide Three-One you are dangerously low on the glide slope. Slide Three-One you are too low for a safe approach, if the runway is not in sight climb straight ahead to an altitude of three thousand feet, acknowledge."

"Three-One, runway in sight."

"Bullshit!" Sergeant Jackson was standing beside Robb looking out into the darkness and the rain. "He can't possibly..."

The silence was almost deafening between the beeps that came loudly from the emergency speaker. To the ashen faced men in the tower it was the sound of ejection beepers, two of them emanating from somewhere in the direction of the end of the runway. Then came the explosion that rocked the entire building. Pale faces turned to look at each other in shock and disbelief. Immediately the sirens sounded their wailing song as the fire trucks roared from warm garages into the cold rain.

It was Sergeant Jackson who finally picked up the phone. "Where?" He paused and rubbed his forehead vigorously. "Oh shit. No, we heard two beepers; they must have gotten out on final. No idea. Roger." He turned slowly to the other men in the room. "The plane crashed on base!" There was a rasping urgency in his voice. "Just beyond the post office; they think it hit the hospital."

Robb's face went suddenly white and his eyes opened wide with fear. "The hospital? Oh no! Dear God, NO!" For only a moment he stood transfixed, then he turned and ran wildly for the stairs. The pounding hammered in his heart and echoed with each step through his anguished soul. The man that ran dazed toward the crash site was not a man; he was little more than a machine, driven compulsively from the stupor of a panicked brain. He crossed an open field and headed for the post office. As he rounded the corner he stopped suddenly and stood trembling before the blazing inferno that roared violently into the dark sky. The wailing sirens and the frightened screams of people in shock echoed faintly through the pounding of his heart. He stood for a momentary eternity and stared blankly at the horror stained sight. Great orange arms leapt through the sky and lashed at the storm's darkness while small black silhouettes ran and shouted at each other or merely stood silent before the awful splendor of destruction. In shock his mind slipped, arose, and slipped back again into the numbing pit of fear, but his heart cried out and the mind responded, and he began to run again through the rain toward the searing heat and the screaming voices.

The first group were being covered with a large piece of gray tarpaulin; only their feet extended to give meaning to the shapeless mounds that lay side-by-side like stacked cordwood. The tall captain opened his mouth to speak, but no sound came from his throat. His eyes went automatically to the feet, but the blurry image would not focus. Again he tried to force them to see, but they were blind to death. So he ran away from the mounds, unknowing and afraid -- afraid because he did not know.

He ran and stumbled and rose and ran again through the black silhouettes before the fire. Frantically, he forced his mind to concentrate. Where would she be at 1330? When was she scheduled off shift today? Did she have surgery to perform today? Had she said anything about her schedule other than meeting him after his shift? When did she stop for lunch? On he ran, circling the inferno as black shapes screamed and ran in confusion. Finally he spotted one lone man standing placidly among the chaos. Robb ran to him. "Where's surgery?" The man turned slowly and looked at him but said nothing. "Where's surgery, dammit!" Rain pelted the man's face, but the blank eyes stared back without comprehension. The man stood mute, slowly turning to look at the blazing fire before him. Robb backed slowly, then turned to run again as the rain blurred his vision and the wind fanned the panic in his breast. Suddenly he stopped; before him was a small man with a large burden. It was Phillip; Kerrie was in his arms, her dark hair matted with blood. Phillip's eyes were large; he was breathing large gulps of air as if drowning; the look on his face was one of shock. Robb looked at the burden in Phillip's arms. This time his eyes perceived the sight his mind would not accept. His mind had slipped again and backed desperately from the nightmare of reality. Phillip stumbled forward and fell to his knees, still holding Kerrie. Robb knelt beside the soft, smooth body of the smiling woman his mind saw and grasped her and pulled her to him, and the hoax ended. The numbed soul was silent in its prayers, and the whimpering heart cried in disbelief, and the trembling body shook. He gently touched her cheek as Phillip struggled in vain to stand.

Nubat Royal Thai Air Force Base

The three men sat in the small conference room, leaning on the worn table, silently staring at their coffee cups. All three wore flight suits;

one of them, Lt. Colonel John Sampson, Squadron Commander of the 23rd Tactical Fighter Squadron, had a g-suit loosely hanging around his waist. His flight suit was wet with perspiration; small beads of sweat glistened in his short hair and across his cleanly shaved face; he looked tired. Overhead a florescent light bulb blinked intermittently in the drab, dark room. It was obviously a room that had never been visited by women. The shelves were either bare or covered with stacks of the interminable government forms. Ashtrays were scattered around the room; most were half full of broken cigarettes, lending a stale stench that mingled with the odor of sweating bodies to permeate the walls and the furniture. After a while, the smell took on its own aroma and simply became a part of the room, a part of the job.

The men rose when the door opened and the tall thin colonel walked into the room, followed by an older colonel in khaki uniform. Colonel Jim Hawkins, the wing commander, walked with the confidence of a man who had succeeded at most things in his life. He moved like he thought, quickly and accurately. Like the other three pilots in the room, he also wore a flight suit, but his was clean and neatly pressed. "As you were, gentlemen." He sat at the end of the table and placed his coffee cup before him. The older colonel sat at his right and surveyed the men before him, envying them their flight suits. His uniform also had a pair of wings on his left chest, but George Cook had not passed a flight physical in over seven years. Now he was relegated to managing the base and all of its facilities. It was a job he did well; it was not the function he desired. As he took his seat, the commander spoke. "Okay, Howard, what happened?"

"McKinney lost it on final. Then he panicked and punched."

"Extenuating factors?"

"Weather was shit." The three men watched the commander as he sat, grim faced, and absorbed the information.

"Are he and the GIB alright?"

"Nav has a broken leg."

Lt. Colonel Sampson spoke without looking at the other squadron commander. "Why'd he attempt an approach in that storm?" There was anger in his voice and it was not concealed. His dislike for the major was obvious and shared by others.

The colonel sipped from his coffee cup and then spoke quietly, watching McKinney's squadron commander. "Howard, I reviewed the tower tapes just a few minutes ago, the tower told him to abort the approach. Sergeant Jackson was in the tower. He's the best."

"I guess he thought he could make it."

"He screwed up, and a lot of good people are dead as a result." Howard Shelby looked at this coffee cup and simply nodded.

I've convened an investigation board to check this out. Jim Flannigan will lead from Nubat; a team from the Pentagon will arrive in four days to assist. Until then, I don't want Mckinney in the air."

"Colonel," Sampson spoke quietly, thoughtfully, weighing his words carefully, "it might be a good idea to get Mckinney off base for the time being."

"That's right, you have a captain who was very close to Major Jernigan."

"She's the surgeon in a coma? How bad is she?"

"Doesn't look good. She's hanging on, but barely; still hasn't regained consciousness."

"Sir. I don't think it would be a good idea if Captain Barker were to meet McKinney in the bar." He looked into the eyes of his boss. "He was in the tower when McKinney was told to abandon the approach."

"Damn!" There was a long silence in the room. "How's he doing?"

"Not too well. Andy is keeping an eye on him. He's a good man—one Mig and a DFC."

"How close were they?"

"Engaged."

"Shit!" He glanced into his coffee cup for a moment then looked up and spoke with authority. "Howard, I want McKinney off base in one hour. Have him moved to Udorn. I'll call and alert Harry that he's coming." That topic closed, he turned to the older colonel. "George, status?"

"I've got a temporary hospital set up in Hanger One. Two mobile operating room trailers are being shipped from Clark as we speak. They should arrive within the week. I'll have three contracts for a new hospital within five days. My guess is it will take three to four months to get back to full operation."

"What about personnel?"

"We still have one surgeon and an adequate staff to function until replacements arrive. Until then, anything serious goes to Udorn."

"Any other infrastructure damage?"

"Well, we lost several vehicles and the hazardous materials shed. Biggest loss was the hospital equipment—other than the people, of course."

"Thanks, George; sounds like you have everything in order." He turned to the other men in the room. "Impact to flight operations?"

"One crew, one aircraft."

George spoke up again. "I'll take care of that."

"Okay gentlemen, back to work." As the men rose to leave, the commander pulled Sampson aside. "John, keep an eye on Barker. If he bends just a little, I want him out of here. We need one hundred percent from these men. Ninety just won't do."

"I understand."

"They were engaged?"

"It was real. They were both head over heels."

"Maybe we'd better go ahead and ship him back."

"Maybe, but I promised Andy I'd let him handle it."

"Andy's good with the troops. I trust him."

"So do they."

"Alright, tell Andy to give it a shot; but one slip—just one—and I want him out of here."

"Right."

"And John, if he leaves, we'll take care of him. We'll make it a good assignment. It won't hurt his career."

"Right now I don't think he's much worried about his career."

"Yeah, you're right." He placed his hand on the other man's shoulder and they walked out into the operations area together.

*   *   *

Dr. Phillip Brady walked across the officer's club to the table in the far corner where the young pilot sat with his head resting on his folded arms. Across the table were several empty glasses and one that had spilled, wetting his arms and the sweat stained flight suit.

Phillip looked at Robb briefly, and then with a determined face he grabbed the pilot and hefted him from the seat. Overestimating his own strength, he managed to dump the semiconscious pilot onto the floor--much to the amusement of the other pilots in the room. Phillip pointed to two of the younger lieutenants who obediently lifted the captain and carried him across the room and out the door. Phillip followed and directed the trio to Robb's hooch. After depositing their load the two younger men left to return to the bar. Phillip remained briefly, checking the young pilot. After a few moments he left, and walked to Colonel Bennett's room.

"Colonel?"

"Hi Doc, can I help you?"

"Just wanted to let you know that Captain Barker will not be flying tomorrow. He's DNIF—sick."

"Come in Phillip. I've been worried about Robb, too. How's he doing?"

The doctor's face was etched with his own pain, but he spoke with great care. "Not well. I'm concerned too."

"He's had a rough time. Wayne, the boy, and now Kerrie. Just how much can a man take?"

"Before he breaks?"

"Before he breaks." The colonel fished in his pockets and produced a pack of cigarettes. Lighting one, he continued. "What can we do to help him?"

"To start with, take him off the flying schedule tomorrow."

"Done. Then?"

"I'm not sure, but let me try first."

"What's your plan Doc?" The colonel peered at the young doctor through the thick blue smoke that trailed toward the roof of the tiny room.

"I wish I knew, Colonel. I guess you'd say I'm just going to "wing it"."

"Will you let me know if I can help? He's been through a lot of shit. I'm not sure any of us can understand where his mind is."

"Perhaps I can try."

*   *   *

The fog of sleep and booze drifted lazily in his mind; slowly it cleared, allowing the pain of remembering. Robb rubbed his eyes. He felt terrible. His body cried out at the surfeit of alcohol that still coursed through his body. His head ached; his limbs felt like lead; and nausea crawled inside his stomach. He needed a doctor.

And one sat silently, half asleep, in the chair opposite his bed in the small room. The awareness of this fact jarred Robb to sudden wakefulness. He recoiled from the man seated across the room and peered at him with strained and unbelieving eyes. "Phillip?"

"Are you going to live?"

"What time is it?" He tried to jump from the bed but managed only to sit on the small bunk.

"Don't worry, you're not on the schedule today."

"I'm not? What do you know about the flight schedule?"

"I took care of it. You're officially DNIF. It's okay, really."

Robb fell back into the bed and covered his eyes with his forearms. "I feel like shit."

"You don't look too good either."

As the memories came crashing into his mind, a loud moan came from his throat.

"You're going to get through this, Robb."

"How the fuck would you know?"

Phillip looked at the man before him and wondered why he was there. Certainly he felt nothing but contempt for Robb. In some small corner of his being he hated the sad soul trying to recover from his drunken stupor. Phillip looked around the room; for the first time he noticed it. He could only imagine what Robb and Kerrie had shared in this very room. He wondered again why he was there, but inside he knew. He was here for her; she had loved this wretched pilot. He was here for her, not Robb. Somehow he could envision her watching him. She would be smiling; she would be proud of him; mostly, she would finally understand how much he truly loved her, even now. Slowly Phillip stood and stretched his thin body. As he turned toward the door he spoke without looking back. "You're going to make it because you're a man, but mostly you're going to make it because that's what she would expect of you. As soon as she comes to, she'll be calling for you, and you don't want to look like a drunk when she sees you. Now get your ass up and follow me. We've got to clear her trailer. Two new surgeons are on the way as we speak.

Besides, when she recovers, she'll need all her stuff." Robb lifted his arm from his eyes and watched the door close behind the doctor.

Robb called after the smaller man. "Phillip, do you really think she'll make it?" There was hope in his voice.

"Sure, she's tough. She'll make it." Phillip lied.

The two men stood before the small trailer in silence. Each had a cardboard box under one arm. Finally Phillip looked up at Robb, squinting in the bright morning sun. "I thought there might be things you'd want to keep." His voice was distant—very far away from his own ears.

"Yeah."

Together they opened the door and walked in. Unlike the warm bright day outside, the lifeless room was dark and cool. Only the sound of the air conditioner interrupted the silence of the small trailer. Phillip walked to the metal cabinet and opened it slowly. There were three shelves and four drawers facing him. He looked back at Robb who stood in the middle of the small kitchen/living room. His face was pale. "Are you going to be alright Robb? I can do this."

"I'm okay." He choked the words.

Phillip looked at the makeup and cosmetics on the first shelf. He began putting them in a plastic bag he had brought in the box. "I'm just going to pitch this."

"Right." Robb had not moved. He stood looking around at the familiar room. Finally he turned and walked into the bedroom. The bed was neatly made. Over the back of the single chair was her favorite nightgown. He knew why it was there. Instinctively he turned and rushed to the small refrigerator beneath the tiny sink. He reached inside and pulled the bottle of wine from the bottom shelf. He moaned aloud and began to weep uncontrollably. The tall pilot sat back upon the large couch and began rubbing his hand across the coarse fabric. Phillip watched him for several moments and finally walked over and placed his hand on Robb's shoulder. After an awkward silence, he spoke.

"Why don't you let me finish this. I'll keep any personal items you'd want." Robb rose, nodding, and walked back into the bedroom; he folded the nightgown carefully, then taking it and the bottle of wine, he turned for the door. Before stepping outside he stopped to look back at the small man standing in the room. He felt the need to say something, but he only stood watching Phillip's back. At first the movement was small, but as the confused pilot watched, the doctor's back shook slightly then broke into convulsions. Robb realized that he was crying, uncontrollably. Slowly he closed the door and walked back into the room.

"Phillip?" Phillip blew his nose loudly without answering, his back still turned. Robb stepped forward and placed his hand on the other man's shoulder. "You've lost a special friend, too."

"Fuck you."

"What?"

"I love her too." As he spoke, his voice broke; it was barely audible.

Robb looked at the other man incredulously. "You do?"

Phillip turned to face him slowly. "Yes, I do. I've loved her from the first time I saw her." It was almost a whisper.

"Damn." The two men looked at each other in silence for several minutes.

"She never knew." There were tears streaming down his face.

Robb stood shocked, looking at Phillip. At length he spoke. "Damn Phillip, you don't know shit about women." Robb rubbed his eyes with his hands. "She cares about you, a lot."

"She does?"

"She told me you were the finest doctor she had ever worked with. She admires you a great deal. She also said that you were one of the bravest men she knew."

The thin doctor stood silently looking at the floor in the small room. Finally he spoke, very quietly. "But she loves you."

"Yes, but she cares about you, too, Phillip--just in a different way." He lowered his eyes to the dull linoleum floor. "Damn, I miss her."

"Me too."

Robb awkwardly reached and put his arm around the thin shoulders of the doctor. Phillip was crying softly. Robb tried to speak but found his own voice hoarse and broken. He stood there patting the weeping man as Phillip babbled on. "It almost killed me when I realized she was in love with you. I knew I had no chance, but I wanted her so much. I never knew I could care about someone like I feel about her."

"I know. She really is special. It would be hard not to love her." They each dealt with their own grief for several minutes. Finally Robb spoke. "Phillip, you gonna be alright?"

"I don't know." It was a choking voice filled with pain. He reached for a handkerchief and again blew his nose loudly.

"You're going to be okay. That is what she'd want. You--in the hospital, operating. That's what she'd want."

"And you flying."

"Yeah." Robb looked back at the small bed for a long time, then at the nightie over his left arm, his mind flooding with memories. "Phillip, what are her chances? Really?" The small doctor only looked at the floor, saying nothing. A shudder passed through Robb's body as he stared at the silent man before him. Finally Phillip raised his head and watched the dark cloud that flowed over the man before him. He knew the demons that were parading in Robb's mind, but he could only guess at their intensity.

"We're going to make it, Robb. Both of us. That's what she'd want." Phillip's voice was thick and broken. "And damn it, we're going to do it for her." He paused for several moments then resumed.

"Let's get out of here; we both need breakfast. We get through today, then tomorrow, then the next day—one day at a time." He pulled Robb's shoulder gently. "She'd want it that way." The tall pilot turned slowly to the thin doctor who looked into his face. Somehow that gave Phillip strength, and that strength flowed through to his new friend. In that moment two very different men found an understanding of each other that would build a friendship that would last a lifetime.

Phillip looked at his watch suddenly. "Damn, it's 0855!" Robb looked wearily at the other man but said nothing. "Go put on your Khakis." The order sounded funny coming from Phillip. It took Robb several seconds to comprehend what he was being told.

"What time?"

"Ceremony starts at 0930."

"Ramp in front of Ops?"

"Yes."

Robb smashed his fist against the wall in the trailer, startling Phillip. "No khakis! I'm wearing my goat skin."

"Goat skin?"

"Old nickname for a flight suit—Kerrie liked it."

"Memo said Khakis."

"Fuck 'em. I'm a pilot."

"Then I'm going in my hospital greens. Fuck 'em, I'm a doctor."

"Great idea." Both men smiled suddenly. Robb walked across the small room and swept up the small doctor in his arms with a great bear hug. "You know, Phillip, you're okay."

"She didn't pick losers."

"No, she didn't."

Three minutes later the two men walked from the dark room into the bright sunlight of the early morning. It was the first day of many that they would struggle through, each bearing his own burden, each knowing that somewhere another man struggled with a similar cross.

Across the base Colonel Bennett keyed his portable radio. "Johnson, how's it going?"

"Captain Barker just left with a bottle of wine—unopened—and what looks like a nightie."

"How about the doctor?"

"He left with him, and colonel, they don't look too good, Sir."

"Thanks, Sarge. If they don't return in ten minutes, you're cleared back to the ramp."

"Roger."

The colonel sat back in his chair and threw the portable radio on his desk. "Shit!" He rubbed his temples vigorously then rose. "Teasdale!"

"Yes sir." The young sergeant rushed into the colonel's office.

"Go find Captain Barker. Tell him he's in my flight this afternoon. Tell him he's replacing Campbell. Campbell's sick. Got that?"

"Yes sir"

"Git!" In a second the young man was gone, leaving the colonel staring out the window of his office. In a moment he turned and walked to the door of the office and shouted at the junior clerk in the office. "Brown! Get me Major Campbell. I need to talk to him ASAP."

"Yes Sir." The young man rose and rushed out the door.

*   *   *

The men stood in the bright morning sun sweating. The enlisted men and staff wore khakis; the pilots wore mostly flight suits with a few in ill fitting khakis. In the middle of their loose formation stood a small flight surgeon, wearing hospital "greens." They stood silently watching the sky above them or the concrete beneath their feet as an older major spoke solemnly, barely audible. Robb stared at the stacked caskets on six small trailers—eighteen in all. He knew Phillip was staring at the same thing, both wondering if time would add yet another to the list.

They stood, some waiting to return to their work, others in respect for people they hardly knew. The formations resembled the uniforms. Those in the khakis were lined correctly in straight rows, the men and women standing "at ease." The pilots stood in loose groups, in various poses. They flew in close military formations, but "military" demeanor curiously stopped when they were on the ground. They stood like men watching a parade. It was this awkward formation that hid the tall captain's movement as he reached his left hand to support the sagging doctor whose knees were beginning to buckle slightly.

"Hang in there, Phillip. Breathe deeply."

"Right." The voice, like the man was small and weak. Phillip had spent 28 hours in surgery after the accident. Additional surgeons had arrived only this morning.

The chaplain said his final prayer; a colonel spoke briefly; somewhere to the right of the formation a sergeant shouted "Dismissed!" as only a sergeant can; and men began to walk away—back to their life, back to the war. Robb stood there long after the others had left, staring at the caskets on the trailers. A hand settled on his shoulder. He did not turn; he knew the owner. It was Colonel Bennett. Together they watched the activities across the ramp. A crew of men stood beside the caskets, waiting to load them on a C-130 aircraft. But first the severely injured would be flown out on another aircraft, already taxiing toward the runway.

The three officers watched silently until the plane gently climbed into the sky and disappeared on the eastern horizon. It was Robb who finally spoke. "I've got a flight at ten hundred hours. I've got to go."

"I thought you were off the schedule today."

"No, I'm flying." He turned and literally ran toward the Ops building.

The colonel watched briefly then followed Robb toward Operations. He caught up to him just as the young captain was entering the building. "Robb." The younger man turned. "Do you need a few days R&R?"

"R&R? Me?" He frowned. "No, Sir. I need to fly. I wish I could fly three sorties today and six tomorrow."

"I understand."

"Am I in your flight today?"

"Yes."

"Are you concerned about me?" He paused, looking at the older man, both a bit embarrassed.

"No, I'm not. But I am responsible for you, your navigator, and that aircraft, and I don't like to take risks."

"That's fair. But Colonel, you don't need to worry, I'm ready."

"Of course you are. Now get your ass in there and figure how to provide secure employment for North Vietnamese bridge engineers." The C-130's engines caused them both to turn suddenly. The jovial tone vanished rapidly. Both watched as the final loading was completed. The large cargo door closed slowly. They turned and walked into the Ops building as the large camouflaged plane taxied toward the runway; neither man saw the giant aircraft accelerate down the 6,000 feet of concrete. Neither saw the large wings soar through the hot morning air and lift the heavy burden. If only human burdens could be lifted as easily. At 1005, Tomcat 2 lifted off that same runway, and as the fighter's powerful engines pushed the smaller wings though the morning air, they lifted the plane and, for a few hours, the pain that weighed upon the young pilot's heart and mind. And below, in a makeshift hospital in one of the hangers, another man stopped to listen to the roar of the planes overhead. He was preparing for a simple operation. Phillip looked at his own thin hands and fingers. For an hour they would be his wings. They would perform as his mind directed, and he would have another patient's face tomorrow morning to add to the long list in his mind. But occasionally he would pause and look up at the masked face in the operating room opposite his own. It was the wrong face, the wrong eyes. How she had marveled at his skill. It had given him such joy to see the excitement on her face as he performed his magic.

"Doctor?"

"Yes?"

"We're ready."

"Oh yes, I'll be right there." He pulled on his mask. "Another day at the office." He had heard her say it so many times. Yes, another day at the office, he thought and turned to walk into the makeshift operating room.

*   *   *

High above the dark jungle below, the planes headed northeast through the growing white columns of clouds. Robb was totally absorbed with flying and the freedom of concentration. He knew he was being watched, but by a friendly professor. He also knew he would pass this test. For him, it was not a question of could he fly. No, it was much simpler. He *must* fly. It was the only way to maintain the reality he was struggling to hold onto. Robb was no threat to himself or his navigator while commanding this powerful plane. Without it he might be. Kerrie had never been a part of this world for him. She was no specter in his mind during flight, but how he dreaded the nights without her. She lived in his memories in the hooch, walking across the orphanage yard, dancing across the porch, but she was not here at 20,000 feet. She did not cheer the attacking planes or scream encouragement for the crippled birds.

She never heard the curses for the gunners, the grunting words at 6 g's, or the excited alerts of the navigators when the Migs challenged the invaders. No, she lived mostly in his nights, a beautiful memory in the dark. But at 20,000 feet he was safe—and in control—until tonight.

"Tomcat lead, I've got the target at 2 o'clock."

"Roger, Two has a fix."

"Three."

"Four."

"Well, gentlemen, let's earn our pay."

Near Skovorodino, The Soviet Union

The bored soldiers jumped to their feet as their captain ran into the warehouse. He was obviously excited. "Quick, load everything on the train. We leave tonight."

Kochkin walked quickly toward Sergei, concern on his face. "What's going on?"

"A government inspection team is due to check this plant tomorrow morning."

"Where did you get that information?"

"From me." The colonel walked into the light and all of the men immediately stood to attention. "Now, get ready, we leave tonight."

The old sergeant pulled Sergei aside and spoke quietly. "Where are we going, Captain? I need time to plan."

"There is no time. We're going to have to plan on the way. I already have another warehouse near the port. If we can just get there undetected."

"But we can't get there in one night."

"I know, but we have to leave now. We have no choice. We'll think of something on the way." Sergei placed a large map on the small table and bent over it with his friend and the colonel. In the dim light they studied it carefully. "What do you think? About 2000 kilometers?"

Finally the colonel straightened and looked at the other two men. "That is going to require at least three nights travel. We can't start until darkness has settled and people are inside for the day. There are just too many people living around here. With the current rail schedule, we can only get eight or nine hours of travel time per night."

"I'm especially worried about the other end—near the port. There are far more risks there." Sergei chewed his pencil as he talked.

Kochkin spoke carefully; he was not yet comfortable around a full colonel. "You're right. We must leave as soon as the sun starts to set. We'll have the missiles covered with tarps. Hopefully they don't blow off on the journey."

"Be sure we leave no evidence of having been here in this warehouse. The inspectors will be here tomorrow."

Kochkin watched the colonel carefully. "Sir, is it possible that we have been discovered? Could that be the reason for the inspection?"

"My sources say this is routine. I trust my sources."

"Couldn't the inspection be cancelled?" Sergei was looking at the colonel.

"Not without risking a lot of questions." The senior officer looked directly at the sergeant as he spoke; he knew it important to make him feel at ease. It would be a long journey, and they had to work as a team.

"Then we had best get busy." Sergei began to fold the map.

"Of course we will succeed. That is why I selected you." The colonel smiled. "And that is why you selected Sergeant Kochkin. Of course we will succeed my old friend. Have we ever failed yet?"

"Not yet."

"Then today is not a good day to start, is it? Call the men together and let's get this underway." The captain nodded, but he was still worried about the trip. Where would they spend the daylight hours? How could they find warehouses along the way? So many problems.

The sun had just disappeared behind the snow-covered trees when the door to the old gray warehouse slid open with a groan and the train backed out into the winter evening. It would be about fifteen kilometers back to the main rail line. Once the crew switched the points the train could back onto the main track and then proceed forward toward Vladivistok. A light snow was falling and was further aggravated by a wind that blew from the north, obscuring the tracks about twenty meters beyond them. Kochkin drove the train slowly due to the poor visibility. Sergei stood in the blowing snow on the front of the engine, watching for obstructions on the track, while the colonel stayed in the engine cab where it was warm. Ruchinsky cursed the weather, and he cursed the inspectors who had disrupted his plans. He was a military man with military training. He knew the value of good planning, and he realized they had not had sufficient time to plan as well as he would have wanted. He was taking risks, hoping for success. He didn't like risks, and he didn't like hope; he liked certainty. Three of the soldiers stood on the flat car behind them, peering into the snow. Sergei shouted at them above the swirling wind. "Watch for the switch. If we miss that we will be diverted onto the parallel siding. That could cost us precious time. It has a hand signal beside it, about three meters tall."

"Captain, is there a light?"

"Out here we are lucky to have a signal at all. There is no light. Watch for the signal. It is on the right side of the track." The train moved slowly toward the junction with the main rail as the storm grew in intensity. Sergei looked at his watch and cursed. Precious time was being lost. At least the storm should clear before morning.

If they could just get out of the local area, he had a chance to find a new site by daybreak.

"Captain, there! The signal is there!" Sergei turned and shouted to the crew in the engine. At once the train started to stop, the wheels whining on the old track.

"Quickly, switch the points." Two men climbed from the train and scrambled down the track in search of the rail switch. Minutes passed and suddenly raised voices were heard in the darkness. His troops were arguing with someone further down the tracks. Sergei jumped from the train and signaled for two of the young soldiers to follow. Dmitriy reached inside his coat, checked his pistol, and followed his men. Shielding his eyes from the blowing snow, he approached to find Sergei arguing with two men dressed in strange uniforms. "What in hell is going on here?"

"That is what we want to know. Who are you and why are you moving this switch."

"It is government business. I'm in charge of this operation, and I don't answer to civilians. Now get out of our way, or I'll have you shot."

The man studied the older officer's uniform carefully. "Listen colonel. We also work for the government. We are rail inspectors for this district. We have control over these switches, and they are not to be moved without our approval. Even the military knows that. You should have gotten approval before you reached this sector. We will have to report this tomorrow. What is your name?"

Dmitriy pulled his pistol from his coat and shot the man in the face. Turning quickly, he fired twice and felled the second as well. The startled young soldiers looked at him in disbelief. One of them was shaking visibly. "Alright, load these government workers on the flatcar. What are you waiting for, throw that switch." The gunshots had brought the entire group of soldiers to the rear of the train. Sergeant Kochkin came running up a few minutes later.

"What happened back here? I heard shots." He looked at the two bodies being loaded onto the flatcar. "Oh shit."

"No problem sergeant. We'll dump them along the way—a hundred kilometers from here in some desolate area; they'll be covered in two feet of snow before morning."

Sergei looked at his colonel with admiration; this is how officers *should* act; this earns respect. "They were idiots, and they were delaying our mission. Now get back to the engine, and let's get moving." As the men scattered to throw the switch, Sergei followed. "Be sure to place it back in the correct position after we are passed. I don't want any evidence we were here. Understand? And throw some snow on that blood."

"Yes captain."

The old switch was more difficult to move than expected. The cold and years of disuse had combined to frustrate the efforts of the two men sent to accomplish the task. Finally Sergei and two others came to the rescue, and brute force ruled the day. As the train finally rolled off toward the east, the cold colonel stood in the warm engine and looked at his watch. "Damn! We've lost almost forty-five minutes. Can you make this old engine go any faster?"

"I'm not worried about the engine, colonel. I'm worried about our cargo and these rails. I would advise against pushing this too much."

"I understand, just hurry as much as you can."

Through the night the train rolled ever eastward toward the sea. As the tracks began to turn toward the south and Vladivistok, Dmitriy studied his maps. "I'm afraid we're going to have to pull onto a siding during the day. There are several trains on this track that we will have to avoid; night is our only safe time to head east. At least we have several sidings along the way that are relatively deserted. There's one forty kilometers outside of Zavitinsk and another at Vyazemskiy. We've got about five hundred kilometers remaining to Zavitinsk, and if we can make it to Vyazemskiy on the second night, that will put us in a good position to reach the port on the third night."

Sergei studied the colonel's face. "When we get to Vladivistok, we will pull into an old meat packing plant on the west side of the city. It can't be any colder than this godforsaken place. If we get off the main track each night before daybreak and secure the tarps, we may be able to keep this undercover. Other trains will pass us, but a small freight train with freight under tarps shouldn't raise any concerns."

"Yes, but hide the troops, or dress a couple in the clothes of the rail inspectors. That might be useful. Have them checking the train as the others pass." Sergei's face brightened at the idea.

"Good plan." He motioned to one of the young troops who was huddled in the cab for warmth. "Tell the men to strip those bodies and then throw them off at the next bridge. Try to salvage the clothes, and get rid of the blood. Civilians don't bleed in our government. That job is left for soldiers like us."

"Yes sir." Reluctantly the soldier rose and climbed from the cab.

The train proceeded steadily through the night as the men on board planned their strategy, cursing and peering into the blowing snow before them. As they pulled onto the siding near Zavitinsk, the tired soldiers looked up to see stars shining through the cold winter evening. The storm had passed. As they pulled the tarpaulins tight around their cargo, the morning sun broke over the snow-covered trees to shed some warmth to the frozen landscape.

CHAPTER EIGHT

Nubat Royal Thai Air Force Base

His hand moved slowly to her face, his eyes glued to hers. Patiently it moved across her cheek and down her neck. He sensed her inhale deeply, then hold her breath as his fingers moved softly over her chest to her breasts.

The brown eyes were so large. They literally caressed him as she stood before him. His left hand reached and brushed the soft brown hair from her right temple as she continued to look straight through his eyes and into his soul. Robb felt the blood pounding in his temples. Small beads of sweat formed on his brow. His entire body tensed with desire. He caressed her nipples; she gasped slightly. Perspiration ran down his right side and tickled his flesh as he continued to stare into her eyes—the large brown eyes. He was aware of his own breath, of hers; he felt his own desire; he felt hers as well. Slowly he caressed her body as the two moved closer together.

Finally he could stand the closeness, her warmth, both of their desire no longer. He reached for her to engulf her, to grasp what he wanted, what he so desperately needed. And she was gone. He awoke with a cry. "Kerrie!" But she was not there. A voice shook him into consciousness.

"Robb? Robb? Are you okay?"

"Huh?" He sat upright in his small bunk and looked bleakly into Joe's sleepy face. "What?"

"You okay, buddy? You were dreaming."

"Yeah, Yeah, I'm alright." Robb stumbled from the bed and began walking about the small dark room. He was rubbing his eyes viciously. A month had passed and Kerrie remained in the coma. There had been no progress; hope was fading.

"Can I get you something?"

"No. No, thanks." He fumbled in his locker and began dressing. "Think I'll take a walk."

"Want company?"

"No. It's after one o'clock. Go back to sleep." The tall captain walked to the door and stood for a long time; finally he walked back to the locker and felt around in the dark. He found the pistol he was searching for and quickly dropped it into his pocket then left the room. The heat of the night and the tension in his own body combined to drench his clothing in sweat. He walked rapidly, a man with purpose, for twenty-five minutes. He passed the planes without looking at them. The men working on the aircraft didn't stop their labor to observe the tall man walking by with a great sadness on his face. The bomb crews, too, passed quickly, tending to their tasks. They never looked back into the red, vacant eyes. They were too busy. No one noticed as he passed the revetments and walked off into the darkness toward the runways.

Robb walked over a hundred yards beyond the edge of the long concrete runway before sitting in the tall damp grass. Immediately south of his position about 150 yards away were the parking revetments where the F-4s rested between their flights. In this area the crews refueled the aircraft, performed minor maintenance, and loaded them for their next mission. The revetments were large steel structures shaped like horseshoes. They were fifteen feet tall and the metal shells were filled with concrete. The revetments were lined in rows to allow easy access, but still provide security for the planes. A lucky rocket might get one aircraft, but no more than one. It was dark, but the full moon cast vague shadows in the night as he stared up at the stars above him. In the distance, however, the bright lights surrounding the revetments cast an eerie glow on the busy ramp, in stark contrast to the dimly lit jungle behind. He was amazed at the sounds that echoed from the deep forest surrounding the base; the cacophony was so different from the mechanized sounds of the flight line. Behind him birds, insects, and animals called and screeched in the darkness. Before him were the sounds of engines and equipment and the occasional human voice. He could not hear what they were saying, but he could recognize the emotions—anger, laughter, urgency. A loud scream echoed through the jungle behind him; was it sex or attack, life or death? The familiar smells of the base were also gone. Robb had never thought about the smells of the jungle until his experience behind enemy lines. Somehow the smells were different here. How could that be? He dug a small amount of the moist soil and held it to his nose. Would this be different than Colorado? Oh yes. It was very different. The smell was pungent and strong, filled with life and death of organisms he did not recognize and could not see. The dry rocks of Colorado were certainly different. Overhead, jets roared into the air while others circled, waiting their turn to land. He watched two of the fighters turn final and land, one 200 yards behind the other. How he loved the planes. The sheer thrill of flying still excited him. But now everything was different; she was gone. He had touched her body, and the blood had covered his fingertips. He had screamed and called to her, but there was no response. How could he ever forget that moment, how could joy ever enter his life again? More importantly, how could he live with this pain? What had life to offer but more total despair?

He sat reflecting on the lives he had touched. How many were mere memories now? How many of his friends were gone, lost forever in an explosion of light and fire? How many others unknown were also gone, dying atop a gun site somewhere in the jungle? Tears welled into his eyes. "Why, God? Kerrie is so beautiful, so loving. She didn't deserve this." It was a cry from the center of his being. But, perhaps, neither did those small, frightened men deserve their fate who tracked his aircraft as it soared over their homeland. Who really deserved to die so young? And who deserved to live? Who wanted to live in this pain? He felt the coolness of the .38 revolver in his pocket. It was the same gun that had killed before, on that hillside in North Vietnam. Who had they been? What had been their dreams? Had they loved someone? Who was weeping for them? And what had happened to the kid with the shoulder wound? Had he lived? Did he really care? Did anything really matter in this madness?

He ran his fingers across the barrel of the gun, admiring the craftsmanship. What did he want, what had life to offer? It became, in the final analysis, a simple equation. Did the value of his life equal the pain? What had life to offer him now? What was the pain he must bear, and how long could he stand it?

Visions of a beautiful, lovely face danced into his mind. She was smiling; she was so happy to share the moment of love. He remembered her face as they had reached the climax of their lovemaking, the summit of love. Her eyes were so large; the expression was so different than he had expected. It was one of utter surprise. He smiled involuntarily. She had seemed shocked at the total euphoric loss of control. Afterwards there was always the smile, the joy. But not at that moment. It had been her gasp that he would remember, the surprise. The unexpected joy that neither could explain--that he would never forget. That moment when both were truly one. And her face--that beautiful face--full of surprise, mixed with joy. Had he ever seen that much joy before? Yes, once.

The first time she stood before him naked. Yes, that was it. His own gasp, his own shock, joy.

The darkness in his mind returned to the smell of burning jet fuel, the sight of an unconscious body, the same body that afforded him such joy. That same body that gasped, wide eyed, at the moment of love's greatest sharing. How could his mind ever forget those moments? How could he ever conquer this world of darkness and insanity?

The gun in his hand was comfortable. It rested there, a weight that was silky to his touch--like her body had been. The mind worked its particular magic, and the darkness of the evening once again became the darkness of the tiny room where they had lain, curled together on the small bunk after an evening of lovemaking. How soft she had been. How he had loved her. While she slept he had lain there, afraid to move, memorizing, memorizing every moment, every touch, every hair falling across her shoulders. How many times had he stared at her sleeping figure--the curve of her hips, the softness of her breasts? How many times had he counted her eyelashes as she slept? Was there a memory that was not stored, forever, in this mind? How could he live with these now? How could a man walk through the daily life of the living with such a burden on his very soul?

He felt the weight in his hand and looked at it carefully. Did it have a serial number? Would that be listed on a report somewhere? The same gun taken into combat used to take his own life?

Robb looked into the dark clouds as another F-4 roared overhead. The sound jarred him somewhat. "Damned fool--too low!" He watched the aircraft flare and touch down in the evening darkness. Two large puffs of smoke arose and slowly dissipated over the gray runway as the large plane disappeared into the darkness. "How beautiful." he thought, "a piece of metal, but beautiful, like Kerrie. A thing of touch, of feel. A machine of passion. It can bring such joy-

-and inflict such pain." Two more aircraft passed overhead. His right arm was relaxed by his side, the pistol limp in his grip. He watched the big birds soar and land--coming home to roost. Home? Would, could, that ever have meaning again? The fourth aircraft, too close to number three, accelerated into a "closed" pattern. He watched, evaluating each approach. And what about his own approaches? Was there an ending to this pain? Could he bear up? What had he endured already? Wayne. Chusak. Now Kerrie. "Why, God?" he screamed into the night. "How could you allow this? Why? Why?"

The gun lay loose in his hand as he examined it again. It would be so simple, so easy. Peace. It would be peace--forever. He would never awake and realize all over again the pain that awaited him each morning.

A hand touched his arm. Robb jerked to his right. No one was there. To his left--no one was there. In panic he rolled to his right, tumbling to a crouched position, the gun on guard, ready. No one. Slowly, in fear and panic, he lowered the gun. He felt the blood throbbing through his temples. Every nerve sent messages to his brain. His eyes reached through the evening haze. He felt her presence as real as the mist on his face. "Kerrie?"

He lurched to his left, his fingers outstretched into the darkness and fell face down in the damp grass. Slowly he crawled to his knees and began to sob. The tears flowed from his eyes, his choked cries muffled in the night. Finally he rolled to his back and lay looking at the stars overhead; he was drained of strength, drained of emotion. He lay there, empty, staring at the night sky. Flight after flight circled overhead and landed on the runway that stretched away from him to the West. He lay back in the soft grass, staring up at the profusion of stars overhead. For a long time he watched them, until finally they blurred in his vision as his eyes slowly closed in restless sleep.

The subtle brain worked its own magic and suddenly he was riding along a narrow shady road on a bicycle. Kerrie rode beside him and laughed. Then they were stretched beside a small stream watching the tumbling water spill and splash over large gray rocks, his head in her lap. She was smiling the contented smile that he had come to love so much. Then they were in the trailer as he reached and felt her hair, soft upon her shoulders, as it reflected the light of their favorite candle; he touched the softness of her body next to his as they hid in the small room. His fingers reached and caressed the blushing cheeks and moved slowly down the curve of her neck to the warmth of her breasts. Slowly they made their way along the gentle slope of her side and along the soft flesh of her stomach. Silently the lips followed the fingers until they had crossed her entire body and memorized the warmth of every curve, every softness, each downy hair. Then, as always, the heat of their passion consumed them, and the soft milky flesh became distorted and finally crumbled away into ashes. Robb forced his eyes open to prevent the next picture from forming in his mind. It was one he had lived with constantly since the afternoon of the crash, and though it was becoming less distinct with the passing days, it still brought a deep moan of anguish from the pit of his stomach when it crept into his mind to torment him. It was a reality he could not bear, one he was struggling with when a movement to his left startled him, a quiet whisper and the movement of something through the tall grass. It was a human voice, but it wasn't speaking English. Robb rolled quickly to his stomach and raised his head carefully. One, two, three men--sneaking in the darkness through the grass toward the revetments. Another movement, this time fifteen yards off to his right. Then another farther to the right. Sappers! They were headed toward the busy revetments. Robb could see the outline of the guard standing atop the nearest revetment, but the guard was looking into the revetments, not toward the threat that crept toward him and his charge.

Robb reached into his pocket and withdrew the pistol. If there were enemy soldiers on his right and his left, they may well be heading toward his own position as well. He reached into the damp grass and found the wet soil below. Quickly digging a handful, he smeared it across his face, the back of his hands, and through his blond hair. The moon was bright; he didn't want to be seen. Crawling slowly in the direction of the revetment, Robb watched carefully for more soldiers, especially behind him. In all, he had noted three on his left and four or more on his right. There were probably more that he had not seen; he was sure of that. Why doesn't that guard look this way, he thought. Could he even see them? Their only weapon is stealth. If they can get close enough to kill a few airmen and toss a few bundles of explosives over the revetment walls, they might get four or five of the aircraft. If they are lucky, some of them might be refueling or reloading, and that might get four or five more.

The guard looked northeast briefly then turned back to watch the activity within the revetment. The enemy moved in quick darts through the grass. They were crawling and crouching as they moved in the shadows of the moon. The soldiers on Robb's left gathered a mere 50 yards from the revetments, huddled together behind a small group of bushes that grew in the grassy field. They were pointing at the guard on the revetment and other guards further down the ramp. The group on the right were still in the heavy grass, crawling further to the right, spreading out. Their plan was becoming obvious. Each had a small pack on his back--explosives. Of the seven men that Robb had seen, it appeared that only three had weapons--AK47s. The remainder were there for the sole purpose of destroying the aircraft. Weapons would only slow them as they entered and exited the target area.

Robb crawled more quickly now. The enemy were totally absorbed with the revetments. None of them was expecting someone from behind. He was within 20 yards of the enemy soldiers when one of them with a gun stood and aimed at the guard standing on the top of the revetment. Robb could wait no longer. He was forced into a decision he would have rather avoided. He pointed the revolver and fired twice. The first bullet struck the sapper in his neck, pitching him forward. The second bullet hit the pack on his back, exploding the contents. The three enemy never realized that they had been followed; they died together immediately in a loud and violent explosion.

A siren sounded and voices began shouting and cursing on the other side of the revetments. Immediately, the other enemy soldiers rose and began running toward their targets, shouting and firing at the guards. Robb stood, amazed at the attack taking place before him. Where had these men come from? How long had he sat in the field? He had never seen them until they were already past his position in the grass. He watched, stunned at the sound of shots, explosions, and the cries of angry and dying men. The bullet that whizzed past his right ear should have shaken him into action, but it did not. He simply turned and looked at the man who had fired at him. The soldier was fifty yards away and clearly visible in the flashing searchlights that combed the area. Each was seen, then lost in darkness, then the lights flashed across them again. The man fired in his direction again; Robb neither heard nor felt anything. Slowly, deliberately, he raised his pistol and aimed as the spotlights crossed the dark field and illuminated the enemy soldier. He fired once, and the man fell backward into the shadows. Robb began to walk toward the fallen soldier. What else should he do? He wished silently that the man had been a better marksman. He wanted out of this life, out of the pain. Perhaps the soldier lying in the grass was the fortunate one. It was then that he heard the F-4's. Something deep inside his mind analyzed the situation and relayed the danger to his consciousness. The F-4's were attacking the enemy, and he was in their midst. His legs began to move. Suddenly he was running toward the jungle. The first aircraft came in low, just above the trees. The growl was one he recognized—a Gattling gun. Six thousand rounds of 20mm ammunition per minute ripped through the evening sky. Everything in the path of that plane would be chewed to bits.

The decision was not conscious; perhaps survival is instinct. Either way, the young captain sprinted into the jungle as he heard the second plane turning off to his right. Robb saw a large hole ten yards away just as the F-4 was bearing down on the enemy positions. With a sudden burst of energy, he dived into the pit as the F-4 roared overhead. It was about four feet deep and wider than he had anticipated. He rolled, spitting dirt, to see two enemy soldiers standing before him, their hands up in surrender. Robb looked at his hand; his pistol was pointed in their direction. They were boys. He guessed them to be 10 or 12 at most. Both were wide-eyed and shaking with fear. Robb almost laughed. The entire horizon lit up suddenly with a giant fireball that splashed southwest for several hundred yards. Napalm! The two boys cried out in terror as they witnessed the destruction behind them. Were they soldiers, or were they simply boys watching the war against the invading Americans? What did they understand about international politics? For that matter, what did he know about that himself?

They shifted their eyes from the burning inferno to Robb then back. Was their father, brother, or uncle out there? God help them if they were. Robb lowered his pistol and spoke to the boys. "Go home!" They stood, looking at each other then the tall American seated in their pit. Neither moved. Robb shouted at the two. "Run, dammit! Go home!" There was confusion on their faces. Robb used his left hand to motion someone running. He then pointed at the boys, then the jungle. "Now go!" They looked at him briefly, then clambered out of the hole. In a moment both were running into the jungle. "Live, grow up, have children!" He shouted after them as he, too, climbed from the ditch. "Stay away from this fucking war!"

The sounds of gunfire and men shouting persisted, but they were more random now. The napalm attack and the Gattling guns had cleared the attackers rapidly and decisively. Robb began running toward the base. Two men passed him, racing in the opposite direction. He watched them over his shoulder; neither stopped to give him a second look. They were running as fast as they could. Robb then noticed that neither had a weapon. He turned and continued to run toward the base, watching for the American and Thai guards lest they mistake him for an enemy. Almost immediately, fire from the revetments began to rip through the grass around him. He immediately hit the ground and started crawling to his left as fast as possible. Machine gun fire rattled through the night. The distinctive sound of an AK47 answered. Two hand grenades exploded. A loud explosion ripped through the night--but it was outside the revetments. More fire: rifles, machine guns, another grenade. Then silence. Robb continued to crawl briefly, then stood to survey the situation. The fire from the napalm was still burning to his left. He started running in that direction since most of the gunfire from the base was directed to his right. He ran quickly but stooped over to minimize his exposure to either of the opposite groups firing into the night. He could hear the fighting to his rear, but only the blazing fire roared ahead of him. He skirted the fire on the opposite side from the base. This would prevent his silhouette from framing him against the bright light of the burning hell. Robb could feel the heat on his face, but it was the sound of the fire that surprised him. He had not expected such a roar from the flames. On he ran, stumbling once, then running again. Finally he stopped to gulp fresh air into his burning lungs. He had run approximately two hundred yards with his boots and fatigues, and his heart was pounding with the adrenaline rush of fear and excitement. As he stooped, gasping, he heard another gasp, similar to his own behind him. He turned rapidly, pointing his pistol at the sound. Down the barrel of his pistol he focused on the inert figure of a man—or what remained of a man after being caught in a napalm attack. The smell of the burned flesh and the blackened figure took Robb immediately to the scene beside the hospital as he had sorted through the bodies from the crash. He struggled with his mind to focus on the soldier and the reality before him. He blinked and then looked again down the barrel. It was shaking wildly. Robb slowly stood, the pistol at his side, hanging limply in his hand. He walked slowly to the wheezing figure lying on the ground. The man appeared to be pointing to something beside him. Robb looked beyond the figure and saw what remained of an AK-47. A loud moan issued from the dying man's throat as Robb determined the message the man was trying to convey. The pilot reached for the weapon beside the burned soldier and dropped it immediately. It was hot and burned his hand. The man wheezed loudly and cried out in pain, pointing again at the weapon. Robb raised his own pistol and aimed it at the man's head. The figure relaxed, and the eyes looked at Robb; they were pleading. Slowly the man nodded, yes.

Robb's eyes filled with tears as the man waited for the bullet to end his pain. "May God forgive us both." He tried to aim the pistol with a shaking hand, but he could not steady the weapon. The man moaned again; Robb placed his left hand over his right to help control the shaking .38. As he focused on the sights of the pistol, he became aware for the first time that night that he wanted to live. He would bear the pain, but he wanted to live. Robb wiped the tears from his own eyes and fired once. The figure before him jerked slightly then ceased to move. Robb turned and walked slowly away, still silhouetted by the angry flames behind him. The soldier's pain was over; he knew his would last a lifetime.

Spotlights raked the area; an armored vehicle plowed through the grass in his direction. A jeep followed with a 30-caliber machine gun mounted in its rear. The airman manning the gun was swinging it in all directions as the small convoy proceeded toward him. He looked nervous and ready to shoot. Robb crawled into a small ditch and began shouting. "Help! Over here! Help!" The guns and the lights swung in his direction. "I'm American! Don't shoot!"

"Get up; and keep your hands above your head!" Robb shoved the pistol in his pocket and stood slowly, hands above his head. "Shit, Captain, what are you doing out here?"

"Protecting your ass." He walked toward the jeep. The men watched him carefully as he approached. When they were sure he was okay, they swung their weapons away.

"Were you the one that fired that first shot?"

"Right."

"Let me shake your hand, Captain. You saved some lives and maybe some airplanes tonight." He paused as Robb crawled into the back of the jeep. "Captain, what the hell were you doing out here?"

"Taking a walk."

"I'm glad you brought your weapon."

Robb pulled it from his pocket and looked at it. It was empty. "Yeah, me too."

"Can we drop you off somewhere?"

"Yes, the club. I need a drink."

"No sweat, we'll buy the first one."

The exhausted man sat awkwardly in the back of the bouncing jeep. The smell of the thick growth surrounded him. He was suddenly aware of life--the sound of the jungle, the lights of the base, the full moon overhead, the small cloud that crept across the sky. Slowly he placed the gun into his belt and looked again into the night. Lights danced across the sky--stars, silent sentinels watching the red and white flashes of the landing planes, tired men returning from the war. A few hours of peace before the horrors of war resumed.

The touch again, caressing his cheek. He felt her presence; it was as real as the evenings he had held her. Her presence surrounded him. "Kerrie?" he murmured. Nothing but the sound of another aircraft overhead, the roar of powerful engines responding to the touch of a man, and he felt his very soul responding to a touch, soft, and beautiful--like the soft Thai evening. As the Jeep bounced along through the darkness he felt it, like a blanket covering his body, the rush of cool breeze across his face, the peace.

*   *   *

The next day after the attack on the base, Robb rose early and walked to the O'club. He ordered three scrambled eggs, a bacon, lettuce, and tomato sandwich, a plate of grits, and lots of coffee. When he had finished, he walked into the bright Thai morning a renewed man, but a different one. One of the majestic qualities of humans that separates them from other forms of life is their amazing resiliency. The injured and bleeding body repairs itself and covers its old wounds with new tissues. It is much the same with the heart and mind; they, too, repair in time, but they, too, are left scarred. As the mark of an old wound is forever a reminder of painful moments in the past, so also, scars in the heart revive old pain when stirred. But time erases much while the body paces through the hallways of time, waiting for the memories to fade. The nights of crying out in his sleep were over; he had found a new way to handle his pain. Months had passed with no improvement; he was finally accepting the fact that Kerrie was lost. He walked a little more slowly; he talked hardly at all; he never stopped for a beer after flying; and he devoted himself exclusively to his work. He attacked every possible job with a vigor that bordered on anger. When he finished all that he was assigned, he did the work assigned his friends, and when that was finished—often for the third time—he searched out additional duties on his own. He could always be found at the squadron working on some obscure map, or plotting courses, or rebuilding the squadron lounge from the bottom up. He became an expert at scrounging materials from nonexistent suppliers and in general took over the entire squadron's unwanted chores. It was even rumored that once he had been found helping the houseboy sweep the building.

These activities were met with mixed reactions from the other members of the squadron. Only a small handful knew the reasons for the outburst of energy that sent Robb crawling exhausted into his bunk after each long and weary day. In their silence those few carried each load he carried, drew each map, wrote the same reports, and flew the same missions. And they, too, crawled exhausted into their bunks each evening.

As he raged through his work and plodded through the sting of memory, his mind slowly began to numb with the hurt. There were always, however, moments of unprotected weakness when a memory could reach a sharp finger of pain to irritate the sensitive wound. Then as the anguish welled up he dashed his body again into oblivious work, work that had no beauty and often no purpose. There was no satisfaction in the effort, save the effort itself. Man's ability to reason and communicate enables him to lie and deceive. This talent has been so perfected that he has even learned to deceive himself. The paradox doesn't end there; man has applied his vast intellect to the process and refined it further to benefit himself. Therefore when a man deceives himself it is generally for his own welfare, the practical infant of the conspiracy between the intellect and the subconscious. For Robb Barker, they were working overtime, to protect him from himself.

*   *   *

Dear Robb,

I know you are in love, and I'm sure we aren't the most important thing you have to think about, but your Dad and I haven't heard from you in months. Drop us a note now and then—you know how your Dad worries.

I am so happy you found Kerrie. She sounds like such a fine young woman. If my son loves her, she must be special, indeed. I can't wait to meet her.

Love you.
Mom

Dear Son,

Your mom and I haven't heard from you in a long time. I guess you must be really busy. Just wanted to say hello and let you know we're thinking of you.

Be careful son. We all love you, and we wouldn't trade you for all of Southeast Asia.

Dad

*   *   *

Robb stood in the dark revetment and faced the yellow ladder. The large fighter plane stood silently waiting, waiting for the touch of the pilot. Without him, it was merely a large metal structure designed by the sheer intellect of American engineers.

Robb looked at the plane before him. To him it was so much more than just an accumulation of metal and technology. It was pure beauty, a creation of wonder. The thrill of flying was still so alive in his breast. Yet the loss of so much he held dear left him a weaker man. He reflected momentarily on all that had been dear in his life. The years of training, the sheer joy of hurdling through the clouds, unfettered. Then the other side of the ledger began to grow as death entered his life and touched those he loved.

His hand reached out and grasped the yellow ladder. Six steps to climb, six steps to the cockpit, a place he knew, a place he fit, a place he belonged. He knew he could climb that ladder again; he certainly had the strength in his limbs to do that. The question was not physical strength; the question was whether he had the mental and emotional strength he needed.

The crewchief passed on his rounds of checking the aircraft. "She's ready, Sir."

"Thanks. Nice work Jack. I'll take good care of her tonight." Both men looked up into the sky as a flight of four pitched out in perfect order. Lead, two, three, four--six to eight g's each. Pros, he thought, just like me. He swung his body onto the ladder and started up; as he climbed he heard a voice; it was Wayne's. "Can you believe they pay us for this?"

"No." he said without thinking. "We are the luckiest men in the world." With great effort he stepped from the ladder and slid into the cockpit.

The flight of four F-4s taxied to the end of the runway. Inside the fighters the pilots sat forward, looking at the entire world from their positions on the nose of the powerful aircraft. Robb thought about the power in his hands, the left holding the throttles to the two powerful General Electric J79-GE-15A engines. His right hand gently stroked the control stick that extended from the floor between his legs. He grasped the handgrip with three fingers and his thumb. Together these hands control a mach 2 fighter. But it is the mind that tells them what to do. I must maintain my concentration.

The four aircraft moved into position on the end of the runway and began their run-up checks. "Lead."

"Two."

"Three."

"Four."

"Tower, Wildcat flight requests clearance for takeoff."

"Cleared Wildcat. Good hunting."

"Roger." One by one the aircraft lurched off into the damp jungle air. Robb watched the lead aircraft begin his roll. Five seconds later his left hand thrust the two throttles forward, then beyond the indent into afterburner. Immediately the roar of the engines jerked the plane forward. Robb felt his body thrust back into the seat. In seconds the plane, fully loaded, sprang from the runway into the afternoon sky. He felt, once again, the singular thrill of flying this powerful bird.

Underneath his mask, a grin broke carefully across his lips and spread throughout his soul. He was alive; he was flying; he would and could find some measure of joy again. It was tenuous, to be sure, but the joy was there. The thrill was still intact.

"Wildcat lead level at 25 thousand."

"Two, Roger, closing on your left." The professionalism in his voice hid the excitement in his heart. There were shadows to avoid; there were memories and demons to fight, but Robb Barker knew for the first time in weeks that he would survive those demons and those memories which would someday be bearable to recall. He pushed the throttles expertly with his left hand while his right guided his plane to a precise rejoin on the lead aircraft. It was perfection. Within seconds his aircraft was closed to mere feet from the lead's left wing. Lt. Col. Sammonds glanced left and saluted in appreciation. In Wildcat Two, the pilot nodded back; underneath the mask, the grin grew wider.

*   *   *

Lt. Col. Andrew Bennett walked slowly through the darkened halls of the 23rd Squadron Operations Building. It was small, dark, and extremely cold, another tribute to American engineering. Outside it was still dark, but the heat of the previous day remained, in stark contrast to the cold drafts of air that flowed unobstructed through the empty halls. The colonel barely noticed the light in the office to his left as he shuffled down the hall. He was barely awake, and though it was morning, he was still tired. "Damn," he muttered to himself, "just can't do this like I used to." Four months of combat during the day and beer drinking in the night with only four to six hours sleep before beginning again was taking its toll. The young guys could handle this; he was approaching forty-six, not an old age at all, but old compared to twenty-eight, the age of many of his pilots. He desperately wanted, and even more desperately needed, a cup of coffee. How much of that did he drink now? Twelve cups? Twenty? Too much, which he suspected contributed to the stomach problems he had been struggling with for the past few months. Probably should see the flight surgeon about this, he thought. No. Too much risk. He might take me off flight status--DNIF (Duty Not to Include Flying) How could you command a fighter squadron if you were DNIF? Abruptly he stopped his pacing. His mind was registering slowly this morning, but it was functioning at some level. Light? He turned and stuck his head in the office behind him. "Captain?"

Robb looked up from his work, saw his Ops Officer, and stood. "Yes Sir?"

"As you were."

Robb relaxed and turned to the older man. "Looks like you need a cup of coffee, Sir."

"Looks like you've already had one."

"Two, it's good; made it myself."

Bennett stretched, noted the sensation in his right knee and right shoulder, winced slightly, then looked at his watch. "Shit. It's 0400. What the hell are you doing here now?"

"Same as you, Sir, working. Martin's down with the flu and Don Houston's on emergency leave. Schedule needs some work before the AM launch."

"I see. What's the story on Houston and Martin?"

"Houston's dad--heart attack. Sixty-seven, retired Navy. I have a letter for your signature on your desk. Don's a good man."

"Yes he is. And Martin, out long?"

"'Bout four days is my guess. This Asian flu is tough. I'll keep an eye on his status and keep you updated. It hit him last night."

"Flight surgeon aware?"

"It's in his report. He'll know at 0600."

"Good." He yawned hugely. "More coffee?"

"Good idea, this one's cold, like this damned office. Alaska couldn't be any worse."

As the two men walked down the hall, the colonel looked at the captain carefully. What he saw troubled him. There were circles under his eyes; his face was much thinner than he had remembered, and it was obvious Robb had aged significantly in the past few months. The young man who had arrived at Nubat seven months ago had changed. He was older now; perhaps he was wiser; perhaps not. "How are you doing Robb?"

"Fine sir, I'm flying every day."

"No, I mean, how are you doing?"

The younger man did not reply immediately. He considered his response carefully. "Okay sir. Okay."

"No you're not. You're working too hard, and you look like shit. Almost as bad as me." Both chuckled at that. "Let me rephrase it, Robb. Is it getting better each week?" He reached and put his hand on the young Captain's shoulder. "You've had a tough road, son. I just want to know which way you're going."

"I'm okay, really."

"Good. And if I get a cup of coffee in the next three minutes, I'll be fine too."

* * *

The seven men sat silently in the rear of the pickup. The colonel sat forward in the cab as the vehicle rumbled along the ramp toward the revetments where the planes were parked. Everyone was watching

Robb who sat alone looking into the distance. Colonel Bennett looked aft and caught the eye of Will Stanton, the navigator flying with Robb today. The colonel had quietly met with Will before the flight was briefed. Bennett signaled thumbs up as both he and Will studied the back of Robb's head. The tall black major glanced back and signaled thumbs up in reply.

Kerrie was still unresponsive after two months, and Robb had not emerged from the shell he had closed about himself. He still worked day and night; he flew every day; he seldom slept, and he looked frightful. Robb was a big man, but he had peeled fifteen to twenty pounds easily by the colonel's estimate. Colonel Bennett was worried, and justifiably so. Robb was nearing a breakdown. But the colonel had one more card to play. His old friend had helped before. Maybe she could work one more miracle.

Robb flew two sorties that day. When he walked back into the operations building at seventeen hundred hours he was stumbling with fatigue. "Get some rest, son."

"I will, Colonel; let me check tomorrow's sorties first. It will only take a few minutes."

Colonel Bennett was studying the schedule with the young captain when the door opened quietly behind them. The colonel's tired eyes glanced up quickly and stopped abruptly on the figure standing in the doorway. Robb had been explaining the morning sorties for the following day. The look on Colonel Bennett's face caused Robb to turn rapidly in his seat.

Framed against the bright hallway was the figure of a tall woman, completely in black. "Sister Estelle."

Col. Bennett moved from behind the desk and started for the door. "Good evening, Sister. Robb, I'll drop back later." In a moment he was gone.

Robb stood and looked at the older woman. There was unmistakable sadness in her eyes. "I'm sorry it has taken so long."

She spoke quietly. She wiped quickly at her right eye. "How are you Robb?"

"Honestly? Not very well."

"That's what I've heard."

"Who?"

"I have my sources." She forced a small smile.

"And you?"

"Let's just say that I've had my own problems too--a small spiritual crisis." She faced him and spoke directly, without emotion.

"You?"

"Don't you think nuns question God too?"

He looked at her with a degree of surprise on his face. "Are you okay now?" He asked finally as he walked around the desk and pulled two chairs together in the small room.

"I'm recovering--like you."

"Yes, I understand."

They both sat in awkward silence before the nun finally spoke. "Miss her?"

"Yes, more than I ever thought I could miss anything." He looked up into her eyes. "I really love her."

"I know." She took his right hand in both of hers. "She loves you too."

He nodded, dropping his eyes to the floor. "It just hurts so much. She's everywhere in my mind. I see her smile; sometimes it is almost like I could reach out and touch her." His face suddenly reddened. She patted his hand softly.

"I know. I lost something too--for a while. My faith was severely tested in this."

"But you're okay now, right?"

"Yes." Tears dropped from her eyes to the front of her habit. Robb reached and patted her hand; then after a moment she rose and began pacing the room as he watched her. "I thought I had this one all figured out. I was the one pulling the strings--or so I thought. I forgot to put it all in God's hands."

Robb watched her in confusion. "Dammit, He really didn't handle this one right." His voice was a hoarse whisper. "Why? She's so beautiful, so good. How could He allow this to happen?"

"I don't know, Robb. I've struggled with those same questions over more graves --tiny ones--than I can count. How could a child be allowed to suffer? I finally became reconciled with the fact that I simply don't understand the Will of God." She paused, looking at the young face before her. "But Robb, I do trust Him." Their gaze both fell to the worn linoleum floor. He finally rose and walked to her, taking her in his arms. They stood silently, giving and receiving comfort from the other.

"You are a strong man, Robb. You've lost a lot of people you love this year. I was worried about you."

"Is that why you came?"

"Partially. But also because I'm weak now, too." She wiped her own eyes with a plain handkerchief that she extracted from her sleeve. "I knew if you could bear up under this; well, so could I." She smiled at him bravely. "But you've got your flying to keep you busy."

"That's nothing compared to forty-seven kids."

"I suppose not, which reminds me, I'd better be going."

"Sister, say a prayer for Kerrie--every day."

"I do." She reached and touched his cheek, "and for you too." She paused a moment and he could see her internal struggle. Finally she spoke. "Robb, there's another reason I came."

"Somboon?"

"Yes, he misses you. He's little; he doesn't understand."

"I miss him too." The young man smiled weakly. "I guess I've been all wrapped up in myself."

"As any human would in these circumstances." She reached

and placed her left hand on his cheek, lifting his face until their eyes met. "Somboon had grown to love her, too. He's also grieving."

"I don't know what to say to him about Kerrie." he admitted.

"Come see him, Robb. You will find the right words; just follow your heart."

"I will; I promise."

"Soon?"

"Sure, and Sister, give him this till I get there. Okay?" He reached into his pocket and produced a small gold cross on a gold chain. "He'll understand."

"Of course."

He kissed her gently on the cheek, and she turned and disappeared out of the door.

Col. Bennett returned a few moments later. "Shall we finish the schedule?"

"Yes sir."

"How about some coffee first?"

"Right."

As they sipped the strong, hot coffee and studied the list of aircraft, crews, and armament, the colonel observed. "I see we have a flight of four with high-drags for Rat Fink Valley tomorrow."

"Roger. Takeoff at 1000 hours."

"Damn, that's over target just after noon. Shit!" The captain nodded and continued to study the pages in his hand. "Less than 450 feet and less than 450 knots in a fucking gun arcade. Who's leading that flight?"

"I am." The younger man spoke without looking up from the sheet in his hands.

"The hell you are."

"Know anyone who could do it better?" The younger man managed a grin.

"You bet your ass I do. Hand me that schedule." The colonel scribbled on it briefly and handed it back. "You're number Two. I'm leading this one."

"Roger that. Three and four?"

"King and Travis."

"You want to win the entire war tomorrow?"

The colonel smiled and slapped Robb on the back as he left the room. "We might just do that."

* * *

Dear Son,

I'm so sorry to hear about Kerrie. I could see in your letters how much you love her. I wish I could be there to help you through these difficult days. I know how close you two are. She loves you too, Robb. That is a blessing for you both. Remember son, where there's life, there's hope. I know you won't give up on Kerrie; you know she's still fighting. In the meantime keep the beautiful memories in your heart, and they will bring you comfort. I wish I could carry this for you, Robb. God bless you; we love you.

Mom

Dear Son,

You know I'm not a man who knows how to express things. I'm just an old engineer who likes to fix things that are broken. How I wish I could fix Kerrie and your broken heart right now, but that will simply take time. God gave us pain to bear in our lives, but He also gave us the greatest healer of all—time. She's young, and she's strong, and she has a lot to live for. We'll keep both of you in our prayers. Some day when you're my age and have a son of your own, you'll understand the helplessness I feel right now.

Fathers fix things, but now I can only watch your pain and wish I could take it away.

Fly safe son. Mom and I love you.

Dad

Dear Robb,

I really don't know what to say. I know you loved Kerrie a lot. It was written all over your letters. She must be quite a woman. Is there anything that I can do? You've had far more than your share of hurt this year. You hang in there kid. One day at a time, Robb; one day at a time.

I know this is the most difficult thing you've ever had to face, but you're a tough guy and you'll get through. She would want it that way. Keep remembering that. She's a doctor; she spent her life healing others. Let her love and her memories keep you strong.

You know that I haven't been to Mass in ten years or more. Well, yesterday I went and got on my knees for all of us. I had a lot of questions and few answers, but I'll keep working on that. Dammit, she healed everyone else; now it's her turn.

We all love you,
Jason

*   *   *

The happy sounds of children at play filled the afternoon with excitement. Three adults walked around the large building, searching every nook in the shrubs and every low branch on every tree. Finally they spotted him, sitting alone, watching the other children at play. His large eyes were closed as he sat with his chin resting on his forearms which were crossed over his knees. Letok turned and left as soon as Robb and Sister Estelle spotted Somboon. The older nun looked at the young child and then at the man beside her. She was worried about both. It was not quite clear to her which needed the other more.

The din from the children ceased momentarily as they studied the strange man with their mother. After a moment their attention left the giant man and concentrated again on their play. The change in the noise level was recognized by the small boy, and he opened his eyes momentarily to discern the cause. Immediately he saw the American and jumped to his feet. He stood for only a moment then started running toward the two adults. Robb stepped forward cautiously, then he too started to run toward the child. Half way across the playground he reached and swooped the small boy into his arms. Sister Estelle watched them, smiling as the two hugged each other. Robb held him at arm's length and studied the boy carefully. There were tearstains on the smiling face, the boy's tiny arms reaching frantically for the man's neck. After a brief silence Somboon began to chatter without pause, and when Robb turned to look back at the nun, the child grabbed his face and turned it back to his own. The man began to laugh at the child, and the boy laughed back in return.

Sister Estelle approached and smiled broadly at the two. Somboon chattered to Robb and then to her. His small voice was ceaseless. Robb watched in amazement until finally he stopped and looked long at the nun. They had been chatting when suddenly her face changed visibly. "What did he say, Sister?"

She looked at him for a few moments searching for words. "He asked about the Doctor Lady." Sister looked directly into Robb's eyes, waiting for some reaction. The smile faded slowly from his lips.

"What did you tell him?"

"I told him she she was hurt and is being cared for by other doctors but misses him very much."

The young man nodded and walked toward the waiting truck with the small boy still clinging to his neck.

Later that evening two pilots stood over the sleeping boy and pulled the sheet over his thin shoulders. "Are you planning on keeping him here?"

"Just for a day or so. He needs to be at the orphanage while I fly. I just think it would be good for him to know I haven't deserted him."

Joe smiled at his friend and patted him on the back. "He's a neat kid; looks just like you. Same blond hair, same blue eyes, same pale skin."

Robb grinned at his friend. "Yeah, same good looks."

"Right." Joe grabbed a magazine and started out the door. "If the president calls, tell him I'm in the library."

Robb bent and stroked the hair of the tiny boy. It was the same bed where he and Kerrie had made love. If only they could have their life together. He tried to imagine Kerrie holding children of her own. The thought made him smile, though it hurt so badly. What he had left was this tiny child that they had agreed to take as a part of the family they wanted to build. Was that all that remained of that dream? Was that even a possibility for him now? He pondered that in his mind as the vision of the beautiful woman moved gently into focus in his mind. Somehow he could sense her; he could touch her in his mind. She was leaning on her elbow, looking into his eyes as they made promises about their future together. Now only the promises remained. He touched the boy's hair as the look of sadness on his face changed to one of determination. Finally he spoke in a voice that was quiet and broken. "You and me, kid. You and me."

Dear Jason,

I'm sorry I haven't written in several weeks. I've just been so busy. Thanks for your support. You're a great brother.

It has been difficult without Kerrie. She's so special to me;

I still haven't heard anything, but I'm going to be okay. And Jase, let Mom know I'm okay—and tell Dad he letter meant so much. I know it must have taken him several days to write those paragraphs. Just tell them I'm fine. I'm flying a lot; thank God and Col. Bennett for that. I'll write more later—got to run to a briefing.

                                             Robb

                          *   *   *

The colonel walked briskly into the pilots' ready room and scanned the assembled pilots and navigators as they shed their equipment after their flights. He quickly found the man he was seeking. "Robb, see me in my office as soon as you can." With a nod he was gone.

Robb stepped into the colonel's domain with a sloppy salute and stood somewhat at attention. Without looking up from a stack of reports the colonel spoke. "At ease." He finished the page, made a note on the top of the report and set it aside. "You better get packing, captain!" There was a wide grin on his face.

"Sir?"

"Plane leaves for Hickam in half an hour. It connects with a courier flight to Andrews Air Force Base." The captain's face was one of complete confusion. "Get moving. I think you need an R&R."

"Andrews!" Slowly the message was sinking into Robb's consciousness. "Really?"

"I've fixed the schedule. You've got three days at Walter Reed. Now get on that flight." Before he could finish his sentence Robb had turned and was running down the narrow hallway.

"Thanks, Colonel."

Bennett watched him running through the ops building and smiled to himself. "Don't mention it."

Walter Reed Hospital near Washington, D.C.

The exhausted captain walked slowly toward the bed, then stopped and stared at the woman he loved. She was hardly recognizable with the various tubes that were attached to her body. Her head had been shaved, and small brown hairs had begun to grow back, partially covering a scar on the top right side of her head. She lay there, silent, unmoving. The older nurse who had escorted him onto the surgical floor watched him carefully. She was not at all certain what his reaction would be. She did not trust men in general, and this one didn't appear all that stable to her. He was pale, thin, and there was a look of pain in his eyes, one she had seen too frequently in her chosen profession. She slid a chair across the floor toward the stunned man.

"Can I get you anything? Water?"

"No, thank you." He never took his eyes off the inert figure in the bed as the nurse turned and walked slowly from the room.

As he reached to touch her, he realized that his hand was shaking, almost uncontrollably. Could that be possible? His hands had maneuvered a mach-2 aircraft through combat and monsoon storms. How could they fail him now? He stood searching for some part of her that he could touch, some part that was not burdened with the life support systems that kept her alive. This was the woman he loved, would always love. Again he reached his shaking fingers to touch the limp hand stretched motionless on the bed. It was not the warm hand he remembered. For a moment he was once again sitting in the ash of the burning hospital, holding her, screaming obscenities into the night sky. All he felt was despair for the situation facing him. But his heart stood fast, and he leaned carefully and kissed her on her cheek.

The nurse standing in the doorway watching the captain was a major. She had seen the best and the worst that life had to offer.

She had entered her profession a young and impressionable woman intent on helping the world, on relieving some of this world's suffering. But the job had slowly hardened her, not because she had learned to care less for the people she served, but rather as a way of protecting a gentle heart from the harsh reality of the medical world in which she worked. Margaret Thompson had worked with countless patients. She had celebrated life, and she had mourned death. The defenses she had built up around her own heart had taken years, and they were strong. They were strong because they were also necessary.

Margaret watched the man carefully and tried to measure his reaction. He was at least ten years younger than she, and he looked as vulnerable as any man she had watched in so many similar situations. She was glad he did not understand the charts that were hanging from the bottom of the bed. That information would be enough to destroy him, she surmised.

So many faces crowed into her mind, so many patients, so many shocked visitors. Some simply broke down and ran from the room, unable to absorb or process the damage they witnessed. Some simply turned and walked slowly into the world they had left outside; most never returned. One had walked sadly to his car and killed himself with the same weapon he had taken into combat. How would this tall captain react? She had certainly seen it all. She looked quickly at her watch and hurried down the hall.

"I love you." He whispered into her ear as he pulled the chair beside the bed. He sat slowly onto the worn chair, still looking at the inert woman beside him. He sat there and held her hand and talked to her softly for over an hour. He talked about Somboon, the base, the people they knew there, and he talked about them and their future. Frequently he would wipe his eyes; once he even laughed while telling a funny story about the children at the orphanage. Slowly his shadow crept across the floor and started climbing the opposite wall. Finally he was silent; he bent closer and kissed her cheek again.

Major Thompson walked quickly toward the nursing station. It was late and she was anxious to finish her paperwork and go home. Abruptly she stopped in mid stride and turned to stare into the small room. Earlier in the day she had watched the captain's tentative move to touch the injured woman's hand; then she had watched him sitting quietly crying as he stroked her hair. He had spent hours talking to her as he sat beside her, holding her hand. It was as if he were having a normal conversation with someone he loved. But it was the soft strains of the lullaby that had caught the old nurse's attention and slowed her gait. There he was in the bed, holding her in his arms, her head resting on his breast as he sang to her gently. It was only after several moments that she realized the lullaby was foreign. The words were strange, but the melody was beautiful as it floated across the room. His voice was not beautiful, and it was frequently interrupted by the emotion in his heart, but it was the most beautiful music Margaret Thompson had ever heard. She watched him; there were tears streaming down his face, but he was smiling. The nurse's eyes widened suddenly, and she took in a deep breath. Yes, she had seen it, or did she? Had he sensed it? She was certain the woman's eyes had opened briefly. Or was it just her imagination? She walked quickly into the room to check the machines that measured her patient's tenuous connection with life. Yes, there. One small blip—or was it? Or was it?

Margaret walked back into the hallway, stopped and looked back for a brief moment. Then she did something she had not done in years. She walked into the women's room, buried her face in her hands, and wept unashamedly.

PART THREE

DISCOVERY AND DECISIONS

CHAPTER NINE

<u>**Somewhere over North Vietnam**</u>

Joe's last transmission was short and tinged with anger. "Fuck!" Less than two seconds later the navigator's ejection seat erupted into the sky. Seconds later, Joe felt the sudden jolt of the seat leaving the burning aircraft. The sudden shock of his seat being propelled up the guide rail dazed him momentarily. His entire body sagged into the accelerating seat. A flash of pain shot from his left hip through the small of his back. With the accelerating g's pushing him into the sky, he could not even grimace. The weight of his own skin increased nine times its normal amount and pulled downward with the rocket accelerating beneath his seat. He did not feel his legs being automatically restrained, nor did he notice the automatic actuation of the emergency oxygen system. He was below the eleven thousand five hundred foot barometric setting in his seat, so two seconds later the time release mechanism released his lap belt, leg restraint lines, shoulder harness, and parachute restraint straps. The drogue gun fired, deploying the drogue chutes, which in turn deployed his parachute. As the large nylon chute opened, he was jerked away from the seat, the last semblance of the plane that crashed burning into the dark green jungles. A moment later he was hanging from his harness below a billowing parachute, drifting lazily toward the menacing jungle. It had happened so fast that the sensations of the g forces and the pain in his back blocked all other memories of the ejection. He became aware of only one other sensation; his right leg was wet and warm. Then came the fear; out of the haze and the shock it came, settling through his mind, rendering his body motionless. He hung there, in panic. "This cannot be happening! It isn't happening!" But the jungle below was moving up to meet him--very quickly.

His chute caught the top branches of a very tall tree, suspending him over seventy feet above the jungle floor below. He hung there, motionless, looking beyond his feet at the ground so far away. Far to the south, he heard intermittent explosions of 500-pound bombs. Were they from his own flight? No, he decided, they were too far away. He was trapped and alone. He looked above him, through the tree limbs to the bright sky above. How peaceful it looked, how friendly. Not like the dark, unknown jungle below the dense covering of trees. It reminded him of his home. How often he had lain on his back in the small field behind his home northwest of Chicago, staring at the clouds and the blue sky. He had known then that he wanted to fly. It had always been there waiting in his mind, a desire he could not explain, but one that he knew he must satisfy. It had been there as long as he could recall and was a part of him, a dream he never fought, one to which he knew he must ultimately yield. But the surrender had been beautiful. Like a new love, it had heightened every sense in his body and mind. In many ways it had tamed his very soul. The first time he left the ground in a small, noisy aircraft, tugged aloft by a raucous propeller, he had known that it was right. When he had flown his first jet, he understood the joy and exhilaration that he had only imagined. The joy, the excitement, even the pride--it had all arrived at this point in time, in this tree, above the dark danger of the jungle below. For the first time in his life he wished he had never flown.

The deep bellowing moan of the F-4 above him brought him back into the reality that he faced. Rifle fire erupted nearby. The enemy troops were firing at something--Pete? The F-4? Joe looked down again at the jungle floor below him. He was a sitting duck for any soldier in the area, and he had the parachute above to advertise his position. He looked desperately in all directions; he knew he had to get down from the treetops to the forest floor. His mind was screaming in panic. "The tree trunk--must reach that or a limb to climb onto!" Like a small child in the park, he started to swing. It took a few moments to establish his motion, but each arc brought him closer to the tree. On the sixth arc, he nearly grasped the trunk. His fingers touched and slid across the damp surface of the tree. "One more inch!" Joe thrust backward as hard as he could; the parachute gave way; and he fell toward the ground. Instinctively, he screamed.

Thirty feet above the ground, the parachute caught another limb. It could not stop the ultimate goal of gravity, but it slowed his fall, and he tumbled onto the jungle floor, unhurt. The parachute slid down the limb and covered him in the damp jungle. For a moment he lay there shaking and breathing deeply. More rifle fire-- nearby. Joe began to scramble, dragging the parachute behind him. It caught in the underbrush, pulling him to his knees. He knelt there momentarily, gulping air and cursing quietly. Turning quickly, he pulled the parachute from the brush and clutched it to his chest.

More rifle fire. Now he could hear their voices shouting in the distance. Joe sat up and looked around, shocked that he couldn't see. It was dark! How could that be? He reached to rub his eyes and struck the sun visor on his helmet. Cursing, he raised it and looked in the direction of the shouting. It was moving in his direction. Had they seen his chute? Had they heard his scream while falling from the tree?

A large thicket of bushes and bamboo was directly in front

of him. It appeared to be greater than 20 feet in diameter. There was one small opening at the base before him, about 18" high and equally wide across. Above that, the bamboo was thick and dense. He quickly began crawling toward the thicket on his hands and knees, holding the parachute under his belly with his left hand. Arriving at the thicket, he shoved the parachute into the small opening and started to crawl after it. Something in his mind stopped him. Tracks? Had he left tracks? The idea buoyed him greatly. His mind was functioning. He was in control. "I'm going to be okay. I'm not going to panic." Quickly he unbuckled the parachute harness, shoved it and his helmet into the small opening and retraced his path for twenty-five yards. Carefully covering his tracks as best he could, he returned to the thicket with several branches of dead leaves. He crawled into the thicket, pulled some of the dead leaves into place behind him, and covered himself with the remaining limbs. Exhausted, he lay shaking on the decaying wet leaves and waited, as sweat streaked the mud he had rubbed onto his pale face.

The voices in the jungle resumed their shouting, but they were different; the urgency and anger were gone. They were cheering, the unmistakable sound of men celebrating. Joe wondered if they had hit another aircraft; no, no chance, not with rifle fire. Had they found his trail? Had he dropped something? His knife? His pistol? Slowly his hand moved down and touched both. He slowly brought the gun from its holster and looked at it carefully. Had he loaded the damned thing? He looked at the revolver's cylinder. The unmistakable brass bullets were there, six of them.

More shouting--closer now. Then the sound of Pete's scream sent a shaft of ice through Joe's body. He lay there choking in the thicket. They had Pete.

The voices grew louder. Then he could hear the sounds of their movement through the thick underbrush. They were laughing, dragging the injured navigator along. Pete was coughing and moaning and cursing. As they walked along, the soldiers took turns hitting him with the butts of their rifles. Joe curled into a small ball under the dead leaves. Only a bloodhound could have found him. The soldiers passed. Joe could see their legs. One of them had jungle boots--obviously Pete's. Pete stumbled, or was tripped, and fell face forward. Joe could see his back as he fell. They kicked him repeatedly. He screamed and tried to get to his knees. As he did, they kicked him again, and he fell backward.

Joe could see the blood on his face. He covered his eyes with his left hand and squeezed them shut. It was the last time he saw Pete alive.

The soldiers laughed and taunted the prostrate figure. His arms were bound, and a two-foot piece of cord was tied to his ankles, enough to allow walking, but not long enough to allow an escape.

Finally, tired of kicking him, the leader took his knife and knelt over the stricken man.

Joe had sealed his eyes, but the screams flooded every cell of his being. He lay in the thicket, shaking, eyes closed, sobbing quietly--listening to the savagery of man to man.

*   *   *

Robb lay exhausted on his bed and stared blankly at the ceiling and the dark walls. How many times had he lain on that bed and stared at the ugly ceiling and the lone bulb that hung suspended in the small, dark man-made cave? How many hours had he struggled with his mind to restrain it from the mental hysteria that drummed around in his brain, aching to climb out and shake his senses into a dizzy oblivion? Tonight it was different. An emotion that had not seized his breast in many months was twisting his lower gut and wrenching it into his stomach.

He raised his arm and placed it over his eyes, but still he could not close out the burning sensation that lighted his mind and set off the myriad of fireworks that frightened him. Joe's small voice over the radio still rang in his ears and echoed through his mind. Joe had been afraid; he had been near panic. That surprised Robb; he knew that Joe would need all of his faculties functioning at their peak efficiency to make it through the long night until the helicopters could make their way back in the morning. Robb studied the plastic water bottle in his hand carefully, then with a sudden lunge he threw it across the hooch to bounce and spill over the stack of dirty clothes that grew beside the door.

The sudden outburst seemed to snap the line that controlled the emotional vacuum that Robb had built around himself over the past few months. Without realizing it he had opened the small door that led to the inner workings of his soul. The doubts trickled in unnoticed and distorted the unknown into one gigantic lie that towered darkly over the faint glimmer of hope that shone deep within his breast. And this invited the monster, fear, to join the parade, but first fear painted its nightmarish masterpiece upon the scaffolds of the mind and hung distortions from every helpless neuron. Then was welcomed the long despised comrade, despair, and together they danced through the muck of their own creation.

Joe was more than just a good friend to Robb; he was more like a brother. He had been the rock upon which the flimsy foundation of Robb's reserve had rested. Wayne, Chusack, Kerrie; always there had been Joe there to hold him within the boundary of sanity; always there had been Joe to make him laugh, to help him forget for the moment. The hours crawled slowly through the darkened room as his mind rolled back the crumpled sheets of time and traced a friendship that had grown with much laughter and the occasional moments of truth.

The soft knock at the door dispelled the parade that marched through his mind and sent the participants scurrying back into their hidden cells to await release again. It was Colonel Bennett. Robb sat up abruptly and stared at the older man. He forced his senses to listen and understand, though he was afraid of what they might hear. "Any word?"

"No, not since the cover left. We're going to get 'em at 05:15. Briefing is at 02:30. I'm leading; you're number two." Robb didn't answer; he only nodded. "Don't worry, son, we'll get 'em out." Without waiting for an answer, the older man turned and left into the night.

The first light of day stretched sleepily across the horizon as the eight officers climbed awkwardly into the rear of the pickup truck. There was always a laziness in the early morning air; the earth was still, waiting for the burning sun to climb slowly over the lush green jungle and heat it with hell's own fire. Only the short nervous syllables from the sleep scarred faces broke the silence of the monotonous jungle hum. Colonel Bennett climbed into the cab of the truck, still chewing his breakfast cigar. In the gray dawn light his face shone from the recent shaving like a polished mug. Only two small wounds betrayed his sleepy hands and bleary eyes. Robb sat huddled next to the cab and stared blankly at the waking jungle across the runway. He looked around sharply as his navigator spoke his name. "Wake up Robb, here's 622." He climbed from the truck and walked quickly across the ramp toward his waiting aircraft. The acrid stench of JP-4 fuel bit at his nose and welcomed him into the revetment. The ground starter unit coughed several times and then spit a huge belching black plume high into the morning air. It whined loudly and woke Robb from his half sleep. He concentrated on where he was going—to get Joe.

The four jets stood smugly against the creeping jungle and strained at their brakes. The roar from their powerful engines stirred the soft morning air and awoke the sleeping jungle. Then there was the relative silence as all of the engines idled. One last check, a head nod, and they were off, leaving only the quiet murmur of the waking forest. The aircraft began to roll slowly down the long concrete strip; the afterburners kicked roughly, and Robb felt the familiar reaction of his own body being thrust back into his seat. The aircraft accelerated faster and soon, like Robb's mind, was racing towards the East and Joe. It had been a long time since Robb had been so nervous about a flight. Long before he had aligned his aircraft along the narrow strip of concrete he had felt the sweat of his body soaking into his flight suit, sticking it damply to his back. He refused to think of the possibilities of what lay ahead, so he did what he always did—he concentrated totally on flying and the mission he was supporting.

Three hours later that morning a large helicopter hovered above the trees and dropped a cable harness through the green canopy. A weak voice on the radio said "Okay," and the rescue team started the wench.

Captain Joe Wilburn hung limply in the "collar." The thickset sergeant reached a hairy arm covered with sweat and grabbed the pilot, struggling against the acceleration of the "Jolly Green Giant" as it climbed to safety. "Got him. We're on our way to Nubat."

"Great work Guys. You're cleared. We're on our way for a rendezvous with a gas whore."

"Good hunting."

*   *   *

The large crowd stood quietly as the camouflaged helicopter hovered overhead and began to descend slowly. Like a giant grasshopper, it settled and relaxed in the morning heat. The engine coughed and stopped. The waves of heat rising from the exhausts joined those from the parched pavement and rose skyward to join the growing clouds that would soon blossom into thunderstorms, storms which would eventually cool the baked earth that had given them birth. Robb edged his way through the sweating mass of men and reached the front of the crowd. He had grabbed several beers from the icebox in the squadron; this served as a ticket to allow him the privilege to be the first to greet the returning compatriot -- the lamb that had been lost was found, and the entire base had turned out to celebrate the return to the fold.

Joe emerged from the belly of the giant helicopter and was met with a great chorus of profanity and laughter. He swung gracefully to the ground, hand outstretched to meet the sea of hands reaching for him. In the age-old tradition of men, the handshakes came first and the drinking came second. It was when he took the beer that Robb got his first good look at his friend. He was muddy, and his dark beard was grizzled and matted with his own sweat. These were expected, but it was not these that Robb was looking at; it was Joe's eyes that stopped him and stirred something deep within. Robb looked carefully at his friend, and his own mind backed slowly away from the stranger he saw before him. The eyes were frightened, and behind them was a darkness that hid something Robb could not understand, something that left him disturbed.

The sea of men laughed and shouted in the heat. Their lost comrade had been snatched from under the enemy's nose and the time for thanksgiving was at hand. From the parking ramp the rowdy mob moved by pickup truck parade to the howling officer's club where the party would continue -- this time for the returned pilot and also the man who had not returned. Pete Grendel was listed as missing in action; he had not been found. The petite Thai barmaids raced back and forth from the bar to the tables carrying trays of drinks that weighed heavily upon their tiny shoulders. Their tight skirts reached nearly to the floor and only permitted movement from the knees down. In these skirts and the high-heeled slippers, they glided comically under the large loads of drinks.

Joe was somewhere in the middle of the tightly packed throng when he noticed Robb making his way toward the rear door. Joe held his drink above the threatening arcs of swinging elbows and the moving mass of bodies, made his excuses, and turned abruptly from the eager group that had pressed around him. Dodging through the crowd, he called for the big blond man who was nearing the door. "Robb! Wait a minute." Robb had just finished an imported American beer and was looking for a place to put the can.

"What's up?"

"Where you going?"

"To get some beauty rest; I need it."

Joe edged him into a corner and shouted above the noisy chatter of happy drunks and a blaring record player. "You still don't approve of these parties, do you?"

"Maybe we'll find Pete tomorrow -- now that would really be a cause for celebration."

Joe looked silently into his drink for several moments before speaking. "Maybe so." He looked up into Robb's eyes; the same mysterious unknown that had chilled Robb before was still there. "I don't like this party either, but I can't go to the hooch now. I need this party, and I'd appreciate it if you'd stay for me--not for Pete if you don't feel that way, but for me." His eyes fell back to his drink, and he spoke slowly. "I don't want to talk about it tonight, and they keep bugging me." He made a sweeping gesture with his arm. "Stay with me, Robb, just tonight."

Robb smiled slightly. "Okay Joe, If you want me to drive off the new guys, I'll do that with pleasure. But it's going to cost you a beer." Joe smiled thankfully and draped his arm over the big man's shoulder. He seemed desperately relieved and alone in the crowded room. He began drinking bourbon and switched to gin, then to vodka, then back to bourbon. He began drinking about noon; it was seven o'clock when it finally caught him.

Jack Treadeau tugged at one boot as Robb untied the other. The major looked at the sleeping figure and laughed. "Damn, I thought it was never going to catch up to him. He never even got drunk until he passed out,"

Robb glanced at the snoring figure. "Yeah, it was almost as if he were fighting that bottle. Joe likes to drink, but tonight there was no fun in it for him. He drank like a man who only wanted to get drunk."

"And forget?"

"And forget. Well, I guess he's got a lot of nerves that need soothing; he's been through his share of hell for the past couple of days."

"You're right about that; you should know if anyone does." Major Treadeau moved the green trash can beside the snoring man's bed. "He might need this--just in case."

Robb nodded. "No doubt he will. Thanks a lot Jack."

"No thanks to me, thank you. It's a good thing you stuck around -- I agree with you on the celebrations by the way, but I generally go anyway, it's easier than arguing viewpoints on principles when we all feel generally the same loss. But anyway, it's a good thing someone warned you that you might be needed."

Robb looked back at the man on the bed then toward the departing figure. "As a matter of fact, I was warned." He waved into the darkness. "See you tomorrow; don't stay up too late reading Chaucer. If the zips don't understand plain English, chances are they won't understand Old English either." A laugh rang back through the darkness and was his only answer.

*   *   *

Time entered its rut again. The days dragged themselves slowly through the humid jungle heat and each was just like the one it followed. Men labored in the sticky pools of their own sweat by day and drowned all consciousness of life in alcohol at night. Bleary eyed and nauseous they crept back to the busy ramp in the dawn's coolness and prepared for another day at war, another day of dropping bombs on some unseen enemy, another day of missing home, another day of driving the body while the mind slept. Some days, however, were different. Some days were marked forever in the mind, an indelible brand, burned forever on the soul. It was the day Hugh was killed; or the day that the chopper crashed and killed Ben; or it was the day John heard about his little girl's death back home; it was a sad day. Or it might have been one of the few happy days -- remember the night the USO team the O'club? But most days were the same. They were hot; they were long; and most of all, they were lonely.

Robb had expected the change that he initially saw in Joe, or at least most of the change. He had anticipated that it would take even carefree Joe a few days to get over the experience of fear. So he said nothing when Joe spoke little or not at all in the evenings; he only shrugged when Joe went straight to the hooch after his flights and discouraged all bids to get him into the bar; Robb watched his friend drink himself into an uneasy sleep each evening without a smile. And he said nothing; he only watched the eyes. Always they were guarded and silent. So, Robb stood quietly, waiting and watching his friend. The blinding rays of the sun stung his eyes and caused small white wrinkles across the sun burned brow, small scratches of white spreading outward from the corners of his eyes. Robb had aged over the past eight months, and the passing time had matured more than just the lean hardness of his body. There was more patience behind the cool eyes, more of a wisdom in the slow smile, more of a gentleness in the strong hands, more of a silence that comes from waiting.

The wrinkles dug themselves more deeply, and the jaw set more tightly as the eyes squinted into the sunlight. They were focused on a dying man, a friend who was drying up inside and choking himself slowly to death. The shaking hands reached slowly for the yellow metal ladder that stretched upwards to the giant machine's brain -- the cockpit. The eyes closed tightly and a shudder shook the torso. Joe Wilburn looked up again to the top of the ladder; his teeth ground together as his face set itself determinedly against the mountain that lay ahead. But the shaking hands gave him away. Joe stepped back down from the first rung of the friction proofed ladder and looked incredulously at his own hands as they quivered violently. Again he reached for the step and stopped abruptly after the first. Slowly he stepped down, lowered his head, and let his arms go limp. Robb ran toward him. "Joe, are you alright?" He put his hand on his friend's shoulder.

"I don't know. I don't feel so good." Joe never looked up.

Robb looked at Joe and then glanced around at the other flight crews climbing into their aircraft. Suddenly he reached into Joe's flight bag and withdrew all of his flight data sheets. He turned to the young navigator who was already in the backseat of the aircraft performing his preflight checks. "Jerry, think you can catch me up while we taxi out?"

"Sure, no sweat. Joe sick?"

"Right." Robb swung up onto the ladder and began to climb toward the cockpit. He turned and looked back at Joe. "Get a little rest, Joe. I'll cover the flight and meet you for a cool one later."

The dark headed man looked up at the sunburned face beneath the tousled blond hair. "Thanks Robb." He turned and left without looking back. That evening he passed out with a bottle of bourbon cradled awkwardly in his arms.

Somewhere in the Pacific off the coast of the Soviet Union

Dmitriy watched the buildings disappear from sight. The familiar browns and greens of his life in the army were merging into an endless gray-blue world of sea and sky. It was a cold, crisp morning, the sun climbing through the sparse clouds that hung above the horizon like small lace curtains on a naked Russian window. He hated ports, but he hated ships even more. Seamen were such slobs. They had no discipline at all; they looked like rats; and they smelled like pigs. He reflected again on his good fortune to be in the army. Almost immediately the smile vanished. Dmitriy recognized the implication of this mission. It was a decision he had made after very little deliberation. And for the first time in many years, he began to doubt a decision. Was this one an act of courage and defiance, or was it the act of a desperate and sad old man? He carefully thought through the potential impacts of what he had done, and they were frightening. He might well initiate a nuclear confrontation in a world already struggling in a painful war. Was that a just tribute to a loving son, or was it a betrayal of all he knew to be right. Was this an act of strength or terrible weakness? He reached into his breast pocket and produced a flask of vodka. All of his second guessing was meaningless; he knew that. He was taking the missiles to North Vietnam. It was too late to turn back now. He looked at the flask briefly and then took a quick drink from the clear liquid; he thought back to his early training in military strategy. How often had he been told, "When a decision is made, proceed! In war you have no time for second guessing every decision. Some will be right; some will be wrong, but proceed. Indecision loses battles."

Sergei stood beside his leader and considered the mission as well. A dark thought had entered his mind. What if headquarters doesn't know about this mission? Could it be so important that only the colonel knows? Hadn't the colonel said that he should tell no one, not even members of his own staff? And why was Sergei now officially listed as being on leave? He pondered these things as the salt spray dampened his coat and hair. What if? What if? So many things to ponder. The slow rocking of the boat was foreign to his land based legs. Nausea rose in his stomach and caused him to abandon the deck. He looked up into the chilly morning sky and then walked stiffly down the metal stairs toward his small and ill smelling bunk. "This is best handled with some of the fine vodka the Colonel donated," he vocalized. He had promised to abstain from the vodka until the mission was complete, but without it, he might never survive the next four days aboard the rocking, stinking ship. He considered that and smiled; it was excuse enough for him, and he noticed it was good enough for the colonel as well.

As the two soviet officers walked aft toward their bunks, a large black plane was turning south to parallel the Soviet coast for his regular reconnaissance run. The pilot of the SR-71 Blackbird checked his altitude at 60,000 feet and slowed his speed to Mach 2.5. He checked his instruments carefully, watching the counter move toward 0. When it clicked down to 3.0, he pressed the camera button. At 2.5 one cannot be too careful, he thought, three seconds margin for error. That should be enough.

Dmitriy took one last look at the cold, clear sky above and stepped inside the freighter. Finally he was on the last leg of his mission. In a few short days the missiles would be safe inside North Vietnam, and he would be on his way home.

Nubat Royal Thai Air Force Base

Jack Treadeau was a good man. He was one of those blessed with a sincere love of life and mankind. Jack was the type of man who becomes involved with the lives of his friends. His was not a loud concern, but a very real one that shines like a flare in the night. He watched the pain and the suffering of those around him, and the hurt he saw attached itself to him. The sharpness of the pain humbled his own soul as it stabbed his friends. He was concerned, and this made him vulnerable; he suffered much. Jack had seen the change that had dulled the eyes and grayed the pallor of Joe's face.

He had seen the spirit slowly dying and fading from a once colorful personality. He saw the fear that drained Joe's reserve, and he saw the ravages of too much booze, too often. As he watched a great sorrow clouded his own mind, a cloud of pity at watching a good friend sink slowly into a pit – one he was digging for himself. He had watched Robb climb slowly from the pit of demons that had dragged him down; now Joe was fighting a similar battle. Joe was on his third bourbon when Jack walked through the door of the tiny hooch. "Hello, Joe, Robb. How are you guys doing? Missed you at the bar tonight."

Robb smiled broadly at the welcomed guest. Jack was tall and thin with a "flat top" haircut that was never quite flat. He always seemed to bring a little laughter that enlivened those around him and set them at ease. "You surely get around well for a man who's old enough to be a major." Robb laughed at his own joke and looked over to see if Joe had responded. He had not.

Jack looked directly at Joe. "How's it going, smiley?"

Joe tossed down the rest of his drink and began pouring another. "Okay, I guess."

"I hate to see a man drink alone. Mind if I join you?"

Joe looked at the older man for a long moment as if deciding. "Sure, if you want." He pulled a dirty glass from the top drawer of the bureau and inspected it carefully above the small lamp over the bed. Shrugging slightly he poured the brown liquid into the dirty glass and handed it to Jack. "If you want ice or coke, there's some of both in the refrigerator."

"You drink that stuff hard?" Jack was looking at Joe's drink.

"I can take it." Joe shot the other man a defiant look, one that expressly let him know that he did not care to discuss his drinking habits further. The men sat in embarrassed silence for a few moments. As the silence became oppressive, Jack spoke very slowly and quietly. "Joe, the colonel wants me to write up a Distinguished Flying Cross for your flight the other day," He looked hopefully at the wavering man across the room.

"A DFC? What for?"

Jack looked quickly at Robb and back at Joe. "Well, we think you deserve one."

Joe laughed sarcastically. Jack continued, "besides, Pete didn't have one, and if we're to get one for him, it has to be done within the week. It would be nice for…"

Joe's eyes flared and his face turned suddenly red with emotion. "Look dammit, I don't want one of your cheap medals. Write one for Pete if you want. Write one for yourself if you want, but don't bother me with this heroic crap. I know how medals are earned, and I know how you guys hand them out. Well, I don't want one! As far as I'm concerned you can take the lot of them and cram 'em!"

The outburst caught the other two men completely by surprise. They sat wide-eyed and shocked. When Joe had finished, he poured another long drink for himself and downed it with one gulp. As he poured another, Jack got up slowly and walked out the door without a word. He only paused long enough to deposit his half-finished drink on the small refrigerator.

Robb Barker looked after the back of his friend as he walked quietly from the room. The door closed softly, and a sudden quiet settled that neither of the remaining men seemed willing to break. Robb looked at Joe a long time before he spoke. "Why did you do that?" The words were almost a whisper.

"Do what?"

"Embarrass one of the few real gentlemen we've got in this stinking hole, that's what. Jack is one of the nicest guys around, and he happens to take that thankless job seriously. What's bugging you, Joe? What the hell is wrong?"

"Now don't you get on my back too!"

"Somebody should." Robb's voice had lost some of its earlier patience. "And don't you think you've had enough of that?" He pointed to the bottle on the table.

Joe's voice came back quickly, harshly. "Now listen dammit, don't start trying to mother me. All I need is a brave fighter pilot for a mother."

Robb grinned weakly and tried to break the mood of the conversation. "Well, if you keep drinking that rot gut, you're going to need a doctor, not a mother's loving care."

"If I want to drink that's my business." He paused briefly. "Why don't you guys just mind your own business?"

The taller man turned sharply and looked down at his friend who was lying back on his bunk with a glass of booze balanced on his chest. He nodded his head as he spoke. "All right, Joe, all right, I'll mind my own business." He turned and started for the door but Joe's words stopped him.

"I've got my problems; you've got yours. I've got booze; you've got Kerrie." Robb stopped, but he did not turn around. "What are you so high and mighty about. We've all got weaknesses. You ought to know that." Joe got up and reached for the half empty bottle. He rocked slightly back and forth as he stood there, cursing himself as he spilled bourbon on the floor. "So I have bloodshot eyes and my hands shake a little, so what? At least I don't lay in bed and whimper at night!" Joe spit the words out viciously, striking the only way he knew. The accusations had barely passed his lips when they collided with Robb's right hand.

The blow lifted Joe slightly and drove him against the wall. Blood streamed from his battered mouth and covered his dirty, stained undershirt. He sat there stunned and stared at the big man over him. He said nothing, but his eyes spoke for him. Robb had expected hate, fear, anger, but not what he saw – complete resignation. He had reacted instantly, and already he was sorry. He knew Joe was drunk, and he knew Joe was carrying something that he could not bear alone. Now the eyes were changed, finally! The fear and the confusion were gone. Joe looked like a little boy who had just been punished; his eyes were strangely sad. He looked pitiful, lost.

Joe wiped his mouth on the back of his arm. The blow had sobered him somewhat. "I shouldn't drink so much." He grinned weakly and looked at the spilled glass on the cluttered floor. "I just need it to forget."

"But you don't need it, Joe. You've got to get over this. So you got shot down, so what? That's your one time for the war. Now you don't need to worry about it again. So they got lucky, but you got back didn't you? You beat it out there in those jungles, all by yourself. There's nothing more to be afraid of."

"How in the hell would you know?"

Robb was beginning to lose his temper again. He could feel the heat rising into his temples and the sound of his own voice surprised him. In an exasperated motion, he thrust his arms into the air and shouted. "Dammit Joe, do you think you are the only son-of-a-bitch who has ever been shot down? If you remember back a few months, I spent a little time down there too, so don't try to snow me with this self pity crap." He paused and watched Joe's face for some sign of understanding; when he saw none, he continued. "So you got shot down; so have a lot of other guys. Be thankful, thankful that you got back; be proud of what you … "

"Proud?" Joe dropped his head into his two hands and bent forward. Again he shouted the word through great heaving sobs. "Proud?" Robb sat down on the opposite bunk and stared at the weeping man; his face was puzzled. "Proud of what? Of being the yellowest coward in…" Joe was sitting on the edge of the bunk, bent over with his head resting on his forearms, which were supported by his knees.

Robb spoke hesitatingly, quietly. "Hell yes, proud. Any man who went through what you did has a right to be proud."

"Hell yes, proud! A proud son-of-a-bitch! I'm a brave fighter pilot. I look after my friends…"

"That's what friends are for. You've damn sure looked after me enough."

"Have I?" Joe raised his head; the blood and the tears mixing on his chin dripped into a small pool on the floor and ran slowly into a crack in the worn boards. Joe's face was contorted with anguish; his body shook. Suddenly he seemed to gain control of himself. He straightened up and looked into Robb's eyes. Very quietly he spoke. "Ask Pete Grendel how brave I am."

Robb looked sadly at the anguished man sitting on the opposite bunk. He sat in silence waiting for Joe to continue. He didn't. "Look Joe, you can't blame yourself for what happened to Pete. Face it, you're the best damned pilot in this squadron. Those gunners just got lucky. Things just happen that way. Besides, we might find him yet; who knows, his radio might be busted or maybe they took him prisoner."

Joe was holding his head in his palms again, staring at the small puddle of blood on the floor. "His radio wasn't busted, and they didn't take him prisoner." His voice broke into deep racking sobs and the muscles on his neck knotted with the pain that burdened his soul. With a sudden shriek of anguish he lifted his face and looked imploringly at the ceiling of the dim room. The sound that came from his throat was that of unbearable pain, an unthinkable sin of self-guilt and torture. "They killed him!"

The rasping voice tore at Robb's insides and wrenched at his heart. The anguish within Joe's soul frightened him; the ugly truth that was dawning in his own mind numbed his emotions even more and left him cold with the shock of the truth. "You saw Pete?" Joe only nodded as he gasped desperately for air. Robb walked over to his friend and carefully put his arm around the bent man's shoulders. Vainly he tried to still the retching spasms of his friend's body as

Joe vomited the stale booze over himself and the bunk. Joe spat repeatedly and gasped violently between convulsions.

Robb patted his back and spoke helplessly. "It's all right Joe, Everything is going to be all right."

"Sure it will. And I can spend a lifetime forgetting."

"You'll get over it."

"How? Tell me how?" Joe spewed saliva over himself and sputtered slightly as he coughed out the words. Every muscle of his body tightened and knotted as he cried out at his friend. "You don't know what it's like Robb. I watched them butcher him, and I couldn't move." The raw voice came more quickly as Joe poured out his burden. "I saw them, Robb; I watched, and I couldn't help him. I just couldn't. They tied him and butchered him, and I couldn't move. I couldn't move." The last words were little more than a whisper.

Robb grasped the wailing man and shook him gently. "Joe, don't do this to yourself. It's all over now. It's finished."

"But I should have helped him. I should have done something, but I couldn't move. I just hid like a coward. I was so afraid." The grating voice shook like the man. Robb felt weak; the stench from the mottled bed mingled with the sour smell of vomit and dried blood in the dark room as the two men sat staring at the floor.

"Listen to me, Joe," he broke into a shout. "Listen to me will you? You've got to forget it. It's over; it's done; he's dead, but you're still alive. You still have to live – with or without that ghost – so forget it."

Joe lifted his face. The eyes were red and puffy; around his mouth the vomit and blood had dried into a thin veneer, broken only by the streaks of hot, salty tears. "How can I forget what I saw? I tried not to look. I hid my face and covered my eyes, and I prayed I wouldn't see any more. But, Dear God, I couldn't stop the screams. I couldn't shut them off. I prayed he'd stop. I begged for him to stop." Joe's voice lowered and became barely audible. He was talking to no one – to himself – to everyone. His eyes glazed slightly, and he whispered softly as he babbled on. "I really couldn't move. The screams, the screams. It took him so long to die." Suddenly he was silent; with a jerk he raised his head. His eyes opened wide; his face became a mask of fear. He was still hearing the screams.

*   *   *

Robb had finished cleaning the scarred floor and was wringing his rag into a small coffee can when Joe began to moan loudly in his sleep. The garbled mumblings spilled from his mouth and fell incoherently upon Robb's worn nerves. The tall man looked sadly at the crumpled, broken figure that lay writhing upon the foul bed. The mucus, blood, and vomit had caked into his hair and covered his face like a blotchy rash. Robb looked at the filthy rag in his hand, at the man on the bed, and then to the floor. He rolled Joe over on his back and started to sponge his face with the rag. The man sputtered and coughed then began to scream again. Robb grabbed the bottle of bourbon and tossed half a glass of the burning liquid down Joe's parched throat. He drank greedily, like a small child in the night. The booze settled the shaking limbs, and Joe sank deeper into oblivious sleep. Robb looked at him a long time and then slowly poured a long drink for himself. He downed it quickly and carefully placed the bottle beside the bed. Unconsciously he rubbed his knuckles and stood over the sleeping man. He felt his own eyes burn and became acutely aware of the sharp pain in his own breast. "You poor son-of-a-bitch! How have you lived with that this long?" Robb shook his head sadly, wondering. "Oh God, how will he live with it for the rest of his life?" He looked at the bottle beside the bed, picked it up, and replaced it immediately. Wearily he lay back on his own bunk. The naked bulb and the naked girls on the wall swung softly in the dim room. He looked at the big breasted brunette pouting prettily beside him. "Funny," he thought, "Yesterday she looked happy; tonight she looks sad and ridiculous."

*　*　*

Colonel Bennett sat looking at his desktop and the item Joe had tossed on it. When he looked up at the unshaven captain there was a look of confusion on his face. "What's this about, Joe?"

"I'm through flying."

"What?" There was a sound of incredulity in his voice.

"I'm through flying."

"Why?" The colonel looked carefully at the man standing before him. Joe had not shaved in two days, and his flight suit was stained with sweat and various other liquids that could ill be defined. The combined smell was revolting even from six feet away.

"I can't handle it anymore." Joe stood awkwardly, staring at his wings as they lay on the desk.

The colonel rose slowly, walked around the captain, and closed the door of his office. He returned to his desk but remained standing. "Captain, you get your ass back to your hooch and clean up. When you report back in this office, you look like an officer, not some fucking hippie. You understand?"

"Yes sir."

One hour later the two officers stared at each other across the colonel's desk. The colonel narrowed his eyes and watched the younger man carefully. "You care to talk about this?" He held the pair of wings in the air.

"No, sir."

Bennett stood silent for several minutes, looking straight into the eyes of the younger man. "Look, I don't know what's going on in your head, but I'm going to give you a few days to straighten it out." He picked up the wings, walked around the desk, and placed them in the breast pocket of Joe's flight suit. "In the meantime, you keep these. I don't know another man who could wear these like you have. Now, get your head back on straight and get back into that cockpit where you belong." Joe started to speak but the colonel raised his hand, halting him. "Go ahead; I can keep you DNIF about a week." The older man opened the door. "You've got seven days to work this out; then I want you to report back here Thursday at 1700 hours. And be ready to talk. Dismissed." Without speaking Joe left the room. After he left, Colonel Bennett sighed deeply and reached for the cigar that lay smoldering in the ashtray on his desk. He took two puffs, thinking, then placed the cigar back in the government-issue glassware and walked to the door. "Brown, get me Captains Brady and Barker. I want them here—now!"

"Yes sir."

The colonel smiled at the young airman. "You do good work, Brown."

"Thank you sir."

*   *   *

Robb entered the hooch and slammed the door behind him. Joe was sitting on his bunk, reading a magazine. "What the hell is going on, Joe?"

"I see the good colonel has spoken to you." Joe was clean-shaven and sober. His flight suit hung on a nail by the door. He was wearing his shorts and a T-shirt; both were clean.

"Of course he did. He's worried about you. Dammit, he cares about us."

"Yeah, he does." Joe tossed the magazine into the chair by his bunk. "He's okay."

Robb pulled the chair into the middle of the room and sat down. "This is not the answer, Joe. Grounding yourself is not the way."

"I wish to hell I knew what the answer is."

"I don't know what it is either; but I sure as hell know what it isn't."

Joe swung his legs over the edge of the bunk and sat with his elbows on his knees and his head in his hands. "I don't know what to do. I don't know how to get back in that plane. What can I do?"

Robb stood and began pacing around the small room. "Shit, I don't know. Just keep trying, I guess. Dammit Joe, flying is the only thing that saved my sanity. You'll become a prune if you sit here in this room."

"I'm trying; I'm really trying." Joe had not looked up. His voice was small and weak. "Every time I step on that ladder, I hear screams in my head." Robb ceased his pacing and looked at his friend, trying to envision the ghosts that haunted his mind. He sat beside him and put his arm over Joe's shoulder.

"It's alright, buddy, we're going to beat this—both of us." Somehow, someway we are both going to get through all this shit. Joe nodded in the affirmative, but he never looked up as Robb left the room.

*   *   *

After the bourbon soaked, blood smeared evening both men purposely avoided any direct reference to what had been said. Robb was much like a new, embarrassed bridegroom; he didn't know what to say or do, and it all seemed so stiffly formal. He worked hard at being normal with Joe, but the harder he worked the more the sounds of his own voice disgusted him. Joe, too, skirted the subject initially. Robb never mentioned the incident, and somehow Joe seemed to know that he wouldn't. It was Joe who finally broached the matter several days later.

Robb was struggling with a letter home. He hated letters; he always found it hard to think of things to write; his spelling was atrocious; and his handwriting was almost illegible, even to himself. He absentmindedly stuck the point of the black U.S. government issue ballpoint pen into his mouth and colored his tongue. "Joe, help me think of something to tell my folks, will you?" Joe lay on his bunk staring at the ceiling. He was more relaxed and a great deal of the tenseness had left his face. His eyes had lost the fear; now they were blank. It was almost as if his spirit had died that night and left little more than a sad robot -- one that could feel little, one that could not cry and therefore could not laugh. He had even quit drinking, entirely, for fear that it might release the demon within him again. He was a dead man--working, sweating, existing -- but he never laughed anymore.

"Here we are in a war, and you can't think of anything to write about. If you were a civilian you probably couldn't even talk."

Robb smiled and threw down the pad and pen. "How about a coke or a beer?"

"No thanks ... Robb?"

" Yes?"

"I'm sorry what I said...about Kerrie. Maybe she's going to make it; you deserve that." He spoke quietly but very deliberately.

Robb sat down on his bed and looked carefully at his feet. He finally looked up at Joe and silently said a quick prayer. This was his moment; he knew it. This was his big chance to help the man that he loved like a brother. He laid aside his beer and began speaking very slowly, very deliberately. It was obvious that he was searching his own mind and soul for the words that stumbled from his lips. "You know, Joe, eight months ago I thought I had all the answers; now it's just too much for me to understand. I really don't know anymore. I can only remember what someone told me when I first got here. You soon get to the point that it doesn't make any difference any more.

It all becomes a great big emotional tangle, and the logic of it all becomes unimportant. It's like he said, your job is to live to go home as nearly the same as you were the day when you came." Robb turned away for a moment. "It seems we both have our crosses to bear."

"But you can't go home the same." It was a simple statement.

"You're right; you can't. Every man over here who has fired a rifle, or dropped a bomb, or stacked a casket, or cried out in his sleep, or watched a friend die -- none of us, nobody goes back the same. We all have a burden to bear. I'll never hold a pistol without seeing Wayne dying in my arms. I'll never look into a winter fireplace without seeing Kerrie's face in the blazes; I'll never smell the stench of blood without hearing Chusak gasping for breath. And you've got a heavy load to carry too. Each one is a little different, like the people who struggle with them, but all of us have our own private little hell from this place. And it's a hard road. Believe me, I know. But you can learn to laugh again; perhaps I'll even learn to love again, and you know, in some ways it makes life a little more precious, a little more beautiful." He paused, his pacing and looked straight into the face of his friend. "But it hurts sometimes—no, often—and a song, or a smile, or a memory can cut through you like a spear – and sometimes, sometimes you just wish you could forget." He reached and picked up a small picture laying face down in his locker, looked at it briefly, then turned rapidly and left the room.

CHAPTER TEN

<u>Washington, D.C.</u>

It was two o'clock in Washington when the balding major laid the report on General Patrick's desk. "You'd better check this one, sir. Looks serious." The tired face of the general looked up from the paperwork on his desk. General John Patrick was forty-five years old, a West Point graduate, tired, and frustrated. He looked fifty-five.

"Okay, put it on the stack."

"Sir, I think you'll want to check this ASAP."

"Oh," he was a little surprised, "Must be serious, indeed." He lifted the report and noticed it had several photos attached. He perused it quickly; his eyes widening as he read. "When did you get this?"

"Twenty minutes ago."

The general rubbed his eyes with his palms. He needed new glasses, but right now he had to act. "How many people have seen this?"

"Only you and I, sir," he paused a moment and reflected, "and whoever processed the film."

"I'll handle this with the chief. And Mark, this is Top Secret with Need-to-Know." He paused, looking again at the report. "And I'll determine the Need-to-Know."

"Yes sir."

After the major had left, John Patrick rose from his large, cluttered desk and walked to the door of his office. "Marge, get me a cup of coffee please--no, make that a pot. It's going to be a long afternoon."

"Sure, General."

He walked back to the window of his office and shouted over his shoulder. "And Marge, get Miles Compton on the phone over in intelligence; tell him I need to see him as soon as he can get here." Outside the snow was falling lightly. It was a cold winter day in the capital, the sky dark and threatening. Snow was beginning to accumulate on the landscape and outline the bare trees outside his office. The day, like his spirits, was wrapped in a sense of foreboding. He felt trapped in the office when he really wanted to be standing on some flight line, leading other men into the air. How he missed the excitement and the camaraderie of young men excited about their work. In spite of the snow, he could see the glow of the lights of Washington on the horizon. It was a city of action, the nerve center of the free world. Men and women across the nation begged for assignments inside the beltway. They were drawn to the power, the excitement, and the money. General John Patrick wanted none of it. He would have been far happier with any address that ended in the letters A.F.B(Air Force Base). He watched the large flakes floating lazily to the ground. They were the last of Winter; Spring would soon bring warmth and new life to the city, but he would still be trapped in this office. The idea depressed him. But he was a general, an officer in the service of his country, and much like the priest who takes his vows of obedience, he, too, had taken his own. He would work where the Air Force sent him, and he would do the best job he could. Duty and Honor had been branded in his brain, in his training, and his education. It was his life; it was his commitment. He turned slowly and sat back into his chair.

He rubbed his eyes again, then cursed them. If they had remained strong, he'd still be flying, probably a wing commander in Vietnam. He had made brigadier before most of his classmates, but many of them were still in a cockpit, flying, like he so wanted to do. "Damn this desk job, damn the star on my shoulder, and damn my eyes." He was a fighter pilot, a warrior, not a desk jockey--and here he was, trapped behind the desk. John Patrick was a disciplined man. He did not graduate with honors at West Point by being undisciplined. He allowed his mind its brief moments of regret, but he controlled the anger that burned in his soul. With absolute control he forced his mind back to the report on his desk. What to do about that?

The pictures were taken by a SR-71 "Blackbird" traveling more than Mach 2 and at approximately 60,000 feet. Still, the images were sharp and clear. It had been a cloudless, cold day, perfect for aerial photography. He studied the rail cars carefully. Their cargo was covered, partially. Some detachment of troops had done their job sloppily. Clearly visible were the tail of two missiles and the nose cone of a third. The approximate length and size of the missiles dismissed any of the surface to air missiles that were plaguing US aircrews two thousand five hundred miles south of Vladivistok. These were obviously surface to surface. He guessed SR-04's. There were four of them on the railcars, covered by bright green tarpaulins. "What are those doing in Vladivistok?" he wondered. The next photo caused him to sit upright in his chair. The same green tarpaulins were covering a similar cargo of two more missiles being loaded aboard a Soviet Freighter at the docks in Vladivistok bay. "Oh shit. They must be going to North Korea," he thought. Then he looked up in surprise. "This is not even a military dock," he murmured. The general grabbed his phone and punched two numbers. "Major Compton? Well, find him. And tell him to get to my office as soon as he can. Yes, General Patrick. And, dammit, hurry!" He turned to see his secretary standing in his office, holding a large pot of coffee and several cups on a tray.

"I've already called Major Campbell, Sir."

"I know, Marge." He smiled at the woman before him. She was his own age, plain, slightly overweight, and wonderful. He admired her, and secretly, he felt a closeness to her that even his own wife did not share. "Sit down, have a cup of coffee with me."

"I really have a lot of work to complete if you want that budget report out today."

"Damn the report. Have a cup of coffee with me--that's an order." He smiled at her, and she smiled in return. "By the way, can I officially give you orders?" She sat the coffee on the edge of his desk, carefully clearing a space from the chaos that existed there.

"I suppose; you *are* a general, and you *are* my boss."

"Good, I'll have mine..."

"With cream and one sugar." she interrupted.

"Right, and you take yours black, with one sugar." Her look of surprise pleased him. Their brief interlude was broken by a short, crewcut Major who knocked once on the door and stepped smartly inside at attention.

"Come in Miles." He sipped the hot liquid. It was just as he liked it, strong and hot. "Grab a cup of coffee; you're going to need it." He looked at his watch; it was 2:35 in the afternoon, or 1435 military time. There was much to do.

*   *   *

Miles Campbell stole a quick look at his watch. It was 1540, but with luck the meeting would adjourn soon. He had a date with his daughter tonight, and for once this week, he planned to leave work on time. Few things in his life took precedence over his work; Cindy was one of those few things. His dedication to his job had cost him his marriage; it would not cost him his daughter's undying admiration. The general was standing in front of a flip chart covered with arrows, scribbled notes, and ranked suppositions. "I want constant surveillance on that ship. Whatever it takes, do it. Day and night. I want to know when it leaves port. I want to know its heading in open sea. I want to know its speed. I want a list of potential ports. I want to know what they have for lunch on that rust bucket. I want it all, everything. Any questions?"

"No sir."

"Major, we may be looking at another hot spot, perhaps even another theater of operations." He grimaced. "And we've got our hands full with the one we've got."

"Wish we had a President and a Congress with balls." The major blurted it without thinking. He was immediately sorry for saying it, watching the general for reaction.

Patrick looked up wearily. "They've got their job; we've got ours." He would have liked to add "They are worried about elections, and we are worried about winning a war," but he didn't. Instead, he placed his hand on the Major's shoulder. "Good work, Miles; I know I can depend on you." He was complementing the major's skills which were well known; he was also sending a message that the inadvertent exclamation was forgotten. The relief on Campbell's face was evident.

"Thank you sir."

As the major left John Patrick lifted the phone on his desk and pressed the one button he hated.

"General Armstrong's office."

"General Patrick here. I have a Priority One that needs his attention."

"I'm sorry, the chief is at a luncheon with the President and a committee from the Hill. He should return shortly after 1500. Shall I have him call you then?"

General Patrick's face was red with anger, yet his voice was calm and professional. "Yes, and Wanda, please remind the chief that this is urgent, Priority One."

"Of course, General."

"Thank you," He hung up the phone and shouted at it. "Damned politicians--all of them!" He turned to see Marge standing in his door.

"More coffee, General?"

He laughed quietly and smiled at her. "Maybe I've had enough caffeine already."

"Perhaps. They say it makes the mind more perceptive." She smiled in return. But he did not see it; he had grabbed a pen and was scribbling names on a list as fast as he could. "Marge, I need to see all of these men in my office at 1600 hours. I don't care what excuses they give. I want them *here*. Tell them all it is Priority One." He settled into his large leather chair and took a long sip of the hot coffee. It settled his agitation. "Thanks Marge; this is great. And so are you."

Margaret Harris smiled at the man seated across the desk. She was nearing her forty-sixth birthday. Her young figure had spread, and her lovely breasts had finally fallen victim to gravity. The green eyes that once sparkled with mischief were now framed by small wrinkles that even the makeup could not hide. Only the hair had survived the changes of time. The sun streaked strawberry blonde still shone as brightly as ever, and the few gray strands that dared emerge were quickly plucked. To most, Marge Harris would be considered an attractive middle aged woman. To Marge, the goal was different; the ideal was to be found in the magazines that constantly lay with her purse beside her desk. The ideal was beautiful and young. Tom Wolfe was right, you really can't go home again. The view of the world around her was very different than the one she watched in the mirror. Only her complete devotion to General John Patrick added luster to an otherwise dull life. What she lacked in reality, she found in her dreams. Somewhere in most of them was a tall, distinguished looking general. Marge knew John Patrick's exact age, where he was born, what he liked to eat and read, even the size of his shoes. Now she was perfecting his moods. "Thanks." She turned and walked to her desk, reflecting on her blessings. She had him ten hours a day-- often more, but always limited to these walls, to his work. His wife had much less of his life, but she had a part of him Marge longed to know but probably never would. When she picked up the phone, there was a sad smile on her face. "General Patrick, I noticed that Miles Campbell is not on this list; shall I invite him also?"

"No problem, I've already briefed him. He'll be there."

* * *

Eight men sat around the large briefing table. It was littered with dirty coffee cups and filled ashtrays. A cloud of smoke hovered overhead, partially obscuring the lights above. Major Miles Campbell stood before a screen, pointing at various items on the projected images. "General Patrick, North Korea does make the most sense. We know there are four missiles with a range up to 1700 kilometers. That would certainly cover all of South Korea. But we also have to acknowledge that to be an assumption. What if the destination is different?"

"Like what? Japan?" Several of the men laughed.

"What about North Vietnam or Cuba? Or China?"

"Cuba makes no sense at all. We've been through that with them before. They know we have that area covered like a blanket. They couldn't import a bazooka without us knowing its serial number. China and North Vietnam make no sense either. They would probably not want that technology to fall into Chinese hands. These are the same missiles they use to keep the Chinese in check. Korea, however, would allow them to open a different front for us. It could divert our air power even if they only use them as a threat. It has to be Korea."

"I agree with your assessment on Korea, but North Vietnam might be different. Suppose they go there?"

"What potential targets would they have from there?"

"DaNang, Clark in the Philippines, any of our bases in Thailand." Campbell was among superior officers, but not superior intellect. "The question--if it is North Vietnam--is not where, but why. Why would they use these missiles?" He looked back at the screen for several moments. "What would they gain by escalating the war? The Vietnamese or the Soviets?"

"That's what I want all of you to think about tonight. Try every scenario. Miles, call our Intel folks and see what they know. Something this big couldn't get through the Kremlin without a whisper somewhere. Get Intel on this ASAP. We'll continue to monitor this ship; it left dock at 0635 this morning. Estimated speed is twelve knots. It should commit to North Korea by 0500 tomorrow at the latest. Either way, gentlemen, we've got work to do. Report back here at 0800 tomorrow. Any questions?"

"One, has the chief been notified?"

"Not yet, He's been out, but I have an appointment with him in thirty-five minutes."

"Good luck."

The general smiled for the first time since the men entered the room. "Thanks."

Nubat Royal Thai Air Force Base

With a swinging leap, Robb grasped the side of the pickup and swung himself into the rear of the truck. The hot metal burned his hands slightly, but he ignored it as the truck rumbled along the soft gooey asphalt. On his left there were several small boys, no more than nine or ten years old, splashing water and mud over the backs of two gray water buffaloes. Like boys the world over, they were shouting and had mud flying in all directions. They were dousing themselves as well as the large beasts standing in the small drainage ditch. Though their laughter was shrill and excited, Robb knew that this was no game but rather a basic necessity imposed by a humorous twist of nature. These regular soakings were essential to save the water buffaloes from the terrible heat in the fields, for the beasts have no sweat glands to provide a means of cooling themselves. Therefore, they must have some substitute—a regular dousing as they work. When the ditch was full of water, as in the rainy season, the animals would merely lay in the muddy water and soak up the moisture; in the dryer season, they were accommodated by their handlers—usually young children.

Robb looked at his own clothing and saw that already it was beginning to show the stains of perspiration soaking through, and he had been in the sun for less than ten minutes. It was hardly conceivable to him that man or beast could labor long in that stifling heat. He had often watched the crew chiefs and the load crews as they left their work on the flight line. After ten or more hours of grueling work, the men would leave the blistering concrete to return to the cool clubs near their billets. There they would drink beer until the pace and the pressure of their work fell from their brains and their bodies. These men had a tremendous job to perform—and under the worst conditions. Hour after hour they would work to meet the ever-demanding schedule. They worked and lived by a schedule. It told them when they could sleep (for some only in the heat of the middle of the day), when they could eat, when their jobs must be rushed, when their planes must fly, and when they could expect to see them flying close together as they returned after another successful mission. They knew their planes; they knew their own capabilities; and they got the maximum out of both. Occasionally they even knew the respect their pilots felt for them or the ultimate importance of the job they were doing. In their minds, they were told to do a job, and they did it extremely well. The glory and the risks would go to the pilots, but every person on the base knew that the mission depended on these young men who labored over their aircraft in the hot jungle sun.

Late one evening Robb had seen one of these young men standing beside an empty revetment crying. His bird had not returned from its mission. It was hard to say whether he was crying over the loss of the two men he had strapped into the plane just three hours earlier or the plane itself, or the possibility that perhaps, just perhaps, he might have forgotten one small bolt, one small gage. He was probably weeping over all three. He had lost three friends that day, and he would never know if he could have been partly to blame. The pressure these men felt was proportional to the awesome responsibility that was theirs. The most critical test any pilot could face would be encountered in combat. Not only were there enemy defenses to be met but also the very act of flying was under the most difficult circumstances. The planes were heavily loaded with ordnance and extra fuel, and with the difficult aerial maneuvers required in combat, this extra weight and drag cut dangerously into the safety margin designed into each plane. All of these factors demanded the highest skills of the men who flew the aircraft and also the crews who maintained them. Small oversights or small discrepancies that might be overlooked in normal flying became critical elements for planes that left for battle with enemy gunners hundreds of miles from the base.

The heat was probably the smallest problem to plague these men. Like the pilots, they also had a war to fight; only they fought theirs on the hot concrete ramps. And like the pilots, they too had to release the pent up pressures that cooked within them during the long hard shifts in the blazing sun or the blinding rain. Robb had been to some of their parties, and he was sure that he would not soon forget them. The concerted efficiency of the workday could easily transform into the wild abandon of release, the relaxing intermediary before the process began again the next morning.

With the same easy grace with which he entered the vehicle, Robb swung himself over the tailgate of the truck and entered the long, low building which held the many briefing rooms, Wing headquarters, the Command Post, and the intelligence "cave." Clem Roberts had arrived early and was absorbed in studying a large photograph with a small, but powerful, magnifying glass. Colonel Bennett walked into the briefing room behind Robb, a wispy trail of blue smoke trailing from the long cigar that was clenched between his teeth. The colonel was of medium build and medium height, but the set of his jaw and the piercing gaze in his dark eyes set him apart from most of his contemporaries. His hair was dark and curly on top; on the sides it was quite gray and cropped close to his head, leaving his temples almost bare. The cigar was as much a part of him as the impish grin, the long, straight nose, or the profound insight into the men with whom he worked. This was a man who demanded your all, and, likewise, you could expect his all. That was why he was a respected leader. Some have lofty goals and vision while others step forward to lead their troops to victory. Bennett could always be found at the front of the battle, not cheering from behind. "Got any good targets today?"

"Yes sir." Major Roberts pointed toward the large photograph, which was really a lot of smaller photographs taped together. "This isn't on our frag order, but there's something interesting going on near our target." As both of the officers leaned over the mosaic, Clem handed the older man the magnifying glass. "It's a water tower." The major shifted the mosaic around toward the colonel, searched momentarily, and pointed out the prize. "There, near the coast."

"A water tower?"

"My guess is it's full of fuel." Look at those tracks leading to the tower. Why would trucks be visiting that tower so often? And note that there are three anti-aircraft sites protecting it. Why would they do that if it were just a water tower?"

"Well those trucks certainly aren't taking on water. They gave up the steam engine too long ago for that." The colonel studied the picture carefully. "Well, I'd certainly be the last man to brief a flight to hit a water tower; however, discretion and valor are reputed to be connected somehow, and I distinctly remember being told at Command and Staff School that a good commander heeds the advice of his younger officers." He paused and grinned over the remains of his cigar. "Anyway, you never know when there may be trucks around that tower, and if you accidentally hit it while aiming at trucks or gun sites in the area, well, certainly no one could criticize that." The grin vanished with the wrinkles around his eyes. "But let's not publicize this, Clem. In order to take the initiative we have to gamble now and then—not just our lives with the enemy, but also our careers with the brass. You've got to cover your ass in case you make a mistake—and if you fly over here for a year, you're bound to make a few. Let's just hope this isn't one of them. Understand?"

"Yes sir."

"Now what do you think it will take?"

"One pod of rockets."

"It's yours." Clem smiled and winked at the colonel. "And Clem, in case you miss, I'll have a pod handy as well."

"I won't miss."

*   *   *

The three officers leaned wearily against the long bar as the colonel ordered beers for them all. "Dammit, Clem, I owe you this one. That was one of the most beautiful sights I've seen in years. That was damn fine work. What a fire."

"Thank you sir. I just figured those zippers were up to something. There just couldn't be any reason for them to drive up to that thing unless it's full of gas."

As the bartender, a pert young Thai girl with long black hair, handed the drinks across the bar that was almost as tall as she, the colonel raised his glass. "Well, they won't be using that fuel stop for a long time now. It burned like a son-of-a-bitch didn't it? Here's to the biggest secondary I've seen in this war."

Robb left the two older men after the first beer and joined Joe and Tom Cantrell for dinner. Robb, Joe, and Tom were returning to the hooches after a terrible third-rate movie when Robb heard his name called. He squinted into the darkness. "Where the hell are you, Clem?"

"Over here on the beach."

Robb peered across the maze of lawn chairs and chaise lounges and sure enough, there in the middle was a broad grin below a tuft of short blond hair. Clem was obviously a little high, and it was with some misgivings that Robb crawled over the tangled chairs in the dark and sat down carefully on one of the reclining chairs. "You been in the bar all this time?"

"Hell yes, I've been sober for three months—since ol' Jerry Mulligan went down—so I felt it was time to tie one on." One of the forward air controller pilots walked by and made several comments about drunks talking in the dark; Clem threw a partially full beer can at him and knocked over one of the several bicycles parked beside the small hooch in which the FAC's lived.

"Damn drunk; some kind of idiot, wasting good beer like that."

Clem and Robb laughed out loud. "That's Casey Morgan; you ever see his pictures of his wife?" Clem's voice had become suddenly serious.

"No, she pretty?"

"Pretty! She's a living doll." Clem whistled in appreciation of the other man's wife.

"You married Clem?"

"I was. We got divorced two years ago tomorrow." There was a sudden sadness in his voice that betrayed a deeper bitterness than he would admit.

"You don't sound too happy with that."

"I'm not."

"I'm sorry to hear that." Robb groped for words, not knowing what was appropriate.

"I guess I'm sorry too." Deep inside the drunken pilot was struggling with a reopened wound that had never quite healed. "Frankly, I still love her."

Robb was shocked by the admission. It did not seem possible that this man, always smiling and happy, could be tortured by a problem hidden so securely behind the façade of carelessness. Clem had carried out the deception well, but the cost to his own peace had left him susceptible to his own weaknesses. Only a great deal of time could ever cover the hurt that he felt inside. And even now, old memories were ever lurking behind every moment, every thought. Vainly the younger man searched his mind for a solution. But how could you solve an issue when you didn't even understand the problem. Perhaps in the heart. "Why don't you go back to her?"

"Go back?" Clem spoke the words slowly, savoring their meaning. "I can't."

"Why not? You just admitted you love her. Could she still love you?"

"I think so. Yes, I'm sure she does, down deep."

"Then go back and try over again. Clem nothing is so big or so horrible that it can't be forgiven between two people who really love each other."

Clem drank from a fresh can of beer that he pulled from a wet cardboard box beside his seat. For long minutes he sat in silence and pondered the other man's suggestion, while Robb squirmed in discomfort. He felt a little silly and somewhat embarrassed. Here he was trying to act as a marriage counselor—and he didn't even know what had caused the split in the first place.

"Robb, maybe you're right. I've been trying to convince myself to do just that for two months now. What the hell, we made it once; there's no reason we can't make it again." With a lunge, Clem threw the half full can of beer into the darkness; it fell with a resounding crash on the tin roof of the FAC hooch and soon brought irate curses and threats from the inhabitants. Clem laughed. "Damn ghetto, a man can't even choose his neighbors anymore. See you tomorrow, Robb, I've got a letter to write."

With a relieved smile, Robb followed Clem around the darker edge of the latrine to avoid the volley they would certainly receive if they were seen by the laughing mob who were already tossing cans and chairs onto the patio.

Aboard the Russian Freighter "Kamkara" in the Pacific Ocean

Dmitriy Mihail Ruchinsky stood on the bow of the freighter and breathed the clear ocean air. It was so different from the air below in the ship. There everything smelled of grease, of greasy food, and of greasy men. His distaste for sailors had not changed. It was here, on the bow, that he realized one small reason for men to go to sea. The clear salt breeze blew across his face and refreshed him. It was also a good place to think. Down below it was impossible to think. The stink and the noise were enough to make most men sick; Sergei had been sick several times on this trip, much to the amusement of the sailors. Ruchinsky turned slowly and relished the last wind in his face and then slowly walked back across the deck. From above, the captain of the ship nodded to him. The captain knew little of the man below, but he did recognize his rank and his cargo. Only an idiot would not have recognized his cargo. Innokentiy was a good captain. He was old and tired of the strain of dealing with the men, but he still loved the sea, and he loved his ship. It was his ship, even though the government shipping bureaucrats thought it was theirs; they really didn't understand, but that was okay. He directed the ship and everything and everyone on it. It was his ship. And Innokentiy checked the freight it carried carefully. This voyage must be an important one. He was proud that his was the ship chosen for such a mission. Surely someone must have finally recognized his skills and his ability. He smiled; his grandchildren would tell stories of this voyage. He looked back at the colonel. Surely he must be a man of position to be given command of such an important task. Innokentiy would treat Colonel Ruchinsky well. A man like that might make a difference in one's position. Already he had given him the best berth with the best bed. And the food— Innokentiy had ordered the cook to bring out the best food and the best vodka for the army colonel. Innokentiy would insure that the colonel was impressed.

Sergei watched his leader and rousted the two young soldiers who were slumbering at their posts, threatening them with firing squads if he caught them asleep again. He also checked his cargo well. They were covered by tarps, but they were still somewhat exposed to the elements. Thus far the weather had been cooperative, but still he worried. Will these things work if they get wet? He wondered. And what about the salt air? He scratched his itching scalp and cursed the soldiers again. Finally satisfied, he returned to the bow of the ship where the colonel looked off to his right and watched the coast of China in the distance. Surely they did not know of his mission. What would be their reaction if they did? To his left he looked off into the distance at the ocean. He could see nothing there except water, but he knew there was more than water there. Somewhere in the distance would be the US fleet. He wondered about their navy. Did their sailors stink and eat filthy food as the men below? He guessed that sailors were the same the world over. He loathed them all.

Sergei turned abruptly at the sound of loud voices behind him. He recognized the voice of one of his guards. Sergei was a very deliberate man, but he could run when the need arose. He was almost running down the deck toward the shouting. From above the ship's captain saw the commotion and rushed aft as well. He arrived at the cargo area just after the Sergei.

"What the hell is going on here?"

"This idiot sailor was nosing around our cargo. I told him to leave, and he told me to eat shit." The young soldier was half the age of the smiling sailor.

"This child should be with his mother. He's not old enough to be weaned yet," sneered the older man. The young soldier stared back with a mixture of anger and fear.

"What were you doing around these things?" Sergei motioned to the missiles.

"Just looking around to see what toys the army has. Anything wrong with that?"

"What were your orders about this cargo and this mission?"

Innokentiy spoke up when the sailor shrugged. "The orders were to stay off this deck unless directed by me." Innokentiy nodded to Sergei.

"Do you normally disobey orders?" Casually, Sergei unbuttoned his heavy overcoat.

The older sailor's smile faded. He had had enough of them. "Fuck you! I'm not in the army. I don't have to listen to this crap. You can eat shit, too." He turned toward the missiles in defiance of Sergei's authority.

"If he takes one more step toward that cargo, shoot him." Dmitriy walked forward and spoke to the young soldier in a calm and steady voice.

"Sir?" The soldier looked at the colonel and then at his captain.

"I said shoot him if he is fool enough to disobey orders." Unlike the other men on the deck, the colonel's voice was calm. The old sailor turned immediately to face the army officers. His expression was one of contempt. The sailor spat on the deck, then took one more step toward the missiles.

"Kill him?"

"Yes, like this." Sergei pulled the pistol from his coat and fired one bullet into the sailor's chest. The man stood there for a moment, staring at Sergei in disbelief. He started to talk, but only blood flowed from his mouth. Slowly he crumbled to the deck before the shocked men standing around him. Dmitriy turned to the soldiers. "Throw him overboard. Then we'll see if sharks eat shit."

Sergei had made his point; he was also wise enough to keep his gun ready should any of the others object. They didn't. He turned to the Captain of the ship. "That was unavoidable, but you know the importance of this mission. No one can compromise this mission. No one! Do you understand?" He was speaking to the captain, but he was watching the assembled sailors.

"Of course." Innokentiy watched as the soldiers threw the body overboard. "He was a fool. I told the entire crew to stay away from this area."

Dmitriy stepped forward. "You did your duty, captain; he should have listened." Once the body was disposed of and the guards were back in place, he walked slowly back to the bow of the ship. Sergei had made an example for his troops; and he had confirmed who was really in command on this ship. He was proud of his captain; he was becoming a fine young officer. Ruchinsky had learned a powerful lesson from his own drunken father, a lesson that had served him well during his entire life, and one that Sergei was learning as well. The power of violence lies not in physical harm to the victim but in the fear it creates in the observers. Throughout history select men had perfected converting the selected use of violence to the controlling tool of fear. He had studied them well, and he had mastered their techniques. He could still recall the long terrible nights as a boy, listening to the drunken man who screamed obscenities and beat his helpless wife. At fourteen he could stand the violence no longer and had killed his own father with his own hands. The local police had assumed the murderer to be some passing drifter. No one suspected a young boy of such violence. A year later, he had joined the Army. That was where he had found his life. His father's influence, in the end, had been a good one. Dmitriy smiled as the salty wind blew across his face.

CHAPTER ELEVEN

<u>Washington D.C.</u>

He was President of the United States, the most powerful man in the world, but he looked more like someone's grandpa, a tired and sad grandpa. Large dark circles were under his eyes; his jowls drooped below his chin, adding to the perpetual look of sadness on his face. He was well groomed, his hair combed straight back; he would have fit well in some small Texas Chamber of Commerce. Beneath that old gentlemanly face, however, lurked a brilliant mind, albeit a very weary one. "Well, gentlemen, what's up?"

The three star general rose and looked around the room. He was the junior military officer present. "We're sorry to disturb your schedule today, sir, but this one is important. What we have is a commercial Russian freighter, the Kamkara, out of Vladivistok, apparently on its way south with a load of short range ballistic missiles. We have counted four on deck; there could be more in the hold." He stopped briefly to allow questions. When there were none, he continued. "We've been tracking this ship for ten hours; it could be on its way to North Korea, China, or North Vietnam."

As the president spoke, his lips barely moved. "Any idea what they're up to?"

"No sir. Frankly it doesn't make sense."

The national security advisor interrupted. "Mr. President, we've checked all possibilities. We've contacted the Soviet ambassador; we've polled our underground sources—it seems the Soviets know nothing about this. In fact, we've just been informed last night that they are desperately checking the story as well."

"What's your assessment, Howard?"

"Well, there are a lot of things here that just don't add up. Why would the Soviets take such a big risk? This isn't like them. They are much too smart to do something like this. And why would missiles like that be shipped on a common freighter? And in broad daylight? We spotted these with a blackbird. Surely the KGB knows our flight path is along the border. It just doesn't make sense."

"Any internal politics going on in the Kremlin? Could someone be stirring the pot?"

"Our sources say everything is cool."

"Damn!" The President sat back in his chair and ran his fingers through his thinning hair. "Damn!" After a few moments of silence he looked back at his National Security Advisor. "What do you recommend, Howard?"

"Mr. President, we've got a serious problem. That is a commercial Soviet freighter, and we don't attack commercial ships on the open seas."

The president spoke quietly, rubbing his temples as he spoke. "What are our options?"

The general stepped forward and continued the briefing. "Option 1, we can sink the ship before the missiles are delivered. Option 2, we can intercept it on the open seas and turn it around. Option 3, we can appeal to the Soviets to turn it around."

The security advisor spoke up again. "If, indeed, they really didn't know about this, number three would be the best option. They could take care of it without us getting involved."

The president rubbed his forehead with his fingers. "That would be the easy way, for sure. General, if we had to sink it, how would you do that?"

"On the open sea it would be a piece of cake, Mr. President. We would use aircraft off of one of our carriers parked in the area. We also have large guns in the battle group, as well as subs in the area."

"Is this thing guarded at all? Does it have escort ships?"

"No, Sir. It does have a couple of anti-aircraft guns aboard, but they're practically useless."

"Damn!" The president looked at each of the faces in the room then back to the general. "And you're sure there are missiles on that ship. There could be no mistake about this?"

"No mistake sir. Would you like to see the photos?"

"No, that's not necessary. You guys know your business better than I do. If you're convinced, that's good enough for me." He nodded to his security advisor on the right side of the table.

"Howard, any ideas?"

"Let's give the Soviets a little more time. My guess is that if they discover a renegade operation, they'll turn it around or sink it themselves. And this almost has to be a renegade operation. Shipping missiles on a commercial freighter with tarps over them is not in their ops book, I'm sure."

"Sounds good to me. How long do we have, general? When does the shit hit the fan?"

"It's hard to say, depending on where it's going. We have at least twenty-four hours, but we'd have to hit the ship before the missiles are offloaded. Once they are ashore we could lose them forever."

"If they got ashore, what are our risks?"

"Again, depending on their destination, with four missiles they could take out Clark in the Philippines, Nubat, Udorn, NKP, Da Nang, Saigon, Seoul, Tokyo, or whatever their choices might be."

The general looked at the faces of the men in the room. His point had obviously been made.

"And you don't know if they are nukes or not?"

"They look like nukes, but frankly, we don't know for sure. For our purposes, we must assume that they are."

"Twenty-four hours?"

"Yes, Sir."

"Howard, get on those Soviets. If I need to use the red phone, let me know. I want hourly updates on what is happening. Let's get back together on this tomorrow morning. Thank you gentlemen." The President rose and walked to the door. He stopped for a moment and walked to the coffeepot in the corner. Two generals quickly grabbed cups and began serving coffee. The President handed a cup to each of the advisors standing beside him then took one for himself. He sipped it quickly, looking at his watch. "Gentlemen, we've got a meeting with Senators Thompson and Garnett." And the three turned and rushed for the door.

Five minutes later the phone rang in General Patrick's office. "Patrick here."

"No decision; they're waiting to see what the Rooskies will do."

There was a long pause, then, "Okay, thanks Wanda. Let me know if anything changes."

"There is a meeting in the morning—situation room, zero seven hundred."

"Will the boss be there?"

"Yes."

"I need to see him before he leaves tonight."

"I'll work you in. Let me juggle the schedule a bit." She paused briefly; the general could hear paper shuffling. "Let me call you back."

"Thanks."

Nubat Royal Thai Air Force Base

The tired pilot stood leaning against the dark revetment wall and stared into the soft night air. Perspiration ran down his cheeks in small rivulets and eroded the thin film of dust that clung to his face. He raised a hand and flicked at the small drops that formed on the tip of his nose. It was dark, and still the heat was oppressing; under the g-suit, pistol belt, survival vest, and the parachute harness, his body drained itself relentlessly in the attempt to maintain a steady temperature in the stifling heat. The night breezes were cooler, but the heat of the day, stored in the concrete ramps and the steel shelters, rose in waves and engulfed the men working there. The maintenance men walked back and forth in armless shirts or completely naked from the waist. The flight crews could not afford such comfort; their bodies struggled under the burden of the paraphernalia of war, and their bodies cried out, sobbing salty tears that streaked them and marked their clothing with great white stains.

An ugly black bug crawled into the light from the corner of the darkened revetment. Robb studied it carefully as it edged slowly across the hot cement. By turning his head toward the repulsive object, he could hear the faint scraping noise of the hard body as the insect lifted its black shell and transparent wings to straddle a small wire left absently behind the large aircraft. Behind the awkward bug was another, larger, with threatening mandibles, dragging along in the same direction as the first. The smaller turned and the larger followed. First to the right, then to the left; still the larger bug followed, slowly closing the gap between them. The wings never moved; neither of the two struggling forms made an attempt to fly—they only crawled across the rough concrete. As the larger drew nearer, his large mandibles began a threatening pinching motion before him. The smaller of the bugs lurched forward and gained a slight advantage in his race, which Robb was beginning to understand was a race for survival. Bleakly, he watched as the two small creatures approached a pipe that lay perpendicular to their path. The smaller of the two reached the pipe first and began to climb over. Three struggling pairs of legs grasped at the greasy pipe. Two legs holding on the pipe, two suspended in mid air, and the third pair struggling on the ground, trying to push the awkward body into the air. The larger insect continued his relentless pace and slowly narrowed the space between the crushing pincers and the struggling prey before him. The smaller insect struggled harder, the hind legs straining, the front legs grasping, pulling. Suddenly the middle pair of legs grasped the pipe and aided in the effort. Now all of the tiny appendages were functioning together, working as a team. Four pull, two push; slowly the hulking body inched up the large pipe as the attacker pressed its pursuit. Mid way up the pipe, the front legs slipped and then the middle ones. The hind legs strained and pushed violently, but the battle was lost. The inevitable laws of nature pulled the thrashing insect to the ground and left him helpless on his back. The tiny legs waved and flagged the air as the larger bug slackened his pace.

"Hey man, what in hell are you doing?" Robb turned to face the bright smile and the blond bushy hair reflecting the bright lights that shone over the ramp.

"Hi Clem. Why aren't you in our flight tonight? I thought we were going to be partners again after the past week or so."

"Well, the way I figure it they couldn't afford to concentrate so much of their talent in one flight."

"Hell yes, that must be it." Both men smiled. Robb turned his head skyward to test the night wind, checking the sky with an experienced eye. "Viz is pretty good, east and south, but I don't like the looks of those dark ones to the north."

Clem swung his head to gaze into the darkness of the evening sky. As he spoke, his large Adam's apple bounced with the rhythm of his words. Even in the semi darkness, the scars on his cheeks stood out as small dark pits that had healed from without, forever leaving their mark of a hard and difficult period that would never be forgotten, mirror images of the deeper furrows they had left within. "We'll be back before they hit." He nodded his head for emphasis.

"Damn, I hope so; I hate like hell to fly in these monsoon storms. I guess I'm even more afraid of them than those zip gunners."

Both of the men turned and walked toward the open entrance of the busy revetment. In silence they watched the spectacle before them. Trucks and vehicles of all sizes roared back and forth, up and down the long rows of aircraft parked in the dark revetments. A tall airman on a short weapon-loading vehicle roared by with a large bomb hanging precariously from two strong steel chains. Another followed closely behind, carrying a much larger bomb, a CBU bomblett bomb. Robb's mind flashed to the scene from the revetment a few moments earlier and he smiled. Clem looked at him with a question but said nothing. It was their way, as it has been with all men prior to battle, to withdraw within themselves. In their silence there was strength and resolve. Their friendship, though decorated with the glitter and brightness of laughter, was founded on the bedrock of comradeship, a deep and trusting appreciation for the other and the individuality of his contribution to the mission. Tonight, they would be in separate flights, but still they would function as part of the same team. They depended upon each other and upon the other men who composed the team which would again prepare them for battle. Here the stakes were real; there might not be another game or another season. Their game tonight would not be watched by millions on TV sets; no audience would cheer the diving, screaming planes; huge purses would not go to the victors; and no one would cry as bodies tore and ripped apart against finely manufactured steel. Still they climbed into their crafts and buckled their tired, sweating bodies to the powerful monsters beneath them.

And as they climbed into their cockpits, they looked at the men across and down the line of planes. These were great men, despite the small muscles, the balding heads, the crooked noses or funny walk. They did not look like a sprinkling of the finest of America's youth, fit and ready. Quite to the contrary, they were a varied and diverse mixture—like the country they fought for. There were fat and wrinkled men here, men who laughed and proudly showed the clippings of their sons' feats of courage on the friendly fields of strife. They fought in order that their sons and their sons' sons could run before the screaming crowds and the multitudes watching from far distant places and bask in the glory of an awed nation of sports fans. There were those among them who had recently run those same fields and those who had never basked in one moment's glory but had only watched. Together these opposite and unlike men formed a new team each night. Everyone played; there were no stars. Each man knew himself, and after a few missions he came to know those sitting across from him at the briefings. These were welded together into a team with a common purpose, a team separate from and greater than its members. The team was relentless; it demanded a man's all, and it got it, for each man depended upon the team for his own survival, and he knew that the team was no stronger than he was strong. He was its weakness, and he was its strength.

The men sat in their planes, and they looked at each other. They waved in the dark, or they made obscene gestures, and in their looking, their waving, their gestures, they said, "I trust you, and you can trust me." They fought together, and sometimes they died together.

Lights flashed across the opposite revetments as another truck rounded the corner and made its way ever so slowly between the bomb ladened racks. The truck rolled nearer, stopped several revetments down, and discarded two crews who lumbered toward their waiting planes. Out of respect for the men and the job they were to perform, the crew chiefs stopped their work and turned to salute and greet the sweating officers. Together they would survey the forms for the aircraft, forms that the chief had studied, memorized, and stuck indelibly in his brain. It was his bird on the ground; he knew her intimately. His plane was his pride and his responsibility; the relationship between man and machine demanded that he seek out the inner workings of the other. Deep into the bowels of their planes the maintenance crews would dig. When they emerged, they would be covered with the blood and the sinew of the remarkable giant. Its power and its intricacies were awesome, like the dedication and care that the men felt for the throbbing, roaring piece of metal. With the awe grew dedication, and from that grew a devotion that bordered on love—the abnormal fondness of man and machine. Together they functioned as one entity with one mission. The groaning machines, bearing their burden high above the ground, responding to the slightest touch of the men who mounted them, shrieking, rasping machines flinging through the damp jungle air. Occasionally they were hit; they moaned and gasped like a dying man. Sometimes they did die, thrusting those who flew them high into the air in a last desperate act. And while the pilots were left to find their own way back to the earth, the planes dashed themselves into the rocks and hills and trees and rivers and burned hideously, destroying themselves in their own fuel, while their pilots floated like silent ghosts toward the earth below. Ears that listened to the great engines, fingers that probed deep inside the hardened skin, palms that felt the well known throb of a familiar friend—these would not be idle long after the big bird went down. Soon they would find another sound, another throb, another deep dark body to know, but the heart would be sad, and the mind would not understand the sadness.

As the lumbering truck gained momentum, Clem looked briefly at the approaching vehicle and then at his friend. "Robb, I thought about our discussion last night—about me and Joanne." He paused, waited, and when the captain said nothing, he continued, thinking carefully on each word. "Well, I figure you were right, and, damn it, I'm going to try it again. Like I said, we made it once; we loved each other once; and I believe we still do. There's no reason we can't make it again if we're willing to try."

Robb smiled at this friend and shuffled his feet subconsciously. His boots made black marks on the grayed concrete. "I'm glad to hear that Clem; it's good to see you resolved. You courted her and won her heart once; there's no reason you can't do it again—a guy as suave and handsome as you." He smiled broadly and slapped his friend's shoulder in an effort to relieve his own discomfort at sharing such a serious decision in another man's life. "You might enjoy the chase; hell, it was fun the first time wasn't it?"

Clem's broad white teeth flashed in an impish grin, and a childish sparkle shined in his light blue eyes. "I haven't been this happy in a long time." The truck stopped with a jerk before the two men and its cursing load scrambled out the rear. Clem spoke rapidly and confidentially as the crews approached. "What I said is just between us, okay?" Robb nodded as Clem continued. "You should see the letter I wrote today—the one I was working on in the briefing. I haven't written in two years; she probably thinks I'm dead, but when she gets this…I asked her to give me another chance. We'll start back at the beginning; maybe this time we can get it right."

Clem joined the other pilots walking down the ramp as Robb started his preflight. As he neared the tail of the craft, he remembered the bugs and flashed his light onto the dark pipe. It stood alone in the darkness, deserted.

$$* \quad * \quad *$$

The fighters stood at the end of the runway and strained at their brakes. First one engine and then the other was run up to full power, never both at the same time, for even without afterburners, both engines at full military throttle were too powerful to be restrained. The roar was deafening. Across the short taxiways lines of maintenance men lined the revetment walls and watched their birds scream and howl in anticipation of the night's mission. The seriousness that had carved deep lines of strain into their faces and drawn tight their eyes and lips only a few minutes ago was gone. It had rolled along the taxiways and onto the mile long stretch of pavement that lay like a dull ribbon across the green rolling earth. The deadening roar stopped. Now it was only moments before the big jets would lurch forward, faster and faster down the white ribbon, and finally the blazing afterburners would ignite and thrust the planes into the air. For the present, there was only the relative silence. At a run-up of 85% power the pilots would make one last check: exhaust gas temperature—470 degrees, fuel flow 4000 pounds per hour, flaps—one quarter, oil pressure—37 pounds per square inch. Only the flight crews and the tower broke the evening silence. "Dragon, flight of four, ready for takeoff."

"Roger Dragon, winds two five niner at ten, cleared for takeoff. Good hunting." With a thundering roar, the lead aircraft dipped forward slightly as the mighty engines roared to 100 percent power. The brakes were released and it raised its head slightly and began to roll slowly away from its comrades. Through the darkness two large streams of fire burst from the plane's aft end; the craft lurched forward and rolled faster. Across the base, those who did not see the engines' afterburners ignite stopped momentarily from their work and looked up, for the night rocked violently with the thudding ache of exploding fuel that could be felt and heard for miles. The temperature immediately behind the aircraft climbed to above three thousand degrees Fahrenheit as the engines sucked from the seventeen thousand pounds of JP4 fuel in the aircraft tanks. The immediate thrust sent the plane down the runway at an increasing speed. At seventy knots the rudder became operative for steering;

at eighty knots the control stick was pulled back full aft; at one hundred seventy knots the plane left the runway and entered its more familiar environment, the endless skies. As the planes climbed east, they flew from darkness into the bright sunlight as morning crawled slowly over the dark jungle below.

The men on the revetment walls watched with a mixture of delight and longing as the planes rolled and then raced down the long runway, nudging each other and smiling as their own craft jumped into the blackness. Slowly they turned and walked away as the glow of the engines finally faded from sight. The mission was on its way; another three hours logged on the engines; another series of g's on the airframe; another three hours to wait. Thirty minutes to the tanker; fifteen minutes to refuel; twenty minutes to the target, a half-hour to work the target, then the process begins over again, this time in reverse.

✳   ✳   ✳

High above the dark jungles, a lone plane lumbered through the sky. "Hillsboro" was a RC-121 aircraft, the controller for the central sector. It was an old aircraft, propeller driven, carrying fifteen to seventeen men whose sole job was coordination of the fighter sorties. While the plane was old, the equipment onboard was the latest. Hillsboro was the eye in the sky. It had sophisticated radar capability that monitored every aircraft that entered its considerable coverage. Somewhere far northwest of them, Dragon flight was rendezvousing with Camel 3, one of the four tankers flying the numerous tracks that crossed Thailand and Laos. Already, Hillsboro had talked to Dragon lead and had confirmed that Dragon was, in fact, a flight of four F-4D's loaded with high drag 500-pound bombs. Estimated time off tanker was also relayed, giving a little lead time for the shadowy figures inside the large plane to review the strike plan for the evening and weigh divert information arriving from the numerous forward air controllers flying in their individual areas, as well as sortie requests coming in from Talltale and Longbow, the sister ships for the southern and northern sectors respectively. When the need arose, flights could be diverted instantly to more lucrative or more pressing targets throughout the theater of operations. Theirs also was the job of coordinating all search and rescue operations during the initial stages of response. Once the Jolly Greens, the large rescue helicopters, or the Fireflies or Sandys, the forward air controllers, got to the scene, Hillsboro could only listen and coordinate backup firepower from additional flights that could, when necessary, be diverted to the crash site. But today there was no divert. Dragon flight was fragged with high drag bombs for Rat Fink Valley. It was a target many men feared.

$$* \quad * \quad *$$

The tired navigator stood on the hot concrete ramp peering at the camouflaged fighter aircraft beside him as perspiration drained his body and soaked his flight suit. His right hand was raised to shadow his eyes from the bright sun overhead as he peered at the tail of the plane. It was heavily damaged with several holes through the vertical stabilizer and approximately half of the rudder missing.

"Damn, that was close!"

Robb climbed down the ladder and joined his friend. "Shit, he only hit the tail. Must have been a new gunner, Jack."

"He was a five level for sure."

"*Was* is the operative word my friend."

"Yeah, I guess you're right." The two men walked out of the revetment and signaled a passing crew van.

"Hey Robb, that your plane?" One of the other pilots motioned to the damaged aircraft.

"Yeah, some guys just can't take a joke."

"How'd it fly with that damage?"

"Frankly, you could hardly tell the difference. In fact, if my nav hadn't pissed in his pants I probably would never have known we were hit."

Jack Trudeau hit Robb on the shoulder playfully. "And if my pilot would take a few less risks, the mechanics would work a lot less overtime." The crew van stopped to pick up another crew. As they got in, the looks on their faces stopped the mirth abruptly. Six men returned from a flight of four aircraft. Colonel Bennett and his navigator climbed in last. He sat heavily on the long bench along the right side of the van.

"We lost Clem Roberts and George Tremball this morning."

Robb snapped his head toward the colonel. "Clem?" There was disbelief in his voice. The colonel nodded. "Any chutes?"

"No, no chutes." Bennett was tired. His face was drawn, and he looked much older in the dim light in the back of the truck.

"Shit!" The sudden shout startled the quiet men in the truck. Robb had expressed the emotion every man in the truck was feeling. The men looked off into the distance and cursed quietly; then they became silent and looked at their feet; then they again looked away. They didn't look at each other; they didn't speak. They followed the age-old tradition of men—on the outside they stood firm, while on the inside the struggle for control raged. The mouth might occasionally quiver, even a tear might well in an eye, but it is understood that men will not look at each other or cling to each other in pain. They simply grit their teeth and look even farther into the distance. If one's lips do quiver, it's okay; no one will be looking at you anyway. A flick of a tear is easily done if everyone is looking at clouds on the horizon. With great will the men forced their emotions deeper still into their minds and hearts while waiting—waiting for the pain to become anger. Men know how to deal with anger, and anger is socially acceptable in their brotherhood. So the young pilot threw his helmet against the side of the panel truck and then kicked it into the wall again. And they all cursed; then they became silent. Perhaps repressed suffering is understandable; it certainly is the most difficult.

The men fell forward as the truck stopped abruptly. There were no laughter or curses as they climbed heavily to the ground. Colonel Bennett turned toward the headquarters building and spoke to the remainder of his flight without looking back at them. "Jack and I will take care of the debriefing. We'll see you in the bar later."

The crews stacked their helmets on the long padded table and then edged their way wearily down the long crowded rows of lockers. Robb's locker was near the aisle, so he waited before entering the cluttered passage. The personnel equipment sergeant sidled over; he was silent a long time before he spoke, as if testing the mood of the sweaty crews. "Captain Barker?" Robb looked up but did not reply. "Sir, were there any beepers?"

"No." His voice was not harsh or even emphatic, rather it was tired.

"They call it all off?"

"No, they'll continue to check for beepers."

"Think they got out?"

"No…they didn't get out."

"Damn." Turning slowly, he shuffled away.

The sweat stained equipment clung damply to his body. With an effort, he flung it off into a heap on the tile floor. A stream of cold air flowed from a nearby air conditioning duct and caused him to shiver slightly as he reached for each piece of his equipment and mechanically hung each in its place. Jack Treadeau passed quietly by and patted Robb once on the shoulder; he knew the friendship Robb had shared with Clem, and he understood the loss Robb felt. Robb nodded and glanced aside. It was then that he saw the combination lock hanging open on Clem's locker across the aisle. He stood and looked at the locker for a long time. His memory merged with the present and the past as he considered the tragic loss he had experienced that evening. He had lost a friend, and it had happened so suddenly, so finally. Clem had been talking about his future, and now he was gone. A deep anguish filled him and he struck savagely at the cold hard locker. The bitterness and anger welled up inside him and echoed distantly with the clattering crash of the gray metal door. Then he saw it through the partially opened door—the letter, the key to open a door of hope. It was a last tribute to a dream, to the belief that when he is willing, a man can always try again.

A trembling hand grasped the letter; tired eyes stared at the soiled envelope. Perhaps she thought he was dead already, as Clem had said; maybe inside she knew. What difference did it make now? What good was there in opening old wounds, reviving old memories and dashing them again against the harsh reality of death? Clem loved her; he had said so himself; he wouldn't have wanted her burden to be any heavier—even in the knowledge of his love. It could bring little joy now; it could bring a lifetime of regret, and that would be so unlike Clem.

Robb was dropping the last few pieces of torn paper into a trash can when a voice boomed through the building. "Truck leaving for the club." He answered quietly. "Be with you in a minute, just as soon as I finish a favor for a friend."

CHAPTER TWELVE

Washington D.C.

At 0559, the last of the officers entered the room. Behind him, the door was closed with a "no interruptions" sign posted outside. The smell of coffee permeated the room. Partially devoured pastries lay on plates scattered around the well-lacquered table. Fresh ones were stacked on a small table in the corner, along with the large pot of coffee. The pot was not marked; only one pot was on the table. There was no demand for decaffeinated from this group.

At 0600 the general rose. He looked tired. He had little sleep the night before. Several classified calls on his special phone, a rush meeting at midnight, and a half hour of his wife's complaining about his work schedule had left little time for rest. By 0300 it had become clear that the freighter was headed for deeper water. It was not on its way to North Korea. "Where the hell are they going?" Every possible scenario had been checked. The freighter, even its captain, were checked. Both were frequent visitors to the Vietnamese port of Vihn. At 0400 the intelligence guys reported their findings. Nothing! If the Soviets were sending new armaments to North Vietnam, their government didn't seem to be aware. They did score one victory, however, they had excellent photos of the missiles being loaded off the train at the rail yard. Earlier that morning, Miles Campbell had noticed a Soviet Army Officer, a captain, in one of the pictures. He appeared to be supervising the operation. So, surely the Army knew. Or did they? The Soviet government is a large and often unmanageable bear. Could it be possible that the Army was working alone, without the knowledge of the government? That seemed highly unlikely, but Campbell had decided to confirm his suspicions by requesting intelligence to check out that officer. Another set of photos had shown him smoking on the back deck of the freighter Kamkara. His connection with the missiles was unmistakable.

"Gentlemen, we have intelligence reports on the freighter. It appears to have four SRBMs on board, and, " he paused for effect, " it's not going to North Korea."

"We can thank God for that."

"The question now is, where is it going?"

"And why isn't it under escort? That freighter isn't armed at all except for a couple of triple A guns."

"Damned good question." Campbell scribbled notes on a pad lying on the table before him as he stood. "Damned good point."

"Has the chief been briefed?"

"Yes, the President, too."

"What's their direction?"

"None.... yet."

"Diplomatic channels?"

"Working." General Patrick flipped on the projector and flashed several pictures of the freighter on the screen."

"Why don't we just sink the bastards?"

"You're not the president."

"Oh yes, a minor technicality." All of the men smiled.

A knock at the door stopped all conversation in the room. The general quickly extinguished the projector. Miles stuck his head through the door and retrieved a package. Thanking the courier, he turned to the group and began opening the package. When the door was secured, the meeting resumed, but most eyes were on the major. "Well, well." He looked up at the general. "Sir, we may have our answer."

"Go ahead."

Miles walked to the front of the room and took the pointer the general extended toward him. He moved a viewgraph machine into place on the conference table and focused it with one of the viewfoils from the package he had been handed. As it came into focus, it showed a younger Sergei Vladislav Iskhakov with lieutenant stripes on his shoulder boards. His name, rank, serial number, even a brief history was written on both sides of the portrait--in Russian. Without being asked, Miles began to read the information in English. As he neared the bottom, he paused, closed his eyes in concentration then continued. "...assigned to the Eastern Sector mobile tank command." He looked blankly into the distance, thinking, then resumed--but not reading the chart. He faced the group "which is commanded by Col. Dmitriy Ruchinsky. Remember him General Patrick? He's the one of those who got busted in the big political shakeup last year. Two years ago he was equivalent to a two-star. Then he went off the deep end. Six months later he shows up in command of an insignificant division in southeastern Siberia."

"That must have hurt. That's almost as bad as a tour at the Pentagon." Everyone laughed.

The general stood and accepted the pointer as the captain sat down. "Gentlemen, could this be a renegade action?"

"Highly unlikely."

"Yes, but that would account for the Kremlin's ignorance."

"Are you that confident that we would really know if the Kremlin did or did not know about this?"

A man in a dark suit in the back of the room spoke immediately. "Yes Sir."

The general reached for the phone on the small table beside the door. "Wanda, I must see the chief immediately."

"I'm sorry general....."

"Before she could continue, Patrick interrupted. "Wanda, Find him. Now! This can't wait. I'm on my way up and will be there in ten minutes." He turned to Campbell. "Miles, get me the scoop on Captain Iskhakov and the entire chain of command from there to the general staff. Go deep. You know what I mean. I need everything we've got on him."

"Yes sir."

"Gentlemen, report back here at 0800. The President is to be briefed at 1000, and we have a lot of work to do first."

As they walked out of the meeting, the major stopped the general briefly. "Sir, you realize the implications of this?"

"You bet I do, Miles. If those are conventional warheads, they could kill a lot of people. If they're nukes, we could have World War III in the making."

"Has the chief told that to the president?"

"I don't know, but I damn sure hope so."

Nubat Royal Thai Air Force Base

Lt. Colonel Andrew Bennett sat hunched over his desk. Ostensibly he was reading one of the numerous reports that crossed his desk each day. A closer examination, however, would reveal eyes that were focused far beyond the paper in his hands. Andrew Bennett was troubled. He had a war to fight—no, he had two wars. One enemy was clear—that war he could handle. It was the internal war, the one within his own unit, that troubled him most. He could handle the Migs or the antiaircraft missiles. But how could he manage a group of finely trained young men who had suddenly turned brittle.

He reached for the cold cigar that waited patiently in the ashtray on his desk. He glanced at it and then thrust it violently into his mouth. The sour taste of the tobacco had not changed as he chewed it slowly—thinking, taking inventory.

He had the finest pilots a commander could ever want. He had lost five men, pulled three others from the jungles, watched his men celebrate four "kills." Six distinguished flying crosses and numerous Air Medals were in process. Then the unraveling had begun. The losses had damaged the squadron's confidence. The monotony of war had replaced fear and courage. This worried him most. The men were tired.

The older officer considered each of his men carefully, jotting notes on a pad of paper:

> Dick O'Brian—rotating back to the states to recuperate.
> Robb Barker—Mig--Wayne/killed boy on ramp/Kerrie—
> watch him—could be shaky.
> Joe Wilburn—great pilot—three Migs—but the fire is
> gone! Why?
> Clem Roberts—He struck a line through the name and
> frowned.

The list continued with the final four entries simply question marks for the new replacement pilots. The tired eyes looked at the list for a long time, then he rose and walked to the window of the small office. He watched two flights of planes takeoff. Finally he turned and walked back to his desk. He sat silently, still playing with the cigar lodged securely between his front teeth. After a few moments he replaced the cigar in the stained ashtray and picked up his pencil. He scribbled another name on the list—A. Bennett. He stared at it briefly and then rubbed his forehead with both palms. He looked carefully at the pencil and the hand before him. It was the hand of an older man. The skin was no longer smooth. Wrinkles and a few scars danced among dark sunspots—or were they age spots? He held the hand up and watched it. It was still strong, and it was steady, but it was no longer young. He wondered how long it would function with the efficiency he needed to fly with men half his age. He ran his right hand through the close wavy hair on his head. It was thinning with each year, and the bald spot in the back was clearly evident. But his eyes worried him most. They bothered him constantly until he finally had to get glasses. He hated the glasses, but he hated the headaches more. He even wore them to fly now. Age was surely creeping up on him, of that he was sure. Someday—someday they would take him from his beloved cockpit and assign him to a desk. How would he handle that? Could he? A steady hand wrote another question mark beside the last name.

"Col. Bennett?"

"Yes, come in."

"Lieutenant Donaldson reporting for duty, Sir."

"Glad to have you on board, Lieutenant. I hear you're a good stick."

"Yes Sir, the best." The young man was grinning.

"The best?" There was an exaggerated tone of incredulity in the colonel's voice.

"Damn right, sir. The best." The grin grew wider.

The older man smiled and looked at the young man carefully. "Lieutenant, I rotate back in six months. Until then, never, never, ever claim to be the best pilot on this base less people laugh at you." Both men were grinning now.

"Of course sir."

"Where are you from son?"

"Wyoming, sir."

"Outstanding, I've never met a man from Wyoming I didn't like. Must be the fresh air out there."

"Thank you sir."

Bennett shuffled through a stack of papers and handed the young man several sheets. "Review these carefully. I'm assigning you to Major King's flight. Watch him; he can teach you a few tricks, I suspect."

"Yes sir. I met Major King already—at the bar."

"As I would expect. He's a great stick, and I don't use that term loosely."

"I know Sir. He said he was second only to you."

The older man looked up quickly. "He did, did he. Many men have made that same assertion, I'm told."

"Yes sir."

"Did I mention that he's bright, too?" The colonel studied the dossier before him. I notice that you're a lawyer."

"Yes sir, Georgetown, '66."

"A lawyer, and you're flying airplanes over here?"

"Damn right, sir. If I were the President of the United States I'd resign for the opportunity to fly Phantoms over here. I can be a lawyer when I'm old; this is the only opportunity I have to fly fighters. How many men get a chance in their lives to do this?"

Bennett looked up at the young man for several moments before he spoke. "You're right; not many." He smiled to himself. "And thanks for reminding me." The colonel walked around the desk and shook the lieutenant's hand before he saluted and left. Bennett watched him go and then walked back to his seat. Picking up the pencil, he erased the question mark by his own name and smiled. That done he stood, stretched, and walked confidently out the door. He turned to his clerk as he left. "Dan, if anyone calls, tell him I'm flying with my men."

"Yes Sir, Colonel."

With a smile he walked down the hall. He was forty-six years old, and he was still flying a first line fighter into combat with men who respected him. Life is good, he thought, and I wouldn't trade places with the richest man in the world or any general in the Pentagon.

Douglas M. Fain

<u>Washington D.C.</u>

The President was bent over his cup of coffee, holding it with both hands. The steam rose in circles around his long nose, causing him to blink his eyes. He slurped it loudly as the general stood to speak.

"Mr. President, gentlemen, the freighter Kamkara is approximately eleven hours from the port of Vihn. It is maintaining a constant heading of 185 degrees and a speed of twelve knots. Two P-3 aircraft off the USS Forestall are tracking the ship around the clock. We have the fleet notified to stand by. There are aircraft from the same carrier and three Air Force bases in Thailand available with thirty minutes notification and two subs moving into intercept position. Fleet Admiral Wilson is standing by awaiting orders. He has all assets in place except the subs; they will be in place in approximately three hours." He turned to the National Security Advisor and nodded. "Sir."

"Mr. President, I have personally spoken with three members of the Soviet General Staff and the Secretary of State has personally discussed the matter with the Soviet ambassador. Their entire chain of command is aware of the situation. Pictures have been sent and are in their hands. We are awaiting their comments." He paused for a moment and added as an afterthought, "Officially they deny any such thing could exist."

"Do they recognize the time constraints? We can't wait all week for these guys to make up their minds."

"We've made that perfectly clear, Mr. President."

"Did they give any indication of when they would move on this?"

"No Sir; they did not."

"What was our official request?"

"That they turn the ship around and have it return with its cargo to Vladivistok."

"Did you explain any consequences?"

"No Sir, I did not. I left that presumption to them."

The president considered that proposition for a moment. "Good idea, Howard."

The general showed several slides of the ship in progress. One was an older picture showing portions of the missiles under the tarpaulins. He gave details of the missiles, their range, weight, speed, and finally their destructive power if armed with either conventional or nuclear warheads. When he finished, the men looked at each other and cursed under their breath. Finally the president spoke. "When do I have to give the word, general?"

"About eight hours, Sir. We will have all units standing by. Both naval forces and our air bases in Thailand will be on alert."

"Thank you general. Good work as usual. I know our troops will not let us down. Let's make sure we don't let them down. That is all gentlemen." The president rose and left the room.

Ten minutes later General Patrick sat perspiring beside his phone. When it rang, he grabbed it quickly and thrust it to his ear. "Patrick."

"Still on hold. All units are to be on standby. Looks like a naval operation."

"Any more meetings set up?"

"Two thirty sharp. Situation room."

"That's cutting it close."

"I'll keep you informed, general."

"Thanks, Wanda. I owe you."

"You bet you do. And I won't let you forget it, either." There was mirth in her voice, but not in his as he hung up the phone. "Damn, still no decision."

Nubat Royal Thai Air Force Base

The squadron was quiet for the first time in over twenty hours. The night flights were out and would not return until almost 0400.

The heat lingered, draping the base in a humid blanket of tepid air. Outside the Operations Building the air-conditioners droned through the evening, chilling those inside with mechanically cooled air. Joe Wilburn turned off the lights behind the operations counter and walked slowly toward the front door. It was late, and he was tired, not from physical exertion, but from the boredom of a day spent behind the counter, logging flights and scheduling maintenance. He was bored. The voices in the hallway echoed through the vacant building—stopping Joe in his tracks. "And what's up with Wilburn, Andy?" Joe stepped quietly back into the dark operations center and listened as the two colonels approached down the hall.

"I told him to stand down a few days. He looked tired. He'll be back on the schedule in three days."

"Did he ask to stand down?"

"No, he's the best pilot I've got. I just don't want to burn him out."

"Are you sure, Andy? He looks alright to me."

"You pay me to manage the pilots, John; three more days. Okay?"

"Look, we can't afford any slackers. If Wilburn doesn't fly, someone else carries his load. You look tired yourself. How many sorties did you fly today?"

"Two."

"You can't continue to do that. It's your job to run this squadron. It's Wilburn's job to fly. Now, be honest with me. Has he snapped? If he has we'll get him out of here in two days."

"He's alright John; three more days."

"Okay, but if Wilburn isn't in the saddle in three days, I want him out of here. I don't care how many Migs he has. Understood?"

"Understood."

The two colonels walked out the door into the warm evening air. From the dark room Joe watched them leave; after several minutes he followed them out into the darkness. Across the street the ramp was lit by large floodlights like a high-school football field. It was busy with men working in the evening heat. Joe stood for a few moments then crossed the road, drawn to the light like the swarms of rice bugs surrounding the large floodlights around the ramp.

The tired captain passed the busy airmen and nodded to their waves. He skirted the racks of bombs and the maintenance crews, finally stopping in the shadows before one of the planes in the rows of revetments. Two young sergeants stood at the tail of the craft, discussing electrical schematics stretched across a folding table. They failed to notice the captain staring at the large fighter. Joe walked tentatively to the nose of the aircraft and reached to touch it as he moved toward the ladder. Slowly he reached and grasped the ladder with both hands. For a long time he stood there looking up at the open canopy; finally he placed his boot on the bottom rung and hoisted himself to the first step. As he stood there, the ladder was transformed in his mind. He stood in the jungle, surrounded by the laughter of men; then came the screams. He grabbed the ladder tightly and clung to the metal structure, his entire body trembling. As the voices in his head laughed and screamed louder, Joe stepped back onto the ramp and walked quickly away from the plane.

Washington D.C.

Margaret Harris watched her general pacing in his office. Without thought she glanced briefly at the floor, half expecting to see a path worn between the desk and the window at the far end of the office. She knew John Patrick very well; she knew he was struggling over something, something she had not yet identified. She wondered if the concern on his mind were personal or professional. She almost hoped that it was personal. Maybe, just maybe…

The phone rang four times before the general even noticed it.

Finally he lifted the receiver. "Any decision yet?" He listened to the brief answer. "Dammit!" He slammed the phone onto its cradle and rose slowly to resume his pacing. "Marge, get the chief on the phone." She eyed the nervous man before her as she dialed the number. As she answered the secretary on the other end, she pointed back to the general's desk.

"Hi, Wanda. This is Marge; is General Armstrong available for General Patrick?" She pointed quickly at the desk.

"Hello Sir, this is John. What's the status on our decision?" Patrick rubbed his forehead with his left hand as he listened. "General, we've got to have a decision! This can't wait much longer; the risks are enormous. Is there anything that can be done to convince him?" He rubbed his forehead harder, finally slamming the phone again into its cradle. "Damn politicians—all of them. Damn!"

Marge walked into the office with an empty cup and a full pot. "Coffee?"

"Thanks." When he looked up Marge stopped abruptly, spilling coffee on herself and the floor. She had never seen such an expression on his face.

"General, are you alright?"

He looked at her, through her. Finally he lowered his eyes and rubbed his forehead with his fingertips. "Yes, I'm okay." He took the coffee, sat back in his chair, and sipped at the strong, hot liquid. "Sorry, I'm just impatient with people who won't, or can't, make a decision. Do you realize how few people make the important decisions in life? Most people just watch, spectators to the world."

"You've never had that problem." She looked at him carefully. "And your decisions are good ones."

"Well," he smiled at her, "most of them, anyway." Very slowly he pushed the coffee away. "Actually, I think I've had enough caffeine today."

She walked around the desk and did what she had never done

before; she placed her hand on his back. She wanted so much to put her arms around him, to take away the cares. "You look tired; why don't you leave early."

"I'd love to Marge, but I've one more decision that I need to make today."

"It appears to be difficult."

"Yes, it is." He looked up at her. "Perhaps the most difficult I've ever made." He rose and walked again to the window. "It involves duty and honor." He turned and looked at her. "And those are the most difficult."

"Must you decide today?"

"Yes." It was simple; it was direct.

"Can I help?"

"No, no one is willing or can do this but me."

She looked into his eyes for a long time before she spoke. "You've already decided haven't you." It was a statement.

He looked at her, amazed. Was he that easily read? "Yes, I have."

"Then it's done, isn't it?"

He spoke slowly, still looking at her. "Yes, I suppose it is."

Her eyes looked into his and settled the torment inside. "Then there's no sense agonizing about it any longer is there?"

"You're right, of course." He smiled at the wise woman before him. "Marge, what would I do without you?"

"You'd be lost forever."

"You're right." He crossed the room, put his arm around her shoulder, and walked her to the door. "You're always right." He smiled at her. "Phone a courier for me; then I'll go home."

She walked dutifully to her desk and withdrew the large Pentagon phone book. He did not notice her wince at the word "home".

*   *   *

Andrew Bennett stood alone in his small office. He was looking down, frowning. It wasn't the scuffed flight boots that held his attention; it was the protruding belly in an otherwise thin frame. "Damn!" he uttered aloud. Must be the beer, he thought. Got to do something about that. Guess I'll start skipping lunch. He pondered that a moment. Well, at least every other day. Ice cream? No, that might even take precedence over the beer; well, the last few each evening anyway. He sensed a movement behind him and turned slowly, sucking in his stomach as he did. When he faced the sergeant his stomach was flat.

"Good morning, Sir."

"Good morning, Tom. Is Jefferies being suited up?"

"Yes, Sir. He's getting into a g-suit now."

"Is he ready?" The two men traded glances. Both knew the purpose of the question.

"Well, Sir, he's a little nervous."

"We'll be in a safe area."

"Oh, it's not that. He's not worried about combat. He'd probably like some of that. He's afraid he'll get airsick."

"He won't be the first to throw-up in a fighter." The colonel smiled. "But don't worry; I'll take it easy on him."

"The men really appreciate your doing this for them, Sir. It makes a big difference in their paycheck." He paused momentarily. "It makes an even bigger difference in their morale."

"Hell, why should they pay taxes on their re-up bonus? Let someone else pay for this war—not the guys fighting it."

"You bet."

"Well, not only do we get him a combat exclusion on his taxes this month, we'll also get him an indoctrination flight in his own bird, and over North Vietnam as well. He can tell his kids about this."

"Thanks again, Sir."

The colonel walked over and placed his hand on the other man's shoulder as they turned toward the door. "You know, I enjoy this too. A beautiful morning to fly, and they won't even shoot at me today. By the way, when do you re-up, Sarge?"

"Two more months."

"Remind me a week before. I don't want you flying with King. He's a madman." They both laughed.

"Sir, any chance to see some real action? You know, not just a milk run?"

The colonel's smile vanished and was replaced by a thoughtful look as he considered the request. "Probably not. The GIB's (Guys in Back) are trained to help us up there. Frankly, I need all the help I can get when the shooting starts."

"I understand. It's just that I've sent you guys out to do battle for seven months. All of us out there on the ramp naturally wonder what it's like. I'd like to be able to say I fought in this war."

Bennett smiled as he started toward the door. "You do, Sarge; believe me, you do." He rubbed his forehead in thought. "I do know a bridge in route Pack Four. It should be lightly defended. Let me think about it." He turned to the younger man. "Now let's keep this between the two of us. Okay? I'll think about it."

"Thank you sir." The sergeant's face broke into a smile as they walked out of the small office and down the narrow hallway toward the personnel equipment area. As they entered a young airman walked out to meet them in full combat attire—g-suit, survival vest, pistol on his hip, flight helmet under his right arm, and a very broad grin upon his face. The two older men smiled at each other. "You know, Sarge, this is what makes it all worthwhile." He turned to the young man. "You ready, Son?"

"Yes, Sir!"

"I'm proud to fly with you today, and by the way, you can expect some stick time, too. After all, Two-Seven-Three is *your* plane. There

is only one name on any Air Force fighter, and it's not the pilot's."
The young man beamed. "Anyone got the camera? It's time for your
"hero picture" to send home."

"Yes, Sir." Meekly the airman produced a camera and handed
it to the sergeant.

"Two-Seven-Three ready?"

"Yes, Sir."

"Then let's go give her a spin."

The flight was scheduled for an hour and a half; after refueling
over northern Laos, it lasted over three hours. The fighter flew alone
across Laos and then entered North Vietnam. This would satisfy
the bureaucracy. Airman Joe Brown had flown into a combat zone
in a fighter aircraft; his $8,000.00 bonus for re-enlisting was now
tax-free. But the flight meant much more than simply numbers in a
bank account. Today Joe Brown had flown his own bird, the one he
knew and loved, the one with his name on it. It was his day—their
day—Joe and Two-Seven-Three. He had felt the power of the large
engines; he had experienced the exhilaration of gliding through the
clouds; he had held his breath as the craft plunged toward the ground
and then climbed rapidly back into the skies. It was a sensation of
wild abandon that he had never known. It was one few men know
and one they never forget. But these two men experienced another
thrill that would surpass even the physical sensations of flight. As
they crossed the border into enemy territory, a small voice on the
aircraft guard channel interrupted their conversation.

"This is Copperhead One, does anyone read me?"

"Son of a bitch!" Bennett's voice was filled with excitement and
shock as he reached for his radio dials. "Copperhead One, this is
Doughboy One. I read you loud and clear."

"Colonel?"

"Hang in there Clem, we'll get you out. Are you alone?"

"Negative, Bravo is with me."

"Any injuries?"

"Negative, but I'd sure like a beer."

"I'll have a case on ice. Standby while I call for help." And thus began another rescue mission, another coordinated effort of helicopters, fighters, and controllers. It was an effort of danger and great personal satisfaction for those men who spent their careers saving others.

Word of the rescue spread quickly across Nubat. Cheers broke out in briefing rooms, the dining hall, and base ops. Aircrews rushed to operations to get the latest information. Forty-seven men cheered loudly when the radio in ops relayed Hillsboro's announcement. "Mission complete; good work Jolly!"

"Roger, Hillsboro, Jolly Three is headed home with two thirsty warriors."

*   *   *

The party in the O'club that night was particularly chaotic. Since both crewmembers were rescued, especially after four days "in the weeds," there were no shadows to darken the festivities. The party began at 1645 and was only stopped when the eight-hour rule came into effect. The drinking stopped eight hours before the first take-off in the morning. There would be many red eyed crewmembers the next day, but their physical discomfort would easily be forgotten in the excitement of welcoming their friends back from enemy soil.

Throughout most of the evening, Clem had remained in the bar. The alcohol quickly overcame his tired body and by midnight, his awkward movements betrayed his fading control. Finally Robb and Col. Bennett escorted him from the bar and deposited him in his bunk. It was noon the next day when Robb approached his friend in operations. Clem was leaning over one of the large briefing tables, rubbing his eyes. "Hi, Clem, did you survive last night?"

"Barely. Damn, I didn't realize it until this morning, but I must have hurt my back on ejection. I feel like an old man. My back hurts like hell!"

"Maybe you'd better let Phillip check it out."

"No way. I don't want to be DNIF first thing when I get back. Just doesn't look good."

"Yeah, guess you're right. By the way, how'd you guys get out without anyone spotting your chutes?"

"On the way down I spotted the clouds north of the target and figured if we punched in them low enough, we might not be spotted by the zips." He smiled. "Guess it worked."

"I'll say. We thought you guys bought the farm."

"For a few minutes, I thought the same thing."

Robb looked at Clem for a long moment. It was obvious that he was searching for words. "Clem, I need to tell you something. I tore up your letter. We thought you didn't make it. Somehow at the moment it seemed the right thing to do."

"It was."

"You're sure?"

"Of course, If it had been the other way around, I'd have done that for you." Clem stood and looked into his friend's eyes. "While I was hiding in that stinking jungle that was the biggest concern on my mind. I was thinking of how painful that letter would be if I didn't come back. I would have hurt her one more time." He gathered the papers he had been working on. "I should have known I had a friend who'd look after me."

"Maybe you can re-write it," Robb offered.

"No, I'm not going to do that."

"You're not?" Robb was surprised and disappointed.

"No, I've got a better idea. When I get back I'm going to tell her in person. By the way, want to be my Best Man?"

"You bet!"

"We probably should celebrate, but I did enough of that last night."

"I've got a better idea. Let's go flying."

"You're right; that's celebration enough."

Walter Reed Hospital

She opened her eyes and stared into the darkness of the small room. One lone ray of light pierced the shades over her window and slowly traced an arc on the opposite wall. Kerrie was aware of the passage of time, but that was of no concern. Something told her that time mattered little. She let her mind drift as she tested her physical senses. Pain? No, only a slightly dizzy feeling that dulled and slowed her thoughts. She glanced to the far wall and saw that the light ray had moved even further. Morning? Was it morning? And what was this place? She looked back across the room and studied a dark shadow that stood beside the glowing beam. She recognized it; it was an IV stand. And how did she know that? This must be a hospital. What did that mean? She relaxed and let her mind drift again. The darkness was peaceful, but that one ray of light called to her. Curious, she watched it again as it danced on the far wall. Where did it come from? Why was it there? A sound in the hall surprised her. Was that a voice? Her mind became alert and began processing the information more rapidly. She was in a hospital—but why? Oh yes, she was a doctor; she must work here. She relaxed and closed her eyes again. She was where she belonged.

When she opened her eyes again, the darkness was gone. The one small beam had filled the entire room and caused her to squint her eyes. A strange voice spoke to her. "Well, well; good morning!"

"Where am I?" The voice was small and weak.

The nurse's head jerked sharply toward her patient as her eyes widened. "Oh my gosh, you spoke! You're awake!"

"Where am I?" The voice was stronger now, insistent."

"There was an accident…"

Vihn Harbor, North Vietnam

They were the first American planes Dmitriy had seen. He watched them streaking across the sky, headed northwest. He suspected that they were off the carriers, but it was hard to tell for sure. He watched them in fascination. He stood on a slow moving freighter carrying missiles to North Vietnam while American fighter jets flew overhead—and he was safe. He watched as they disappeared over the horizon. How fast they flew. How dangerous they might be, but Dmitriy knew they were no threat to him or his cargo. It was against their rules of war—not his—thank goodness. He wondered about power and decided that in the absence of will, there is no power. The largest and strongest is powerless without will, and the smaller man with a bigger will generally wins. He reflected on the encounter with the rail inspectors and the insolent sailor. He had demonstrated clearly to his men that he had both the power and the will. It had worked. Now they all feared him. But he did not fear the planes flying overhead. The leaders in the United States were cowards who lacked will, so they made rules that would not let their side win. How stupid they must be. He smiled that he did not fight for such men. Ruchinsky was a soldier first and last. He understood that when leaders lack courage, their men die inglorious deaths on the fields of battle. He was a man willing to make decisions and then carry them out. He hoped Colonel Tran was just such a man as well.

Chapter Thirteen

Nubat Royal Thai Air Force Base

The captain evoked a lot of stares as he walked through the squadron building. He was wearing a dress uniform, not fatigues or a flight suit, and he had a briefcase handcuffed to his right wrist. He proceeded to Colonel Bennett's office and knocked twice on the door.

"Come in." The colonel looked up to see the young officer standing at attention before him. "At ease." He studied the young man with amusement. "Can I help you?"

"Sir, I'm Captain Martinez, and I have sealed orders for your eyes only." He fumbled with the handcuff and then the briefcase. "It's from General Patrick."

The smile on Bennett's face evaporated as he rose and waited expectantly for the packet. "Yes, he alerted me you were coming."

"Yes sir. He said the directions would be clear but that I was to stay in case you wanted me to courier anything back." He handed a thick, sealed packet to the colonel and stood awaiting instructions. Bennett pulled a knife from his desk, slit the seals on the package, and walked slowly to the door of the small office as he studied the contents of the packet. "Sarge, please take Captain Martinez down to the snack bar and buy him a cup of coffee." He turned to the

captain. "I'll be with you in a moment." When they had left he
closed and locked the door and spread the sheets across his desk.
The instructions were clear, so like his old friend. "Review all of
the material in the packet and call me. My office phone is on the
third page." Bennett calculated the time difference, eight hours, and
reflected on the man waiting on the other end. He knew the time
difference was irrelevant; John would be there. The phone would ring
twice and he would answer. Putting the thought aside, he studied
the notes, the pictures, and finally the letter.

Andy,

By now you've seen the pictures and the notes. This is important,
and it's Top Secret. Those missiles may well be nukes. We have no
idea what they are up to, but the implication is too great to ignore.
You will understand that better than anyone. I have run this up the
flagpole and still am waiting for direction. The president has been
briefed, and I'm sure he's weighing all the alternatives. If a decision is
not made by the time those missiles are offloaded at Vihn, it will be
too late. I'm doing all I can to get a go-ahead to sink that ship. You
can imagine the politics in a decision to sink a Russian freighter. My
concern is what we will do if the brass waits too long. I'm nervous.
The chief is our official spokesman—enough said there. He hasn't
changed a bit since graduation—still more of a politician than a
military man. I'm worried.

So, I've done a lot of soul searching, and I've made a decision. If
the war needs a decision, I'll make it if no one else will. We've got to
take that ship out. If we don't get the go-ahead by Friday morning,
I want you to sink that ship. I've included written orders to do so. I
don't know how well that will cover your ass, but it should be worth
something—I am a general officer. Andy, I realize the risks for
both of us; I'm willing to do this, but you may not be. Weigh this
carefully and make your own decision. If you decide that you cannot

participate in this, I'll understand. Believe me, my own decision was not easy. I only ask one thing. If you decide not to do this, please burn all of this material and just keep it between us.

I'm not appealing to our friendship but rather as one officer to another. If those are nukes and the North Vietnamese go nuts, a lot of our people are going to die, and the world will face a crisis that will make the Cuban blockade look like a Sunday picnic. We've simply got to sink that ship before those missiles can get inland. The President still has time to make the right choice. However, if no decision is made by Friday, then I'm afraid we will just have to sacrifice our careers to do what's needed.

One last thing—I'd give this office, my parking space, and these stars just to be able to fly on your wing when you go after that ship. Okay, call me.

John

Bennett studied the papers on his desk again, stood and looked out the window for a moment, then reached for the phone.

"Andy?"

"Hello, John. I got your invitation to the party. I'm really excited about it and look forward to coming."

"You'll be there?"

"Wouldn't miss it for the world."

"You're sure?" The voice of the general was suddenly very serious.

"I'm sure."

"If the boss agrees to buy the beer, you'll be the first notified."

"This should be a fun party, wish you could be here."

"So do I." There was a slight pause. "Andy, good luck."

"Thanks, John, I'll talk to you later." Bennett took the pictures and several sheets of the material and folded them into his breast pocket. The others he placed back inside the packet and walked them down the hall to the paper shredder. "Sarge, see that this gets burned immediately." The colonel walked out into the bright Thai sunlight, past the cascading waves of bright fuchsia bougainvillea and out on the flight line. This was where he did his best thinking. He walked slowly around the planes without seeing them, his mind working the implications of the call he had just placed. It would certainly end John's career and possibly his own. He also recognized the logic in what John was saying. They both understood the risks of nuclear missiles in North Vietnamese hands. The politicians must be pissing in their pants about now. But Bennett knew how they would procrastinate. Already they had saddled him with rules of war that would not allow him to win. Now they were going to risk thousands of lives for some political solution that would be too late. John was right, but the price would be high. Had he done the right thing? Bennett wasn't sure, but he had given his word to his friend, and he would complete his promise. He stopped pacing and looked up. He had made the decision; that was done. Now he had a lot of work to do to implement it. Maybe he would be lucky and the orders would come through. He walked back toward the squadron with a determined look on his face.

Washington, D.C.

"What's up Margaret? Jeff said you wanted to see me." The face that looked up from the Selective typewriter spoke volumes to the smiling major.

"We need coffee, Miles. Five minutes." She looked furtively around the room.

"See you." Three minutes later the two stood alone in the coffee room off the main hallway.

"We've got a problem."

Miles filled a third of his cup with cream and two sugars before adding the thick black coffee. "And that is?"

Margaret Harris looked carefully over her shoulder to insure their privacy. She stirred her coffee nervously and reluctantly answered. It was clear that she was uncomfortable with divulging the information but equally afraid not to. "General Patrick ordered a strike on the Russian freighter this morning."

"What? Are you sure?"

The secretary looked down into her cup as she spoke. "He said we couldn't wait any longer."

"Oh shit! Why didn't he tell me?" The major turned away from his friend and closed his eyes in concentration. Carefully he set his coffee on the table in the small room then slowly answered his own question. "He was protecting me. Of course! Anyone involved in this will be in deep shit!"

"What'll we do Miles?" For several minutes he pondered without speaking. Finally he opened his eyes and spoke. There was a smile on his face.

"We're going to very quietly cover Patrick's ass. That's what we are going to do." He turned back to the nervous secretary; he was smiling, in control. "Alright, who did he call?"

"He sent a courier to Colonel Bennett at Nubat. Bennett and the general are old friends from West Point. Bennett called him back to confirm the request."

"And you conveniently listened in." Marge's face turned bright red; he noted the change. "Hey, thank goodness you did."

"Can we help?"

"Sure, all I have to do is to make sure the real orders go to Nubat – not DaNang or Udorn or the navy."

"Can you do that?"

"Of course. Look Marge, I've got an IQ of 163 and I work amid imbeciles. All I have to do is outsmart a bunch of colonels. That's easy." He smiled at his own bravado. "And Marge, thanks for telling me. Patrick was right; he just jumped the gun. He should have been patient."

"Do you think the real orders will come through?"

"Oh yes. The President will give the order, or the Soviets will sink that ship themselves. Either way we're covered."

"You're sure?"

"Wanda, have I ever been wrong except for the time I guessed you to be thirty-three?"

"No." She smiled at the brash young man.

"Look at it this way. One—Nuclear weapons in the hands of the Vietnamese would be a major policy change for the Soviets. Two—The Chinese won't be very keen about nucs on their doorstep either. Three—Use of those nucs by the Vietnamese could potentially draw all of the nuclear powers into a confrontation. Nobody wants that. And, four—The Soviets have really been blindsided. They are as shocked about this as we are. My guess is that there are a lot of red faces in the Kremlin right now, pun not intended. My second guess is that it's a race to see who sinks that ship first. I've just got to make sure the orders are routed to Nubat, that's all. And there will be orders; the President has no other choice. Even he realizes that. Well, I'm off to discover how combat frag orders are processed." He patted the woman's forearm. "Don't worry Marge, everything is under control."

"Thanks Miles. You know, the general is really lucky to have a friend like you."

"No Marge, friends like *us*. See you." The young officer walked confidently down the hall as the secretary watched, still nervously stirring her coffee.

Nubat Royal Thai Air Force Base

The three men stood before the small hooch and counted handfuls of Thai currency. Each baht was worth about a nickel, so a considerable number were necessary to purchase any of the items downtown, despite the fact that everything was cheap. For the most part they had rolls of large bills known as "Red Barons" by the Americans. Each of them was worth about five dollars US. Just inside the open door, Robb Barker was splashing aftershave lotion over his face. Coke and magazine in hand, Joe sat across the room, expressionless. "Joe, you sure you won't go with us?" The silent man looked over the top of his pop can and nodded negatively. "C'mon Joe, we've got a good group going tonight; it'll be good for both of us. Have a few beers. We've all got late briefings tomorrow. We can raise hell till three if we feel like it. C'mon."

Joe nodded again. "No, thanks just the same, but I think I'll just read a little and hit the sack."

Robb shrugged and walked out to join the group in the yard. After a brief conference outside, Jack Treadeau stuck his head in the door. When he spoke, there was strong authority in his voice, one of quiet strength. "Joe, grab some duds and let's try some of that Thai formaldehyde they call beer. Hop to. The merchants downtown are in dire financial straits—they need a fresh transfusion of good old American cash, and since you are a rich foreigner, it's up to you to help solve the world's economic woes. Hurry, half of the financiers from the West are waiting outside." The brooding man looked silently at the older man standing in the doorway. He sat down his half-finished drink and started to rise. Before he could speak, Treadeau interjected, "Go with us Joe; we'd really like you to come."

Joe's dark eyes flashed; he squinted perceptibly at the luke warm can of coke and with a sudden movement pushed it across the small chest beside the bed. "Okay Jack, I'll go." For the first time in months, Joe smiled. It was a slight smile, and it disappeared almost immediately. "Will you ask those bankers to wait for me a few minutes, and I might need to arrange a loan of a few baht."

Jack smiled triumphantly. "I've got you covered." Without speaking further he turned and left.

*   *   *

The five men strolled casually towards the crowded bus stop. Each was clad in his own hand carved shoes and personally tailored trousers and shirt. Across each breast pocket was embroidered the initials of the wearer; only the colors and the initials themselves distinguished the men from each of his friends.

The war, like the baggy green flightsuits, had been put aside for the night. Except for a few references, the war would be forgotten for the evening. Other topics would be discussed, things that had been stored safely in the back of their minds, shelved for evenings like this. Countless lost moments had seen the list of these memories inventoried; long hours behind the duty desk or spent sitting in the darkened tower at night had passed quickly, traveling back across the time and distance of the mind's deepest recesses. Each man had his own memories: that deliriously happy week at the lake with Joan and the kids; the burning warmth of that last night with Betty; the carefree days back at the fraternity house during football season; that beautiful new machine—"I hated to leave that Corvette worse than some of the guys hated to leave their wives. What a beautiful car." The idle mind reached deeply into the archives of a relatively short life and replaced the boredom of the moment with the excitement and thrill of past and imagined events. And these became reality. They inspired, depressed, and excited young men who were trapped in a sudden pause in their lives. Most of the private worlds were indeed private, but some of the topics were suitable for discussion and so were dragged out to be aired before the friends around the table. They discussed cars, politics, families, investments, sports, women, pay, booze, books, and sometimes they even discussed themselves. On the nights out they mostly tried to avoid the war—that occupied far too much of their time as it was, and it would occupy far more for the first few months after they left it; sometimes they just grew tired of it. There were some who didn't, and they mostly kept with their own crowd. To them the war was a new experience in which they had proven their questionable manhood. It took months to get over the discovery of one's own personal courage, especially when it had been doubted.

The tiny pink baht bus looked much like a toy as it bounced down the worn dirt road. A young boy in a tight khaki uniform braced himself in the aisle and plodded toward the rear of the bus, handing out tickets that he punctured with a sharp thumbnail, receiving in return two baht from each of the men. Around his neck he wore a small white towel to absorb the dusty perspiration that rolled intermittently from under the band of his small billed hat. He wore no socks and his tennis shoes were held together with small, neatly tied bits of colored string. Robb nodded to the boy. "Sah Waht Dee."

The boy smiled a large smile showing perfect white teeth. "I fine; how you too?"

Major Treadeau grinned broadly. "You know, some of these people speak as well as some students I've had in freshman English."

"And spell better."

"No doubt."

The small talk grew larger as the men secretly watched Joe. He nodded affably and smiled at some of the jokes, but he never entered the conversation. He sat watching the passing countryside, the small shacks on the edge of town and the growing thunderstorm that was moving in from the Southeast. The towering gray clouds grew darker and stretched upwards of forty thousand feet as they grew in the afternoon heat. Large billowing puffs of cloud sprang from the main body and thrust themselves across the sky like blurry appendages. Already the anvil top was forming high in the air, and slight, lacey wisps of clouds shot out from the top of the buildup, pointing in the direction of the winds aloft. With the exception of the occasional crashes of deafening thunder, the giant grew perceptibly, but with silent motion. The unseen power that thrust the seething growth higher and higher into the atmosphere worked quietly, as the results of its toil loomed larger and darker over the horizon. Joe watched the clouds with the eyes of a pilot. To him they were not a beautiful creation to be admired; they were, rather, a combination of elements that could be as destructive as any weapon the enemy possessed. To him it was a threatening monster, a force that could destroy, a force he could neither understand nor conquer—much like the dark cloud that grew within his own breast and enshrouded his spirit. The laughter and happiness of the men around him were as remote as the faintest wispy clouds drifting elegantly from the top of the giant buildup. They were also equally inaccessible.

The small bus bounced through the heavy cloak of dust and turned from the small road to a slightly larger one leading to the center of the town of Nubat. The plodding water buffalo gave way to the bus and the speeding taxis; there were fewer animals on the road as the smells of the town grew heavy in the air. Loud motorcycles and slow three wheeled bikes known as samlors crowded the busy streets as the stench grew more oppressive. Sewage and refuse flowed down the small drain that passed parallel to the sidewalk; it was open to the air with only boards to cover it. Frequently even that protection was missing. The peculiar odor was a combination of the sewage, the highly spiced food that was cooked by the small vendors along the sidewalks, and partly from the rotting jungle that surrounded the small island of civilization. Near the northern section of town there was a more progressive area. The newly constructed night clubs and restaurants were built to accommodate the rich Americans who had arrived at the base. The local beer was cheap; the music was loud; and there were always empty tables and available girls. The names for the clubs had come, ingeniously, from the titles of the American girlie magazines. These magazines held a special role in the lives of the local population. The poorer segments of the populace would cover their drab dwellings with any color picture they could find. Since there was no stigma attached to having a nude pin-up in the house, they were exhibited prominently. It was always a matter of extreme awe for the Thai people to see pictures of America's large breasted pinup girls. The Thai girls, while renowned for their beauty, are quite petite. The raw sex of a thirty-eight inch bustline was almost incomprehensible, yet the idea was having its effect on changing the mores of the Thai population around the American bases. Tight sweaters, mini skirts, and mod shoes were coming into style, and for once, the larger girls were the most popular. They used little makeup; their complexion combined beauty of color and smoothness of texture; their eyes were naturally dark and large; their hair, naturally mod and straight; and in many cases, they were no larger than dolls in a toyshop.

The bus had barely stopped as the men swung to the ground, following each other in single file like paratroopers jumping into a sky of people. The tall Americans moved slowly through the scurrying crowds shopping along the narrow wooden sidewalk. The shops, like the town itself, were a combination of the old and the new. Flanking a new, modern, air-conditioned jewelry store would be an open-air stand selling the handmade wares of the city's tradesmen. An occasional mongrel dog would pass cautiously and eye the taller men. The thin animals sulked carefully in the shadows, watching for a few morsels of charcoaled squid or perhaps even a piece of discarded crust. Animals are seldom pampered in a land where people are often hungry.

Jack Treadeau led the group as they turned from the main section of town and edged their way single file down several small alleys to the spacious courtyard of the "Blooming Lotus," one of the better restaurants that had sprung up to handle the booming American demand. They were met at the gate by three young men who bowed very low and politely ushered them into the dimly lit room. Entering the front door, the bar was on the far left; a small stage with a piano was on the far right; and between was a confusion of tables and chairs arranged randomly and served expeditiously by a battalion of waitresses wearing tennis shoes and bobby socks.

The waiters immediately recognized Major Treadeau as the titular head of the group. As such he was seated in the center, not at either end of the long table. One of the older, corpulent Thai gentlemen walked over from the bar to exchange pleasantries with the group and take the wine that several of the men had brought. Good wine was cheap on the base; in town it was practically nonexistent, so the men always carried their own and had the waiters ice it for them. In return for this slight service, the owner, who was collecting the wine, usually enjoyed a glass for himself and joined the group in a toast. It was a ritual that had grown up with the base.

The meal began with large platters of steaming spring rolls and small delicate bowls of a spicy sauce and extremely sharp mustard. With these came the wine and the toast to good health. The small rolled delicacies had hardly been finished when large stacked trays of lobster and kobi steaks were brought to the banquet. More wine and an ample supply of the potent Thai beer cluttered the narrow table. Only the pleasure of drinking interrupted the consumption of the stacks of food. For an hour they ate and drank. The meal was finished at about the same time that the entertainment began, and while the empty plates were being removed to make room for the miniature cups of black coffee, the room began to pulse with the sounds of amplified music with a haunting mixture of earthy western soul and a shivering oriental beat. The swaying reverberations soothed the body while the steady flow of wine and beer calmed even Joe's bruised mind. A shapely Filipino singer was cooing to the smoky room as Robb slipped, unnoticed, from the transfixed group and headed toward the back of the room. As he returned, the overweight owner walked around the edge of the room to the small stage. He whispered silently to the leader of the small band and left. Two songs later, the beautiful young woman was urging the audience to join in. "Can anyone play the piano?"

The men at the long table took the cue and began pointing at Joe. Other than possibly flying and drinking, music was Joe's greatest passion. He was an avid piano player and had played in this same restaurant several times in the past. He protested, but the men behind him refused to take no for an answer. With cheers and shouts, they bodily hoisted him into the air and deposited him before the piano. He sat stiffly on the small wooden stool and stared blankly at the howling mass of men. When the pretty singer rubbed her breasts against his cheek and kissed him on the top of his head, he dropped his eyes to the worn keys on the instrument before him. He did not grab at her as the old Joe would have done, instead he reached slowly for the keys while his forehead sparkled with tiny beads of perspiration. He had made an earnest effort to join his friends that evening; he had finally laughed and joked even though it lacked the sincerity he had shown in the past, but he was progressing. He had been making the first steps toward the long journey of rejoining the world he had once known. He touched the keys lightly as if caressing them and finally began to play. The entire room was cheering when the first notes rang sharply into the smoky room. With eyes set, Joe began to search the instrument. The muscles in his jaw tightened and knotted; his eyes narrowed; and his fingers reached tentatively and began to move across the keyboard. He guided the piano, and it sang for him. First it shouted the joy of Dixieland; then it cried with the blues; then, the ballads. Joe hammered the piano, and it wailed louder and louder in its frenzy. The crowd took up the beat and tapped their feet on the new teak floor. The music grasped them all; life in the room stopped. The waiters cowered against the far walls and watched the mad group of Americans as they worked up the spirit of their homeland. Joe never looked up. Harder and louder he banged upon the instrument; faster and faster the tempo rose; every muscle in his body tense with the battle he was waging. The shouting stopped; the foot tapping ceased; even the accompanying combo laid aside their instruments to stare; the men looked from the storm on the stage to each other and back to the man and his music. Joe still had not looked up. All were silent, only the mounting crescendo of the piano dominated the room. The music finally reached its frantic peak; then it subsided, and suddenly Joe smiled, and the smile broke into a grin, and the grin to a laugh.

*   *   *

The evening had been long and loud. What the drinking and singing had failed to accomplish, the samlor race finished in grand style. Each of the officers had contributed a Red Baron for a grand total nearing $100 US. That pot was held by the owner of the Blooming Lotus for the Samlor driver who could get his charge to the front gate of the US base first. All along the route there were cheering men, upset vehicles, cursing drunks, military police, and general chaos. Somewhere along the way the group got separated. Robb and Jack found themselves twisted into the spokes of two colliding bikes and eventually walked the greater portion of the way back to base. It was two AM, and the wet road steamed with the rising heat. They staggered along, supporting each other physically and morally. Finally a pickup of air policemen stopped and offered them a ride. The two young air policemen escorted the two staggering officers to the back of the truck grinning sheepishly. "Hop in the back with the others, gentlemen."

"Jack, I sure hope colonel Bennett doesn't hear about this."

"No sweat, Robb. He won't hear about it. I think he's out for the night."

"Colonel Bennett?"

"Rog, that's him you're sitting on."

"Well I'll be damned."

It was noon the following day before the pair met again. The waitress placed two hamburgers and coffee before them and smiled at the two men with their chins resting on the table. Robb looked at the hamburger and winced as he lifted the top bun. "I can't stand to look." He struggled with the napkin dispenser and finally gave up, wiping his hands on his flight suit. "Why do we do things like that to ourselves? We're grown men; we ought to know better than that. I thought I was going to die this morning."

"Yes, but it was worth it. I haven't seen Joe smile in a several weeks."

Robb grinned suddenly, remembering. "You're right. I was beginning to be really worried about him, but, by damn, I think he's got the most of it licked." He stared out the window thoughtfully. "It was almost like you could see him fighting with that piano last night. It's funny, booze couldn't do it, but music could."

"Robb, do you know what's been bugging him?"

Robb stared down into the brimming cup of coffee. "Yes."

"Want to share the load?"

"No thanks, Jack; this isn't one you can easily share." He paused to sip the steaming liquid. "He's ahead of the war, that's all that counts."

"His war?"

"Yes." The two men ate in silence for a while. Raising his cup in an inverted position, Jack nodded to one of the regular waitresses and then produced four aspirins. He pushed two toward his friend and swallowed the other two himself. "You've changed too, Robb."

"Haven't we all."

Washington, D.C.

The White House chief of staff adjusted his tie, knocked once, and walked into the Oval Office. "Mr. President, the Soviet freighter *Kamkara* is turning into Vihn harbor."

The president stood before the windows behind his desk looking out at the cold winter day. "What you're telling me is that the generals are getting nervous."

"Yes Sir. I've got a handful of them in my office, and their patience appears to be wearing thin." The chief watched his boss's back.

Finally the President turned to face his friend. "They want action."

"Damn it, they just want an easy answer."

"Don't be too hard on them, John. Every one of them has fought for this country. They've got their scars. Those casualty reports most see as numbers are often their friends. They feel responsible for those kids."

The Chief of Staff looked at his boss and shook his head affirmatively. "Yeah, you're right."

"Have we heard anything from the Soviets yet?"

"No, but you can bet they're up to their ass right now trying to find out how those missiles disappeared."

"If they really don't know about this, it ought to scare the hell out of them and us. Look at this from their point of view. Suppose the Vietnamese were to set off a small nuke over Da Nang or Clark Airbase. What would the Americans do? Nuc Hanoi? Then what? This could easily get out of hand. What we have here is another Cuban Missile crisis all over again."

"That's a no-win for everybody."

"Right."

"Then why haven't the Soviets given us the go-ahead to take it out?"

"My guess is they're trying to determine how to do it themselves then deny the whole affair."

"Well they damn well better get in gear. Time's running out."

"Yes it is. That's why our team out there is getting nervous."

The two men looked at each other in silence for a short moment.

Then the younger asked the question burning in his mind. "What is your decision, Mr. President?"

The President leaned over his desk placing both hands flat on its surface. He leaned toward his friend but continued to look at the center of the desk as he spoke. "Well, John, you're going to pour both of us a strong bourbon. Then we're sending a message to our Soviet friends telling them that we are certain they have probably resolved the problem of the missiles on that ship by now, but in case they haven't, we will do so immediately. Tell them we appreciate their efforts in this situation and that the actions we take will not be announced to the public. We also feel it would be in both countries' interest if they do the same. We regret any loss of life that may occur but feel the gravity of the situation left us no alternative. Etc. Etc."

"Then?" John walked across the room with two strong drinks.

"Then we turn our boys loose on that ship."

"They don't have much time, Mr. President."

"I know. I also know that those generals out there already have at least a dozen plans and adequate resources in place to do the job. Shit, John, there are probably three flights of bombers circling that ship right now." The President sipped his drink and smiled. "You know, we've got good men over there. I wonder how long this war would last if we really unleashed them, really turned them loose."

"Sometimes I think you'd like that."

"Yes, sometimes I think I would. I'm getting tired of losing." Both men drank deeply from their drinks. "Oh well, another war, another time." The President walked back to the window. "John, assemble the troops in the situation room in thirty minutes."

"Yes Sir."

"And John, remind me to tell the generals how proud we all should be of their boys over there."

"Their boys, sir?"

"Right, *our* boys."

$*$ $*$ $*$

The president looked at the men in the room. He wondered whether he looked as tired as they did. He sat stiffly in the chair at the end of the table and nodded at the general standing at the opposite end. There was a tension in the room that was obvious to all.

"Mr. President, the ship is approaching Vihn Harbor. Assuming they wait for the tide before moving into the docking area, we have four, maybe five hours."

"What you're saying is that you need a decision."

"Yes sir."

The men sat quietly looking at the president. There were no smiles in the room. An Army four star addressed the briefing general. "What is the soonest they could get to the dock?"

"Three hours."

"Can the sub take it out now?"

"Airpower is the best answer that close to the harbor."

The president looked at his advisors seated beside him. "Any luck with the Russians?"

"No, seems they're waiting to see what we're going to do. They don't have any resources in place to take care of that ship anyway. They are really screwed too. My guess is that they are scrambling like hell right now."

The President rose, leaned on the table, and stared down at it for a long time. Finally he spoke. "Now I know what Kennedy must have felt like." He looked up; there was fatigue and frustration on his face. "Sink the ship. There is too much at stake, and we really have no other option." He looked up at the generals at the end of the table. "You guys are my experts. Get it done, and let me know when it's over. But gentlemen, this is to be kept quiet. We have nothing to gain by rubbing the Soviets' nose in this mess." He pushed back his chair and started for the door. "Thank you, gentlemen. And good luck." As he walked out the door, the Air Force chief stood and looked at the chief of staff.

"Our planners have been working on this all night. I've got two thousand pound guided hobos at Nubat. Seems like that's the best bet."

"I agree, but I'll have a batch of naval sorties in the air as backup."

"I've got plenty of firepower. But thanks, I'll let you know the details in thirty minutes."

"There's not much time."

"I know, the orders are on my desk waiting for my signature. I'm on my way there now."

"Wish you could fly that sortie?"

"Damn right, but we'll give it to a younger man with better eyes."

"Good plan." The generals walked out of the room and walked briskly to their waiting drivers for the short ride to the Pentagon. Each was glad for the decision. Each wished it had been given earlier.

CHAPTER FOURTEEN

Nubat Royal Thai Air Force Base

Col. Bennett rose quickly from his seat. He had been watching the phone all morning. It was Friday, and he knew that the command staff had scheduled a meeting with the President later that morning. He had hoped that the decision to attack the Kamkara would have been made much earlier, but it had not. He also knew his window of opportunity was growing short. He had little faith in the politicians; they had failed before; obviously they failed again. He stopped only briefly to look at the picture of his wife on the corner of his desk. She was smiling; they had enjoyed a great life together. He wondered if he would ever see her again; he wondered if she would understand his decision if he didn't. Probably she would. They had spent a lot of years together and she knew him very well. He looked at his watch, looked back at the phone and hurried down the hall to the equipment room. He called to Joe behind the counter in the operations office as he left.

"Joe, I'm waiting on a very important call. Come get me if a call comes in." He was putting on his g-suit when Joe raced down the hall.

"Colonel, you're wanted on the phone."

Without even zipping his g-suit, Bennett ran to his office and grabbed the instrument. "Bennett here!"

"Is this the 23rd Tactical Squadron?"

"Yes; I'm the ops officer of the 23rd." He recognized that the call was long distance.

"This is Lt. Colonel Schultz at Walter Reed; I have a Dr. Jernigan here from your outfit. One of my nurses asked me to call. Dr. Jernigan responded to vocal stimulus last night. It's not a lot, but it is significant. Major Thompson, our nurse, said Captain Barker should be advised."

Disappointment quickly turned to excitement as Bennett processed the message. "Yes, that is Captain Robb Barker, her fiancée."

"I'll be damned." The colonel reached for a pad and paper. "This is great news. Give me your contact information." Frantically he scribbled the information and tore the sheet from the pad. "Thank you, colonel. Captain Barker will be in touch ASAP!" Bennett smiled as he rose, speaking to himself. "Well I'll be damned. That's great!" He turned toward the door and stopped at the ops counter. Joe was completing schedule changes behind the desk.

"Get your call, colonel?"

"No, but Kerrie seems to be improving. That was Walter Reed."

"That's great."

"Yes it is. When Robb comes back in, have him check the note on my desk. I've got to run to my flight, but tell him he should leave as soon as possible. He has my approval." He looked at the phone on the counter for several seconds then rushed out the door.

*   *   *

The frowning colonel climbed quickly into the front seat of the F-4. As he entered the cockpit, he stopped briefly to look at the young navigator climbing into the seat behind him. He wondered what fate he had ordained for the young man. By tonight they would both be dead, or they would be standing by for a general court martial. What a strange world; what a predicament in which he found himself entangled. He pondered his responsibilities as a commander, as a man. He had managed to save two other crews from this ordeal, but he could not spare this man. He needed the help on this mission. General Patrick was a man of integrity; he could depend on him to carry the responsibility as far as he could. Bennett also knew that Patrick could only protect him so far. He would be embroiled in the repercussions; he could not avoid that.

Automatically he began running through his checklist. This was not the time to have a malfunction; this mission was far too important. As his mind and fingers clicked through the familiar list, he pondered the consequences of his actions. Would they put him in jail? Highly unlikely, he concluded. What was the worst they could do? Ruin his career? A twenty-five year Lt. Colonel? That made him laugh out loud. No, there was always the other one, the one he dreaded most—loss of wings and sidelined to a desk job somewhere to finish his career. In that case he would simply retire early and leave the job that had been his life. There might be a dishonorable discharge; that would be tough, but it was the loss of flying that would hurt the most. He had paid a very high price to stay in the cockpit; it would be a shame to lose that now. For the moment it was time to put his thoughts aside. It was time to complete what he had committed to do. Dishonorable discharge or not, Andrew Bennett was a man of honor. He had given his word and had committed to do what he felt was right. He had waited for the message that never came; obviously the president had not made a decision. There was no turning back now. He looked into the mirror fastened inside his canopy and studied the busy man in the rear cockpit. Roland Gamble was a competent navigator; he was also single. It seemed ridiculous, but for some reason it just seemed the right thing to do. The mission came first; his responsibility to his men came second only to that.

The colonel looked up and saw the young crew chief standing forward at the left side of the plane, looking up at him. He grinned back and gave the proud sergeant a thumbs-up. If this is my last flight, he thought, it might as well be the best. He keyed his mike, "Nubat tower, Tiger one, permission to taxi?"

"Roger Tiger one, cleared to taxi to runway 035. Wind 4 knots from 020. Altimeter two-niner-niner-eight." The young sergeant stood before the fighter and began giving directions with his arms as the plane pulled slowly out of the revetment. Several of the crewmen standing nearby stopped their work to watch the plane accelerate slowly across the hot pavement. It was an awkward looking sight, an F-4 with two guided bombs, one under each wing. The large 2,000 pound "hobos" would dwarf any other weapon on the base. It was a dramatic sight as the sergeant stopped his backward pace and saluted smartly as the plane passed him. Inside the plane, both crewmen saluted back. In the front cockpit, the pilot wondered if he would, indeed, return that day to the same revetment, the same crew chief. Time and fate would tell, he thought. For now there was work to do, and a great deal of concentration would be required to insure that this was not just a wasted opportunity.

"Tiger one, this is the tower. Are you a flight of one?"

"Roger that, tower. Two mechanicals; I'm joining another flight," the colonel lied.

"Roger Tiger one. You are cleared for takeoff. Good hunting."

"Thanks, Tower." A few seconds later the large fighter glided into the warm humid air and began its climb to the northeast. As it did, Bennett reached to the Litton Inertial Navigator and input a set of coordinates from his kneepad. He turned slightly to his starboard and pushed both throttles forward.

*   *   *

Robb sat in the truck and watched Colonel Bennett salute his crewchief as he taxied out. He was disappointed. He wanted to fly—even in combat. Today he was prepared and excited about the flight. It was always fun to bomb bridges. The truck jerked to a stop and Major Williamson climbed in with his navigator. "You abort too?"

"Yeah, Line chief met me at the plane with a red streamer hanging from her belly."

"Me too." Robb squinted into the bright sunlight of the hot afternoon. "Damn, I've never seen that before. Is the Colonel going out alone?"

"Looks that way."

"That's strange. I would have expected him to find at least another plane to go up with him. We were going after a bridge today."

"Maybe tomorrow."

Robb walked into the Operations room and banged his helmet on the worn counter. "I need a plane!" He was shouting and smiling at the same time. He was just beginning to get louder when Joe entered the room with a handful of papers and reports.

"What are you doing here?"

"Busted plane. Williamson too."

"That can't be."

"What do you mean; they both were down."

"The colonel is going to Vihn alone?"

"No, we were going for a bridge up in Route Pack Four." Joe looked at his friend for a moment and then thrust a decoded message in front of his face. "Oh shit!" Robb stood silently for a moment then began talking very quickly and loudly. "When did that come in?"

"About five minutes ago."

"He didn't know. Dammit, he didn't know. I thought he was acting strange in the briefing. I'll bet he is going after that damned ship. He pulled a fast one on us."

"Of course, that must be it. He was waiting for a special call that never came this morning. He kept checking all morning." Joe's face broke into a smile. "He did get a call about Kerrie."

Robb grabbed the edge of the counter and braced himself as his legs became weak beneath him. "Kerrie?" His voice was small and frightened.

"She's better. He left the note on his desk."

Robb dropped his gear and ran to the colonel's desk. He scanned the note and then walked slowly back to the ops area, studying the frag order Joe had handed him. As he entered the operations area, he stopped and looked at the two pieces of paper in his hand. For a moment deep furrows creased his forehead, then he looked up, and the furrows were gone. He carefully folded the colonel's note and placed it in his breast pocket then vaulted onto the counter and grabbed the radio from its charger. "Sergeant Lander, this is Ops. Get in here on the double. ASAP! Now!" He replaced the radio and began pacing back and forth. "Joe, he didn't know that order was approved. My guess is that he's on his way to Vihn right now with two "hobos" to bomb that ship."

"Alone?"

"Alone!"

"Shit. If this order is correct, that place will be crawling with Migs and enough triple A to fight off a squadron of F-4s." Both men were staring at each other when the sergeant walked in.

"Lander, read this. Fast." The man scanned the order quickly. "Is that where the colonel is headed? Did he tell you to red tag our planes?"

"I have no clue where the colonel is headed. I'm just the line sergeant."

"He didn't see this order; Sarge, he's on his way alone."

"What order?" He read the paper quickly. "What is this all about?"

"He left before he was cleared to sink that ship. My guess is that he tried to keep us out of this, and we all know why."

"He told me to keep my mouth shut on this one."

"Sergeant, the rules have just changed. The colonel is flying into a hornet's nest alone. Are any of the new E models cocked?"

"One is. I can have another ready in five minutes."

"Make it three. Damn, where's Williamson?"

"He left, probably for the club."

"Well, I can't wait. Try to find him; tell him to try to catch me on the flight line."

Joe interrupted. "You can't go alone. The Migs will be swarming over Vihn. Hillsboro says there are over a dozen there. They must be protecting something on that ship."

"I don't have a lot of choice. The colonel is five or ten out already. He's going in alone; I've got to catch him. Go to the squadron and find whatever help is available." Robb turned for the door and was walking quickly away.

"Then I'm going with you," Joe shouted across the room. "Catch Williamson's nav. Tell him to grab his gear. We're heading out."

A voice from the equipment area shouted back. "I'm already suited up. I'll meet you on the ramp."

Robb stood in the doorway looking back at his friend. "Are you sure, Joe?"

"Damn right. I owe Bennett, and I'm not letting you go alone. Now we'd better hustle."

Minutes later Joe stood before the yellow ladder and steeled his mind. He looked over at Robb and waved as his friend scrambled up the ladder of his aircraft. Joe looked up at his own plane; he knew that the plane was sixteen and a half feet tall at the top of the tail, but he had never realized just how tall that really was. He looked again at Robb, took a very deep breath, cursed quietly, then ran up the ladder as fast as he could. The voices in his mind screamed and laughed, but his muscles responded and forced his body up the steps to the cockpit. When he reached the top rung there were tears in his eyes and a grimace on his face. With great effort he pushed his body over the precipice, first standing, then seated in the pilot's seat. He placed his right hand on the control stick, while his left hand grasped the throttles and held them tightly. Closing his eyes he sat there as the battle raged in his head. Perspiration ran down his forehead and puddled in his eyebrows as the oxygen mask on his face floated on a film of sweat.

Deep inside his mind amid the shrieking voices a small musical note echoed faintly within the din of noise. He was surprised by this interloper in the echo chamber in his mind where the demons played. Joe listened carefully. The note faded but returned. Softly, slowly it played and teased him; finally it grew into a melody, and the screaming voices faded slowly into a muffled sound that eventually became a drumbeat. In the distance the notes called to the reverberating drums. The melody grew in intensity and danced with the drums through his mind. One called; the other answered. Then they joined and grew into a beautiful song. As they did, a small smile broke across his dry lips. He recognized the melody — "Guantanamera." It grew and faded and grew again. Joe concentrated as the melody echoed through his mind, finally silencing the drums, silencing the voices. What was the instrument? Another smile broke across his face as the melody returned. It was a man whistling. Joe sat quietly listening as the whistling spirit walked slowly away in his mind, drifting into the distance, leaving silence, leaving peace. "Thanks, Pete."

A trembling hand released the bayonet clip on his facemask. It fell away, and Joe opened his eyes. Across the taxiway Robb sat in his aircraft. His sun visor was down, but Joe knew he was being watched. He could feel Robb's eyes boring into his soul. With an effort he gave a "thumbs up" to his friend. The other man nodded. Now both were smiling.

It was one of the fastest preflights in aviation history. Two new F-4Es taxied to the end of the runway a few minutes later.

"Aircraft on runway, say callsign."

"Tiger Two and Three; we'll be joining Tiger One."

"Roger Tiger, you're cleared for takeoff."

Robb looked over to the revetments and saw the crews standing on the trucks and the revetment itself, watching the two F-4s as they pushed their throttles forward and roared off into the sky. Joe pulled onto his wing shortly after takeoff and looked over at his friend. Robb could not see his face through the helmet visor and the mask, but he knew Joe was smiling. "Tiger Three, go frequency Baker."

"Roger, Frequency Baker."

"Joe? You up?"

"I'm up."

"As soon as we enter enemy territory, we'll jettison bombs."

"Good plan. I don't think they'll help what we're here for."

"Hot damn! We've got guns this trip. These E's are boresighted very well."

"This could be fun."

"Joe, You okay?"

"I'm okay. Damn this feels good."

"All right guys, we didn't get to brief this very well, but we all know the score. Get on those radars and find trouble before it finds us. All right, go delta, we need some vectors to Tiger one."

The RC-121 turned south on a racetrack pattern over central Laos. Inside the large plane, radar operators tracked the single fighter approaching Vihn harbor. "Tiger One, this is Hillsboro Four. Squawk seven-up." Bennett dialed the coded numbers into his inflight identification system. "Roger, Tiger One, I have a contact. What is your current heading?"

"Zero, eight, niner."

"Zero, eight, niner?"

"That's a roger."

"Tiger One, be advised that we have significant enemy activity in the area around the port of Vihn."

"Roger, I'll be swinging to the south."

"Be careful and call feet wet."

"Roger." The colonel looked at the radio briefly and then reached forward and turned it off. "Roland, did you get that?"

"Sure did. Maybe we'll see some action today."

The colonel smiled. He didn't need his Henry-the-Fifth speech today. His navigator was an Aggie. He was ready. Well, he'd better be. "Get in that scope and keep scanning. We may have company." He peered outside the airplane then swung the plane back to the port, heading directly toward Vihn.

* * *

While Robb and Joe flew to catch their leader, the alert was broadcast across the entire base. The wing commander notified the three squadron commanders who, in turn, notified their operations officers. Within minutes, pilots and navigators were running toward the operations building. Activity on the ramp increased to a fevered pitch. One flight was armed with laser guided bombs; all others were stripped of all armament except air-to-air weaponry. Young airmen ran, worked, sweated, and cheered in the hot morning sun as they downloaded bombs and uploaded sparrow missiles while the impatient aircrews waited.

Colonel Samson had been briefed quickly and led his men to their aircraft. As they taxied out, they grouped into fours and became flights. There had been no time to brief or prepare other than the quick briefings in the van to the planes. Each lead fighter picked his flight's name: Cougar, Rattlesnake, Yessup, Copperhead, Wolf. In the hot waves of heat they taxied toward the long gray runway. On the revetments the airmen stood and watched their planes leave for battle. The large engines roared in defiance and shook the base. One by one they raced off down the concrete strip and leapt into the hot humid morning sky. Every pilot in each of the flights took his turn. As the preceding plane rolled, the next pushed his throttles to 100% while holding his brakes tightly. He checked his instruments one last time while counting silently. RPM, check; EGT, check; Hydraulics, check. Then a glance to the men on the revetments, a quick salute, and with a grin, both brake pedals were released while the throttles were pushed beyond the indent into afterburner. The thrust pushed the eager crew back into their seats as the planes lurched forward. Every man had waited for this moment. He had probably flown over Kep airfield and seen the Migs there—off limits to his bombs, rockets, or guns. The rules of engagement were heavily weighted in favor of the enemy—but not today. Hillsboro had reported over a dozen Migs over Vihn harbor and more on the way; today they were fair game. All the training would be realized on this day. Each young pilot flew eagerly toward their target. They knew three of their comrades were ahead of them on some important mission, and they knew the three were heavily outnumbered by an unusually large group of enemy aircraft. Obviously the North Vietnamese were trying to protect something very important.

The laser bomb crews stopped long enough to be briefed on the mission of the lead aircraft approaching Vihn Harbor. They would finish the job if the three ahead of them missed. But that mattered not at all to these young pilots. They wanted a crack at the Migs. Finally the Migs had come out to play. Well, today it wouldn't be a game of tag. No rules! That was what the flight leader had said. "Find them! Destroy them!" The search was on.

"Copperhead, we'll jettison tanks on my command as we approach the target area. Copy?"

"Two, copy."

"Three."

"Four."

"Alright men, hang on. We're in a hurry today. Wolf, take my right; Yessup—left. Rattlesnake, you follow with Cougar."

"Roger, Rattlesnake is two for takeoff. Save a few for us."

"Cougar, are you heavy?"

"Roger that."

"Were you briefed on the target?"

"If Tiger misses, we'll get the target. We're ready."

"Copy. Good hunting. We'll run interference. Rattlesnake, you're shotgun for Cougar. Just get that target."

"Will do, Copperhead."

✳   ✳   ✳

The port city still was not in sight when the call came over the radio Guard channel. "Tiger One, if you read me, you have four bandits heading in your direction from your eleven o'clock position. I repeat. You have four bandits heading in your direction from your eleven o'clock position. Acknowledge."

Bennett changed the channel back to Hillsboro's frequency. "Roger Hillsboro, I read you five-by. Did you say four bandits?"

"Four and they are closing fast. They're about twenty-five out now."

"Roger, and thanks." Over the intercom the colonel's voice was fast and tense. "Do you have them, Roland?"

"Sure do! I'm locked on one now."

Bennett acted quickly. "One's away! Now, quick, lock on another."

"Done!"

"Two's away."

"Locked on three."

"Three's away."

"Last lock."

"Four's away."

"Tiger, this is Hillsboro. I have two blips remaining? What is your status?"

"S.O.L. I'm Winchester."

"Turn hard right and get the hell out of there!"

Bennett looked into the mirror at the young navigator. "Good work, son. We got two of the bastards."

"Are we out of missiles?"

"I'm afraid so."

"Then let's get the hell out of here."

The colonel squinted his eyes in concentration. What were his options, one heavy plane with no weapons against two enemy fighters? He couldn't fight them and his chances of evading them were slim. Yet he knew he had to get that ship. He had made a serious error in judgment; he needed the rest of his flight. Now he faced odds that put his mission in jeopardy. As he struggled with the options, the colonel caught the movement off of his right wing. An Aim 7 missile streaked from behind him and passed on his right. Almost simultaneously, two more passed on his left. As the young navigator began to cheer in the back seat, two F-4Es pulled into formation on either side of the colonel's plane. "Well, I'll be damned!"

"Tiger One, this is Hillsboro. Splash number three. Number four is turning east and may be damaged."

"Tiger One, Tiger Two and Three request permission to join."

"Thought I left you guys back at the ranch. What are you doing here?"

"Approval came through."

"It did?"

"Roger that."

"Are you briefed?"

"We're up to speed. Lead on McDuff."

"Thanks for coming."

"Wouldn't miss this for anything." The colonel recognized Joe's voice.

There was a long pause before the colonel spoke to Robb. "Two, did you see the note on my desk?"

"It's in my pocket."

"Well, we've got the first string here, so let's go to work. Keep in those scopes; there's bound to be more Migs where those came from." He looked at the plane off his right side. "Today we fight; we'll celebrate tomorrow."

Vihn Harbor, North Vietnam

Colonel Ruchinsky watched the small boat approaching off the starboard bow. He didn't recognize anyone in the delegation, but he knew their purpose. They were his welcoming party, the local leaders sent to measure both him and his cargo. He knew these men were not to be trusted. Dmitriy frowned; even the ocean smelled of sewage. He hated Vietnam, and he distrusted the Vietnamese. To him there was little difference between these cunning creatures and the enemy flying overhead as the ship had approached the harbor. There was but one man to whom he would deliver the missiles, Colonel Tran. He alone would be trusted with this cargo. He concentrated on the small boat bouncing across the waves. Watching it brought a slight nausea to his stomach and reminded him how he hated the sea and boats of all sizes and descriptions. How he longed for the solid soil of home, resting securely under two meters of snow. How different it was from the stinking, steaming jungles of Vietnam. He smiled for the first time in days. His mission was almost over. In less than a week he would be on his way home, home to Dasha; that made him smile.

Several jets circled high overhead. Dmitriy assumed they were Vietnamese Migs, a gift from his own country. No one else even seemed to notice. They all knew that Vihn harbor was a safe haven. Everyone knew the rules of war. They had been briefed well. "You can shoot at the Americans, but they are not allowed to shoot back, not here."

Watching the planes had helped settle the nausea for the time being. It had also allowed the bobbing boat to approach, and already the dignitaries were climbing aboard. Ruchinsky stood tall and prepared himself for the meeting.

Hung Cuong Nguyen, Governor General of the province was the ranking man in the group. He was a small man and surprisingly plump for a Vietnamese. His face reminded Dmitriy of paintings of cherubs he had once seen in a museum in Moscow, but the eyes were sharp and penetrating. Such men pretend to be stupid, but their minds are sharp like guillotines. He knew to beware such men. He watched the dark eyes; they made him uncomfortable. He straightened his uniform, dusted his hat, and stepped forward to meet the cherub.

"Colonel, welcome to Vihn." Dmitriy simply nodded, silently counting and analyzing each of the remaining members of the delegation. He noted no weapons in sight, but fully expected others that might be hidden. "Colonel, we have been expecting you. You and your cargo are most welcome here."

"Thank you." He forced a smile and bowed slightly , carefully watching the penetrating eyes of the smaller man. He was surprised that the cherub spoke fluent Russian.

"May we see the cargo?"

"Of course." Ruchinsky led the way down the deck to the tarp-covered missiles. His men stood alert, weapons at attention as the group approached. Sergei stood by the weapons and lifted a corner of the tarp. The governor leaned forward and peered at the missiles. Sergei dropped the tarp quickly and looked overhead as if expecting a plane to fly by with cameras. The older man stepped back and conferred with three others in the group. After several moments they emerged from their huddle and addressed Dmitriy.

"Your ship will be directed to the appropriate pier at the next high tide. We will commence offloading the missiles just after sundown. In the meantime you and your captain are cordially invited to join us ashore. We would like to express our appreciation."

Ruchinsky looked at the men for a moment before speaking. "Captain Iskhakov will remain here with the missiles. I will join you and confer with Col. Tran. He will be here I assume."

"Yes, of course, Colonel Tran will be your host while here in Vihn. He is waiting ashore."

"Thank you."

The sharp, piercing eyes of the Governor General drilled into Dmitriy's as he led the way to the small skiff. Slowly the men climbed into the smaller boat and began their journey toward the shore. Sergei stood on the ship and watched the group leave. He longed to join them and enjoy the Vietnamese hospitality he had heard so much about. He was anxious to discover if the rumors were, indeed, true.

*   *   *

The three F-4s turned starboard to a heading of 020 and began descending. Col. Bennett called the flight to yet another frequency and made a quick inventory. "Armament remaining?"

"Three Aim 7s, four Sparrows, and cannon."

"Two Aim 7s, four Sparrows, and cannon."

"Great. You men know what we're here to do?"

"Roger, Two."

"Roger, Three."

The three planes streaked on toward Vihn in silence until the sector controller finally broke the peace. "Tiger, this is Hillsboro."

"Go ahead, Hillsboro."

"We have thirteen bandits airborne over the port of Vihn. Your intentions?"

Before Bennett could answer, Joe interrupted. "Kick their ass. What else?" Bennett smiled though he was not at all amused with the thirteen to three odds. But that was the old Joe, the best stick in the Wing—perhaps the best in the Air Force. Bennett knew he needed that—the best pilots he could muster. They had to keep the Migs off long enough for him to make one pass. One pass, that's all he would need. The two "Hobos" would do the rest. Four thousand pounds of explosives, driven right through the hull of that ship. That would be enough. But he had to be free for that pass. Obviously the enemy knew the value of the cargo aboard that ship. Thirteen Migs was a formidable force. If only he had another flight of four, but Robb and Joe were all he had. Could the two of them do it? They would have to.

"Two, Three. Fire as soon as we're in range and you've got a good lock. Let's try to improve those odds."

"Roger that."

"Tiger, this is Hillsboro! Three bandits approaching your two o'clock, low, high speed!"

"Thanks, Hillsboro."

Bennett strategized rapidly. "Three, take them, low."

"Roger." Joe banked right and dived toward the ground. As he did, both external tanks were jettisoned. Both afterburners ignited and the E model was gone.

Bennett spoke calmly into his intercom. "INS says we're about 100 out. How does that look to you, Roland?"

"Looks good to me."

"Tiger! Tiger! Three bandits approaching fast, dead ahead!" There was a brief pause as two missiles streaked off Robb's aircraft. "As I was, two, make that two bandits remaining."

The colonel initiated a sharp dive, descending rapidly. As he did, he noticed the two wing tanks being jettisoned from Tiger 2.

"Tiger! Tiger! Two bandits passing your position. Bandits heading 185 degrees." As the Migs passed overhead, the two F-4s streaked northward just above the treetops.

"Splash one!" It was Joe, the old Joe. Both of the other pilots smiled. Joe was still in the fight. "Splash two!"

The planes were silent, but inside the low flying Phantoms the crews were cheering. "I hope he gets five more." The colonel was speaking in the intercom, his voice calm and quiet. In his mind he was measuring his options.

"Three is free in New Orleans. Position one?"

"Ski country, heading for the Windy City."

"Roger, I'm on my way."

"Three, run interference. Get in front."

"Roger, understand."

"One, this is Two. Shall I join him?"

"Negative, stay close."

"Roger." The two F-4s skimmed a ridge and there it was before them, Vihn harbor. It was beautiful, a large blue lagoon surrounded by peaceful green foliage and white sand beaches. It could have been a resort poster hanging on the wall of some travel agency. Immediately the two F-4s began a steep climb. As they did, off to their right another F-4, with both afterburners lit, was pulling upward into the formation of Migs above. Two missiles streaked off the plane, catching the Migs completely unaware. One of the planes exploded and tumbled into the bay.

"Okay Robb, give him a hand. And good luck, son." Robb thrust the throttles outboard, past the indention and into afterburner. He felt the sudden thrust of acceleration as he rushed to join his friend. Bennett continued to climb, checking all of the ships in the harbor. He needed only one—the right one.

Robb looked up at the sky above him. It was filled with aircraft, circling, waiting. He glanced right at the F4E climbing beside him. Like him, Joe was looking at the enemy above, analyzing the odds, the relative position and vector of each aircraft. So this was it, two emotional cripples against at least a dozen or more enemy fighters. Were they crazy? Perhaps. At least they had little to lose. What were their chances? Not good, but they had to give Colonel Bennett one pass—one pass to blow that Soviet ship out of the harbor. One chance to save what? Da Nang? Clark Airbase? Nubat? Bangkok? If only Bennett could get his pass, the enemy planes really didn't matter much. The two "hobos" wouldn't miss.

Robb flew into the maelstrom. He counted six Migs easily and knew there were more. One was banking hard into his 4:30 position. Suddenly it exploded into a large ball of fire. Joe's aircraft flew directly through the fireball from beneath then banked hard right, a Mig in hot pursuit. Robb banked right, too, directly behind the pursuing Mig. He watched the Mig float through his pipper. As it did, he squeezed his trigger, heard the low growl of the Gattlin gun, and watched the Mig explode before him. Immediately he banked hard left and dove toward the sea. As he did, two Migs turned after him.

The colonel watched the battle above him briefly, then turned his attention to the ship in the harbor. "Hang on Roland, I've got the target in sight. Get in that scope."

"Right, Colonel."

"Shit!" He banked hard right as a missile streaked closely off his left wing. Straining hard, Bennett swiveled in his seat scouring the sky for the Mig.

"Eight o'clock, low!" Roland was leaning backwards and had pressed himself to the canopy.

"I see him!" Bennett pulled hard on his stick, lit both afterburners and began an abrupt, steep climb.

Joe was in his environment. Planes filled the sky. Rockets and gunfire were everywhere. The world was screaming at high speed—but not for Joe. He saw everything differently. He knew where every plane was, its speed and direction, and his own path around and through the mass. The F4-E was a remarkable bird. For the first time in his career he had a gun he could depend on. It would shoot where he aimed, unlike the gun pods on the D models. Joe was having fun. As long as he had ammunition, he considered the odds fair.

Bennett was straining to look over his shoulder at the Mig on his tail. If only he could jettison the two giant guided bombs under his wings. If only he had a gun or a sidewinder. If only—if only. The Mig had turned sharply and was climbing after him, shooting wildly. Bennett knew the Mig couldn't climb with him, but what about the two 2,000 pound bombs he was lugging aloft? The afterburners were doing their job; the F-4 accelerated upward while the Mig climbed behind.

Robb glanced back at Joe and suddenly something strange happened. The world slowed before him. The enemy aircraft moved slowly across the sky, their flight paths easily discernable. Amazed, he looked at his own instruments. He was pegged at 6000 feet per minute, straight up. So this is how it is for Joe, he thought. He's had this all along. Amazing. He glanced to his right as Joe's fighter passed in a sharp bank. Somehow Robb knew that Joe was smiling, watching the same slow motion world outside his own aircraft. Robb watched two Migs turn at his four o'clock. Instinctively he broke hard into them and sprayed 20mm fire across another as he dove toward the bay. He sensed Joe breaking left as two Migs followed him in the climb. He watched three others break toward him, diving fast. The E model strained hard at nine and a half g's as Robb pulled out of the dive, climbing past the enemy fighters. He hit both afterburners and watched the ground recede behind him. He sensed that Joe was on his left. He looked left and the big camouflaged plane was climbing beside him. Joe looked over and spoke quickly. "Robb, break into me—low—now!" The two planes crossed each other very close, dragging their respective pursuers behind them. The Migs were intent on their prey and crossed right through the other Mig formation's flight path. Two collided and burst into a large fireball, distracting the remaining enemy pilots.

"Robb, break hard right!"

"Got him!"

Joe watched the two Migs split before him. Another was turning from his left; he banked hard left and fired off a sparrow. He watched the Mig turning behind him and smiled, knowing he could out maneuver the novice he had observed for the past few minutes. He decided that he might even be able to get the Mig to shoot down one of his own comrades with a little fancy flying. Then he saw the F-4 with the awkward bombs climbing to his left. A Mig was chasing him from behind, firing over the F4's right wing. "Damn!" Joe banked left, right in front of the Mig chasing him and blasted the left wing off the Mig pursuing Colonel Bennett. In the process, the E model took several hits from the amateur who got off a lucky burst as Joe wheeled before him. "Shit! Todd, you okay?" Nothing. "Todd!" Nothing. "Hang on Man! Hang in there!" Joe wrapped the stick left and the plane responded. He engaged both afterburners and pulled back on the stick, and the plane climbed immediately. Disengaging both afterburners Joe looked over at the Mig beside him. They were suddenly canopy to canopy, watching each other, climbing together. "Okay asshole, try this!" Joe dropped his landing gear and speed brakes simultaneously. The giant fighter stopped accelerating immediately and fell behind the Mig. Joe threw up the landing gear handle and thumbed the speed brakes. Now he was directly behind the Mig. One burst from the Gattlin gun and the enemy aircraft disintegrated before him. He yanked the aircraft left and saw the smoke trailing from his own fighter. "That's how a pro does it, asshole!"

Bennett saw the E-model bank toward him. In his mirror he saw the Mig explode. There was no time to cheer. He had a ship to kill. He threw the stick left and began a steep, fast descent. "Roland, quick lock onto the ship I'm diving at. Quick!"

"I've got it!"

"Wrong ship—the other one on the right."

"Got it."

"That's it. Good work." Bennett swung the aircraft left and right with his rudders. The lock was good. "Shit hot! One's away. Now, lock on again."

"Got it."

"Two's away."

* * *

Robb knew they were in trouble. The Mig pilots were no match for him or Joe, but there were too many of them. Surprise had given them the advantage, but the odds were catching up with them now. He had seen Joe's smoke; the enemy were quickly reacting to the attack. He waited for the colonel's bomb release call, then they could try to disengage and flee. That, too, was highly unlikely. He wondered where the colonel was and if he had even made it into the target area. He wanted information, but he was too busy to even ask. He put several rounds through the tail of one Mig but was desperately trying to turn away from two others closing on his right. Straining to see behind him, he watched one of the Migs firing wildly with his cannon. The second followed close behind the first, also turning into his six o'clock position. "Shit!" Robb pushed the nose down, spun over and began a sharp Split S maneuver. The two Migs followed, closing on him rapidly. Suddenly the second Mig burst into flames and began to spiral toward the harbor. The second turned sharply left and lost half of his right wing to a missile fired from behind him. Robb yanked his stick left and saw two flights of F4s engaging the enemy fighters. The cavalry had arrived.

* * *

The Soviet captain watched the air battle from the bow of the ship. It was clearly a mismatch. The Americans were having a turkey shoot. Migs were falling into the bay like leaves on a fall afternoon in Moscow. He paced back to the stern and cursed the sailors watching the battle. "Man your guns, idiots! Perhaps you can find the opportunity to shoot at the enemy. Or would you rather just watch the war? Our Vietnamese may be piss poor pilots, but at least they fight like men. Now get to those anti-aircraft guns. Now!" His face was red; he was waving his pistol and shooting into the air. The young men watched him, then ran to their battle stations lest he go berserk and shoot them as he had shot the sailor on the trip from Vladivistok. Sergei was shaking with rage as he watched the battle above. He had never felt so helpless. Then he spotted the lone aircraft diving toward his ship. As it flew closer he ran to the nearest gun site and pushed the young sailor aside. "Shoot, dammit!" He pulled the trigger and a clip of 37 mm rounds fired off into the sky. Brown puffs of smoke blossomed to the right of the fighter bearing down on his cargo. Another string of 37 mm rounds flashed through the sky—again missing high. One of the young seamen stopped abruptly as he hauled ammunition for the gun site.

"What is he doing? Is he attacking us?"

"Keep shooting! This is a Soviet ship. They'd never attack us.

This harbor is off limits to them." Sergei peered carefully at the approaching fighter. "They...wouldn't...dare..." Sergei's voice trailed off in disbelief as the men aboard Kamkara watched the two large bombs fall from the wings of the F-4D and glide directly toward them. The plane banked left then rolled right, circling the ship. It was obvious the pilot was watching his target.

Sergei stood in his gunner's seat on the gun site and looked forward at the missiles under the tarps. Then he looked back at the two large missiles gliding gracefully toward the ship. Sergei was still standing on the gunsite, screaming obscenities as both bombs ripped into the ship.

The small skiff bumped repeatedly against the dock as the Vietnamese officials stood in shock watching the Kamkara sink into the harbor. Some cursed; one fired his pistol into the air at the American fighters. Dmitriy simply watched in silence. He understood war, and he knew this battle was lost. Finally he sat down and pulled the flask from his jacket. He took one last swallow and tossed the silver container overboard. Like his dreams, like his son, like the missiles, it sank slowly into the blue water and was lost forever.

*   *   *

Bennett watched the retreating Migs and the pursuing F-4s. Aim 7 missiles filled the sky as many of the Migs exploded in retreat. Four headed east over the ocean, but Hillsboro had a flight of navy jocks waiting for them five miles out to sea. Breathing hard, the colonel watched the two Paveway II Electro Optical Bombs smash through the hull of the ship. The ensuing explosion rocked several ships nearby. The secondary explosions he guessed to be the missiles. In less than three minutes the entire ship sank; the two large two thousand pound bombs had blasted the ship into a burning mass of molten metal.

Bennett saw the small skiff that was nearing the shore. It had slowed to watch the attack. Perhaps there were dignitaries aboard, maybe the crew of the ship, but it mattered not. He had expended all of his ordnance on the freighter. That was his mission; now it was time to go home. Suddenly he felt tired, old, and exhilarated—all at once. Robb and Joe—where were they? He knew one had taken a hit protecting him, but he didn't know how bad it might be. Now it was time to find his men, assess the damage, and head for Nubat.

"Hillsboro, this is Tiger 1, squawking Bingo. Pigeons to Two and Three?"

"Roger Tiger 1, I have your squawk. Two and Three are 263 degrees, 45 miles."

"Thanks Hillsboro. You guys were pros today. Two, do you read me?"

"Roger, Two and Three are limping home."

Bennett checked his fuel gage as he pushed both throttles to 100%. He punched off both external tanks and accelerated toward his flight. "One's joining from your five o'clock."

"Roger."

"Three, status."

"Not good Colonel. Hydraulics are dropping steadily. Left engine is out; right is running rough. GIB is hit."

"Fire?"

Robb spoke first. "Roger. Wing root, left side, but it seems to be subsiding."

"Visible flames?"

"Affirmative, and lots of smoke."

"I have you in sight and will close on the left." The crews watched the D model glide smoothly into formation on the left. Both crewmembers were staring intently at the damaged plane on their right. "Two, move out so I can take a look."

Robb extended his position on Joe's right wing without reply and watched as the colonel slowly rolled up, over, and around the damaged aircraft. When his inspection was complete, he moved out into a loose formation on the left. "Two, any word from your nav?"

"No, sir."

"Are you okay? Any hits?"

"I'm fine. What's Todd's status? How's he look?"

"Bad, son, real bad. Has he moaned or made any sound on the intercom at all?"

There was a long pause. Finally Joe answered. "No." It was a small voice, one he hardly recognized as his own.

The three planes flew southwest. Joe was fighting the plane as best he could with full right rudder and right aileron. Slowly the aircraft was descending toward the jungle below. Billowing black smoke trailed behind and slowly faded into the hot jungle air.

"Three." It was Colonel Bennett. "Can you climb at all?"

"Negative, I'm just trying to maintain five thousand."

"We're at four-three now."

"I know, but I've still got burner on the right."

"Stay away from that unless you have to use it. It's just too risky, son." He paused momentarily. "Hillsboro? Tiger. Pigeons to the border."

"Straight ahead. I estimate ten minutes."

There was a long silence, then the colonel spoke. His voice was very deliberate. It was obvious that he had considered his words well. "Joe, you aren't going to make it to the border. I want you to punch out. Your plane isn't going to hold together much longer."

"Bullshit!"

"What?"

"Bullshit! I'm taking this baby into Udorn."

"You can't make it, son."

"Colonel, if I punch out, Todd is dead. I can see his shoulder in my mirrors. He's slumped to the right—under the railing. If we punch, it'll cut him in half."

"I know son, but Todd is already gone."

"How do you know?"

"If you try to bring this in we'll lose you both. Todd's dead. Punch out. That's an order."

"Fuck your order! I'm bringing Todd back."

For the first time, Bennett's voice rose with anger and frustration. "Dammit, Joe, He is covered with blood. He was hit by 30 mm cannon fire. He hasn't even moaned. Your plane is going down. Your going with it doesn't help anyone. Now, I'm giving you a direct verbal order to punch out. You got that!"

"Fuck you,…sir."

Robb interrupted the conversation, his voice calm and slow. "Joe, I know why you're doing this. Todd's gone. I checked him, too, Joe. He's gone." He paused momentarily then continued. "And this isn't going to bring Pete back. Do you understand? You don't need to do this, not for Todd or Pete. Joe, they're dead. Pieces are falling off of your plane. You can't make it with this one. Do what the colonel says and punch out."

"I'm bringing this piece of crap home. Don't you guys understand? I can't punch. I can't kill Todd. He might be alive. I just can't do it." He paused and then added. "And neither would you guys."

Before the colonel could speak, Robb spoke again. "You're sure about this?"

"Damn right I'm sure. This is for Todd; it's for Pete; but most of all, it's for me."

"Okay Joe, I'm on your wing as far as you take me." There was a long silence. Then the colonel spoke.

"Shit. Me too. Good luck, son."

They watched the man in the cockpit between them fighting the dying plane. They were silent, but each was praying and cursing at the same time. Below them, the silent jungle loomed dark and damp in the afternoon heat. It slid past imperceptibly, a sea of trees below the clear blue sky. Joe fought the plane expertly. He nursed and cursed the dying machine. Three minutes later, fifty miles short of the Thai-Laotian border, Joe's plane began to lose altitude rapidly. Joe looked quickly into his mirror. Behind him he could see the helmet of his GIB, "Hang in there, Todd. We're going home, buddy!" He struggled violently with the vibrating stick, cursing through clinched teeth while the altimeter continued to move in a counter clockwise direction. For the first time, he looked at his two wingmen. He couldn't see their faces behind their oxygen masks and sun visors, but he knew they were nervous. Over the intercom he continued to talk to the inert figure behind him. "Okay, Todd, we're going to show them how it's done, how a pro does it. We're the best, Todd. We're the best." Joe looked again at the altimeter. Col. Bennett's voice interrupted his thoughts.

"Joe. You're losing altitude—fast!"

"Hang on Colonel!" Joe pushed the right throttle slowly forward and beyond the indent into afterburner. "Come on, baby!"

The plane lurched toward the clouds above, then exploded in a blazing ball of fire. Four startled crew members watched helplessly as the fireball sliced through the afternoon sky and crashed into the jungle below. Tiger 1 and 2 banked hard right and circled the crash site twice. No one spoke; finally the colonel turned southwest and headed toward Nubat.

EPILOGUE

Washington, D.C.

Miles Campbell walked into the general's office and sank into one of the chairs before the commander's desk. "It's finished."

"Successful?" The general continued reading without looking up. He was hunched over a pile of paper that cluttered his desk; a half eaten sandwich lay on a stack of reports with a large coffee stain before him.

"Yes sir."

"Good work, Miles. You know they'll court martial me for this." It was said as a matter of fact. There was no emotion in his voice.

"No they won't."

"They won't?"

"Nope." He slid the signed order across the desk. Patrick picked it up and quickly read the sheet. Then he sat upright, leaned back in his chair and reread it, more slowly this time.

"Son of a bitch!" He rose and walked to the window of his office and looked out on the new morning. "And Bennett pulled it off?"

"Two Paveway II's—right down the stack."

"Are we sure none of the missiles were offloaded?"

"Never made it to the dock. They're all scrap on the bottom of Vihn harbor."

Patrick walked quickly to the door of his office and looked outside. No secretaries were in sight. "Damn, How do people get nine to five jobs?"

"They get a civilian job in the government." The younger man laughed quietly.

"Come on, I'm going to buy you a cup of coffee in the cafeteria."

"I save the world and I get a cup of coffee?" Campbell grinned at his boss.

"And…how about a steak and drinks with our wives tonight."

"Now you're talking." The two men rose and started for the door, the general struggling with his dress blues.

"As soon as we get back I've got to call Bennett. Damn, he really did it!"

"He sure did."

"Find me a full bird spot—a good one, a wing commander, a flying slot. He's due to rotate soon. Let's promote him, and I want DFC's for the crews that pulled this off, and not for Achievement; these should be for Heroism." He thought a moment, then continued. " But remember, we can't mention the Kamkara. That never happened."

"Roger that; the DFC's are already in process, and if you tell me to, sir, I'll get Bennett a two star spot."

"You know, Miles, I'll just bet you could." He had a determined smile on his face as they walked toward the elevators. "We'll do that—all in good time."

Skovorodino, The Soviet Union

Dmitriy lay in the darkness listening to the silence that hung like a shroud between him and his wife. It had been two weeks since his return from North Vietnam. He had not slept well since the attack, the sheer horror of the exploding ship etched forever in his mind.

For an hour he had lain there, listening to her breathing. He knew she was not asleep, yet he dared not disturb her. He rolled to his side in the narrow bed and felt the softness of her hip against his own. He wanted so much to broach the gulf between them, but he simply didn't know how to do it. His own life was a tangled web of failure and regret; she was his last bridge to reality and meaning, yet he didn't know how to reach her. As he lay struggling with himself, he felt the tiny twitch in her body, then another, then another. The rhythmic motion of her body increased in tempo; finally he realized that she was crying. The tiny tears overcame the dam in his own heart, and he turned and pulled her to him without speaking. He held her in his arms, cradled against his breast. As she cried, he stroked her hair and kissed her forehead. Finally he spoke. "Do you remember how Nikolai hated vegetables when he was young? Well, you always thought he ate them anyway. Actually, he put them in your flower pots in the dining room."

Dasha sniffled and spoke through her tears. "He did? And you knew?"

"Yes, it was our secret. He would ask for seconds of milk in order to get you to leave the table, then he would sneak the food into the flowers. We would laugh quietly so you wouldn't know."

Dasha sat up in the bed and blew her nose gently. "So that is what you two were up to."

"Once I put my vegetables in the pots as well. That really made him laugh."

"I always wondered why those flowers grew so well."

"It is a wonder that he grew so tall. All he ever ate was meat and potatoes."

"Yes, he was tall, wasn't he?"

"And thin; he obviously didn't take after me."

Dasha lay back beside her husband. "I can recall a very thin young man when we were first married."

"That was before I had your wonderful cooking every day."

Dasha snuggled next to Dmitriy and put her arms around him. "I miss him so much. It is so difficult knowing that I will never see him again. Sometimes I don't know how I will live with that."

"I know, Dasha. I miss him too." He stared into the darkness, holding the woman he loved. "But you know, last night I had this strange feeling as I was standing on the porch. It was as if he were standing there beside me. I could feel his presence. It was so real to me."

"How would you describe the experience? Was it happy?"

"It was peaceful. I think he was trying to tell me to find peace with his death."

"That's going to be hard to do." Her lips quivered as she spoke.

"Yes, but we need to do that." He paused a moment and then added, "for him, and for us, too."

Dasha rolled to her back; Dmitriy could feel the dampness of her tears on his arm. "I'm not sure I can do that."

"Yes, you can. Nikolai would want it. He was a brave young man; he would expect no less from us."

"Yes, you are right. But it is so difficult."

Can you remember his face when we gave him his first dog, the one with the short legs? Or the day he got his wings at flight school? Can you remember his face that day? Exactly the way it looked?"

"Yes, it was shining with joy."

"Keep that face in front of you when it gets hard. Remember his joy in life. That is what he would want for us."

"Yes, you are right." She cuddled against her husband and smiled. "Do you remember the time he hid your hat? You had to report to duty without a proper military hat. You were so angry."

"He could be a rascal."

The night turned into stories, then laughter, and occasionally tears. Finally they lay silent again holding each other, reliving moments from the past, remembering past happiness.

As Dmitriy held her, an old longing awoke within his body. It was an unexpected desire that surprised them both. The softness and warmth of her body had brought back the years of memories of joyous lovemaking in their marriage. She smiled in the darkness as she pulled her gown over her head. That he still wanted her gave her great pleasure. That he wanted her now was even more beautiful to her. Dasha recognized that his pain, like her own, had threatened the tenuous balance in her husband's existence. If she could bring him joy and perhaps also fill a part of the void in his life, that would give her more satisfaction than the act of sex itself. Thirty years of marriage had not dulled their love or their expression of that love. Rather, they were like practiced dancers, understanding the moves and the reactions of the other. With a small laugh, she straddled her husband and bent forward to kiss him. Like a small boat bobbing on the ocean, the two of them rocked gently with the delight of unexpected passion. They were lost in a sea of darkness with only the touch of the other to maintain their anchor to reality. In time, however, the waves grew and the tiny boat was tossed in the swirling passion of the storm. In the night they both cried out, but not for safe harbor. They cried out in joy and pain, in suffering and deliverance. It was an affirmation of their need for each other in the darkness of their lives; it was also an affirmation of the continuance of life.

The joy they shared represented an important turning point in their struggle. The difficult path ahead was apparent, but they had passed a significant milestone on the journey that evening. Their act of love was a celebration of life and of living.

Breakfast was different the following morning. The food tasted better; the two talked about their day; and they held hands across the small table. As he rose, Dmitriy looked at his wife and smiled. "Let's have dinner out tonight. I've heard of a pleasant little restaurant in town. It will not be Moscow, but it should be good food." Dasha smiled and nodded as she held his coat before the door.

*   *   *

As the Soviet colonel walked into his office, his clerk stood to attention and announced two visitors waiting inside. The joy in Dmitriy's heart dissolved rapidly into fear as he recognized the major and the captain as they stood for his entry. They were staff personnel from command headquarters.

"Good morning, Colonel. I hope we may have a few moments of your time."

Dmitriy struggled with his coat and gloves. "But of course. What can I do for you this morning?" He stepped back through the door and called to his clerk. "Bring three coffees, please."

"Sir, are you aware of the incident of a Soviet freighter being attacked in Vihn harbor two weeks ago?"

The older officer studied the two younger men carefully as he sat in his chair. "Please be seated. No, I was not aware of that. What happened?"

"It was attacked by an American aircraft."

"That is outrageous, we are not at war with the Americans. Our government will not stand for such insolence." Dmitriy could feel the sudden rush of adrenaline through his body as panic spread through his heart and mind. Could these two possibly know of his involvement? Were they there investigating the incident?

"Our government is well aware of the attack, but we will ignore it as will the Americans. This incident will not be reported by either side."

"Why?" Dmitriy tried to sound convincing.

"Because it contained four Soviet nuclear missiles that were shipped without approval to the Vietnamese."

"But how?"

"That is why we are here." The colonel could feel the panic rising in his breast. "It is felt that a renegade officer and his sergeant may have stolen the missiles for transfer to North Vietnam. The local authorities there say they know nothing of the transaction; obviously we are not the only ones with renegade officers."

"Have the men involved been identified?"

"We know it was a Captain Iskhakov from this region. By the way, we also have determined that this captain and a Sergeant Kochkin were involved in a number of other illegal activities here. Our guess is that they were trying to sell the missiles. It is also possible that the Vietnamese are lying and knew about the deal all along."

Dmitriy looked at the two officers and quickly weighed his options. These were bright men; they would have done their homework well and would surely know of his relationship with Sergei. "I know Captain Iskhakov and am shocked by this accusation. Are you sure he is involved?"

"Absolutely. We also suspect the sergeant but are not certain of his involvement yet." The major stopped talking to receive his coffee as did the captain and Dmitriy.

"Have you questioned them yet?" Dmitriy asked hesitatingly.

"No, that would be impossible. They are both presumed dead, killed in the attack."

"Dead." There was real sadness in Dmitriy's voice. His voice was barely audible to the two younger men. Dmitriy stood slowly and walked to the window to peer down at the parade ground. Slowly he rubbed his forehead with his fingertips as the reality sank once more into his consciousness. Yesterday morning he would have lacked the strength to carry out the deception with these men. The night with Dasha, however, had changed all of that. He now knew that life still had value. He also realized his own role in pulling her from the desolation that had doomed them both before last night. For the first time in months he could see the opportunity to find peace and even a measure of joy in his life; more importantly, he was convinced he could lead Dasha to that as well. She was all that mattered to him now. But now everything hung in the balance. He had to be clever with these two men. How much did they know? Why were they here?

"The Americans sank the ship. We are told there were two guided bombs used in the attack. There were no survivors onboard."

"There were no survivors at all?"

"None. The Americans were quite efficient in their attack. They used 2000-pound guided bombs. Everyone involved was killed."

Dmitriy sat slowly back into his chair. "Why do you think Captain Iskhakov was involved in illegal activities?"

"We have evidence that he was dealing in stolen military goods, but there are also indications that he and Sergeant Kochkin may have been bringing drugs into the area as well."

Dmitriy looked at the two men for a long while before speaking. "Well, what do you want of me?"

"Actually we just stopped to thank you and Captain Odnoralov. The report you insisted he make on the stolen missiles helped in initiating this investigation. It saved us a great deal of time. We have been able to determine that Iskhakov planned and initiated this operation; we can only guess at his motivation. Yet that really isn't too difficult, given his illegal activities. I just wonder what the Vietnamese promised them — perhaps drugs." The two men finished their coffee and rose to leave. "Thank you again, colonel. Do not discuss this with anyone. This entire episode is understandably embarrassing for the army."

"Of course." He watched them leave then walked back into his office. With trembling hands he poured a large vodka and drank it quickly. Then he sat in his chair and waited for the burning liquid to calm him. He could feel the panic slowly subsiding; in its place was a darker demon, the realization of what he had done. The revenge he sought for Nikolai had been folly. It had denigrated the memory of his son, and now another man who had trusted him was also lost in the attempt to make sense of the brutal loss he had suffered. Dmitriy poured another drink and downed it without pleasure. He was a military man. His job was to make good decisions based on logic and within the confines of his command structure. He had violated both, and he had lost the lives of men in his command as a result. Slowly he rose and walked to the window. He could feel the effects of the alcohol as it drugged his body and his mind. Suddenly he was tired. All he wanted was to go home to his wife and see her smile. After all, he had promised her a dinner in town. Could he tell her that he had failed as an officer, that he had broken his pledge as a leader of men? No, he could not. What he could tell her was that he no longer felt suited to this life. He was certainly old enough to ask for his pension. Perhaps it would be enough for the two of them to live in a small apartment near Moscow. Perhaps that would be enough. It was something he must consider, but not tonight. Tonight he had a date with the only important thing left in his life--his wife. Tonight he would hold her again and seek some semblance of joy in a life of dark shadows. Tomorrow? Tomorrow would be time enough to plan a memorial for Sergei and measure his career against a future he had yet to define.

Walter Reed Hospital

The balding doctor held his forehead in his left hand as he stared at the floor. He was listening intently to the unsolicited consultation of a colleague—who was also his patient. Finally he stood erect and nodded with a small smile. "You are quite right, Dr. Jernigan. I agree." He watched the pale young woman with the large brown eyes as she left the room and walked slowly down the hall.

The experienced nurse was watching them both. "It's remarkable. Her progress is just remarkable."

"Yes, she's progressing much faster than I would have expected." He smiled and made a few notes on a clipboard he was carrying. When he looked up there was a determined look on his face. "I have an idea. Let's put her to work. She's bored and I think this just might be the answer for her."

"Do you think she is ready?"

"Mentally—yes! Physically, I'm not so sure. Let's start slowly."

"Well, we can certainly use the help. We're short staffed right now."

"I know, but let's take it easy until she regains her strength. And one other thing, what is her emotional state. That may be more important than even the physical progress."

The nurse smiled. "You don't need to worry; she's in love."

"Really?"

"Really. He's a pilot at Nubat. He's scheduled to rotate back to the states soon, and that changes everything."

Nubat Royal Thai Air Force Base

The four men stood at attention as the Wing Commander pinned Distinguished Flying Crosses on their chests. They were beautiful medals, blue and white, broken in the center by one lone bright red stripe. Hanging below the fabric was the large cross superimposed by a propeller with sun's rays behind it. The commander spoke briefly about heroism and courage, saluted the four, then turned and left. The entire ceremony was over in less than ten minutes. There was a war going on, and it demanded their attention. As the crowd dispersed, two of the four men standing on the hot asphalt stepped aside. Their eyes were not glued to the medals they had received but rather to the two held tightly in Colonel Bennett's right hand. After an awkward moment Robb spoke. "I would like to write a letter to Joe's folks."

"I'll be writing one for both Joe and Todd tonight. You can add yours when I write to Joe's family."

"Yes sir, I'd like that."

"Robb?"

"Yes sir?"

"I'm proud of you, son. You've had a rough tour over here, but you've handled it like a man."

"Thank you, sir."

"You rotate back in less than two weeks, I know you'll be glad to get back to Kerrie. I hear she's improving."

"We're getting married as soon as she's well enough."

"Be sure to send me an invitation. Maybe I'll arrange a fly-by!"

Robb grinned. "That'd be great!"

The smile slowly faded from the colonel's face. "I'll need your letter for Joe before 2400. I don't like to let these things wait."

"Yes sir; I understand."

An F-4 flew low across the base and pulled up steeply in a victory roll. Both men watched and smiled. "Joe really was the best you know." The colonel said it emphatically as the plane turned north and prepared to enter the landing pattern.

"Yes he was."

*   *   *

Dear Mom and Dad,

Great news, Somboon's paperwork came through. I'll be bringing your new grandson with me when I return in a couple of weeks. My plans are to fly to Walter Reed first; we're hoping Kerrie can be released by then. If all goes well we should all be in Colorado very soon. I told Sister Estelle that she just had to come for the wedding. When I told her your church had several boxes of clothing and toys and was looking for a school to sponsor, she agreed to think about it. I've already bought her ticket, so she really doesn't have much choice now. Oh yes, my new friend, Phillip, has agreed to be my best man. Next to Joe, I can't think of anyone I'd rather have. He's a very special friend to both me and Kerrie. We've all been through a lot together.

Somboon sends his love. We can't wait to get home.

Robb

*   *   *

The sun climbed lazily into the clear morning sky, spreading its warmth to the waking world. Far off on the northeastern horizon small build-ups of fluffy white clouds were already beginning to form. Slowly they would grow as the earth basked under the warmth of the morning sun. By mid afternoon the warmth would turn to unbearable heat that would scorch the earth and leave it breathless in the steaming tropical jungle. And above, the fluffy white cloud would have grown into a powerful and threatening giant, towering forty thousand feet in height. Villagers would view the awesome growth and seek shelter from the downpour of rain that swept along with the pent-up fury of a monsoon storm. Pilots would watch the mammoth growth, too, and beware the air currents that could damage or destroy even the robust design of combat aircraft. Through the day the giants grew and raged and finally would spend themselves in the later afternoon rains, and in their death they would bring some relief from the same heat that had given them birth.

In the mornings, however, the sky was blue and peaceful. The earth awoke from its rest and began again the process of life and death, and only the mournful roar of the sleek fighters returning to the base broke the peaceful silence of the day. This morning was no different. At first they were only four tiny specs on the far horizon. Slowly they grew, then more quickly, until the form became distinctive. And last came the roar of the powerful engines, the song of the Phantoms.

Those who walked along the small dusty village roads glanced at the sky for an instant and then stared again at their bare feet in the warm soil. The newness and the fascination had worn away long ago, and the planes, like the giant thunderclouds, had become a part of their life. But they were still incomprehensible, something beyond their understanding. Slowly the peasants turned and plodded along toward the market, their burdens slung across their backs in large woven bags, while overhead the jets streaked off into the distance, their burdens hanging beneath their wings.

CPSIA information can be obtained at www.ICGtesting.com
Printed in the USA
BVOW071234081111

275589BV00004B/1/P